Fire Hazard

"Who would have thought
dragons could be so sexy?"
—Fresh Fiction

D1008031

Praise for the Novels
of Katie MacAlister

The Unbearable Lightness of Dragons
A Novel of the Light Dragons

"Had me laughing out loud. . . . This book is full of humor and romance, keeping the reader entertained all the way through . . . a wondrous story full of magic. . . . I cannot wait to see what happens next in the lives of the dragons." —Fresh Fiction

"Katie MacAlister has always been a favorite of mine and her latest series again shows me why. . . . If you are a lover of dragons, MacAlister's new series will definitely keep you entertained!"
—The Romance Readers Connection

"Magic, mystery, and humor abound in this novel, making it a must read . . . another stellar book."
—Night Owl Reviews

"Entertaining." —*Midwest Book Review*

Love in the Time of Dragons
A Novel of the Light Dragons

"Ms. MacAlister has once again taken a crazy plot and fascinating characters and tossed them with a lot of fun and a dash of mystery to create a darned good reading adventure. Who would have thought dragons could be so sexy?! Katie MacAlister, that's who. Hail to the powers of the creative author." —Fresh Fiction

"An extraordinary paranormal romance. Ms. MacAlister has created a wonderful world of dragons, demons, and other assorted characters. . . . The dragon men are hot and their mates know just how to stand up to these aggressive alpha males. *Love in the Time of Dragons* is a funny, romantic, and sexy novel. Once I started to read it, I couldn't put it down. Katie MacAlister has another winner on her hands!" —The Romance Readers Connection

continued . . .

"I was sucked into the world of [the] Dark Ones right from the start. . . . This book is full of witty dialogue and great romance, making it one that should not be missed."
— Fresh Fiction

In the Company of Vampires
A Dark Ones Novel

"Hysterical and surprisingly realistic, considering it includes witches, deities, vampires, and Viking ghosts, *In the Company of Vampires* delivers a great story and excellent characterization."
— Fresh Fiction

"Ms. MacAlister has another winner. . . . Her humor is evident throughout the story and cause for more than a few dozen laughs. This book makes the perfect partner for a long winter night."
— The Romance Readers Connection

"Zany [and] clever."
— *Midwest Book Review*

It's All Greek to Me

"MacAlister wins again with her signature sass and steam. . . . This delightful and satisfying read is low on conflict, high on humor, and stratospheric on sexy sizzle."
— *Publishers Weekly*

"*It's All Greek To Me* is a wonderful, lighthearted romantic romp, as a kick-butt American amazon and a hunky Greek find love." — Genre Go Round Reviews

"Full of sassy yet steamy characters . . . lots of humor, and plenty of sizzling and sexy scenes."
— The Season for Romance

Also by Katie MacAlister

Katie MacAlister

Sparks Fly

A Novel of the Light Dragons

A SIGNET BOOK

SIGNET
Published by New American Library, a division of
Penguin Group (USA) Inc., 375 Hudson Street,
New York, New York 10014, USA
Penguin Group (Canada), 90 Eglinton Avenue East, Suite 700, Toronto,
Ontario M4P 2Y3, Canada (a division of Pearson Penguin Canada Inc.)
Penguin Books Ltd., 80 Strand, London WC2R 0RL, England
Penguin Ireland, 25 St. Stephen's Green, Dublin 2,
Ireland (a division of Penguin Books Ltd.)
Penguin Group (Australia), 250 Camberwell Road, Camberwell, Victoria 3124,
Australia (a division of Pearson Australia Group Pty. Ltd.)
Penguin Books India Pvt. Ltd., 11 Community Centre, Panchsheel Park,
New Delhi - 110 017, India
Penguin Group (NZ), 67 Apollo Drive, Rosedale, Auckland 0632,
New Zealand (a division of Pearson New Zealand Ltd.)
Penguin Books (South Africa) (Pty.) Ltd., 24 Sturdee Avenue,
Rosebank, Johannesburg 2196, South Africa

Penguin Books Ltd., Registered Offices:
80 Strand, London WC2R 0RL, England

First published by Signet, an imprint of New American Library,
a division of Penguin Group (USA) Inc.

First Printing, May 2012
10 9 8 7 6 5 4 3 2 1

 REGISTERED TRADEMARK—MARCA REGISTRADA

Printed in the United States of America

PUBLISHER'S NOTE
This is a work of fiction. Names, characters, places, and incidents either are the product of the author's imagination or are used fictitiously, and any resemblance to actual persons, living or dead, business establishments, events, or locales is entirely coincidental.
   The publisher does not have any control over and does not assume any responsibility for author or third-party Web sites or their content.

ALWAYS LEARNING   PEARSON

To my darling agent, Michelle Grajkowski,
because she needs a Baltic book all to herself

Dear readers,

There's nothing worse than joining a party midway through it, when everyone knows who everyone else is, and what funny things they did before you arrived, and worse, you're too late for the really good canapés, and are left with only a Vienna sausage skewered to a sweet pickle and soggy cracker.

Because I hate being stuck with the soggy cracker as much as everyone else, I make sure that pertinent information about characters is included in each book, so that new readers should be able to pick up any book and enjoy it without having read any previous volumes in the series. This book is no different, but I know that some readers prefer to consult a concise table of who's who, and for that reason, I've included a little cheat sheet of characters, locations, and other fun facts in the back of the book.

If you are a longtime reader of the dragon novels, you can nibble on your tasty roast beef and caramelized onion vol-au-vent canapé, and smile knowingly at all the latecomers to the party. If you are new, and wish to forgo the soggy cracker, you can consult the information at the back of the book as needed.

Whether you are a new reader or old, I welcome you to this, the third volume in the Light Dragons series, and hope you enjoy the latest shenanigans of all the wacky dragons, demons, Guardians, and assorted other folk who insist on being a part of the books.

Katie MacAlister

Chapter One

"The lady is here to see you."

Baltic turned at the voice, obviously startled to hear it since he had been alone in the upstairs corridor. "What foolishness is this?"

The heavily varnished wooden paneling that ran the length of the upper floor of the three-hundred-year-old pub melted into a dirt yard dotted with odd wooden figures.

Baltic glared first at the wooden figures, then at the man who approached him. "Ysolde! Why have you drawn me into one of your visions of the past? And why must you include that murderous bastard in it?"

"Don't blame me; blame my inner dragon." I sighed to myself and folded my arms over the couple of shirts I had been about to hang up in the wardrobe, which, like the corridor outside our bedroom, had faded into the scene before us. "Although I have to say, if it's going to make me watch episodes from your past, you might as well be here, too. Who is that? Oh, Constantine. And look, it's Baltic version 1.0, all sexy and shirtless and hacking away at something with a sword."

"I have better things to do than relive unimportant events," my Baltic, the Baltic of the present day, growled, transferring his glare from Constantine, the former silver wyvern and once his friend, later his most hated enemy, to me. "Make the vision stop."

"I would if I could, but they never do until they're good and ready.... Hey, where are you going?"

Baltic, with a rude word, turned on his heel and marched away. "I have spent the last twelve days chasing Thala across all of Europe and half of Asia. I have work to do, mate. You may indulge yourself with this vanity, but I will not."

"Vanity! I like that! It's not vanity. And you can't just leave my vision like that!" I yelled after him, watching with a growing sense of injustice as he disappeared around the side of a small hut. "They're valuable sources of information! Kaawa says we're supposed to learn from them, to glean facts about what is important to us now. Baltic? Well, dammit! He left! That rotter."

I slapped my hands on my legs and spun around as the vision of Constantine approached the other man who stood in a cluster of quintains and man-sized targets.

"Well, I'm not going to be so obstinate that I don't learn whatever it is my inner dragon is trying to tell me. Let's see, what do we have here ... obviously, we're in some sort of a training yard, and since Baltic isn't frothing at the mouth at the sight of Constantine, evidently this vision is from a time when they were still friends. Hello, my love. I don't suppose you can hear me, let alone see me?"

The vision Baltic didn't react, not that I expected him to. The people in the visions my inner dragon self, long dormant and only recently starting to wake up, had provided me were just that—visions of events in the past. I could watch and listen, but could not interact with them.

Constantine, clad in wool leggings and a tunic bearing a gold-embroidered dragon on a field of black, strode past the empty sword-fighting targets to the occupied one, his attitude cocky, while his face was arranged in an expression implying sympathy. "Did you hear me?" he asked as he stopped at the side of the man who was diligently hacking away at the straw and wood target with an extremely big sword.

"I heard. It is of no matter to me."

I spent a few moments in admiration of the interplay of his muscles as Baltic continued to swing and thrust his sword into the target, his bare back shining with sweat.

"It always did make my knees weak to see you wield a sword," I told the vision Baltic, moving around to see the front of him. His face was different yet familiar to me, his hair dark ebony then, his chin more blunted. "I like your hair the dark chocolate color it is now. And your chin, as well, although you certainly were incredibly sexy before Thala resurrected you. And your chest . . . oh my." I fanned myself with a bit of one of the shirts I was holding.

"Alexei says you have no choice. He says it is the command of your father." Constantine cocked one eyebrow at Baltic, moving swiftly to the side when Baltic swung wide.

"You look the same," I informed Constantine. "Evidently being brought back as a shade didn't affect your appearance, whereas resurrection does. Interesting. I'll have to talk to Kaawa about that the next time I see her. Still, you were handsome then, Constantine. But you didn't hold a candle to Baltic."

"My father does not control my life," Baltic snapped, his breath ragged now as he continued to swing at the vaguely human-shaped target. "Nor does Alexei."

I settled back against one of the targets, prepared to watch and learn what I could from the vision.

"He is our wyvern. You owe him your fealty," Constantine said, stiffening. "You must do as he says. You *must* meet the lady."

"Do not lecture me, Constantine," Baltic snarled, turning on him. Sweat beaded on his brow and matted the dark hair on his chest. Constantine took a step back when Baltic gestured toward him with the sword. "You are Alexei's heir, *not* the wyvern himself, and I do not take well to being ordered about."

"Pax!" Constantine said, throwing his hands up in the air in a gesture of defeat. "I did not come to argue with you, old friend. I wanted simply to warn you that the lady had arrived, and Alexei is expecting you to do your duty and claim her as mate."

I had been idly wondering to myself when exactly this moment had taken place—judging by the comments, it predated not only my own birth, but even the time when Baltic had been wyvern of the black dragon sept—but as the two men argued, I had a sudden insight.

"This is about the First Dragon's demand I redeem you, isn't it?" I asked the past Baltic. "This has something to do with whatever it is I'm supposed to accomplish to erase the stain on your soul. But that was due to the death of the innocent, and this . . . *a mate*?"

It took a minute before Constantine's words sank into my brain, but when they did, the hairs on the back of my neck rose. I stalked forward to the two men, glaring at the former image of the love of my life, uncaring that this was only a vision. "You were supposed to take someone else as a mate? Who?"

"I've told Alexei of my decision," Baltic said, snatching up his discarded tunic and wiping his face with it before sheathing his sword. "I have not changed my mind."

He turned and started up the hill of what was obviously the outer bailey of an early stone castle, stopping when Constantine called after him, "And what of the First Dragon? Will you defy him, as well as Alexei? You are his only living son, Baltic."

"I know what I am," Baltic snarled, and continued walking.

"The lady wants you. The First Dragon is reported to desire you to take her as mate. Alexei has commanded it in order to avoid a war. Do you really think you have a choice in the matter?"

The word that Baltic uttered was archaic, but quite, quite rude, and ironically, one his present-day self had spoken just a few minutes before. I watched his tall, handsome figure as he disappeared into crowds of dragons going about their daily business, my eyes narrowing as Constantine suddenly smiled.

"Why do I have the feeling that you know something?" I asked him.

He didn't answer, of course. He just continued to smile for a few seconds; then he, too, strolled off toward the upper bailey, leaving me alone in the practice yard.

"Who was she?" I bellowed after them, achieving nothing but the venting of my spleen. "Who the hell was she?" No one answered me, of course. Drat them all.

"Well, I'm not going to stand for being left clueless about important episodes from the past yet again. I've had it! I'm going to find out what's going on if it kills me. Again. Which it won't. Oh hell, now I'm talking to myself while in a vision. How pathetic is that?"

I looked around me, trying to figure out where exactly I was. It was fall, judging by the color of the leaves on the trees in the little town that straggled down the hill below me. Behind was a large mound flattened at the top, bearing a circular stone and wood tower, all of which was surrounded by a tall wooden stockade. "Motte and bailey castle," I murmured, racking my frequently incomplete memory for the time period of such structures.

All I could remember was that they were popular well before the century I was born. I took a deep breath and marched up the hill to the tower keep, automatically moving around people and objects that weren't really there, all the while muttering to myself about dragons and their stubborn ways, with an emphasis on one ebony-eyed wyvern in particular.

The stone and wood keep wasn't much to look at, not nearly so grand as my father's stone keep had been. I paused before the door to the main tower where I knew the keep's owner would reside, and considered who might live there. "Has to be the black dragons, since Constantine mentioned Alexei. And Baltic wasn't yet the heir, which means he probably slept in the garrison with all the other soldiers and unmarried men."

When I was a girl living with the humans I thought of as my family, my sister and I were strictly forbidden from ever stepping so much as one toe into the soldiers' barracks. Many were the times that we lay together in bed, speculating just what went on in the forbidden lower level of the keep, but a healthy respect for our mother kept us out of such a tantalizing spot.

Later, when Baltic and I finally found each other, and he had built Dauva (his stronghold in Latvia), I stayed out of the men's quarters by habit. Although I could have claimed the right as Baltic's mate to visit it, it had never occurred to me to break the rules and see just what went on in such a place. My upbringing had been too strong to overcome.

"We've come a long way, baby," I paraphrased as I strode into the lower level of the keep, looking around with interest. There were pallets everywhere, stuffed with straw and strewn with items of clothing and armor. Some men were asleep on them, while others huddled in a circle dicing, and farther into the smoky, ill-lit room, another group squatted next to braziers, clutching tankards and talking quietly to themselves. "This is somewhat disappointing," I told the visions of dragons from the past. "Where are the racy sights of naked men doing terribly immoral things that my mother always swore were what went on down here? Where are the camp followers enticing men into lustful acts? Where are the orgies?"

"The human woman who raised you had no knowledge of dragonkin," a voice said loudly behind me.

I spun around to see Baltic—my Baltic—in the doorway, his hands on his hips as he glanced around the room.

"Came back, did you? I knew you couldn't stay away from the past."

He rolled his eyes at the teasing note in my voice, striding over to me. "I returned for you when you did not come with me, as a proper mate should."

"Uh-huh. So, which pallet was yours?"

"Why do you care?"

I smiled up at his frown. "I want to see where you curled up at night."

"Why?" he asked again.

"Because it's something from your past, and kind of wicked, at least according to my mother. It's where you were naked and slept and had naughty thoughts. And speaking of naughty thoughts, just who is this female you were supposed to take as a mate?"

He grabbed my hand and pulled me deeper into the room, where a jointed wooden screen marked a separate sleeping area, affording it a goodly amount of privacy, even if it was not a closed room proper. "I did not sleep with the others. I was accorded a place here."

"Because of your father, you mean?"

He nodded. I sat on the long, narrow bed and looked around the living quarters, bouncing slightly as I did so.

"You had a real bed, one stuffed with feathers, although the ropes holding your mattress are kind of squeaky. Is that the same chest you had at Dauva?"

"Yes. Are you done? I wish to return to the pub. I have many things to do."

I slid my hand down the bear-fur covering of the bed, and leaned back on my elbows. "Did you entertain in this little private room, my love? Did you have girls here?"

He wanted to roll his eyes again—I could tell—but Baltic, always keeping a firm grip on how many times he gave in to that act, instead beetled his brows at me. "Do you wish to know how many lovers I had before you?"

"No. I just want to know if any of them ever shared this little love nest."

"No."

"Ah. Good." I smiled and kicked off my sandals, rubbing my legs and feet along the fur in what I hoped was a seductive manner. "Perhaps you'd like to change that?"

Interest kindled in his eyes even as his lips were about to chastise me for wasting his valuable time. "Are you sure you would not prefer to wait until such time as I was with a lover?" he asked me with a completely deadpan face. "I know how it inflames you to engage in lovemaking while others are present."

"Oh!" I sat up and slapped my hand on the skin. "I do not have kinky sex fantasies! Just because I thought it was kind of fun for us to make love with the vision version of our past selves doesn't mean I am a swinger! I would never want to see you with another woman! Unless it was my past self . . . er . . . I wasn't yet born at the time of this vision, was I?"

"No."

"OK, then. It's just you and me. In your old bed. With the guys in the garrison just beyond that screen."

He gave in and gave another eye roll, but removed his

clothing as he did so. "I will indulge you, but only because we have been separated, and it is the way of dragons to claim their mates upon return."

I giggled as I squirmed my way out of my shirt. "You already did that when you returned at three o'clock this morning. Twice. In a way that left me utterly breathless for hours."

"And yet you seem to have your breath again," he murmured as he whisked off the last of his clothing, kneeling on the bed to stroke a hand up my belly to my breasts.

I reached for him, shivering with pleasure as I slid my hands along the muscles of his arms and shoulders. "I expect you can do something about that."

"Perhaps," he murmured, his cheeks nuzzling my breasts at the same time as his hands busied themselves with removing my bra.

One hand slid down to the waistband of my jeans, about to unzip them, but a sudden shadow looming overhead had me gasping.

The black-haired Baltic of the past stormed into the room, quickly removed his clothing, and flung himself down onto the bed, right on top of where I lay.

"Whoa now," I said, scooting to the very edge, looking down at the naked man who had once been my Baltic. "That startled me. Er ... is he going to be here for a while?"

"How the hell do I know?" Baltic rolled off me, a decidedly disgruntled expression darkening his face.

"Well, he's you. Don't you remember how long you were here?"

The look he gave me spoke volumes, and none of them expounded on the brilliance of my thinking. "No, mate, I don't happen to remember what I did every single day of my more than one thousand years of existence."

"You weren't resurrected until almost forty years ago,

so you missed three hundred years," I pointed out, watching with interest as the past Baltic tossed and turned before lying on his back, his hands behind his head. I couldn't help but glance downward.

"Ysolde," Baltic said warningly.

"I was just looking, not comparing. Besides, I already told you that your resurrected form was a bit more robust, so you have nothing to glare at me about, not to mention the fact that this is the very same body I used to ogle in the past."

"Come," he said, holding out his hand.

"Well, I had planned . . . never mind. I suppose having him right there wouldn't be appropriate."

"Nor desirable. We will continue this in our own bedroom later."

Reluctantly, I climbed off the bed and accepted the clothing Baltic handed me. As we put on our clothing, I glanced back at his former self with a bit of sadness. "Although if you were to lie down in exactly the same spot that he was . . ."

The lecture he gave me as he dragged me out of the keep and down the bailey was potent, but not worthy of repeating, and of course, absolutely unwarranted. "And in the future, you will cease involving me in your visions. Do you understand?"

"Pfft," I told him, pinching him on the behind as he strolled around the corner of the hut next to the practice yard. "You're so limited in your ability to enjoy different things."

"I have more important things to do with my time," he called back as he disappeared.

"Nothing is more important than the job your father gave me. Hey, speaking of that, you never told me who that woman was. Baltic? Who was she?"

"Who's who?" a voice asked behind me. I spun around, staggering slightly when the world spun with me for a few moments, finally resolving itself into a familiar, if uninspiring, bedroom atop the old pub. "Are you all right? You look funny, like you smell cabbage cooking."

"I'm fine, lovey." I smiled at the brown-haired boy watching me with eyes that always seemed far too old for their nine years. "And there's nothing wrong with cabbage, despite your stepfather's insistence that it was put on this earth only to try his patience. That stir-fried cabbage with peanut sauce that Pavel made last night was to die for, which you'd know if you had tried it."

Brom wrinkled up his nose. Always a placid child, if a tad bit eccentric, in the month that had passed since our house had been destroyed, he seemed to have adopted Baltic as a hero figure. I'd caught him more than once watching Baltic closely, as if fascinated with the way a wyvern acted, but I think it went deeper than mere curiosity about the dragons with whom we now found ourselves living. He'd started parroting Baltic's likes and dislikes, even going so far as to spurn food I knew he didn't really mind.

"Are you going into London today?"

"Nice change of subject, and yes, I am." I shook off the last few dregs of anger over the idea that the First Dragon had tried to force Baltic into taking a mate, and finished putting away the shirts I'd bought in a local shop. "Where is Nico taking you today?"

"He wants to go see a history museum." Brom looked thoughtful. "It has ships and stuff, but no bodies, although Nico says there might be some surgeon's tools. When are we going to get our own house so I can set up my lab again? You said you'd start looking right away, and it's been forever."

"Four weeks is hardly forever." I smiled and gave him one of the three daily hugs he allowed. "But I'll ask Baltic again about a house. Would you mind if we lived outside of England? He's likely to want to be near Dauva in order to oversee the rebuilding, and I hate to make him travel between here and Riga all the time."

"Are there mummies in . . ." His face screwed up in thought.

"Latvia?" I finished. "I have no idea, although it is close enough to visit St. Petersburg, which I know has some fine museums. Whether or not they have mummies is beyond me. You can ask Nico, though. Perhaps he'll know."

"OK. Will he come with us? Because he's a green dragon, and not in Baltic's sept, I mean."

"I'm sure Drake will give him permission, since he's agreed to let Nico tutor you for a year. Oh, you haven't had your allowance yet, have you? Let me get my purse."

Brom's expression turned painful for a few seconds before his shoulders sagged, and he said with obvious reluctance, "Baltic gave it to me this morning when he got home from Nepal."

"Uh-huh. And were you going to tell me that, or just let me give you more?"

His lips twitched. "Well . . . no. But if you wanted to give me more, that would be OK."

I laughed and gave his shoulder a little pat. "I'm sorry to have burst a burgeoning scheme to get money from both of us, but you really don't need more than *one* weekly allowance."

"How am I going to buy supplies when we get a house?" he asked as I herded him before me back into the narrow hallway. The floor and walls, wooden and uneven, made me feel as if I were walking at an angle. I didn't complain, though; I found the small pub run by some human friends of Pavel, Baltic's second-in-command, charming and quaint in its Elizabethan Englishness. Baltic insisted we would be safe there should Thala, his former lieutenant, decide to try to kill us again. I had no doubt that he would keep us safe no matter where we were located, but like Brom, I was growing tired of such a transient lifestyle, and I yearned for my own home where we could settle down once and for all.

"When we have room for you to set up another mummification lab, I'll buy you some supplies. Although, really, Brom, couldn't you find some other hobby than mummifying animals?"

"You said it was illegal to mummify a human," he pointed out as I tapped on the door to his tutor's room. "Besides, I don't know where to find a dead person."

Nico, an auburn-haired, studious green dragon who had charge of Brom's education for the last few months, greeted me and grabbed up a small backpack. "Did Brom tell you that we're going to the naval museum today?"

"Yes, despite the fact that it won't have bodies." I shared a smile with Nico before reminding Brom to behave himself. "I won't be back until just before dinner, but Pavel said he was going to cook up something special, so be home by six."

"Absolutely," Nico agreed, and with a glance at his watch, hustled Brom down the stairs. I heard the rumble of male voices drift upward after them, and waited, wondering how best to broach the subject of my vision.

Baltic appeared at the head of the stairs, his hand quickly whipping away from his pocket as he spotted me.

"You didn't!" I said, frowning as he approached, Pavel on his heels. "Baltic, really, it's too bad of you!"

Guilt chased across his face, followed immediately by a look of pure seduction as he swept me up in his arms and bathed me in dragon fire. "*Chérie*, what is it you're frowning over? Could it be that you have missed me in the last five minutes as much as I've missed you?"

"Whenever you call me *chérie*, I know you're feeling guilty about something," I said, melting against him even as I giggled a little. "Of course I missed you, and not just for the last five minutes. It's been a hellish twelve days while you were trying to find Thala, not only because I was worried sick about you, but because you weren't here to drive me wild with desire, but that's not the point. Brom did *not* need more money. And don't deny you gave him some, because I saw you putting your wallet away."

"We've spoken of this subject already," he murmured against my lips, pulling me brazenly against his hips. "If you are good today, I will allow you to have your wanton way with me later."

"If I'm *good . . .*" I released my outrage at such a statement, and almost purred as I let him kiss me, amused that he thought he could distract me in such a way before I realized that he had a very good record of doing just that.

I gave myself up to the sensation of his fire sinking into me, of the hardness of his body against mine, of his scent, that masculine, spicy scent that seemed to kindle my own dragon fire. And when his mouth moved against mine, I knew I didn't stand a chance. I kissed him with all the passion I possessed, making him growl into my mouth as I tugged on his hair, wordlessly demanding more of his dragon fire.

Pavel passed by us, murmuring something about waiting for Baltic in the sitting room, but even that didn't stop me from welcoming Baltic's fire with a little moan of my own. His tongue burned as it swept inside my mouth, his chest and legs hard when he pushed me up against the wall. I clung to his shoulders, rubbing myself against him, pulling hard first on my fire, and when that didn't come, on his, to bathe us both in heat.

"Ysolde, if you do not stop attempting to seduce me in the hallway, I will take you right here," Baltic said in a low voice filled with passion. "And while I would be happy to fulfill this latest of your secret fantasies, we risk shocking anyone who comes upstairs."

I slid one hand down to pinch his adorable behind. "For the last time, you incredibly sexy dragon, I do not have sexual fantasies that are anything but perfectly ordinary, and certainly do not involve voyeurism. And before you say it, no one would have seen us in the keep, not even your past self. I will admit, though, that parts of me are still humming after the way you greeted me this morning when you arrived home. That was quite the homecoming."

"I merely gave you the attention you were due." Baltic raised an eyebrow seconds before he dived for my chest, his mouth and hands hot on my breasts. I squirmed against him, shifting his hands so I could have better access to his chest and wondering if we had time to indulge our need for each other, but at that moment, my phone vibrated in my pocket and bellowed out a recording of one word: "Ysolde!"

Baltic raised his head from where he was licking the valley between my breasts, frowning something fierce. "Mate! I thought I told you to change your alarm sound."

I giggled against his mouth and nipped his bottom lip. "But it's so perfect! Nothing catches my attention more than your saying my name. And speaking of attention, I want to talk to you about that vision."

He ignored the emphasis I put on the words, wrapping his arms around my waist and lifting me off the ground as he squeezed tightly. "You try my patience, woman. I have no time for reminders of what happened in the past. I have lost twelve days chasing Thala, and there is much work that I must accomplish in a short amount of time."

I took a deep breath. "I wish I could ignore them, but I can't. You're not the only one who lost twelve days, my darling. When the First Dragon demanded I salvage your honor—"

"I've told you before that my honor is fine as it is."

"When your father, the godlike ancestor of every dragon whoever was and whoever will be, tells me to salvage your honor, then I'm not about to ignore anything that might help me do just that. Especially since you aren't making it the least bit easy for me."

"If you choose to waste your time—"

"Waste my time? *Waste my time!*" I gasped, shoving at his shoulder. "I cannot believe that you would call my visions a waste of time!"

"You are being emotional, Ysolde," he started to say, but I slapped both hands on his chest with a glare that by rights should have stripped his hair off his head.

"I am not being emotional!" I yelled. The echo of my voice along the wood-paneled hallway was quite audible. Baltic's glossy dark chocolate eyebrows rose. "Fine! I'm emotional! I can't help it. I'm hormonal right now."

"Are you having your female time? You were not earlier. Did it arrive since then? I hope it will be over soon. I do not like having to wait for it to cease," he said, passion firing in his eyes.

"People can hear us downstairs, you know, and you haven't *quite* embarrassed me to death. Would you, perhaps, like to inquire as to the state of my bowels?" I took a deep breath when he looked about to do just that. "What were we talking about that didn't involve my bodily functions?"

"Your being emotional. It is a good thing that I am a wyvern, and thus am able to control my emotions where you cannot."

"Oh, I like that—"

"It is just like that time at Dragonwood when you tried to geld me with your eating dagger. You were most emotional then, as well. You remember that, do you not?"

I frowned for a few seconds as I tried to dig through what remained of my memory. "No . . . at Dragonwood? I tried to geld you? Are you sure?"

"Do you distrust my memory?" he asked. There was something about the innocent look on his face that made me suspicious, but there was nothing I could say to challenge his statement.

"Your memory of the past has never been in question, no, although you didn't remember what you did in the vision we just saw," I said slowly. "If you say I tried to cut off your noogies, then I assume I did so, but I'm also sure I had a very good reason for doing it. What did you do that made me so annoyed?"

"You are going straight to the meeting and back again," he said, totally ignoring my question and setting me down to escort me down the narrow stairs to the main floor of the pub. "The driver will wait outside for you. I would accompany you myself, but the builders are ready to leave the country, and I must check with them before they do so."

"You are getting more and more like Drake Vireo every day," I told him, alternating between annoyance and pure, unadulterated love. I decided it was better to indulge the latter rather than the former, and accordingly gave the tip of his nose a little lick before waving at Pavel as he stood talking to three men whom Baltic had engaged to begin the process of restoring Dauva.

"I am infinitely superior to the green wyvern," Baltic said loftily, nodding to one of the blue dragons he'd hired as drivers for us. "And you must remember that I will do anything to keep you and Brom safe."

"I know that, and I appreciate what it cost you to borrow some of Drake's men to watch over Brom and me while you and Pavel were tracking Thala, but as I told you before you left, we'll be fine. There's no reason for Thala to want to harm Brom, and really, that goes for me, as well. As for you . . . well, she went to the considerable trouble of resurrecting you, so despite that whole situation of her blowing up the house on top of us, I don't think she wants to kill you. I think she was just frustrated, and angry, and felt cornered, and let loose on us because of that, not because of any murderous intent."

"She did an exceptionally fine job of making me believe otherwise."

I touched his shoulder. Although Thala's destruction of the house hadn't killed us—dragons being notoriously difficult to kill—it had done so much damage to Baltic's back that even today, he still bore scars. "Well, I should say she has no reason to want to kill you, so therefore, she can't gain anything by offing me. After all, you're not like the other dragons who cork off if their mate dies."

Baltic, who had been frowning at my slang, instantly switched into seductive mode, something he was wont to do whenever I mentioned the newly discovered fact that he was a reeve, one of the very rare dragons who could have more than one mate. "I would not survive your death again, *chérie*," he murmured against my lips, bathing me in a light sheen of his dragon fire. "Not a third time. It is for that reason I insist that you not see the archimage again."

"We may not have a choice in the matter," I said slowly, brushing off an infinitesimal bit of lint from his shoulder. "I didn't get a chance to tell you earlier, but I reached Jack this morning. Do you remember him?"

"No."

"He was apprenticed to Dr. Kostich at the same time I was—only Jack is a very gifted mage, and I'm . . . well, you know how my magic goes all wonky because I'm a dragon. Jack is now a full-fledged mage, and very talented, from what I heard, but even he says there's just no one of the caliber we need to tackle Thala other than an archimage."

Baltic watched me closely. I kissed his chin, knowing he wasn't going to like what I had to say.

"There are other archimages," he said.

"Two others, and one is out of reach while he's on some sort of a magi retreat. The other is a woman I have had no experience with, and I suspect wouldn't be overly easy to persuade to help catch a highly dangerous, partially psychotic half-dragon necromancer."

"Thala is not that dangerous," he said dismissively.

I pulled down the back of his shirt collar. "Have you looked at your back, lately? That dirge she sang brought down an entire three-story house on top of us, Baltic. You can't do that if you're not able to tap into some pretty impressive power."

He made a disgusted noise.

"I'm just saying that I think Dr. Kostich is going to be our only choice."

"I do not like it." Baltic's frown was, as ever, a stormy thing to behold, but I had long learned to ignore the expression.

"Neither do I, but so long as mages wield arcane power, they are going to be the best bet for combating the dark power that necromancers use. I'm afraid, my delectable dragon, it's Dr. Kostich or nothing."

His jaw worked, since he was no doubt sorely tempted to tell me we'd do without my former employer and head of the Otherworld, but we had few choices open to us.

"You and Pavel chased Thala for twelve straight days and nights," I told him, my hands caressing his chest. "You know her better than anyone. You know what she's capable of; you know how many outlaw dragons follow her. Can we bring her to justice without the aid of people outside our sept?"

"No." I knew just how much it cost him to admit that. He took a deep breath, his eyes sparkling with the light of vengeance. "She has grown more powerful in the last month. I do not know where she is getting the members for her tribe of ouroboros dragons, but we encountered more than thirty of them in Belgium, and another two dozen in Turkey. That she can lose that many members and still have the number of dragons we saw when we finally chased her to Nepal . . ." He shook his head and didn't finish the sentence, clearly frustrated that he hadn't caught her to deal with her himself.

For a moment, I was stunned by what he said. "You ran into fifty-some of Thala's ouroboros dragons before you lost them in the wilds of Nepal?"

"Fifty-eight."

"What happened to them?" I knew from the manner in which Baltic had greeted me upon his return that morning that he had no injuries, so it wasn't likely he'd fought the dragons.

His eyes grew hard and even shinier. "What do you think happened to them?"

"You didn't kill them?"

"Not alone. Pavel was with me."

I gawked at him. "Baltic!"

"They were trying to kill us," he pointed out, instantly quelling the lecture I was about to make. Although I had my doubts that Thala's intentions with regard to Baltic were of the murderous nature, I knew from the past experience that her gang of outlaw ouroboros dragons were much more cutthroat.

"I still don't like it."

"Your heart is too soft," he said, giving my behind another squeeze.

"That is not my heart, and you know full well I don't like killings. Which is why I wholly approve of the plan to bring Thala to the Otherworld Committee for justice. They can banish her to the Akasha, or something appropriate like that."

Baltic made a noncommittal noise that had me glancing sharply at him, but before I could do more than wonder, he said, "You will ask the archimage if there is another who could deal with Thala now that we know where she is."

"I thought you said she disappeared in Nepal."

His lips thinned a little. "She did. But I suspect she has taken control of an aerie high in the Himalayas."

"The one I saw in my vision a few months ago?" I asked, remembering the cold, bleak stone building.

"That is the aerie, yes. It used to be held by Kostya, before Thala confined him there."

I shivered at the thought of being held prisoner in such a stark location. "All of that notwithstanding, I will ask Dr. Kostich, but I can tell you now there isn't anyone else to help us. And stop looking at me like that—I don't want to have to deal with him any more than you do, even though he's really not the horrible person you think he is."

"He is responsible for your death, mate."

"You know as well as I do that he wasn't responsible for my dying a second time. Well, not directly responsible. Besides, I apologized about that, so you can stop looking like you're going to yell at me again. It's not as if I die so often that I deserve a lecture. Honestly, Baltic, you really are becoming just as bossy as Drake, and you know that only irritates me."

"I do not like your going where I cannot protect you," he said in a low grumble that was softened by the look of love in his beautiful onyx eyes. I melted against him, unable to resist the emotions I knew bound us so tightly together. "The other mates should come here, instead of you going into London."

"It's Aisling's turn to host the Mates' Union meeting, and even if it wasn't, I'm not going to live my life hiding in the shadows because Thala is on the loose." I kissed him quickly so as to avoid the temptation his mouth offered, then climbed into the back of the sleek dark blue car. "I'm going to do a little shopping before I meet with

Aisling and May, and yes, I'll be careful, so you can stop fretting. Thala is in Nepal, not here in England."

"There is nothing to say she hasn't escaped."

"You left a whole bunch of Drake's guys to watch the borders, didn't you? Stop worrying. They'll tell you if she leaves the aerie."

"Assuming they see her," he muttered darkly.

"I'm the first one to admit she's powerful, but I don't see her getting out of the country without someone noticing. I'll be back before dinner. If Brom and Nico come home early, remind them that Brom's vacation was officially over yesterday, and it wouldn't hurt them to start on his lessons this afternoon. Oh, and Baltic?"

"Yes?" He leaned into the car.

I grabbed his head and pulled hard on the little core of dragon fire that slumbered inside me, letting it flow out to him as I kissed him again. "Perhaps later we can explore some more of *your* secret fantasies," I whispered, smiling to myself at the look of mingled surprise and passion that flitted through his eyes.

Chapter Two

"To the Wyvern's Nest?" asked Ludovic, the dragon whose services the blue wyvern Bastian had offered as a gesture of peace (and more likely, of apology for believing Baltic had killed so many of his sept members), as he pulled out into the sparse traffic of the tiny little suburb of London and headed in the direction of the main roads.

"Not yet. I'd like to do some shopping first. Er... some special shopping." I cleared my throat. "After that, I'll be going to Aisling's house, not the blue dragon pub. The meeting has been moved since Baltic had a hissy fit at the thought of it being held out in public where anyone might happen to sing a dirge and thereby blow up the building with us in it. Do you know where Aisling lives?"

"Of course," he answered, his light brown eyebrows rising. "We blue dragons make sure we know where *all* the wyverns live."

"That sounds like something Chuan Ren or another red dragon would have said, not the peaceful blues."

Ludovic shrugged. "It is the truth nonetheless. I'm sure you will realize this is not meant to shame or embarrass you, but we trust no one outside the sept."

"And yet you're working for us," I pointed out gently, not wanting to offend him. Ludovic was a nice young man, probably only a few hundred years old, with a personable smile, and a penchant for the latest in high-fashion clothing. He always looked as if he had just stepped off the runway, something I'd noticed had applied to most blue dragons—male and female—that I'd seen since my latest resurrection. "Surely Bastian wouldn't have volunteered you to drive us around if he didn't trust us."

He shrugged again. "It is not for me to question the wyvern; he gives the orders, and I follow them."

I kept silent but thought to myself that the easygoing Bastian ruled his sept with more of an iron hand than I had imagined. That or he inspired some pretty intense devotion from sept members.

"Where is it you wish to shop?"

I bit my lip, a little heat warming my cheeks. "It's . . . uh . . . I'd like to go to a toy store. An adult toy store."

"Adult toys?" he asked, frowning in the mirror at me. "Electronics, you mean?"

"No." I took a deep breath. "Sexual toys."

His eyes widened, a speculative look in them.

"Not for Baltic and me," I told the look quickly. "Well, perhaps one or two things. But I have to replace Pavel's toys."

His speculative look went into overdrive.

"Not that I ever use them with Pavel. He and I don't do that. Or anything, really. Nothing sexual, that is. We like to cook together. . . ." I closed my eyes for a few moments, knowing I was just making things worse. "I need to find a store. You wouldn't happen to know of one, would you? If not, I can call around to find one that doesn't look like you'll get a social disease by shopping there."

Ludovic spun the wheel and sent us out into the traffic heading for the main road into London. "As it happens, I know of a necromancer who runs a shop of the sort you seek. She has many specialty items."

"Specialty? Fetish, you mean? I don't think Pavel's into anything too extraordinary. Although there was that swing contraption, but I assume that was for . . . never mind. I'll try your friend's shop. Is it in London?"

"Yes." He glanced at his watch. "When is your meeting?"

I told him the time and sat back, making a mental shopping list of things I wanted to purchase. By the time that was done, I had to face the sad truth that the inevitable could be avoided no longer. . . . I called Dr. Kostich.

"Good morning, this is Ysolde de Bouchier," I said politely in answer to his terse greeting. "I hope I'm not disturbing you, but I have a matter of some importance I'd like to discuss."

"What do you want, Tully Sullivan?"

I flinched at the zing of pain that followed the use of my human name. Members of the Otherworld frequently avoided the use of full names simply because names have power, and in the hands of people like an archimage, that power could be quite tangible. Not to mention painful.

"I'd like to request your help with a necromancer named Thala. She —"

"No," he said abruptly.

"Thala is Baltic's former lieutenant, the one who sang a dirge directly on top of us, and brought our house down around our ears. Literally."

He breathed heavily into the phone for a few seconds. "I do not have time for the troubles of your husky dragon, Tully."

I dug my fingernails into my hands in reaction to his wholly unsubstantiated jibe that Baltic's dragon form was fat. "This concerns Maura, too, you know," I said quickly, hoping the mention of his beloved granddaughter would sweeten his temper. "Thala is a necromancer, and the leader of the tribe of dragons that—"

"I have just told you that I have no time for your troubles, and I object to being made to repeat it, but I will do so this once: I have far more important things to do than worry about dragons, necromancers, and whatever other trouble you've found yourself in, so I will thank you not to disturb me again."

Before I could explain, he hung up the phone, and I had a very strong presentment that if I tried to call back, he'd simply hang up again. Or worse.

"Oh, what the hell. You live only three times," I said, throwing caution to the wind as I dialed Dr. Kostich's number again.

"Yes?"

"I realize you don't want to talk to me—"

"Then you should know better than to call me. Do so again at your own risk."

The phone went dead in my ear.

"Arrogant, annoying mage," I grumbled as I dialed a third time. "Can't be bothered . . . Look, this is important, Dr. Kostich, so please hear me out."

"As important as being transformed into a tree sloth? That is what I am about to do."

"Threaten me all you like, but I will not be bullied into keeping quiet—"

The murmur of his voice speaking in Latin caught my attention. I listened for a few seconds, recognized the words, and with a snarled, "You are the meanest person I know!" I hurriedly hung up the phone before he could complete the spell.

"Problems?" Ludovic asked when I examined myself for signs of imminent slothdom.

"Just the normal—my life going to hell in a sloth's handbasket."

After that failed attempt at garnering help, my chat with Ludovic while driving into London was confined to unextraordinary subjects, since Baltic's trust—like that of Bastian—went only so far. It had been an uphill battle to get Baltic to accept the offer of Ludovic's services, due to Baltic's steadfast insistence that the day would never dawn when a light dragon would need help from another sept. He gave in only when I pointed out that Pavel and he were the only adult males in the sept.

The Merchant of Venus wasn't what I thought of as a sex shop (small, dark, and filled with both unidentifiable stains and sleazy men in trench coats) and instead could have passed for any brightly lit, clean, modern boutique in a trendy part of SoHo.

"Wow," I said to no one in particular as I entered the store. Facing me was a freestanding wall with black-and-white arty photographs, and a half-moon table bearing a reproduction of *The Lovers* statue. I peered closer at the photos, blinking when I realized the couples and groups in them were not all human.

"Welcome to the Merchant of Venus," a soft, cultured voice said. "I'm Dido. Can I be of assistance?"

The woman who stood at the end of the barrier wall looked perfectly ordinary; she had short blond hair and was wearing a pair of black pants, a red shirt, and a black leather waist cincher.

I realized I was staring and made an embarrassed gesture of apology. "I'm . . . sorry. You look so normal."

She smiled and inclined her head toward the pictures. "Are you interested in poltergeist erotica? If so, we have a large collection of both books and videos."

"That's ... uh ... what's in the pictures?" I fought the urge to look closer, feeling it was better if I didn't know. "Thank you, but I'm here for some ... er ... toys."

"Ah." Dido gestured toward the wall. "Perhaps you will come into the shop proper, and I can help you select something that would be suitable for"—she touched my shoulder, rubbing her fingers together—"someone who has relations with a dragon."

I followed her around the wall, blinking slightly at the bright overhead track lighting, the shelves full of colorful packages, a row of mannequins modeling a number of risqué leather outfits, and the number of people strolling up and down the aisles with shopping baskets on their arms.

"Toys for him, toys for her, toys for the ethereal, or toys for shape-shifters?" Dido asked politely.

"Ethereal?" I asked, surprised. "You mean like ghosts and such?"

"Of course," she said with a little shrug of her thin shoulders. "Spirits have sexual needs, too, you know."

"How do they—no, never mind. It's not important. Why don't we start with leather wrist cuffs? A couple of them, and if you have the ones with sheep skin on the inside, that would be awesome."

"Restraints are in aisle D," she said, leading me to the correct aisle, and giving me a basket before leaving me with a murmur promising more help if I needed it. I spent a fascinating ten minutes picking out a pair of over-the-door wrist restraints to use on Baltic, adding two more sets of regular cuffs to replace Pavel's, which had been destroyed with the house, and after a few moments' thought, tossed one of the under-the-bed restraint systems into the basket for Pavel, as well. "I have no idea if he had one, but he'll probably like it," I murmured to myself. The next forty-five minutes were eye-opening, if

not fascinating, as I strolled up and down the aisles, my
brain boggling at all the items available. I had stopped to
consider something called a vibrating nipple teaser, wondering if Baltic would enjoy it, when I heard a familiar-
sounding voice asking where the spectral whips were
kept.

I put the nipple teaser back and moved cautiously to
the end of the aisle, but I didn't see anyone in this section
of the store but a sales clerk.

"Ethereal items can be found in the blue room," the
clerk said, gesturing to a blue door at the back of the
store. "A demonstration model is available. Do you need
assistance with it?"

"Do I look like the sort who doesn't know how to use
a spectral whip?" a voice asked out of nowhere.

"You are incorporeal, sir, so I can't say what you look
like at all," the clerk pointed out.

"Faugh. I'm just saving my energy. Tell Marsella I'll be
in the blue room, if she's looking for me."

"Constantine?" I said, my eyes narrowing as I searched
in vain for any sign of him.

His form shimmered into view, a surprised expression
on his face that swiftly changed to joy. "Ysolde! My beloved!"

"I thought that was you. Spectral whips, Constantine?"

He looked abashed for a moment before grinning.
"You have no idea how stimulating they can be. But
what are you doing here? Trying to spice up a boring sex
life, eh?"

"My sex life is anything but boring, not that it's the
slightest concern of yours," I said with dignity.

"Is that so?" He poked at the items in my basket, pull-
ing out an object made of plastic, shaped like the letter
C, with knobs on either end. "The Ultimate Man Button
Massager. Man Button?"

"I think that's ... You know...." I waved vaguely toward my behind.

"Prostate?" Constantine asked, his face screwing up in thought. "Really? I had no idea Baltic liked it up the—"

"That's not for Baltic," I said quickly, snatching it back and burying it under the oral stimulator. "It's for Pavel."

His eyebrows rose almost to his hairline. "You mean that you—"

"No!" I took a deep breath, wondering why I was always called upon to explain the obvious. "Pavel had a variety of toys that were destroyed when Thala sang the dirge and exploded our house. I felt bad that he should lose them, so I am trying to replace them with things I think he might like. 'He' being Pavel, not Baltic. Baltic doesn't like toys. At least, I don't think ..." I glanced at the male G-spot stimulator that poked out from beneath the vibrating pleasure wand. "No, he wouldn't like it."

"The things you learn," Constantine murmured before taking me by the arm and moving me out of the way of a couple strolling down the aisle. "My darling, when are you going to let me rescue you from that monster?"

"He is not a monster, and we've been over this before. I love him. I do not love you. End of story."

"You've been brainwashed, that's what it is. You've been taught to believe that he's what you want, and you don't know any better. If you would just place yourself in my hands—"

"Give it a rest, Constantine," I said, suddenly tired from all the stress and strain that had been my constant companion for the last twelve days.

Constantine looked about to argue, but stopped, squinting at me, instead. "You look exhausted. What has that monster done to make you look that way?"

"He left me." Constantine's eyes lit. I hurriedly continued. "Baltic was gone for almost two weeks trying to
track down his lieutenant. Former lieutenant."

"Former . . . ah, the archimage's daughter? The necromancer who raised him?" Constantine looked puzzled. "She was with you last month in Dauva. Why is he
pursuing her now?"

"It's a long story," I said, rubbing my neck.

He watched the movement avidly. "Are you in pain?"

"Not really. The muscles in my neck and shoulders are
a bit tight, is all, and they're giving me a headache."

"Ah. Here. Try this."

He extricated something from a package tucked into
his basket.

"It's a hummingbird. How cute. Although that's an
awfully long proboscis, isn't it?"

"Allow me," he said, switching it on so that the entire
hummingbird vibrated with a dull throbbing hum.

"Thanks."

"Continue. You were telling me about the necromancer."

I absently rubbed the hummingbird massager on a
particularly tight tendon on the back of my neck.
"There's not a whole lot to tell. Thala betrayed Baltic,
tried to kill us—that's why we were in Gabriel's house
that day you stormed in and tried to take the sept from
him—and is up to who knows what with her tribe of ouroboros dragons. And lucky me, I get to try to persuade
a very unpersuadable Dr. Kostich to change his mind
and help us with her."

"I do not know this Kostich," he said, repeating the
name a few times.

"He's the head of the Otherworld, and a very powerful archimage. He's the only one who can handle such a
dangerous necromancer."

"Pfft," Constantine said with a dismissive gesture.

"Necromancers are nothing. They draw their power from dark sources."

I moved the hummingbird to another tight spot on my neck, wondering if the headache that had been threatening for the last hour was going to blossom into a full-blown migraine or not. "I don't follow what it is you're trying to say. What does her source of power have to do with how dangerous she is?"

"I am a shade," he said, touching his chest.

"Yeeees," I said slowly, still not seeing what it was he was implying.

"I am made up of dark power, sweetling. That's what a shade is, and why when we run out of it, we dissipate into nothing until such time as our consciousnesses have gathered up enough power to return to the mortal plane."

"So you're saying that Thala could, what, suck up all your energy and destroy you for good?" I asked, giving the hummingbird vibrator to Constantine when he gestured for it. I moaned softly when he rubbed it along the top of my shoulder line, working it gently into the tight muscles there.

"The opposite, my heavenly body. Exactly the opposite. Necromancers have power over liches; their abilities have little effect on spirits, bound or unbound. I've heard it said that necromancers avoid shades because they simply have no way to control us."

I spun around, staring at him. "They don't? None whatsoever?"

He shrugged and turned off the hummingbird, putting it back in the box before replacing it in his basket. I caught a view on the box of just in what manner the long proboscis was meant to be used, and hurriedly averted my gaze. "Shades are Risen, Ysolde. Necromancers deal with spirits who are not, and it is that from them that they make liches. So no, they have no power against us. Why does this amaze you?"

"Because it means . . ." I bit my lip for a moment, weighing Baltic's anger with Constantine to his over-powering dislike of Dr. Kostich. "Constantine, if I asked you to help us, would you do it? Without telling me every five minutes how much you love me and that I should leave Baltic for you?"

"But I do love you, and you should leave that murder-ing—"

"Without that, would you help us? If I asked you to?"

His expression turned thoughtful, then canny. "With the necromancer?"

"Yes. The animosity between you and Baltic notwith-standing, I think he would prefer to have you deal with Thala than Dr. Kostich. He still hasn't forgiven Dr. Kos-tich for that incident that resulted in my dying. *Again*."

"I will not help Baltic," Constantine said firmly. I opened my mouth to try to persuade him, but stopped when he took my free hand and continued. "But I will do anything that you ask me, my ripe little plum. Assuming you will reciprocate, naturally."

"Reciprocate how?" I asked, amused that even dead, dragons still enjoyed bargaining. "I'm not going to do anything against Baltic."

He made a face. "Unfortunately, I begin to believe your protestations regarding him are true. The help from you that I seek has nothing to do with him."

"Or Gabriel," I said, narrowing my eyes at him to let him know I wasn't going to budge on that point, either.

"The silver dragons—"

"Are happy with Gabriel."

"I started—"

"No," I said, pulling my hand from his to hold it up. "I won't do it. If that means you won't help me, then so be it, but I will not help you try to take the silver sept from Gabriel."

He pouted for a moment, then said with ill grace, "I

love you, as I have said many times. You have requested my aid. By the code of chivalry that binds me to your side, I have no choice but to honor your wishes, and I will do as you ask."

"And in return, what do you want me to do for you?" I asked with no little wariness, knowing better than to fall for that chivalric-code crap. There wasn't a dragon born who didn't try to bargain for every favor done.

He was silent a moment, his dark eyes searching mine. "I do not know when I will need your help, but I feel that time is very near. I ask simply that if I request your help, and you feel morally able to provide it, that you do so in recognition of any assistance I give you with the necromancer."

I bit my lip again as I thought furiously. Baltic wouldn't like my promising to help Constantine any more than he'd like Constantine's helping us with Thala . . . but the needs must when the devil drives. "I agree. So long as it's nothing I'm morally opposed to, I'll help you."

Smiling, he made a move as if he was going to kiss my hand, but a voice stopped him.

"Constantine Norka?" A tall, elegant woman of Indian ethnicity approached us. "I am Marsella."

"Yes, I am Constantine. This is Ysolde de Bouchier, my mate."

"I am not your mate. I am Baltic's mate," I said wearily, smiling politely at the woman as she gave me a quick once-over. "I'm not with Constantine at all, as a matter of fact. I'm just here shopping for a few things."

"Ah." She touched one of the packages in my basket. "The Octopus. An excellent choice. I have heard many good things about it from gentlemen customers."

"Yes, well . . ." I shot a glance at Constantine, and cleared my throat. "That's not for my wyvern. It's for another dragon. I'm just replacing his toys."

"Indeed," she said without the slightest hint of curiosity. She turned to Constantine, saying, "I understand you were desirous of engaging my services. I regret to tell you I am unable to resurrect shades, and even if you were in a form conducive to resurrection, I would be unable to do as you desire. The resurrection of dragons is a difficult feat, one that only a master necromancer can accomplish. I can think of only three such people in existence today, and even then, the materials required to do so are beyond the means of most individuals."

"Quintessence," I said, nodding as I remembered hearing that Thala had stolen Dr. Kostich's priceless quintessence to resurrect Baltic.

"Just so." She gave me a long look. "Do you have knowledge of the resurrection of dragons?"

"You could say that. I've been resurrected twice, now."

She stared at me in disbelief for a moment. "Twice?"

"I sacrificed myself for her the first time," Constantine said, putting his arm around me. I elbowed him sharply in the side and slid away from him. "I don't know how she was resurrected a second time."

"Yes, twice, and it's not something I recommend." I gave Constantine a firm look. "Don't even try to pretend you don't intend to be resurrected simply so you can harass poor Gabriel."

"I am wyvern, not him," Constantine said, obviously ready to go into the familiar diatribe about the silver sept belonging to him by rights.

Marsella murmured something about seeing to another customer, then glided off to another section of the shop.

"I've already told you I'm not listening to any more of that, Constantine. You can't go messing with the septs that way, and that is that."

"Messing with the septs?"

I froze at the mild voice behind me, the world seeming to stop as slowly, I turned around to behold a man who wasn't a man.

It was the First Dragon, right there in the middle of a London sex shop.

And he didn't look happy.

Chapter Three

"Um," I said, not knowing how to greet the more-or-less god who was effectively my father-in-law, and wishing for the hundredth time that I had my memories back so I knew how I had addressed him in my former life. "Hello. I didn't summon you inadvertently again, did I?"

"No," the first dragon said, his all-knowing gaze drifting over to Constantine for a moment.

"I'll just ... er ... get back to what I was doing." Constantine gave a deprecating cough before he suddenly busied himself by examining the nearest item at hand, which turned out to be an exercise ball with some odd attachments. He hastily shoved that back and grabbed the item next to it, bending his head over it as he pretended to be engrossed with it.

I considered the First Dragon for a moment or two. "Since I assume you don't normally visit chic London sex shops, I'm going to assume you're here to speak to me? Or is it Constantine you want?"

We both looked at Constantine. He was absently fondling the betasseled teat of a lifelike blow-up sheep in fishnet stockings. Constantine reddened and shoved the sheep behind him, but he must have flipped on some sort of switch, because the sheep began to vibrate with a loud hum.

The First Dragon turned back to me and opened his mouth to speak, pausing when Constantine's sheep started baaing in what I can only imagine its creators thought was a seductive manner.

Constantine muttered to himself as he beat the vibrating, baaing blow-up doll against the wall in an attempt to shut it up.

"I gather it's me you wish to see." I cleared my throat and tried to look relaxed and not at all worried about that fact. The First Dragon's eyes were hooded, his face stern, causing my stomach to turn to lead.

"You have failed me, daughter of light."

"Baaaagggg . . ."

I turned an annoyed glare on the man behind me. "Constantine! We are trying to have a conversation here. Could you play with your sex sheep somewhere else, please?"

"I'm not playing with it, and it's not mine," he said, shooting little looks at the First Dragon. "I'm just trying to shut the damned thing up, but it won't die."

The First Dragon raised one eyebrow.

Constantine blushed even harder and began swearing softly to himself while alternately throttling the doll and beating it with the exercise ball.

A quick worried glance at the First Dragon sent my spirits plummeting, not that they were in any way buoyed by what he had said. "I'm sorry if I've failed you. I'm really not trying to, but I've had a horrible time trying to figure out just what it is you want me to do."

At a choked noise from Constantine, I recalled to whom I was talking, and made an apologetic gesture.

"That is to say, it's difficult with my memory loss to understand what it is you want me to do. I'm happy to do it. I just needed a little guidance on what it is, exactly." Mentally, I groaned. I sounded as lame as I felt.

His gaze roved over my face for a few seconds, his expression, as ever, unreadable. "If you fail me entirely, daughter, there will be the gravest of repercussions, ones that I will not be able to correct. For your own sake, and for that of all dragons, you must right the wrong done. The sacrifice of the innocent shall not be wasted."

At his words, desperation swelled within me, desperation and fear, topped off with more worry than any one person should have. I wanted to tell him that I was trying, but that Baltic was being his usual dragon self and not giving me any help. I wanted to point out that I was starting at a disadvantage by not realizing what his relationship to Baltic was in the first place, and that if someone, *anyone*, had just taken pity on me and reminded me of things I had known in the past, I might have succeeded by now. Instead, I said the last thing in the world I expected to say to the ancestor of all dragons.

"Did you love Baltic's mother?"

His eyes widened slightly. The air around us stilled, as if all life had ceased but for the three of us.

"It's just . . . I've always wondered. You seem to care about him a lot, and I thought maybe that was because his mother was very dear to you. . . ." My voice, fortunately, trailed off to nothing. The basket handle bit painfully into my hand as I waited for him to either smite me dead on the spot for being so bold, or to answer my question. I fervently hoped he'd do the latter.

"Hope for the future lies within you," he said after half a minute of extremely painful silence. "For the sake of it, you must succeed."

A chill swept over me as he turned away, but before he could disappear, he turned back to look at me, his eyes, so fathomless, not even remotely human. "If I did not, you would not be here."

I blinked a couple of times in confusion, not sure what that meant.

"Why did you ask him about Lady Maerwyn?" Constantine clutched a now-deflated—although still vibrating—sheep in one hand, and the giant exercise ball in the other. "And what did he mean by his answer?"

"Lady Maerwyn?"

Constantine gestured with the ball. "Baltic's mother."

"Ah. I'm not entirely sure what he meant," I said slowly, suddenly feeling the urge to cry. What a tragedy for the father of all dragons to lose his beloved mate. "And far be it from any dragon to just come out and answer a question when it's put to him." I shook the shadows from my head and glanced at Constantine, who still held the giant ball. "How on earth are you supposed to get two people on that at the same time?"

For a second or two he looked at me as if I were mad, then glanced down to the sex toy. "Why would you try to get two people on it?"

"Well, it has two . . . er . . . phalluses on it. That means it's for a couple, doesn't it?"

He coughed and shoved the deflated sheep into his basket, replacing the exercise ball on the shelf. "Not in this case."

"Really? But then what is the second . . ." My eyes widened as I understood. "Oh. That has to be really . . . never mind."

"Not quite your style, eh?" He didn't make another risqué comment, which took me by surprise. Instead, he said in a voice filled with wonder, "The First Dragon visited you. I do not believe he has ever done such a thing without first being summoned."

"And can I say just how much of the world I feel is on my shoulders right now? Don't fail or I what, wipe out

the entire weyr?" I slumped against a shelf full of
strap-on devices in varying sizes, colors, and species. "I
really am getting tired of his dumping everything on me.
I'm half tempted to just do as Baltic tells me, and ignore
him, but unfortunately . . ." I stopped, realizing I was
babbling everything to a man who didn't particularly
care if I fulfilled the task with which the First Dragon
burdened me. "Well, enough about that. My time is up,
and I have an appointment elsewhere. I will talk to you
soon, Constantine. Enjoy your spectral whip and sexy
sheep."

"Ysolde! I am not through discussing . . . blast and
damnation!"

I glanced back to see him fading into nothing. I smiled
and blew him a kiss before he disappeared completely.
He followed me, unseen, to the register as I paid for my
items, but after a few minutes, he ran completely out of
power. With a few impotent snarls of rage, he disappeared entirely.

"And I am so grateful that he stayed in a corporeal
state for as long as he did," I said to myself as I got into
the car.

"Who?" Ludovic asked.

"Constantine."

"The silver wyvern? The former one, that is?" Ludovic
looked startled.

"Yes. He's a shade now. I'm surprised you haven't
heard about it."

He blinked at me a couple of times, then nodded.
"Very well. To the green wyvern's house, I assume?"

"Yes, please." I sat back while Ludovic drove through
the busy London traffic, my thoughts tangled and confused.

Sadly, I was beginning to get used to their being in
that state.

"I'll call if we're done earlier than two o'clock," I told

Ludovic a short time later as he saw me to the door of
Aisling and Drake's London house.

"I will be nearby," he said, bowing in that formal way
of all dragons. His manners may have been smooth as
silk, but the way his eyes watched everyone on the street
belied a background in protection that was comprehensive enough to pass even Baltic's stringent requirements.

I patted Ludovic on the arm before entering the
house. "You don't have to hide in the shadows and co-
vertly watch everyone who walks down the street. In
fact, I know you'd be welcome for lunch at Drake's
house."

He shook his head, his gaze flickering hither and yon,
watching for any potential threat. "This is my job, Ysolde.
I will fulfill my duties in a manner worthy of the blue
dragons."

"He's sooo serious," I told Aisling and May some ten
minutes later, after having spent a few minutes playing
with Aisling's twins before they went down for their
naps. "I know that Baltic put the fear of god into him
about keeping me safe, but he won't even go sit in a pub
when I'm shopping. He has to lurk in darkened doorways and skulk along alleys, waiting for Thala to pounce."

"If I had to answer to Baltic, I'd be skulking in the
shadows, as well," May said with a little laugh, leaning
down to scratch the hairy belly of the demon in large
black Newfoundland dog form that was Jim.

"Aw, yeah, right there . . ." Jim's voice trailed away in
bliss as one of its back legs kicked wildly when May hit
a particularly itchy spot. "You have the best fingernails
of anyone, May."

"I should—they're long enough," May said with a
smile, holding up her hand and waggling her crimson-
tipped dragon claws.

I considered them for a moment. "I'd just like to know
why the shard, the very same one I carried, left you with

the ability to shift into dragon form even though you're a doppelganger, while I, who was born a dragon, can't do so."

"I thought you were resurrected as a human," Aisling said, entering the library, followed immediately by a couple of green dragons laden with trays of food. "Er . . . the last time you were resurrected, that is. I wasn't around for the first one. Lunch, anyone?"

"Hooyeah!" Jim cheered, leaping to its feet and sniffing the trays. "Now that's what I'm talkin' about."

"You will eat only what you are given, and if I catch you mooching off May and Ysolde, it'll be off to the Akasha with you," Aisling warned as the table was laid out with tempting dishes.

"Yeah, yeah, heard it before. You da big bad demon lord, and I'm just the lowly demon. Hey, where's my burger?"

"That *is* your burger," Aisling said, nodding at the chopped-up contents of a plate in a raised dog bowl.

Jim sniffed and wrinkled its nose. "That's not a burger! It smells like cereal and crap."

"It's a vegetarian burger. It's healthy and low fat, and it's just what you need if you're going to lose that extra ten pounds the vet says you need to drop. If you don't want it, you don't have to eat it. Now, let's see . . . Ysolde, our cook heard me talk so much about the wonderful food you had at the *sárkány*, she wanted to make sure you'd enjoy this lunch, so she went all out with the menu. Here we have panfried Tasmanian ocean trout with butternut squash gnocchi, and that is the orange-honey marinated beetroot, ricotta, and pine nuts tossed with a citrus dressing, and over there is a crisp flatbread, topped with Gruyère and ham."

"Oh man! And all I got was a low-fat crap burger!" Jim whined, watching with pathetic eyes as Aisling pointed out each dish. "I love Tasmanian ocean trout!"

"Beetroot, ricotta, and pine nuts," I repeated as we took our seats around the table laden with delicious food. "I'll have to tell Pavel about that. I never thought of pairing up beetroot and pine nuts."

"Bet Pavel wouldn't starve my magnificent form with crap burgers."

"It looks delicious, Aisling," May said as she took a seat next to me.

"Bet Gabe wouldn't, either."

"I hope you like it. Suzanne felt we had some standards to live up to," Aisling said with pride as she skirted Jim and pulled out a chair.

Jim sighed and slumped over so its head was resting in its bowl. "Can I have the leftovers?"

"No," Aisling told it. "Eat your healthy burger."

"You didn't even have Suzanne make me proper fries. These are sweet potato fries."

"You love sweet potato fries, and so help me god, Jim—"

"I'm eating, I'm eating. But if I waste away to nothing and you have to get me another form because this one is skin and bones, I'm going to pick an elephant or something. Then you'll really be sorry when it's time to take me for walkies."

Luckily for Jim, the tempting dishes before us served as an ample distraction to keep Aisling from carrying through with her threat to banish it to the demon version of limbo. A short time later, when we were done moaning that we had all eaten too much of the wonderful lunch, Aisling called the meeting to order.

"On our agenda today—" Aisling stopped as the door to the library was thrown open with a flourish.

"Am I late?" asked the woman who stood there, her blue eyes lighting on the remaining food. "Oh goody, I'm not too late. Is that beetroot? I *love* beetroot!"

"Cyrene," I said, blinking a couple of times in astonishment at the sight of May's twin when she hurried over to the table and helped herself. "I didn't know . . . that is, I wasn't aware . . . er . . ." I cast a helpless glance at May and Aisling.

May gave a weak smile. "I meant to warn you that Cyrene was back in town, Aisling. She . . . uh . . . showed up last night to spend the night with us, and heard Gabriel mention the Mates' Union meeting."

"Butternut squash gnocchi!" Cyrene squealed as she hauled over a chair and sat down with her loaded plate. "How did you know I loved butternut squash? Oh, and the union? Totally fabulous idea, Aisling. I'm so in on it."

"I wasn't . . . eh . . . I didn't think you would be interested in a mates' union," Aisling said, clearly floundering with the rest of us. "Drake never said anything about . . . and you're not really . . . are you?"

"Am I what?" Cyrene asked around a mouthful of trout and gnocchi.

"What she means is, did the K-man lose his mind and take you back, or are you still boinking Neptune?" Jim said, spitting out a piece of parsley garnish. "You gonna eat that last bit of trout?"

"Lose his mind!" Cyrene sputtered, outraged. "As if Kostya would have to lose his mind to beg me on his knees to return to him, which is naturally what has happened since I'm here now, aren't I?"

May, who had more insight into her twin than the rest of us, watched her with a wariness that was telling. "If you're back with Kostya, then why did you spend last night with us?"

"Kostie-kins has been out of town," Cyrene said, waving away the question with her fork. "You know how lonely I get, so I'm sure he'd want me to stay with you until he gets back."

Aisling opened her mouth as if to speak but instead tipped her head on the side as she listened. A slow smile lit her eyes as she said simply, "Well, I'm glad to see you again, Cyrene, although I have a feeling you're not going to be quite so happy in about thirty seconds."

I caught the rumble of masculine voices at the same time May did, both of us turning to the door seconds before it opened and two men strolled in.

"I know you are having your meeting," the man in the lead said, his green eyes glittering with some secret amusement as he strolled over toward Aisling. "But it would be a rudeness for us to not greet May and Ysolde—" He came to a halt at the sight of the fourth person at the table.

"Good afternoon, Drake," I said, watching with interest as his older brother froze with a horrible expression of complete and utter disbelief on his otherwise handsome face. "Kostya, it's nice to see you again. I'm glad you're here, actually; I was planning on giving you a call while I was in town."

"What is she doing here?" Kostya asked, pointing at Cyrene and sucking in approximately half of the oxygen left in the room.

"Kostie!" Cyrene squealed after looking disconcerted for a moment. "You're back! Lambkins!"

Kostya, I noted absently, was looking much more like his old self. I remembered him well from my past as Baltic's former heir, and the man who had stood by him for many centuries—until the day he decided to kill Baltic. He'd always been a darkly handsome man, with the black eyes and onyx hair so common in black dragons. But when I'd been reintroduced to him a few months before, he'd been thin to the point of gaunt, having suffered, so Aisling informed me, from imprisonment and starvation at the hands of lawless, septless dragons.

Now he was looking much healthier, breadth and depth returning him to an impressive figure of a man, and although I'd be the last person to ever apply the word "happy" to Kostya, his expression the last month had been much more relaxed.

Kostya sidestepped Cyrene as she leaped from the chair and tried to throw herself on him. "I am not your lambkins, and I will thank you to refrain from flinging your person at me."

"Oh, Kostie," Cyrene said with a simper, flashing glances around us. "Silly dragon, thinking you ever stopped being my one true love."

May groaned as Aisling rubbed her hand over her face, shaking her head. Drake moved to her side, his hands on her shoulders as he watched his brother. I watched Kostya, too, interested to see what he'd do.

"Silly dragon?" Kostya roared, his expression as dark as his hair as he glared at Cyrene. "You left me! You made me name you as a mate—despite the fact that you *aren't* a wyvern's mate—in front of all the weyr, and then you left me six weeks later!"

"I didn't really leave you. I just had to go do some . . . er . . . work. . . ."

"You told me I was a beast and cruel and wasn't worth the ground you walked on!" Kostya stormed. "You said you hated me, and that you were going away to live with some water god, and you never wanted to see me again."

Cyrene, with another glance at the rest of us, tried to put her hand on his arm, but he snatched it back with a disbelieving glare. "Now, dumpling, I'm sure the others aren't interested in our silly little squabbles—"

"Squabbles!" Kostya bellowed, sucking in the remainder of the air in obvious preparation for continuing at that volume.

"Cyrene, I think now is not the time to have this discussion," May said, taking her twin and pushing her toward the door. "You're just upsetting everyone, and if Kostya continues to yell like that, he'll wake Aisling's babies."

"But I'm a mate," Cyrene protested as May forced her out of the room. "This is a mates' meeting. I should be here."

The door closed on May's soft murmurs, leaving the room highly charged.

"Wow," Jim said, snuffling Kostya's legs until the dragon narrowed his eyes. "Never thought she'd have the balls to try to sweet-talk her way back into your good graces. You're not going to take her back, are you? 'Cause if you are, I'm going to want to have a video camera handy to film it. It isn't often you see a wyvern emasculate himself over a chick."

"Aisling," Kostya growled in warning.

"Jim, silence. Don't you give me that look—you know better than to say things like that, especially to Kostya. Although . . ." She glanced up at Drake. "Although I do admit to wondering if you're intending on taking her back, Kostya. Not that it's any of our business, but . . . er . . . I wondered."

"As did I," I said, noting that Kostya looked as if he wanted to set fire to something. Or more likely, someone.

To my surprise, he shot an unreadable look at me. "Why do you care? You aren't going to try to make me believe you have any fondness for me, too, are you?"

It took me a moment to find the words. "I have always been fond of you, Kostya, right up to the point where you killed Baltic, and then, obviously, I had a change of heart. But lately, I've been reminded that you weren't entirely bad, although I could do without your breaking Baltic's nose all over the place."

"Twice. I've broken it twice in the last few months, and he broke mine as many times, so we're even," Kostya protested, rubbing his nose. He stopped and squinted at me. "You want something from me, don't you? I can tell. I can always tell when a woman wants something."

"Of course I want something. I want my house back."

Kostya took a deep breath. "Dragonwood is mine."

"Baltic built it for me! I designed the gardens!"

"It belongs to the black wyvern, and thus it's mine now," Kostya argued. "Unless you have something of equal value you wish to exchange for it?"

"I have money. Well, Baltic does," I said slowly, knowing full well that all of Baltic's resources were being funneled into the rebuilding of Dauva. Although it went against the grain to buy what truly belonged to me, perhaps Kostya could be tempted into an arrangement. "How much were you thinking of?"

"I would not sell Dragonwood for mere money," Kostya scoffed. "You have nothing else of value to offer?"

"Me, personally? I have my love token." I touched the chain around my neck, the small oval of silver that hung from it tucked warmly between my breasts. "But its value is sentimental rather than material."

"I wouldn't take the love token that Baltic made for you," he said, outrage flitting through his eyes before he added with a grin, "He almost severed his fingers engraving it."

"He told me it was the hardest thing he'd ever done because he doesn't have a single artistic bone in his body," I said, sharing a remembered moment with Kostya, my smile matching his. "He was so proud of it, though."

The smile faded from Kostya's face. "You have nothing with which to bargain, then? So be it." He held up a dismissive hand when I opened my mouth to protest his cavalier manner. "I have relinquished my rightful claim on Dauva; that is as far as I will bend, Ysolde. The matter is settled, as is the situation with Cyrene. I have called next week's *sárkány* for the purpose of rescinding my statement regarding her, so after that time, she will have no formal standing either in my sept or the weyr."

"Kostya, you know how much that house means to

me—" I started to say, getting to my feet, intending on pleading with him.

He shot Drake a harried look, then made a formal bow to both Aisling and me. "I will see you later, Aisling. Good day, Ysolde."

I bit my lip as he strode off, damning him for being so obstinate. "Next time maybe I'll save Baltic the trouble of breaking his nose and do it myself."

"It's tempting sometimes, I admit," Aisling said.

Drake shot her a look.

"Sorry, sweetie, but even you have to admit that sometimes when Kostya gets on his high horse, he's impossible to take."

"And yet right is on his side in this," Drake said, taking the glass of dragon's blood wine that Aisling poured for him. "The house does belong to him."

"It does not—" I started to say.

"Now, hang on here," Aisling interrupted, suddenly looking thoughtful as she turned to me. "Ysolde, I think we've had a breakthrough."

"In what way?"

"Who's had a breakthrough?" May asked as she slipped into the room with a muttered apology for her twin's scene.

"Kostya." Aisling eyed me speculatively.

I frowned, confused. "I don't see how."

"He offered to trade Dragonwood for something. He's never done that before, has he?"

"No," I said slowly, thinking that point over. "He's always been adamant that the house belongs to the black dragons, and as he's the wyvern, it does. You know, I think you're right, Aisling. I think this may well be the breakthrough I've been looking for."

"Yes, but now you need something to trade for it. I don't suppose Baltic would give up Dauva?"

I sighed. "The only things that stand higher than Dauva in Baltic's affections are Brom, Pavel, and me. So no, trading Dauva for Dragonwood is out of the question. I need something else, something of great value that he would want. Hmm."

"I'd offer you the dragon shard that chose our sept, but ... well, I'm not sure that's kosher, so to speak," May said. "Not to mention that Gabriel wouldn't let the shard go."

"No, I wouldn't take your shard," I said, smiling at May. The fact that she, too, had once borne the same shard of the dragon heart, most important relic of all dragonkin, that I had borne so many centuries ago, made me feel especially comfortable around May, as if we were old, old friends. "I can only imagine what the First Dragon would have to say about the idea of us using the shards to buy something so esoteric as a house."

"Jim, will you stop it?" Aisling frowned at the big black demon as it rubbed its nose on her hand. "If you need to go walkies, you are excused."

"Baltic doesn't have any big stacks of gold lying around his lair?" May asked, looking as thoughtful as Aisling did. "Not that I'm trying to pry, but you know how dragons are about gold—I'd think that even Kostya could be swayed by it."

I glanced at Drake, who was watching Aisling with a glint in his eyes that hinted he'd rather be alone with her. "Er ... that's pretty much earmarked for Dauva, I'm afraid."

"No valuable—Jim, so help me, if you wipe your nose on me one more time—no valuable, oh, what do you call them, dragonny things?"

"Dragonny things?" Drake asked her.

"You know, the valuable things. Relics and that sort of

stuff. Jim! That's it! I am sick and tired of you. You can speak again, so go tell Suzanne you need to go for a walk."

"I don't have any relics, and Kostya cleaned out Baltic's lair before we got to it, so I'm afraid anything that was stashed away is long gone," I said sadly, my heart breaking when I thought of my beloved Dragonwood being inhabited by strange dragons.

"Man, Ash, I'm never going to be on your team for charades," Jim said with an injured sniff. "I wasn't doing the pee-pee dance, I was doing the 'I have something important to say but you keep ordering me to silence because you're all bossy now that you have spawn to push around' nose bumps."

"What important thing do you have to say?" she asked, wiping her hand on the napkin. "And it had better be very important."

"It's just a way to help Soldy, that's all. Just a way for her to get back that house she loves so much, the one that acts as vision central for her," the demon answered blithely, sitting down and staring at the two remaining pieces of flatbread.

"What is that?" I asked the demon.

It cocked an eyebrow at the food.

I picked up the flatbread. "If your idea of something important is one of your usual, ridiculous ideas, Jim—"

"It's not! I promise, it's great," it answered, a thin line of slobber creeping out of its furry flews.

"Oh, for the love of Pete. Where's your drool cloth? Not on Drake's nice carpet!" Aisling whipped a napkin around the dog's neck, mopping up its wet mouth before nodding to me. "Go ahead and give it to Jim, Ysolde, but that's your treat for the day."

I gave the dog the piece of flatbread. "And your idea?"

Jim gulped down the appetizer, licking its lips loudly. "Yum. That ham makes the whole thing."

"Jim," I said warningly.

"OK, OK, no need to look like you're going to turn me into a human again," it said, quickly backing up until it was pressed against Aisling. "That was sheer and utter hell being out of my magnificent form. My idea is this: you need something to barter with, right?"

"Yeees," I said slowly, suspicious despite my interest.

"Something fabulous like that thing that May stole from Kostich."

I looked at May in surprise. "You stole something valuable from Dr. Kostich?"

"Magoth—he's the demon lord I used to be bound to—had me steal a minor object," she said with a wry smile. "But I ended up taking a quintessence. For a day. I returned it the next day once I realized what it was."

I goggled at her. "You stole a quintessence? Those are so valuable that they're literally priceless."

"Yes, I know," May said calmly, a little smile on the corners of her mouth. "Kostich set the thief-takers after me for it. That's how I met Savian Bartholomew."

"I may have been Dr. Kostich's apprentice for a long time, but there's no way he'd give me so much as the time of day, let alone something impossibly valuable like a quintessence," I protested.

"I didn't say you should give Kostya that—I just mean that you need something *like* it, something über-valuable," Jim corrected me.

"How am I supposed to get something über-valuable? Hmm . . . Savian . . . I wonder if he could be of help. . . ."

"He *is* a tracker," May said doubtfully. "But I always assumed that meant tracking people or beings or things like that, not so much locating valuable items."

Aisling started laughing so hard, she had to clutch a napkin and mop at her eyes.

"Mate?" Drake asked, frowning at her. "Are you unwell?"

"No, I'm fine," she wheezed, dabbing one last time at her eyes. "It just struck me as funny, that's all."

"What struck you as funny?" I asked, sharing a look of confusion with May.

"Oooh," Jim said, then it, too, snickered. "Good one, Ash."

Drake's eyes were narrowed on her until suddenly he sat back, his expression unreadable, but his eyes glittering with interest.

"I definitely feel like I'm not sitting with the cool kids," I told May.

"I'm right there with you." She turned back to Aisling. "What do all three of you—wait a minute, you're not thinking what I think you're thinking, are you? Wow, that might . . . hmm."

"Great, now I'm it and all by myself." I sighed. "Would someone take pity on the poor, resurrected woman who clearly has missed something of great importance?"

"I'm sorry, Ysolde, I didn't mean to make you feel like a pariah. I was just laughing because . . . Well, it's kind of ironic, really. What I was thinking is that you don't need Savian Bartholomew," Aisling told me. "You need a thief. A really good thief. A master thief, the kind who knows not only where all the über-valuable things are, but how to get to them, and has the ability to do so."

I glanced at May, who shook her head. "My thieving days are over, thank the gods."

"You probably don't remember this, but the green dragons are noted thieves." Aisling patted Drake's leg, pride obvious in her voice. "And there are none better than the wyvern himself."

Drake pursed his lips, idly rubbing his chin. "It is tempting, I admit. I haven't had opportunity to . . . *liberate* . . . anything in some time. What did you have in mind, *kincsem*?"

"I don't know who has all the goodies that might

tempt Kostya, although part of me says it would be a blast to grab something from Dr. Kostich. Still, he'd probably know it was us and make our lives hell, and I can't do that to all the green dragons. We need something that can't be traced back to us."

"I'm not really comfortable with the idea of stealing something," I said reluctantly. "I don't think I could be happy with the house knowing it came at the price of theft. But I appreciate the thought."

"Maybe if it was something taken from someone bad?" Aisling suggested. "Like a demon lord? Or maybe something that was taken from you, and was really yours to begin with?"

"The only things that were taken from us were taken by Kostya, and much as I would be happy for Drake to try to steal Dragonwood back, I think it would be beyond even his skills."

Drake rubbed his chin again, his eyes speculative before he sighed and shook his head. "No, it would be beyond me, despite its being a tempting target. Kostya would not be pleased, either, and although Aisling would not hesitate at enraging him, he *is* my brother, and I would have peace in the weyr."

"I suppose that would be the best," Aisling said with a slump of her shoulders. "There's got to be something, Ysolde."

The door opened at that moment, allowing the tall, elegant man with short dreadlocks, bright grey eyes, and lovely warm brown skin to stroll in. He made a beeline for May, stopping next to her to stroke her short black hair, saying as he did so, "Good afternoon, Aisling, Ysolde. Greetings, Drake. What is it Ysolde is searching for?"

"Heya, Gabe," Jim said, sauntering over to snuffle him. "Still wyvern, huh? That ghost not challenged you for the sept yet?"

Gabriel Tauhou, wyvern of the silver dragon sept, stiffened for a moment, ire flashing in his eyes. "Not for lack of trying." He turned to me, adding, "Has Mayling spoken to you about Constantine?"

"Not yet," May said, moving over to sit on the couch, Gabriel at her side. "I was . . . er . . . saving that for later. Along with the other thing."

"Is Constantine still being impossible?" I asked. Weariness swept over me. "I ran into him earlier today and told him again that he isn't getting your sept, but you know how he is."

"Oh, we know. He hasn't left Gabriel's side for more than an hour or two," May said, leaning into her wyvern.

"I had to sneak out the back of the house in order to escape without him on my heels," Gabriel said, looking extremely martyred.

"We've tried to explain nicely that we have nothing but the utmost respect for him since he founded the sept, and that we'd be happy to have him visit, and that he's even welcome to offer advice—"

Gabriel made a choking sound.

"But he keeps insisting that Gabriel stand down and let him take his rightful place as wyvern. He doesn't seem to understand that he's a ghost. The only time we get any relief is when he runs out of energy and has to go into an incorporeal state to recharge his batteries."

Gabriel slid his arm around May. "My guards had taken to challenging him to sword fights in order to facilitate that event, but after a few weeks of that, he caught on to us, and now simply haunts me every chance he gets, attempting to formally challenge me for the sept. I refuse to accept the challenges, of course, citing the fact that he's not living as my excuse, but it is growing exceedingly tiresome. I wish you would take him back, Ysolde."

"I think Baltic would kill me himself if I did that," I

said with a sympathetic look. "I'm very sorry, though, Gabriel. Perhaps if someone else was to talk to him . . ."

"You're the only one he talks about," May answered. "If you could try reasoning with him again, we'd be very grateful."

"I can try, but I'm not sure he'll listen to me any more than to you. He hasn't thus far. But I'll bring it up with him again. Baltic and I owe you so much, it's the least I can do."

"About that," Gabriel said smoothly, his brows rising slightly in question. "Have you approached Baltic about the curse?"

My shoulders slumped as the weariness swamped me. I struggled to keep my head above it, rising from the table and moving over to the fireplace. "Two weeks ago, as a matter of fact. He's remaining steadfast that there's no compelling reason for him to lift the curse from you guys. I keep telling him that the whole reason behind the curse is moot now that we know Constantine didn't kill me, but he just says it's as good a reason as any, and ignores my attempts to make him understand how it's hurting all of you."

Gabriel's jaw tightened as May put her hand on his, obviously reminding him of his manners. I felt bad watching him struggle to keep from lashing out, knowing just how much the silver dragons wanted Baltic's dramatic curse removed, made at the time of my death, and dooming them all to never having a mate born until a black dragon ruled the sept.

"What I need is some leverage I can use against him," I said, desperately wracking my brain for something, anything I could use to force Baltic into lifting the curse. "Something that he wants so badly, he's willing to give up his long-nursed grudge for it. Something . . ."

The image of an object came to my mind at that moment, a bright, shining object that glowed with white-blue light, something that was indeed so valuable, its reclamation could well force Baltic into a position where he had to lift the curse.

"You've thought of something," May said, her expression going from despair to hopeful in a second.

"Yes," I said slowly, turning to look thoughtfully at Drake.

"Something über-valuable for Drake to steal?" Aisling said, leaping to her feet, excitement visible in her expression. "Something that you can use to get back Dragonwood? Or to use against Baltic?"

I was about to explain when Aisling's words struck me. "Oh. Dragonwood. Yes, it would be valuable enough that Kostya would probably give Dragonwood up for it. But . . ." I glanced over at Gabriel and May, my heart aching. There was no choice to be made, however. Despite the fact that my very soul cried out for Dragonwood, I could never live there knowing I could have saved the silver dragons instead. "No, that would never do. It will have to go to you, Gabriel. Then you can use it to force Baltic to lift the curse."

"I thought you said you wouldn't be happy if Drake stole something for you. Was that just for Dragonwood?" Aisling asked, moving over to stand with me. "Not that I think you're wrong, because I'd totally steal something in order to save the silver dragons. And I know that Drake is dying to have a go at something really difficult— you wouldn't believe how happy the thought of a little thievery makes him—but if it's going to cause problems with you, then we won't do it."

"What is this object that has so much power over Baltic?" Gabriel asked, frowning as his thumb rubbed over May's fingers. "He has Dauva, does he not? He has you. . . . I don't know what else there is that could hold sway over him."

The mention of Dauva triggered a memory of a

month ago, when Baltic had discovered that Thala, his lieutenant, had stolen a very valuable personal artifact from a hidden lair deep in the bowels of the remains of Dauva. "There are two things, actually," I said, carefully picking my words. Baltic hadn't mentioned the loss of his talisman, the item that marked him as a child of the First Dragon, to anyone, not even Pavel. "One is something of which I have little knowledge, and thus wouldn't be suitable to our purposes—although Drake, perhaps one day— well, we'll leave that until such time. The other, however, is something that rightfully belongs to Baltic, and was taken from him by a very unscrupulous method. And yes, it has enough value to him that it might just do the trick."

Gabriel suddenly sat up straight, rubbing at his shoulder. "The sword? The one that Kostich took from him?"

I nodded. "Dr. Kostich blackmailed him to get it, using me as bait, the rotter, and later hid it away in some secret, unreachable, impossible-to-access stash of the L'au-dela." I smiled as everyone in the room sucked in a collective breath. "I think it's time to *liberate* Antonia von Endres' light blade, Drake."

Chapter Four

"What will you give me for it?"

"I beg your pardon?"

Drake's voice was smooth as ever, his face austere, but his eyes were hot with a look that I remembered from centuries before when Baltic acquired new treasures.

"You desire me to steal the light blade so that it can be given to Gabriel, and in turn exchanged for the removal of the curse upon the silver dragons, is that not so?"

"That was the idea, yes," I agreed.

"What will you give me to steal the blade?" he asked.

"Drake!" Aisling whomped him on the arm. "You are not going to pull that negotiating crap with Ysolde!"

"I do not see how such an act will benefit the green dragons," he told her, catching her hand when she was about to whomp him again. "*Kincsem*, you know how these things are done. My services do not come without a price."

"Gabriel is your friend!" Aisling said, clearly outraged.

"And my friend has his mate," he answered smoothly.

"You . . . I don't believe . . . Drake! All the silver dragons are our friends! I can't believe you'd be so heartless, so callous, as to charge Ysolde for saving them!"

Gabriel laughed when Aisling wrestled her hand away from her wyvern, looking as if about to deck Drake.

"I don't mind paying him," I said hurriedly, not wanting to cause any trouble between them. "I don't have a ton of money set aside, but I'm sure we could work out something."

"What are you laughing about?" May asked Gabriel, giving him an odd look.

"Aisling, do not attack Drake. I assure you it's not necessary," Gabriel said, chuckling. "I am not offended by his request for payment. It is perfectly understandable that he should desire payment for what will be a difficult and risky venture. However, I am willing to assist Ysolde if she needs financial help, since she has not had the resources of a sept behind her."

"Oh no," I said, straightening up and lifting my chin. "This was originally my bargain with May for her help in getting Thala free, and although I greatly appreciate your offer, I will pay Drake. Somehow. Er . . . how much were you thinking, Drake?"

"I have money," Drake said, ignoring Aisling when she continued to glare at him. "What do you have to barter?"

"What do you want?" I countered, feeling it was better to have the upper hand when negotiating with a dragon.

"Dauva," he said simply.

"You're kidding, right?" I asked.

He shook his head.

I sighed. "Dauva is not mine to give. What else do you want?"

"What do you have that is valuable?"

"We've just been through this," I said, running my hands through my hair in agitation as I frantically ran over my meager belongings. What I needed was something similar to the light blade, something that had belonged to Baltic and the black dragons, but that had been taken away from us. Dragonwood and Dauva were out. Baltic's talisman was out of the question, even if I knew where it was. The only other thing I could think of having been stolen from the black dragons was the Modana Phylactery, the one-fifth of the dragon heart Baltic had kept in his lair until Kostya had filched it a few months before.

"She thought of something else," Jim said, plopping its big butt down on my foot and leaning on me. "Ear rubbles?"

"Jim, leave Ysolde alone while she's thinking," Aisling said, ceasing muttering at Drake long enough to glance at me. "*Did* you think of something?"

I eyed Drake. I couldn't ask him to steal his brother's shard as payment for stealing the light blade—that would just rack up another debt to be settled, not to mention the fact that Drake probably wouldn't do it. Which meant I had to steal the thing myself. I wondered how hard it would be to get into Kostya's lair. "Yes, I think I have—"

"I knew it! I knew you would be here! You thought to have meetings to find ways to destroy me, did you not? But I have found you out, and now, in front of these witnesses, you will accept my challenge!" A man's voice rolled out across the room before he stalked through the closed door, stopping in front of Gabriel. "You, my godson's brother, you will be my witness that this one, unworthy of bearing the title of wyvern, has accepted my challenge at last and will give back to me the sept I, myself, created."

"Constantine," I said with a sigh, causing the man in question to spin around, a delighted expression chasing away his scowl.

"Ysolde! You are here? How fortunate, since I had not finished speaking to you when you left the shop."

Drake glared at his mate. "I thought you warded the house."

"I did!" She looked as surprised as Gabriel was exasperated. "Those wards were supposed to keep out all spirits."

"I am not an ordinary shade. I am a dragon, a wyvern, and we are not governed by those laws relating to lesser beings," he answered with aplomb before taking my hand and pressing wet kisses to it. "My adorable one, as always, perhaps we could continue our conversation in private?"

I was about to tell him that I would talk to him later, when a thought occurred to me. "You got through Aisling's wards?"

"I believe we've just established that fact." He relinquished my hand when I pulled on it. "My poor darling. All those centuries spent with Baltic have weakened your mind."

If Constantine's shadehood allowed him to get through Aisling's wards, then perhaps he could do the same with any protection that Kostya had on his lair. If so, that would solve my problem of how to get the shard.

I smiled at Constantine until his words penetrated my brain. "By the rood! Did you just call me stupid?"

"Ooooh, so not the way to woo the babes, Connie," Jim said, giving his shoes a quick once-over before cocking a furry eyebrow at the former wyvern.

Constantine, who was obviously about to placate me, glared instead at Jim and said in a thoroughly outraged tone that had Aisling and May both giggling, "*Connie? Did that . . . that . . . what the hell is that thing?*"

"It's a demon, and its name is Jim, and it's a friend," I said, my hands on my hips as I flared my nostrils at him. I wasn't normally the sort of woman who went around flinging her nostrils willy-nilly at people, but this was clearly one of those moments when such action was called for. I half wished for Baltic to be here, just so he could punch Constantine in the face and shut him up . . . but then I remembered not only my agreement with Constantine, but the new idea that had just struck me, and instead I kept my tongue behind my teeth.

"Hiya," Jim said, allowing a little tendril of drool to coil down onto Constantine's shoe. "I'm with Aisling, in case you're wondering."

"I wasn't," Constantine snapped. "And you will not refer to me by that appalling appellation again."

"Nice alliteration," Jim said before yelping when Constantine set fire to its head. It ran toward her, yelling, "Ash!"

"Stop it right now," Aisling said, beating the demon on the head with a pillow to put out the flames.

"Do not give me orders, woman," Constantine said grandly, flicking more fire toward her.

"Oh!" she gasped before starting forward toward him, but Drake was instantly there, his eyes glittering with ire as he shoved Constantine against the wall.

"You would dare lift a hand to me?" Constantine asked him, outraged. "Recall who I am, wyvern. Your father was my friend!"

"My father was a deranged madman," Drake snarled with such menace that I stepped forward, angling myself between the two men. "Not that I ever believed the day would come when I would speak these words, but I begin to believe that Baltic was correct about you all along."

"I think that's one for team Soldy," Jim told May.

"I think that's two for her," May answered.

"All right, boys, that's enough," I said loudly, pushing my way even farther between the two posturing dragons, one hand on each of their chests as I shoved Drake back a step. "Drake, back down. Constantine, you may have been dead for four hundred years, but you used to have better manners than would allow you to act so rudely to a wyvern's mate in his own home. You ought to be ashamed of yourself for setting fire to Aisling's personal demon like that, not to mention trying to pick a fight with Drake. Now just simmer down, both of you! We have plans to make, and I don't have the time or inclination to witness a pissing match, especially one involving fire."

Aisling applauded lightly. "Well put, Ysolde. Hackles down, Drake."

Her husband shot her a look that would have scared the tar out of me, but he moved over to sit when she patted the spot next to her on the couch.

"Plans?" Constantine asked me. "Something to do with what we talked about?"

"No," I said hurriedly, smiling widely at everyone. "Not exactly."

"What—" Aisling started to ask.

"We were making some plans about having Drake find an arcane object," I told Constantine, hoping to distract both him and Aisling at the same time.

"Ah." He made a bored gesture. "I have no interest in such plans unless they concern that usurper of my sept."

I bit back the response that no one had invited him there to begin with, reminding myself that antagonizing him would serve none of us well. I eyed Drake for a moment before speaking. "If I promise to pay you with an item that would be ample compensation for the work you'll undertake for me, will you do it?"

"What item?" he countered, just as I knew he would, blast his dragon hide.

"I'd rather not say right now."

Interest chased away the remnants of ire in his eyes. "I must be reassured that what you have to offer me is suitably valuable."

"Oh, it's valuable. It's so valuable that by giving it to you, I'll have no end of trouble with Baltic."

He narrowed his eyes on me, then nodded. "Very well. I have no reason to distrust your word, but be warned that if the payment is not all that you swear it is, you will hand over Dauva."

My eyes widened at his audacity even as Aisling protested with a gasped, "Drake!"

"I just got done telling you that Dauva wasn't mine to give."

"Nonetheless, an agreement made by a mate must be honored by her wyvern. Do you agree to my terms?" he said smoothly, ignoring Aisling when she continued to voice her opinion of his underhanded tactics.

I bit my lip, imagining what it would do to Baltic if I had to force him to give up his beloved Dauva. I had no choice, however. There was simply no other way, nothing else I had up my sleeve. "I agree," I said slowly, praying that Constantine would be able to do the impossible, and take the shard from Kostya.

"What is this arcane object you seek that requires a large payment?" the man himself asked me, looking somewhat bored by the conversation. "What agreement are you making with Toldi's son?"

"I'll tell you that on the way to my car," I said, grabbing his arm and pulling him after me as I moved toward the door. Constantine, who had been starting to fade into a semitranslucent (and thus incorporeal) state, solidified again with a besotted look on his face.

"Er . . . just a second, Constantine. Aisling, could I have a quick word with you?"

"Of course," she said, gesturing toward a side door. "Private, I assume?"

"Yes. It's ... er ... mate business. Constantine, please do not try to challenge Gabriel. I'll be back in a minute."

May and I followed Aisling into a small sitting room.

"Ysolde does not command me. About my sept, Tauhou—" Constantine was saying as I closed the door.

"What's up?" Aisling asked, propping one hip against a small table.

"I want to ask you a strange question," I said carefully.

"Whoa! Sex talk in private?"

Aisling rolled her eyes at the demon as it entered the room. "Hush, you. What sort of strange question?"

"It's about Drake." I considered how best to phrase my question.

Aisling made a face. "You've known him a lot longer than I have, judging by the vision you had a few months ago."

"I knew him, but didn't *know* him, if you know what I mean. Ugh. That sentence was confusing. What I want to know is whether you trust him."

She blinked at me.

"OK, that one didn't come out right, either." I thought for a moment, trying to find the words that would not offend, yet make it clear what I was after. "If you weren't Drake's mate, and you had something very valuable that could possibly be misused, would you trust him to hold it without abusing it?"

She laughed, to my surprise. "That's an easy question. I did, and I did."

"You did?"

May looked as confused as I felt. "What did you trust Drake with that was so valuable?"

"Have you ever heard of the Tools of Bael?"

May's eyes widened. "You didn't have one of them!"

Aisling nodded. "I did. That was how I met Drake, as a matter of fact. He stole the aquamanile I was sent to Paris to deliver. It turned out to be one of the Tools of Bael."

"I'm not familiar with that. What exactly are the Tools of Bael?" I asked.

"You don't get to Abaddon much, do you?" Jim asked, snuffling me.

"I have enough things going on in my life that fortunately, no, I don't."

"The Tools of Bael are three gold objects that individually allow the bearer to tap into the power of Bael. Or they did. I heard from the Guardians' Guild that they were destroyed shortly before Bael was banished. But before he was, they were objects of great power, and the three of them together had basically limitless power. Enough to topple the mortal world itself."

"And you gave one of those to Drake?" I shook my head. "Before you were his mate? How did you know he wasn't going to use it?"

"Because I knew by then that Drake might be many things, but he has never been power hungry. And he could have done a whole lot more damage than you know—you see, he already had possession of the other two Tools. He had to give them over to Bael a few years ago, but never once did he consider using them. So in answer to your question, yes, absolutely I would trust him with an object of great importance. Were you planning on giving him one, perhaps in payment for a certain task?"

"That's what I'm thinking, yes. It just depends . . ."

"Depends on what?" she asked.

I smiled. "On some things that haven't quite come together. Thanks for the honesty."

"Any time," she said, escorting us back into the library.

"And thank you for the wonderful lunch. My compliments to Suzanne. May, Gabriel—it was a delight to see you again, and just as soon as Baltic and I get settled in a home while Dauva's being rebuilt, I'll have you all over for dinner. In the meantime, Drake, consider yourself employed. I'll be in contact about . . . er . . . things."

Aisling hurried after us as I all but dragged Constantine to the door while saying the necessary polite things, but avoiding the penetrative look Aisling bent upon me.

"Where are you taking me, my forceful one?" Constantine said as one of Drake's redheaded guards opened the front door. "I am not done with the silver pretender—"

"Yes, you are. Thanks, István. It was nice seeing you again. Pavel sends his best to you and Pál. Constantine, stop digging in your feet. I have something I want to say to you."

"Something private regarding our plans?" he asked, following me when I exited the house. "Or something intimate? You wish for me to destroy Baltic once and for all, so that we might be together as one?"

"That is going to get old so quickly. . . . No, I lie; it already *is* old." I scanned up and down the street, spotting Ludovic's car a block away. "Just be quiet for a few minutes and let me talk. I don't have much time, because Ludovic is convinced that every second on the street is a second where Thala is lying in wait to smash me to a pulp, so we're going to have to make this quick."

"I am intrigued, naturally, but I have already agreed to help you, and thus you must now release my arm. I am almost at the end of my power."

"Sorry." I let go of his arm. He faded into nothing. "You still there?"

"Always at your side, my love."

I sighed to myself, wanting to snap at him, but knowing it would do little good, not to mention leaving him testy and less likely to aid me. "You said you got through

Aisling's wards because you're not a normal shade. Does that mean you can do other things that non-wyvern shades can't do?"

"What sort of things?"

"Like, say, break into someone's lair?"

"You desire that I steal from Baltic?" Satisfaction was rich in his voice. "I will move the stars themselves to do that, beloved one."

"Don't be ridiculous, Constantine. Why would I need to break into Baltic's lair? No, what I need from you is much, much more difficult . . . and much more dangerous."

He said nothing as I spoke quickly while walking slowly toward Ludovic's car, obviously playing up to his ego by explaining that I desperately needed Kostya's shard—the one that had been stolen from Baltic—and that he was the only one who could get it for me. By the time Ludovic stood waiting for me next to the open door of the car, Constantine was making pleased noises.

"You wish for me to steal from my godson for you?" his disembodied voice asked.

A woman strolling past us with two basset hounds looked startled before hurrying on. A few yards away from us, Ludovic frowned when I stopped. He glanced around the street before cocking an eyebrow at me.

"Yes, that's exactly what I want you to do."

"That I will gladly do without requiring a further commitment of help from you, but only after I reclaim my sept."

"No!" My fingers itched with the need to throttle him. "Constantine, I don't know what any of us has to do to make you understand this, but I'm going to give it one more shot because you were a good friend to me before you lied to me and dishonorably bound me to you in order to keep me away from Baltic—Gabriel is a good wyvern. The members of his sept—and it is *his* sept, not yours any longer—love him. They will stand behind him no matter what. You can challenge him from here to kingdom come, and they'll still stand behind him. If you persist on this idiotic course of trying to oust him, all you'll do is destroy the sept, because I can guarantee you that if Gabriel were to leave, all the rest of the silver dragons would go with him."

Constantine appeared before me, a pugnacious look on his face. I glanced around quickly, but no one was close enough to have seen his materialization . . . no one but Ludovic, who started in surprise. I gestured to him that it was OK, but still he headed toward me.

"The very same dragons who followed me when I left the black sept!" Constantine snapped, anger and pain and frustration in his voice and expression.

"Yes, those very same people," I said, putting my hand on his arm. "But you've been gone for four hundred years, Constantine. They aren't your followers anymore. They have a wyvern, a good man, one who will fight you to his death to keep them. Do you really care so little about the silver dragons that you would destroy them simply to satisfy your own ego?"

He digested this for a moment. "They are not my sept any longer? I am not a silver dragon?"

Pain lashed him, pain that I knew well. I hugged him, wishing things had turned out differently, wishing I'd listened to Baltic and never had Constantine's shade raised. "I think you're like me—once a silver dragon, and now something else."

"You are a light dragon," Constantine said, looking curiously at me.

For one horrible moment, I thought he was going to demand that I persuade Baltic into accepting him into the sept, but he simply looked beyond me. "But before that, you were a black dragon."

"Yes. I was born silver, but I became a black dragon when I accepted Baltic as my mate."

His voice and expression were contemplative. "Hmm."

Ludovic was growing impatient, gesturing toward his watch even as he continued to scan the streets for potential threats.

"I have to go, Constantine. Is there . . . This sounds so strange. . . . Do you *live* anywhere? Is there somewhere I can contact you about the situation with Kostya?"

"Kostya," he said in that same tone of contemplation, his attention focused on some inner vision. "Yes, I believe that will suffice. It should have been mine by rights, after all."

"Also, do you have a cell phone? Or is there some other way I can get a hold of—what should have been yours by rights?" I asked, suddenly suspicious of the pleased look that spread across his face.

His lips curled in a smile as he grabbed me, suddenly fully solid, and pressed a fast, hard kiss on my lips. "The black sept, of course. Your idea is most excellent, Ysolde. It should have been mine to begin with, but that underhanded Baltic used his grandfather's affection to challenge me for the position of heir, and Alexei gave it to him."

"Whoa," I said, twisting myself out of his grip. "I asked you to steal a shard from Kostya, not take his sept!"

"But now," Constantine said, continuing just as if I hadn't spoken, "I will have my revenge, against Baltic, against Alexei, against all of them. I will take the black sept, and return it to its full glory!"

"Heaven preserve me from dragons with one-track minds," I swore.

Chapter Five

"Savian speaking."

"Hello, I don't know if you remember me, but my name is Ysolde de Bouchier, and I—"

"Ack!" The man on the other end of the phone squawked so loudly that Ludovic, at the wheel of the car as we headed back to the pub, cast a curious glance at me in the rearview mirror. "You're the deranged dragon who has the unnatural interest in my nuts!"

"I am neither deranged nor do I give a fig about your testicles," I said with much dignity.

"You threatened to turn them into toads!"

"It was all a mistake, and I apologized later for that. Besides, it's not like I actually did turn them into anything. It's just that you were being very annoying by telling Gabriel and May that my ex-husband hired you to get me away from them, which was extremely embarrassing considering they were nothing but nice to me, so really, any testicular threats made—and again, I will point out that they were threats only, and not actions—were perfectly reasonable given the circumstances."

Savian Bartholomew, roguish Englishman famed for both his ability in tracking, and his record as a thief-taker for the L'au-dela, breathed heavily into the phone at me. "That point is open to debate. If you didn't call me up to harass my nuts, what do you want?"

"I have a job for you, one involving the location of a stronghold." I had to go carefully here, needing to assess his willingness to steal something from people who occasionally employed him.

"Which stronghold?"

I cleared my throat and idly watched the buildings stream by as we passed into the London suburb where the pub was located. "I don't know that it has a proper name, but it's a place where items of great value are stored."

"I'm not a thief," he warned, his voice rife with suspicion. "If you're thinking to hire me to steal something for you, you can just think again."

"I wouldn't dream of asking you to steal anything that wasn't mine. And as a matter of fact, the item that I do want removed from this stronghold belongs to Baltic, so even if I was thinking of it, it would be perfectly moral to do so. However, all I need is for the location of the stronghold to be found. After that, your job is done."

"You're talking about a dragon's lair, aren't you?" Savian's voice was relaxed now, almost lighthearted. "But wait. May said you're hooked up with that wyvern with the deranged theurgist who almost killed me when I hunted down his lair. Whose lair do you want found if it's not his?"

"It's not really a lair I want found. Well, perhaps it is of sorts, but it . . . uh . . . doesn't belong to a dragon. I'm glad you mentioned May, though. She said that she and Gabriel had hired you to do some things that would have made Dr. Kostich angry had he known about them."

"Now you're blackmailing me?" he asked, his voice rising.

"No, no, I'd never dream of doing that. I just wanted to make sure that I understood exactly what it was that May said, and that you were willing—should the price be suitable, naturally—to do things that may not be looked kindly upon by the L'au-dela Committee. Is that correct?"

"Well, I'm not going to kill anyone, or steal something, if that's what you're asking. But if you are speaking of a greyer area ... I'd be open to discussing the situation."

He sounded intrigued now. I was counting on May's having said his loyalty could be swayed away from the group that ran the Otherworld, and slumped back against the seat in relief. Another glance out the window warned me we were almost home. "Look, this is too complicated to work out over the phone. Can we meet to discuss the details?" I gave him directions to the pub. "Say, an hour?"

"I could do that," he said slowly. "If you promise me one thing, that is."

I sighed. "I assure you that I have absolutely no designs on any part of your genitalia—"

"No, not that, although I will hold you to that promise."

"What do you want, then?" I asked, curious.

"Carte blanche to beat the living daylights out of that lieutenant your wyvern keeps around to destroy innocent people."

I smiled as Ludovic pulled into a spot behind the pub. "I wish I could. There's nothing I'd like more than to see Thala brought down a peg or two, but she's gone to earth in Nepal. However, I think I can say with all confidence that if you were to find her, you could have at her with impunity—as well as a whole lot of my personal appreciation."

"I'll be there at eight," Savian promised before hanging up.

Pavel was busily making dinner in the pub's kitchen when I entered.

"Evening, Pavel. Did Brom and Nico get home?"

"Yes, about an hour ago. Nico went off to deal with a minor family emergency but said he should be back shortly. Baltic is around somewhere, arguing with the builder about whether or not it's reasonable to rebuild Dauva to its original specifications."

"Oh yes, I can just imagine what the locals will think of a medieval castle popping up out of nowhere. I'd better go reason with him." I started for the stairs that led up to our rooms but stopped to sniff the air, trying to guess what it was he was cooking. "Is that . . . roast beef?"

"Roast Angus beef with Yorkshire pudding," he answered, looking up with a smile. Pavel and I shared a love of cooking that amused Baltic, although I noticed he never complained about the fruits of our labors.

"Oooh, so very English. I've never tried to make Yorkshire pudding. Do you need help?"

"No, my friend Holland is due any minute. He'll give me a hand with the starters if I need it."

"We're having appetizers? What's the occas—did you say friend? You mean a friend, like the Casemonts who own this pub? Or a *friend* friend?"

Pavel laughed, dusted off his hands, and to my absolute astonishment, winked. "Holland is a friend I've known for some time . . . but he was involved with someone before."

I tried to look not in the least bit interested in Pavel's somewhat complicated love life. "How nice for you. What are you making now?"

"Langoustine tortellini. It'll be served with some vegetables, green lentils, and a shellfish cream."

"That sounds heavenly. Did you want me to whip together something for dessert? What . . . er . . . what sorts of things is your friend into? I mean, what does he like? Food-wise, that is." I coughed, my face turning red as Pavel laughed again.

"I made roasted-banana ice cream earlier, and we'll have that with cinnamon doughnuts with honeycomb cream, unless there's something else you'd prefer."

"No, no, that sounds fine." I eyed him, wondering if I should dress up for dinner, then realized how strange it was that I was even thinking of dressing for his date. "Sounds like you have everything under control. Which reminds me, I have a few things for you. I'll give them to you after dinner, since you're busy now, and they . . . er . . . I'll just give them to you later. But I do think your friend will like them. At least, I hope he likes them. . . ."

Pavel's lips twitched, but he said in a perfectly sober voice, "I'm sure Holland will enjoy whatever you have for us, as will I."

"Good. Well, then. I'll just go see how many turrets and drawbridges Baltic needs to be talked out of. And maybe I'll run by him the idea of us . . . hmm."

"He said no," Pavel called after me as I hurried up the stairs. I paused and bent down low to look over the banister at him. "I wouldn't mind if you were present, but Baltic seems adamant on the subject."

I swore. "Dammit, he has this bizarre idea that I'm fascinated by the idea of you with . . . and of course, I'm not."

"Of course."

"Not in the least. I mean, I'm happy that you've found a friend again, naturally, because you deserve some companionship. But just because that friend is a man doesn't mean anything to me, nothing at all."

Pavel's eyebrows rose.

"He really said no? To you? Right to your face?"

He nodded.

I ground my teeth and continued up the stairs, intent on informing Baltic once and for all that I had no outlandish sexual fantasies, and the sooner he admitted that, the happier we'd all be. I paused quickly to check on Brom, mentally organizing several arguments that Baltic would be unable to dispute.

Brom's room was empty, although judging by the notebooks, pamphlets, clothing, and assorted detritus usually associated with my son that was strewn around the small bedroom, he had been there recently.

I continued on to our room, dropped off the shopping bags, and collected the laptop that Baltic had purchased the week before; then I headed down the front stairs to the private room that Baltic tended to use as his office.

"... Don't care what you say it used to look like, I'm telling you that no one has a moat anymore. It's all high-tech security these days, dragon."

"I can have a high-tech moat," Baltic insisted, tapping an architectural plan that was spread out on a small round table. "I do not intend for the new Dauva to be anything less than what it originally was."

"I thought we'd been through this already," I said as I entered the room, pausing to glance around it. "Back when you were having the plans for the new Dauva drawn up. Where's Brom?"

"That design had too many faults," Baltic said, holding out his hand for me. "I want it redesigned."

"Two days before we're due to start clearing the land." The builder, whose name was Murphy, stabbed his fingers through his hair. "This is why I don't like working with dragons! You're always expecting me to work miracles."

"Where's Brom?" I asked again as Baltic's fingers wrapped around mine.

"Upstairs in his room. Mate, do you not think that four towers—"

"No, he's not upstairs. I was just up there. Brom?" I released Baltic's hand and went out into the corridor that ran between the main section of the pub and the side rooms, quickly checking the rooms for signs of him. Seeing that they were empty sent a chill down my spine, my belly suddenly feeling as if it had been gripped with a clammy hand. I ran to the main room of the pub, hurrying over to the bar. "Angela, have you seen Brom?"

"Not since this morning, luv," the short, round woman said, wiping off a tap before handing over a pint of dark ale. "Oh, but someone left a letter for you. Let me see, where did I . . . Ah, here it is."

She handed me an envelope before turning to the next customer.

Baltic appeared in the door to the pub, a frown pulling down his dark chocolate eyebrows. "Did you find him?"

"He's not here. Baltic—" A wave of fear crashed over me, making my skin crawl. "You don't think Thala—"

"No. She would not," he said with absolute conviction, but that did little to ease the panic that clutched me. I ran past him to the door of the pub, quickly searching the parking lot and the street for signs of Brom.

"Where has he gone?" I wailed to Baltic, spinning around, unsure of what to do, or where to look for him. "He doesn't just wander off like this, not when he knows how worried I am!"

Baltic had his cell phone to his ear, his eyes darting around the street. "He does not answer his phone. Where's the tutor?"

"Gone off to deal with some family situation." I reached toward my pocket to yank out my own phone, but the letter Angela had given me was still in my hand.

"What is that?" Baltic asked, frowning.

"I don't know. Angela said someone left it for me—" I froze, my horror-filled gaze meeting Baltic's for a moment before I shredded the envelope in my attempt to get the letter out. My hands were shaking so badly, Baltic had to pull the paper from the envelope.

My stomach turned over as I read the words.

> *Sullivan: I have Brom. If you want to see him again, you'll do exactly what I say. If you contact the Watch, or mundane police, he'll suffer. His mobile phone is under his pillow—I'll call his phone tomorrow at noon with instructions, but in the meantime, have that dragon start gathering up gold, because you're going to need lots of it if you ever want to see the kid again.*

It was signed with one word: *Gareth.*

For a moment, the world swam around me in a sickening fashion. I clutched Baltic's shirt, trying to keep from vomiting or passing out, both of which were likely at that moment. Baltic's arms were warm around me, holding me tight and keeping me safe as he murmured words of reassurance in my ear.

"Do not swoon, *chérie.* I cannot find my son if you need my attention, too."

"Brom," I said, choking on the word. Tears streamed down my face as I grabbed his arms. "He's taken my baby!"

"Our son is not a baby," Baltic said firmly, giving me a little shake before turning me toward the pub. "He is smart, and clever, and he will not be frightened by insignificant beings like the one who spawned him. He will know that we will not tolerate this abduction and will reclaim him immediately. Come, mate."

Oddly enough, what Baltic said made me feel a tiny bit better. In part, the knowledge that Brom was everything Baltic said reassured me, but mostly it was the fire I felt raging inside him. Baltic was beyond furious, his dragon fire threatening to slip his control, and I knew to the depths of my soul that he would move heaven and earth to get Brom back.

That didn't stop me from pacing the floor in Baltic's workroom an hour later, however, as he made several phone calls, attempting to locate Gareth. Pavel, with his friend Holland in tow, arrived to say that they'd thoroughly searched the pub and immediate area, and no one remembered seeing Brom or anyone resembling Gareth.

"If he so much as touches one hair on Brom's adorable head," I swore, "if he harms him in any way, I will take his scrotum and pull it over the top of his head."

"If you're talking about me, I'm leaving," a male voice said from the doorway. I spun around to see Baltic who, moving so fast he was a blur, was smashing a tall, angular man against the wall.

"Savian! Baltic, no, that's Savian Bartholomew, the thief-taker I told you about."

Baltic snarled something rude in Zilant, an archaic language once used by the dragons in the weyr, but he released Savian, who gasped and clutched a nearby chair as he tried to get air back into his lungs.

"I have no use for a thief-taker until we find that bastard who forced himself on you to spawn my son," Baltic snarled.

"Are you all right, Savian? Here, sit down. Let me get you a glass of water. And no, Baltic, I didn't mean we needed a thief-taker; Savian is also a renowned tracker. I was going to hire him to find something, but now that's . . ." A little wave of dragon fire danced down my body as the words that just left my lips sparked something in my brain.

"Not another one who can't control the fire," Savian said, accepting the glass of water I held out and moving his feet so my fire, now dancing around my feet, didn't reach him. "What is with you mates?"

My gaze met Baltic's again. "Savian is a *tracker*," I told him again, emphasizing the word "tracker."

"Not just a tracker—I'm the best there is."

Baltic was on him in a flash, pulling him to his feet, although this time without choking him. "You will find my son."

"Who?" Savian squawked.

"Our son, Brom. Do you remember him?" I said hurriedly, my hands clutching each other as I stood before him. "Gareth—he's my ex-husband, the one who hired you to rescue me from Gabriel—he's kidnapped Brom and taken him somewhere, and we can't find any trace of him. We don't even know where he is, or if he's all right, and I wouldn't put it past Gareth to harm Brom!"

"His own son?" Savian asked, his face a mask of disbelief.

"Brom is *my* son; the usurper is nothing to him. Although I myself will see to it that Gareth will die in the most heinous manner if he inflicts hurt upon Brom," Baltic said simply. Savian, with a sidelong look at the hard expression on Baltic's face, edged away.

"That's none of my business, but if you want me to help you find your son, I am at your service," Savian said, finally getting himself out of Baltic's grip enough to make us both a little bow. "You'll find no better tracker than me, if I do say so myself. Now, tell me what you know, and we'll see what we can see."

While Baltic and the others filled Savian in with the details, I paced the long room, feeling itchy with the need to be doing something, *anything* to rescue Brom, little pools of fire trailing my footsteps until I smothered them on the following pass through the room.

The horrible words of Gareth's note kept dancing through my head, making me rage at the same time my stomach turned over with worry. *I'll call his phone tomorrow at noon with instructions,* the note said. His phone . . . the two words reverberated in my head. Gareth's phone! Or rather, his phone number. I still had Gareth's phone number programmed into my phone!

I pulled it out and stared somewhat dazedly at the entry for him. It couldn't be this easy, could it? Could I just call him and demand that he release Brom? I hit the DIAL button and held the phone up to my ear, half expecting to hear a recorded voice tell me the number had been disconnected.

"Yes?"

The voice was so familiar, it took my breath away. Well, the fury that followed that one word took my breath away—it took me a good two seconds before I was able to speak.

"Who is this?" Gareth's slightly nasal, annoyed voice filled my ear.

"If you treat Brom with anything but the utmost care, I will do things to you that you cannot even imagine," someone said in a low, ugly voice, and to my surprise, I realized it was me.

Baltic spun around at my words, frowning as Gareth sputtered, "Sullivan? How the hell did you—dammit, Ruth, I told you we should have gotten a new phone!"

"Where's Brom?" I asked, and then repeated it, screaming, "Where have you taken my son?"

Baltic was at my side, one arm around me, trying to take the phone, while behind him, Savian made gestures at me and said something about keeping Gareth on the phone as long as possible. He pulled out his own cell phone and turned his back on us as he made a call.

"He's right here, and he's all right, although he's not going to remain that way if you don't do as I tell you," Gareth said.

I closed my eyes for a moment, visualizing roasting Gareth alive. "Let me talk to him."

"No. There's no reason for you to speak with him."

"By the rood, Gareth! He's my son! I'm out of my mind with worry! I have to know he's all right!"

Gareth muttered some rude things, saying in a slightly muffled tone, "Get the boy. No, she's insisting on talking to him. Just warn him not to say anything but that he's unhurt."

"Mate, control your fire."

I opened my eyes again to find the tables surrounding us were alight. I tamped down the flames, staring in mute appeal to Baltic.

"It will not help Brom if you lose control," he said softly, and tried again to take the phone.

"Sullivan?"

I almost wept with relief at the sound of Brom's voice. "Are you all right, lovey? Did Gareth or Ruth hurt you?"

"No, I'm fine, although they don't have any interesting books, and I left my field notebook in my room. There's a dead sparrow outside my window, but I can't take notes about it."

I leaned into Baltic, some of the tension easing as Brom complained. If he was well enough to fret over the loss of a notebook, he wasn't harmed.

Before I could say any more, Gareth was back. "Happy now?"

"I can't believe you would kidnap your own child to use against me," I told him, tightening my fingers on the phone.

"I told you this wasn't over when you tried to brain me against my own car," Gareth sneered. "If you think we're going to roll over and lose all that gold you brought in each year, you're stupider than I thought."

"How much do you want?" I asked through clenched teeth. "How much blood money will it take to let Brom go?"

"All we want is what is due to us. All those centuries we took care of you; you owe us, Sullivan." He named a

figure that didn't even register in my by now numb brain.
I was past the disbelief that Gareth would hold his own
child hostage for profit; I just wanted to do whatever it
took to get Brom back. "That'll do for now."

My gaze met Baltic's. He nodded, then made a gesture toward his watch. "You'll get your gold, but it will
take Baltic a day to get it from his lair. Where are you?"

Gareth laughed. "Nice try, but we're the ones calling
the shots. I'll call you tomorrow to see if your dragon has
the gold. And Sullivan—he'd better have it. Because any
delay is going to make Brom very, very sorry."

My fire rose around us in a wall of red. Baltic's arm
tightening around me reminded me of the veracity of his
words. I had it extinguished by the time I finished saying,
"One hair, Gareth. If so much as one hair of Brom's is
harmed in any way, you will regret the day you first drew
breath."

"Just have the gold ready, and save the empty threats.
And don't call here again—I will be the one to call you,"
Gareth said, then hung up.

"He will not harm my son," Baltic said, his breath
warm on my forehead as he kissed my hair. "He knows
we will destroy him if he does. You will cease worrying."

I gave a shaky laugh, hugging him for a moment just
to soak in his strength. "I'm a mother, Baltic. Worry is my
middle name. Gareth may be many things, but he's always had a strong sense of self-preservation, so I don't
think he'd do anything to endanger himself, and that
means Brom is probably going to be left alone. I just . . .
I want him here."

"I know. We will have him within twenty-four hours."

"How can you be so sure?" I asked, watching him as
he moved over to consult briefly with Pavel before eyeing Savian.

The latter held up a finger as he listened to something

being said in his phone before asking, "What's the number of your phone, Ysolde?"

I gave it to him. Savian repeated it, listening intently again, a smile suddenly softening the long lines of his face. "Got him. He called from Spain."

"Spain? We used to live there, but . . . how did he get Brom to Spain so fast? He's been gone only two hours."

"Portal, no doubt," Savian said, thanking his friend on the phone and tucking it away. "I'll check the local ones and see if Gareth used any of them."

"I will come with you," Baltic said, gesturing to Pavel. "Mate, you will remain here, with Pavel's friend."

"If you think I'm going to sit around here worrying myself to death while you big strong men go rescue Brom—"

Baltic cocked an eyebrow. "I had hoped you'd make arrangements, and pack our things, as well as Brom's, so that we can be ready to leave shortly."

"Arrangements?" Fear clutched my heart again. "Baltic, I know dragons avoid using portals because it makes you all discombobulated, but time is of the essence. It would take several hours to fly to Spain, even assuming we could either charter a jet or find a commercial flight that was leaving right away."

The look he gave me sharpened before he marched over and gave me a swift, hard kiss. "You should have more faith in me, mate. We will take the portal to find our son just as soon as we know where he is. See to things here so that we may leave once we have that information."

The three men left, leaving me standing in the room with a man of my height, with brownish blond hair and a little goatee. I stared at him for a few seconds, my mind whirling with worry and fear and anger.

"We haven't been properly introduced, have we?" the man said with a slight Welsh lilt. "I'm Elliot Holland.

And I'm happy to help you locate your son, if you can use my assistance."

I looked him over carefully, too frazzled to care if I was being obvious or rude. "What are you? I mean, you're not a dragon."

"I'm a knocker."

I blinked at him. "I beg your pardon?"

He laughed. "A knocker is a Welsh being, traditionally heard warning miners from danger, although we also have the reputation of being somewhat troublesome. These days, we mostly concentrate on talking."

"Talking to who?" I couldn't help but ask.

"Birds, mostly, although I can understand some four-footed beasties."

I stared at him for a moment, and then shook my head. It didn't matter who he was or what he could do—I wasn't about to turn down an offer of help. "I'm delighted to meet you, happy you and Pavel have hooked up even if Baltic is being a poop about that whole thing, and will welcome your help."

Nico came in as we were stuffing a few necessary items in bags. He was immediately distraught and blamed himself for Brom being abducted.

"I don't have time for this," I said, shoving two bags at him. "I know you're sorry, and you can come with us if you want, but you have to pack quickly."

He was off before I finished the sentence, hurrying with the bags down to where Ludovic was waiting at the car, promising over his shoulder he'd be packed in three minutes.

I briefly explained the situation to Angela before going to stand by the car, rubbing my arms against the chill of the evening air.

Brom would be all right. He just had to be.

Chapter Six

The town of Tarraco was tiny, tucked away in a mostly inhospitable, arid, and mountainous region in the north of Spain. It was also very remote, and as we drove slowly up a dusty, rutted track that led from the town proper, climbing in zigzag fashion to the remains of a medieval fortress perched high above the valley floor, I began to think that Gareth was cleverer than I had previously given him credit for.

"This place is gorgeous," I said, unable to help but admire the Romanesque architecture of the fortress. "I love how the buildings seem to tumble down the slope of the hillside, and how they are clutched by those immense spires of rock. It's as if the fortress were born of the earth, not put there by man. Baltic, I don't suppose you'd consider—"

"No," he said, pointing to the side when Pavel, who was driving our car, squinted in the darkness. "Dauva is not a Spanish castle. There, Pavel. We will stop there. They may see the lights of the cars if we are any closer."

The second car, containing Holland, Savian Bartholomew, and a still-distressed Nico, pulled in behind us. Savian, Holland, and I were all fine despite no sleep and the predawn hour; the dragons, however, looked rumpled and grumpy, as was usual when they were forced to take a portal that utilized a tear in the fabric of space.

"I never understood why dragons have such an aversion to portals," I said softly to Baltic, smoothing back his hair, and brushing out the wrinkles in his soft linen shirt. Even his clothing looked annoyed at having been forced through a portal.

"It disturbs us."

"Yes, but why? Other beings have no issues with it."

"Dragons are superior. Elemental beings don't like portals, either. You will enter the front of the fortress with Nico and Holland, mate. Pavel, the thief-taker, and I will slip in the side. Do you remember your instructions?"

"We are to distract and subdue Gareth, if possible without putting Brom in harm's way, or in the worst-case scenario, draw Gareth and Ruth away for a few minutes so you can locate Brom and release him."

Baltic nodded. "And?"

"And?" I searched my memory for any other facets of the hastily concocted plan that had been borne of the half-hour drive from Tarraco. "I don't remember anything else."

"And you will not put yourself in any danger, or try to deal with Gareth yourself." His hands were hard on my shoulders as he frowned into my eyes. "I will not have you harmed any more than I will my son."

I licked the tip of his nose. "A sentiment of which I approve, and will be happy to reward once Brom is back with us. The same goes for you, too, you know."

"I am a wyvern," he said arrogantly as he turned me and gave me a gentle push toward my team of rescuers.

"Who can still be hurt or killed. You just remember that."

Baltic, who had already moved off into the darkness, lifted his hand to show he heard, before disappearing into the inky shadows.

I turned to my companions. "Shall we?"

We picked our way carefully up the track, trying to avoid making noise that could warn anyone of our presence. Baltic guessed that Gareth would have some sort of security arrangements put into place to detect the arrival of any visitors, but I wasn't so convinced—intricate plans and attention to detail were never my bigamous ex-husband's forte.

"If we're lucky," I said as we walked under a gorgeous stone arched doorway that opened into a grassy area below the bulky tower complex that made up the still-standing section of the fortress, "Gareth will think he's so incredibly clever, no one could ever find him here. I wish I could see the detail of the carvings better."

"Carvings?" Nico looked startled for a moment, then nodded his head as we clung to a drunken line of a curtain wall. "Ah, on the *castillo*. Eleventh century, I believe. Moorish influence. The sun should be up in an hour; perhaps we'll be able to see them then."

I bit my lip, not speaking of the fear that held me in such a painful vice: that we wouldn't be able to free Brom.

We climbed higher, approaching the dark bulk of stone and brick, walking slowly to give Baltic's team time to scale the side walls before any alarm of our approach was sounded.

"Too late," I said ten seconds later as a harsh voice called out in Spanish for us to halt.

We stopped, our hands up to show we were unarmed as two men emerged from either side of a broken chunk of the curtain wall. They were armed with long, wicked-looking daggers, and as soon as they drew close, Nico said under his breath, "Ouroboros dragons."

"Who are you?" the bigger of the two dragons demanded to know.

"I am Ysolde de Bouchier. I want to see my son," I said in my haughtiest tone, wondering like mad why Gareth had chosen to become involved with outlaws, dragons who had been kicked out of, or voluntarily left, their septs, and thus were no longer recognized by the weyr. Gareth had no love for dragons, and for them to be here now . . . The penny dropped at that moment. "You're part of Thala's tribe, aren't you?"

"Come," the man said, gesturing toward me with the dagger. Nico and Holland closed protectively around me, but I shook my head at them and walked in the direction indicated.

"Is Thala here? I always got the impression she didn't get along with Ruth and Gareth, but if they went running to her for protection, then I guess I was wrong. She's here, isn't she? She's the one really behind this kidnapping. I just know it. She must have convinced Gareth to do her dirty work, knowing that Baltic and I would come to rescue Brom. Well, you can just tell her for me that I am not going to let her get away with this. No one messes with my family. *No one!*"

I worked myself up to a fine fit of anger by the time we made it into the main part of the fortress, not in an attempt to intimidate the dragons—I knew full well they weren't scared in the least by us—but in order to keep my fear squashed down to a minimum.

"You go here," the dragon said, pulling me toward the larger of two square stone towers. "La Torre de la Reina."

"The tower of the queen," I translated, looking up as we entered the twin arched doorways. The tower looked to be about three stories tall, the outside illuminated by solar lights stuck haphazardly into the rocky ground.

Lovely twin arched windows, and columns with trapezoidal capitals intricately carved with elaborate scenes of battles graced the exterior, while inside it was much cooler, and scarcely furnished with just a few pieces of sturdy-looking antiques. "All right, we're here. Now, where's my son? Where's Thala? I have a few things to say to her."

The dragons didn't answer me, shoving us none too gently up a curved flight of stone steps. I waited until I reached the first landing to sidle away, asking again, "Where's my son? I'm not moving one more foot until I see Brom!"

"You go," the dragon said, shoving me again.

"Not one more step! And if you touch me again, I'm going to scream my bloody head off!"

"Ysolde," Nico said with a warning, his green eyes glittering in the dim light. "I think perhaps we should go wherever it is they want to take us. You wouldn't want to attract the *wrong* attention."

I bit back the urge to yell for Brom, and nodded, allowing myself to be pushed up more of the stairs. Baltic, I knew, must be in the compound, using Savian's sterling skills to locate Brom. I didn't want to do anything to pull them away from that. This was why, three minutes later, as a very solid wood and iron door was slammed shut on us, I turned to face the two other men who were locked with me in the airless, stifling room. "Great. Now Baltic is going to have to rescue us, too."

Nico and Holland moved quickly over to the shuttered window, pulling open the wooden slats to peer down the wall of the tower. "We can't jump."

I came over to look. "Really? It's only three stories. We could do that easily. I've jumped out of a second-story window without breaking anything. . . . Oh. Damn." The ground beneath the window dropped away dramatically, punctuated with jagged spires of rock that erupted almost painfully from the earth. "Yeah, that's not going to happen."

"Pavel says you are a mage?" Holland asked.

"Kind of," I said, looking at the door. "My magic isn't very reliable, not even after Dr. Kostich lifted the interdict that was meant to keep me from using it."

Holland looked confused. "I thought dragons could not use arcane magic?"

Nico gave him a wry grin. "They're not supposed to. But Baltic and Ysolde seem to be the exceptions to the rule."

"Baltic doesn't use magic very often," I explained. "I was trained by the head of the Otherworld himself, Dr. Kostich, but my magic is . . . well, as I said, it's not very reliable. Still, it's worth a shot. If nothing else, it'll be another distraction, and that can only be good for Baltic."

"I think we'd better get out of the way." Nico hurried over to a large wooden chest that lurked in the corner, big enough to hide a body in, turning it on one end, and moving so that the chest blocked sight of him.

Holland watched closely as I placed both hands on the door, trying to get a feel for its composition, and for any magic that might have been placed on it to keep us on one side of it.

"No wards or anything," I said, shaking out my hands and taking a deep breath. "All right, I'm going to give an unlocking spell a try. Holland, given what happened to Aisling's demon Jim when he stood next to me the last time I cast a spell, you may want to go hide behind the chest with Nico."

"What happened to the demon?" Holland asked.

"It lost its preferred form. Took Dr. Kostich to fix the problem, and I died during the process. Baltic was *furious*."

Saying nothing, Holland just ran for the chest as I

drew a circle on the floor and called the quarters, beginning with the east. "Heart of storms, I call upon you to aid me now. Heart of fire," I said, turning to the south, "I call upon you to give me strength. Heart of tears, I call upon you to give me wisdom." Finally, I turned to the north. "Heart of iron, I call upon you to bend all to my will."

"You might want to duck down," Nico said as Holland peeked over the top of the chest. "You wouldn't want anything to happen to your head."

"Erp." Holland disappeared.

"I wish May were here," I said, taking another deep breath, trying to put all thoughts of worry and fear and anger from my mind. "She does this so much better. Here goes."

My dragon fire, normally banked, grew in intensity as I pulled on it, but that alone didn't give me the force I needed to form my will into action. I knew the quiet place in my mind where I used to access arcane magic was gone, driven out, I suspected, by the dragon that was waking within me. Rather than fight that loss, I simply pulled hard on Baltic's fire, reveling in the power it brought with it as it roared through me and joined with my own lesser fire, merging into a force that lit up my mind. I cast wide my arms and spoke the words, channeling our merged fire as I did so:

> *Threefold and one,*
> *Elements come unto me.*
> *Iron-bound, and oak-hewn,*
> *Portal of strength and denial.*
> *Turn to my hand and let me see,*
> *All that lies beyond.*

The air within the room gathered itself, silence lying heavily over us for the count of four, then with a soft *whump*, the air exploded outward in a brilliant flash of white-blue light, knocking me backward a good two yards into the wall.

"I'm all right," I said, shaking the stars from my head as Nico rushed toward me, helping me up. "I'm fine; just had the breath knocked out of—by the love of the saints!" I stared at the door, wanting to simultaneously scream and throw large, heavy objects around the room in a temper tantrum to end all temper tantrums. "Why can't *any* of my spells go right?"

Holland had moved to the door and was considering it with his head tipped to one side. He reached out to touch it. "It's . . . it's glass."

Mentally, I ran over the spell. "Turn to my hand and let me see, all that goes beyond. Oh, very funny, magic! Ha-ha-ha. *Let me see*, indeed." I marched over to the door, which was indeed now made of glass, thick, wavery glass approximately three inches thick, and bound with the same iron bands as the wooden version.

"At least you didn't change any of us," Nico offered with a little grin before picking up a wooden chair. "Shall we try to break it?"

"You can try, but I doubt if even dragon strength will take down that door. It looks like awfully solid glass."

And so it was. It might have the appearance of glass, but it evidently retained the properties of the oak door, because we didn't even scratch the glass.

Nico, Holland, and I were taking turns whaling on the door with bits of the bed and chairs when two shimmery figures suddenly appeared on the other side of the door.

"Baltic?" I asked, and dropped my bit of broken chair to squint at the figures before I realized that neither of them was even remotely as big as he was.

"What the hell have you done?" a man's voice asked as the door was opened.

I snarled something extremely rude, and lunged for

the two figures. Gareth screamed, then stumbled backward at the same time his wife, Ruth—who I had spent the last ten years thinking was my sister-in-law—leaped at me with her fingers curled into claws, forcing me back into the room.

"Where's Brom?" I bellowed, belching fire at Ruth, who shrieked and started slapping at her clothing to put out the fire. "You bastard, if you've hurt him—"

"You're not supposed to be here, you stupid woman! Why the bloody hell can't you just do what I ask?" Gareth yelled back at me as Nico and Holland leaped forward to keep me from strangling Gareth where he stood in the doorway. "You never listen to me, do you? I don't know what's wrong with you that you can't even follow simple directions! I told you what to do; I gave you very specific instructions, but did you bother to listen? No, you did not. Instead, you had to drop in on us at the crack of dawn, interrupting my sleep. You know how I hate that!"

I stared him down, my fingers itching to draw the most vile spell I knew, but given that was one to cause the unplugging of bowels, I curled my fingers into fists and fought the desire to use the broken chair on Gareth, saying instead, with great deliberation, "Where. Is. Brom?"

Gareth scowled at Ruth as she continued to slap at herself. "What are you doing, woman?"

"She set me on fire!" Ruth snarled, stabbing a finger at me.

I smiled.

"For god's sake, will you two stop fighting? It's enough to drive a sane man crazy." Gareth narrowed his already beady-eyed gaze on me, waving his hands toward us. "Well, you're here. Nothing I can do about that, I suppose, although just once I'd like to see you do what I tell you to do. Still, it could be worse. That dragon of yours had better bring the gold with him when he comes to get you, or he'll find himself going home without his precious mate as well as the kid. If you're done causing havoc, I'm going back to bed."

"I don't think so. I think you're going to take me to Brom in the next ten seconds, or this very badass dragon here is going to beat the crap out of you, while this equally badass . . . er . . . mine ghost will help him."

"Knocker," Holland said helpfully, then cracked his knuckles while looking menacingly at Gareth.

"Sorry, badass knocker." I slid a glance toward Ruth, who had moved closer to Gareth. "And while they're doing that, I'll call down fire unlike anything you've ever seen. I bet you that even an oracle and a necromancer can be roasted alive."

Gareth sputtered in anger while Ruth made some pretty scatological threats that I ignored, but in the end, all it took was Nico's shifting into dragon form, and my setting fire to both Gareth's and Ruth's shoes before they conceded.

"You can see the brat, but the others have to stay here," Gareth spat out, jerking me by the arm, his fingers biting painfully into my flesh.

"We will not leave Ysolde," Nico said, starting toward us.

"You stay or she doesn't see the kid," Gareth snarled.

"It's all right," I said, pulling my arm from Gareth's hold, rubbing the resulting bruises. "You boys stay here. Gareth isn't stupid enough to hurt me, not when he knows Baltic will skin him alive if he even thinks about it."

Gareth made a rude noise, slammed the door closed on a still-protesting Nico and Holland, and shoved me toward the stairs. "Hurry up. I want to go back to sleep, and you're wasting my time."

I walked carefully in front of them, bracing myself for the feeling of Ruth's hands on my back. I wouldn't put it past her to try to shove me down the stairs. Luck, however, was with me, and I arrived at the landing one floor down without injury.

"Maybe you can get the kid to stop his whining all the time," Gareth said, unlocking the door. "Nice job you did raising him. All he does is complain."

I shoved past him and ran into the room, stumbling over a chair when I lunged toward the small bed that sat under one of the arched windows. "Brom!"

"Hnn?" came a familiar groggy sound, one I heard every morning when I tried to rouse my child from sleep. "Sullivan?"

He was warm, and sleepy, and utterly wonderful as I clutched him to me, ignoring the terms of our previous agreement about how many times I was allowed to kiss and hug him on a daily basis. I wrapped my arms around him and held him tight, tears burning my eyes for a few seconds as I thanked every deity I could think of for preserving my son.

"Sullivan, I can't breathe," he wheezed after a minute or so.

"Sorry," I said, reluctantly loosening my hold on him. "Are you all right? Gareth hasn't hurt you, has he?"

"I'm OK. Geez, Sullivan, you've kissed me five times, way over the limit, and Gareth's watching. He's going to think I'm a baby or something."

I laughed, a shaky laugh to be sure, but laughter filled with relief as I let go of him and sank to my knees next to his bed. "If Gareth knows what's good for him, he isn't going to think anything of the sort."

"So very touching," Ruth said with a sneer, looking disdainfully around the room. "My god, you've already turned this place into a pigsty! I can't believe we put up with you two for as long as we did."

"It was no bowl of cherries living with you for the past ten years, either," I said, still holding Brom's hand.

"Ten years? Try three hundred," she scoffed, scowling furiously.

"Three hundred *years*?" I shook my head. "That can't be right. I know you have some pictures of you and Gareth and me in old-fashioned clothes, but I haven't been stuck with you for three hundred years."

Ruth opened her mouth to answer, but Gareth interrupted with a curt order. "Go get the guards to move the dragon and the knocker to another room. I don't trust Sullivan's magic to not screw up the door so they could get out. I'll watch her until you get the others locked up properly."

"She could try something on you," Ruth said suspiciously.

Gareth's lip curled. "If she does, the kid will suffer."

I gave Brom's hand a little squeeze before getting to my feet and moving to stand between him and the man who was biologically responsible for fathering him. I'd never been one to feel hatred for people; that seemed like such an extreme emotion, and one that made no allowances for shades of grey, but the primary emotion I was feeling now was pure, unadulterated hate.

"Why are you doing this?" I asked, feeling that I should at least make an attempt to understand the despicable depths of his mind.

"I had to do something to keep you two from bickering. I had centuries of that, and I don't need any more."

"No, not why did you send Ruth on an errand—why did you kidnap Brom?"

"I told you—we want gold. The gold you owe us."

I shook my head. "You're an Oracle, Gareth. Surely you could make money by practicing your trade. You don't have to resort to kidnapping to get it. Is it Thala? Did she tell you to do this?"

He sucked one of his teeth and looked somewhat bored, leaning back against the door with his arms crossed over his chest. "She contacted Ruth, yes. But we would have done this without her. You owe us, Sullivan. For all those centuries of care, you owe us plenty. We just want what's due us."

"I can't believe . . ." I shook my head again. "Three centuries? That would mean I'd been with you since . . . since I was killed."

"We found you wandering around in the snow, too stupid to figure out who you were or what happened to you," he said, picking his ear and studying his finger. "Ruth wanted to let you freeze to death, or be caught by the dragons who were attacking the castle, but I realized right from the start that you were worth a fat reward. You wouldn't have been brought back by that dragon god otherwise."

"You saw the First Dragon resurrect me?" I was stunned by that thought, although it made sense. If Gareth and Ruth were outside of Dauva when it fell, then they would have had the opportunity to see me wandering around in a postresurrection daze.

"I convinced her it was to our benefit to keep you alive, so we took you with us back to Paris."

"What were you doing in Latvia to begin with?" my curiosity prompted me to ask.

"Did a scrying the month before and saw that there was something valuable to be had there. Since we weren't exactly welcome in St. Petersburg at the time, we headed out that way to see what was what. We had no idea the valuable object was you. What the hell?"

The last of his words rose almost an octave as the world spun around us, a blinding whiteness swirling around and in and through us until I realized that we were in yet another vision.

"Cool," I heard Brom say behind me. "Is this one of those dreams you have where you get to see stuff in the past?"

"Yes. Stay next to me, lovey." I reached back and

grabbed him, holding him to my side as I looked around the small, dark room of the vision. It was cold, very cold, and wherever we were wasn't particularly nice.

"Can they see us?" he asked.

At the same time Gareth demanded, "What is going on? What the hell have you done to me, Sullivan?"

I turned to look where Brom was pointing. We appeared to be in some sort of a small shack, badly made, with drifts of snow coming through the gaps in the boards that made up the walls. A derelict cot was pushed up against one side of the shack, a figure huddled on it covered by what looked like a thick fur cloak.

"I don't understand," the figure said, lifting her head, a confused and dazed expression on her face. It was my past self.

"No, they can't see or hear us." I glanced from the present-day Gareth to the memory of his past self where he stood with Ruth in close consultation.

"It's simple," the past Gareth said, going over to where Ysolde sat. "You're with us. We saved you from bad dragons who want to kill you. We're all going to Paris to keep them from finding you, and let your friends, the ones with lots of gold, know that you're alive. You remember that, don't you?"

"Dragons?" Ysolde said, rubbing her forehead. "There's something . . . something horrible—"

"That's right, the dragons are horrible, and we're trying to help you because we're your friends. Remember?"

Gareth put both hands on her head and muttered what sounded like an invocation.

"What's he doing to you?" Brom asked, pressing closer to me. "Is he hurting you?"

"No, lovey. He was just trying to make me believe something that wasn't true." I looked over Brom's head to where the present Gareth was now watching impatiently. "You really were a bastard, you know that?"

"And you were a stupid cow who believed anything we told you," he answered with one of his unpleasant smiles.

"I believed because you brainwashed me," I said with a disgusted snort, reining in my temper. Brom had seen enough dissent between Gareth and me; I didn't want him to witness any more unpleasantness.

"We had better be rewarded for our trouble," the past Ruth said, coming over to jerk Gareth's hands off Ysolde's head.

"We will," he answered, giving her a sly look. "The dragons will pay well for her once they know she's alive again."

"Thala won't be pleased," Ruth said as darkness began to fill my vision.

"Then we simply won't tell her. She cannot rail against us if she doesn't know the wyvern's mate is still alive. . . ."

The darkness washed over us in a wave of insensibility, wiping away everything that was.

Chapter Seven

The sensation of being consumed by nothingness ebbed away to leave us standing in the exact same positions, but instead of a dim, cold shack, we were once again in a room lit now by the rosy golden glow of a sunny Spanish morning.

"Thala won't be pleased?" I asked Gareth as awareness returned to me. "What does she have to do with the price of tea in China?"

"The price of what?" he asked, looking more irritated than usual.

"It's an expression. Why would Thala care if you and Ruth took me in after I was—" I sucked in a huge amount of oxygen as realization struck me. "She's the one who killed me, isn't she?"

For a moment, I could swear I saw fear flicker in his eyes, but that emotion was soon replaced with familiar belligerence. "I don't know anything about who killed you, and I don't give a damn who did the job. All I care about is getting what's owed to me, and your high-and-mighty dragon had better get his dread wyvern ass in gear and come up with the gold, or he's going to be missing his bit of tail. And I don't mean the one in his dragon form."

I glared at him, wanting to say so many things, but determined to keep as much of it from Brom as was possible. "So what happened after you brainwashed me outside of Dauva? You took me to Paris?"

"How long does it take to get a few guards?" Gareth grumbled to himself as he peered out through the open door toward the stairs. "I could have gone to Seville and back by the time she stirs her stumps. What? Yes, we took you to Paris, fat lot of good that it did us. It turned out that anyone we could have ransomed you to was dead, so we were stuck with you. Ruth was ready to drop you in the Seine, but then you went into one of your funks and started manifesting gold, and we knew we were set for the rest of our lives."

"The fugues," I said, rubbing my forehead before glancing back at Brom. He had gotten dressed, and was sitting on the edge of his bed, watching with silent interest. "They started all the way back then?"

"Why else do you think we'd keep you around?" Gareth answered with another of his unpleasant smiles. "Every six months you'd drop to the floor and go to sleep for a few weeks, changing lead to gold in the process. Everything was fine until you decided you wanted to have a husband and a kid."

I straightened up, ready to leap on him if he said anything unkind toward Brom, and since I didn't want him to pursue that line of thought, I said with a nonchalance I knew would goad him, "It seems to me, then, that I've more than paid you for supporting me, and later Brom. This particular goose will not be laying any more golden eggs."

"How do you know?" He looked me up and down.

"You didn't manifest during your last fugue, when you were with the silver dragons, but that was because they didn't put lead in the room with you, right?"

"No, they didn't, but that doesn't mean anything. The dragon inside me is waking up, Gareth. Slowly, but it's waking up. And that means that whatever weird circumstance that caused me to alchemize gold is no longer there."

"You don't know that. In another few months, we'll know, but until then, we want what's due us." He cocked his head to listen. "Finally. Where the hell have you been, Ruth? It's not enough that Sullivan has to make me get up at this ungodly hour, now you're dragging your feet and keeping me from going back to—what are *you* doing here?"

"I've been asking myself that for weeks, now," a female voice answered, and to my utter surprise, a buxom woman, who was a little bit taller than me appeared in the doorway.

"Maura?" I said, a little spurt of anger following the word. "I imagined you'd be in Nepal with your boss. If you've come here to kidnap or shoot us again like you did in Latvia—"

She raised her hands in a gesture of peace. "I wouldn't dream of doing either, and even if I wanted to—and I assure you I've learned my lesson when it comes to shooting anyone—I couldn't."

"Why?" I asked, my curiosity (as always) getting the better of me.

A man answered. "Because I wouldn't let her."

"Who the hell are you?" Gareth demanded to know as Savian loomed up behind him, a gun in his hand. Before he could answer, Gareth narrowed his beady-eyed gaze on me and added, "Just how many people did you bring with you?"

I reached behind me for Brom, pulling him tight

against my side. "As many as it takes to ensure my son is safe."

"Sullivan!" Brom protested, his face filled with embarrassment.

I loosened my hold on him a little, watching Maura carefully.

"Hullo," she said to Brom.

"Hi," he responded, giving her a thorough once-over. "You shot Baltic?"

"My men did, but I didn't mean for them to do so."

I glared at her.

She coughed and looked away. "It was all very unfortunate. I was extremely upset about everything, and still regret that things turned out the way they did."

"How did things turn out?" Brom asked.

"It's not important," I said, transferring my glare from the untrustworthy Maura to Gareth, who was sidling around her to get out of Savian's line of sight. "What *is* important is what on earth you're doing here. Or, wait, are you still doing Thala's dirty work? Or are you now out for hire, and Gareth has hired you to help him kidnap an innocent child?"

"I do not kidnap children," she said, straightening her shoulders, giving her long brown hair an annoyed flick over her shoulder. "Dragons do not war against children. Everyone knows that."

"Gareth doesn't," I said somewhat acidly. "Where's Baltic?"

"At the foot of the tower, beating back a handful of dragons who showed up with a woman. Where are the others?" Savian asked.

"Baltic?" Gareth ran toward the door. "God damn it, Sullivan, you brought that wyvern here? He's just supposed to bring gold, not come into the fortress himself!"

I listened as hard as I could but didn't hear any sounds

of fighting. Nonetheless, I was worried. Baltic was perfectly capable of handling a few dragons on his own, but
I didn't want him hurt. "Of course Baltic came with me;
he loves Brom. Nico and Holland are upstairs one floor,
Savian. Can you let them out? Baltic probably doesn't
need any help taking down whatever dragons Ruth
found, but I'd hate for him to get carried away and kill
them rather than just disable them."

Gareth's eyes widened with panic.

"Here, you take this, and keep her highness covered,"
Savian said, handing the gun to me after gesturing with
it toward Maura.

"Why? I admit there're a few things I'd like to say to
her about her actions of the past, and more important,
about how her family is worried sick over her, but really,
I don't think we need her."

"We do," Savian said, pushing Maura farther into the
room. "She knows the secret way out."

"Which, if you will recall, Bart, or whatever your
name is, I offered to show to you, so you can stop treating me like a prisoner."

"The name is Savian Bartholomew, and you're definitely a prisoner. Don't let her get away, Ysolde."

"You're making it very difficult for me to do what's
right, you know!" Maura yelled after him as he left the
room and ran up the stairs to the floor above.

"You offered to help us?" I asked Maura. "Why?
You're Thala's second-in-command. And before you say
anything, I should mention that the last time I spoke
with your mother, she was very concerned about your
being so involved with this outlaw tribe that you tried to
kidnap me a few months ago, not to mention all the
other nefarious things you've done."

"Yes, because I'm so very much the queen of nefarious," Maura said, looking strangely drawn. "I offered to
help your wyvern when he jumped me outside because I

do not happen to agree with using children in this manner. And yes, I was Thala's lieutenant, but—"

A sudden explosion outside gave us all a moment of pause.

"That sounded like an arcane compression blast," I said thoughtfully. "One of your tribe must have pissed off Baltic enough that he's using magic."

"Right, that's it. I've had enough of you and your insanity," Gareth said, shoving Maura hard into me, sending us backward until we tripped over a wooden chair and went down in a tumble of arms and legs. "You still owe me gold, Sullivan! I expect it to be delivered."

"By the rood, get off me—thank you. Brom?" I struggled out from under Maura, worried sick for a moment that Gareth had grabbed Brom as he escaped, but luck was once again with me.

"I'm here. You OK?" he asked when I got to my feet and limped hurriedly to the door, rubbing my shin as I did so.

"I'm fine, but your father has escaped, dammit. I hope he runs smack-dab into Baltic."

"I'm fine, too, not that anyone asked," Maura said as she got to her feet. "You dropped your gun, Ysolde."

I took it when she held it out to me, thanking her. "I do appreciate your offering to help us get Brom out, even if it seems otherwise. In fact, it more than makes up for shooting Baltic and trying to kidnap us, so I suppose really, we're even on that score."

"I truly am sorry about all of that," she said, wringing her hands. "At the time, it seemed like the wisest thing to do, but I see now that what we were told about you was all wrong."

"Who told you—" I started to ask, but stopped when Nico, Savian, and Holland thundered down the stairs.

"Brom! You're all right?" Nico asked, coming forward

to clap his hand on Brom's shoulder, their approved method of showing affection.

"Of course. I'm not a baby," Brom said with a scathing look.

"You're far from that," Nico agreed. "I'm proud of you for not being frightened by the situation. I know you must have been worried."

Brom shrugged. "I knew Baltic wouldn't let Gareth and the dragons do anything to me. Is Baltic going to beat up Gareth? Do we get to watch when he does?"

"Our first priority is going to be to get you to safety, my bloodthirsty child," I said.

"Baltic says I get that from you. He says you're the most bloodthirsty person he ever met," Brom said with a rare grin.

"He is utterly and completely wrong." I was unable to keep from hugging him just one more time, ignoring his protest. "I haven't a violent bone in my body. Now, someone needs to go help Baltic."

"Holland and I will go," Nico said as he moved toward the door. "The thief-taker will stay to protect you and the other dragon."

"My cup runneth over with joy," Maura said somewhat acidly.

Savian gave her a sour look. "I'm not thrilled with the job, either, princess, but it's what I get paid to do."

"Mercenary and violent—what a charming personality you have," Maura answered, looking at her fingernails with apparent fascination.

"Better than traitorous and trigger-happy," Savian snapped back, glowering at her.

"I didn't shoot Baltic, you horrible man; the dragons who were with me shot him!"

I ignored them both, bit my lip, and glanced at Brom. Now that I knew he was safe, I itched to help Baltic, sure that my presence would have a steadying influence on him, not to mention I might be able to avert potential disaster with my own—admittedly sometimes wonky—magic abilities. "Savian, I think you should stay here to protect Brom. And keep an eye on Maura, of course."

Savian, in the middle of responding to yet another of Maura's insults, frowned at me. "I don't think Baltic would like you in the midst of any sort of battle, Ysolde."

"Nonetheless, it's where I'm going. Brom, I want you to stay with Savian, no matter what, all right?"

He started to shrug off my hands on his shoulders, but stopped when he got a good look at my face. "All right. But I'm not helpless, you know. I can make stink bombs. I read about it in the chemistry book I found downstairs." He gestured toward the dusty and worn Spanish textbook that sat on the edge of his bed. "Those would be useful."

"Of course they would, and if you have anything lying around up here to make them, then you have my full approval to do so, and drop them out the window at any of Maura's tribe you see."

"They're not my tribe in the sense you mean," she corrected. "I don't lead them. I never did. I was just in charge of a small espionage team, one of whom you evidently turned into a rock, and the other two of whom abandoned me the moment your wyvern got pissed, so really, calling them my tribe is completely incorrect."

"Espionage," Savian said with a disbelieving snort.

Her nostrils flared at him. "I happen to be quite good at it, just as I am quite good at escaping tight situations."

"Really?" He looked thoughtful for a moment, then whisked out a pair of handcuffs, and before Maura could do so much as squawk, slapped one over her wrist, and the other on his own. "There. That will ensure that you don't escape before Ysolde is through with you."

"What the—you can't do this to me!" Maura wailed, struggling to get free from the handcuffs.

"I just did," he answered with grim finality.

"Ysolde!" Maura appealed to me. "This is intolerable! Make him take them off. He can't do this to me! I have things I must do, and I can't do them tied up to this self-aggrandized, puffed-up policeman!"

"Puffed-up policeman!" Savian was clearly outraged. "I'll have you know I've received three commendations from Dr. Kostich himself for my work with the L'au-dela. *Three* commendations!"

"Bully for you. And while we're on the subject of bullies—"

"Can we argue about this later?" I interrupted, heading for the door. "Savian, you should probably take off the handcuffs."

"I will. Later," he said with a dark look toward Maura. She growled at him.

"Brom, stay with Savian. Savian, I expect you to protect him with your life."

"Of course," Savian answered, and I read absolute sincerity in his face.

"Oh, this is just what I need," Maura said, sighing. "For the last time, will you let me go?"

"Not until Baltic says we're done with you. You're just going to have to stay with me while I protect Brom and Ysolde."

"I don't mind helping with that. I like *them*. Ysolde, I will be happy to protect your son, too," Maura said, an annoyed expression on her face as she glared at Savian, jerking the arm connected to his. "I did, after all, go against everyone here to offer to show you where the bolt-hole is hidden, so that you could take him out without anyone being hurt."

"And I appreciate your help. We'll talk later about your mother and grandfather and everything," I told her, and giving Brom a steely look that warned him what would happen should he disobey me, I hurried down the stairs toward the ground floor.

I burst out of the building, braced and fully expecting to find Baltic, Nico, and Holland in full battle with the ouroboros dragons, but I saw . . . nothing.

"Well, this is anticlimactic," I said aloud, looking at a whole lot of empty courtyard. To my left was a smaller tower, while behind me was the tower I'd just left. To my right, the silhouette of the partial remains of a third tower lurched drunkenly against the pinkish orange morning sky. Behind the semicircle made up of the three towers were two small stone outbuildings, the entire area composed of towers and buildings surrounded by the tall stone inner bailey wall.

The air was crisp and cold, and smelled fresh despite the reddish brown dust that lay thickly over everything in sight. The faintest whiff of pine drifted down from the alpine trees that grew on the slopes behind the fortress complex, making me think of clean mountain streams and brisk hikes into the forest. Birdsong rose thinly overhead, peppered occasionally by the cry from a hawk no doubt out hunting for his breakfast.

A scream of absolute rage had me moving before I was aware of it, pelting down a beaten track in the red dirt toward the main gate we'd been escorted through by the ouroboros guards. The gate, an anachronism of metal plate, was closed. It hadn't been when we arrived, which meant someone had closed it. Baltic? Gareth? One of the ouroboros dragons? I hesitated for a moment, unsure if I should open it to allow an easy exit, or leave it closed. Another scream from beyond the gate had me running for it, twisting hard at the intricate sliding lock, and pulling with all my strength to open it up.

A wave of brown beings, approximately four feet in height, with garish clothing and long, thin fingers, washed up the road, a few of the little beings darting out to grab an unwary hare or other small furry animal.

"Negret!" I swore under my breath, and, with super-human strength, slammed shut the door and jammed home the lock. "Negret!" I yelled, spinning on my heel and running back toward the tower where Brom was located.

At that same moment, a familiar voice bellowed, "Ysolde!"

"Negrets are at the gate!" I bolted into the tower and ran straight into a large, hard object that I grabbed with both hands to keep from falling. "Baltic, negrets!"

"I know; we saw them." He frowned down at me. "What are you doing inside the fortress? You were supposed to remain outside, drawing away the guards. *I* was to locate our son."

"It's not a contest," I said, annoyed by his attitude enough to leave my main concern for a few seconds.

"No, but if we make a plan, we should all follow it." He pulled me after him as he exited the tower, Brom immediately behind us. "You must take Brom and escape, mate. I will keep the attention of the attackers until you are well away from the area."

"Are you crazy?" I shook him as best I could, which wasn't easy because he was built like the steel gate out front. "I'm not leaving you here with those little monsters! They're vicious, and cruel, and have an appalling fashion sense."

Savian, Maura, and Holland gathered around us as I tried to reason with Baltic, but he was adamant.

"The half dragon knows of the location of the bolt-hole," he said, nodding toward Maura. "You will take Brom, and go with Savian and her. We will stay here and draw the attention of all the others."

"I have a name, you know," Maura said. "It's only two syllables, and not that difficult to remember."

"Others? What others? More ouroboros dragons?" Suddenly remembering he'd been battling them, I checked him quickly for injuries. Fortunately, he had none.

"No, we destroyed or chased off those who were left." His voice was rich with satisfaction, and I had a startling memory of just how annoyed I used to be over his love for the opportunity to battle. It didn't matter who was his opponent; he just loved to fight.

"You're enjoying this, aren't you?" I said, poking my finger into his chest. "Don't you deny it! I can see how much fun you're having. You always loved to fight with people! I used to beg you not to, but you were never happier than when someone you could beat up wandered near Dauva. You're incorrigible, do you know that? I bet you even found a sword to use while you dealt with the ouroboros dragons, didn't you?"

"Where would I find a sword?" he asked, his voice suddenly persuasive as he held up his hands to show they were empty. "*Chérie*, you are overset. You must calm yourself and lead our son to safety while I distract the attackers."

"Baltic, you left your sword upstairs," Pavel said somewhat breathlessly as he thumped down the stairs, two swords in his hands. "You will want it, yes?"

I glared at the love of my multiple lives.

"Two of the ouroboros had them," Baltic said, not meeting my eye. "Go with the half dragon, mate."

"My name is Maura. Maura Lo. You can even call me Mo if you like, although no one but my mother calls me that."

"Mo Lo?" Savian asked, his lips twitching.

"You do, and I'll deck you," she said, shaking a fist at him and jerking her handcuffed arm again.

I poked Baltic a second time. "If you think I'm going to leave you here to face at least a hundred negrets armed with nothing but a sword, you can think again."

A metallic clang sounded from the gate. Baltic shoved Brom and me toward Maura, before he snatched the sword from Pavel, and raced toward the gate. "Go!" he yelled over his shoulder as he shifted into dragon form, the rosy morning light burnishing the white scales that covered his body.

I didn't argue. I wanted to stay and help him, but he was right—I had to get Brom to safety first. I took Brom's hand and ran after Maura and Savian.

"This way," Maura cried as they dashed around the side of the tower. "The bolt-hole is in the chapel's crypt."

Out of nowhere, two blue dragons in their respective dragon forms burst from the chapel, snarling various obscenities.

Maura yelled something at them when one of them raised a gun toward us. The dragon hesitated, which was his undoing. Before he could blink, Savian and Maura were on them, Savian handily disarming the gun-toting dragon, before knocking him senseless with a swift move that had me more than a little envious. Maura, naturally, had to move with Savian, but she took me by surprise when she leaped on the second dragon, somewhat hampered by being tethered to Savian. Her surprise attack took the second dragon off guard enough that before he could do more than slash through the air with his tail and splash a little dragon fire around, he was on the ground, bleeding and unconscious, but alive.

"That felt good," Maura said, sucking her knuckles after grinning at Savian.

"Friends of yours?" he asked with an answering grin.

"Hardly. This way."

We ducked to avoid the low lintel of the chapel, the cool, musty air inside making my nose wrinkle with the need to sneeze.

"The crypt isn't big—really, I think it was just put there simply to disguise the secret exit—but finding the right bit of stone to push can be tricky if you don't know the pattern."

The chapel was obviously not used much by Thala's dragons; it was full of rubble, with bits of broken masonry, antique painted statues of various saints, and carved reliefs piled up on one side. Two arched windows let in some of the morning light, but it had a hard time fighting its way through the general air of abandonment.

"There," Maura said, climbing over a stone altar and pointing. We scrambled after her, peering down at stairs cut into the stone that faded into blackness. "Watch your step—some of the stairs are broken."

"I'll go first," Savian said, pulling out a penlight from an inner pocket. "Ysolde?"

"Right behind you." I pushed Brom in front of me, my hands on his shoulders as he followed Savian and Maura. Before taking a step into the black maw of the crypt, I glanced over my shoulder, but the two dragons were still flaked out on the ground. "Careful of the steps, lovey."

Brom made a noise of profound disgust and disappeared into the darkness. I followed, clutching the rough stone wall as I picked my way down the uneven steps. A few of them were partially crumbled into nothing, but after a few tense minutes, we were all on the floor of the crypt.

"There are four tombs down here." Maura's voice echoed eerily in the darkness. "The first three are genuine. The fourth one isn't. To the left, Bart."

"Bartholomew. As in Savian Bartholomew, Mo Lo."

I could hear Maura sigh even from the foot of the stairs. "I'm so going to regret ever opening my mouth," she muttered before stopping in front of a large stone tomb.

Savian flicked his light over it, casting into faint relief markings typical of Romanesque design, mostly battle scenes, but some domestic carvings as well, including one of three men involved in an act that looked quite inappropriate for a chapel. "This dog here, this is the first piece. Press the stone and you should feel it click. Then over to the north side, do the same to the snake that's about to seduce Eve. The third is the knights fighting—you press the charger's rear flank. And last, you go back to the stone dog and press it again."

As she suited action to word, the stone gave a loud click. Maura leaned down and shoved, the entire top half of the tomb grinding to the side to reveal a short drop down to an earth and stone passage.

"Cool!" Brom said, peering down into the tunnel.

"Voilà, the bolt-hole. Take the right branch in the tunnel, and it will lead you to an exit about half a mile below the *castillo*. You can't miss it. Now, unlock this damned thing so I can go do what I have to do." Maura held out her arm to Savian.

"We certainly won't miss the turn, because you're coming with us," Savian said grimly, pulling her after him as he entered the tunnel.

"No! I said I'd help you get the boy out, and I've done that. But I can't leave! Thala will—"

"I really don't give a damn what Thala thinks," I said, swearing to myself as I stumbled over a root, stubbing my toe in the process. I grasped the back of Brom's T-shirt, feeling blinder than blind as we crept along the tunnel.

"You don't understand! I can't leave—" Maura's protest came to an abrupt halt when Savian, with a muttered oath, leaned down and flung her over his shoulder.

The next ten minutes were fraught with irritation, mostly due to Maura's complaining loudly about Savian's actions, antecedents, and at one point, the fact that he was holding her leg in a manner he should be ashamed of in front of a small child.

"Really," I told Savian when he at last set her on her

feet, sputtering threats and vague promises of death and destruction, "I think she has a point about the handcuffs. She's done what we asked. You can let her go."

"Just as soon as I know you're safe," he answered, patting his pocket, a slightly panicked look coming across his face. I pushed past him, shoved aside the overgrowth of aptenio, a persistent ground covering plant found everywhere in this part of Spain, and emerged into the full morning sun.

A small clutch of four negrets that were ripping something furry to shreds looked up, staring in surprise at me, blood and bits of fur smeared across their mouths. Beyond them, the hillside was covered with small figures, slowly making their way up the slopes to the fortress.

"Holy—" I spun around and shoved Savian and Maura back into the tunnel, yelling at the same time, "Get back to the crypt! We've got to close it off! Brom, run!"

Gareth may have been Brom's biological father, but, luckily, my genes appeared to be stronger in him, at least so far as his intelligence went. He didn't say a word; he just turned on his heel and ran. Savian stopped muttering to himself, took one look at the pack of negrets ripping through the aptenio to get to us, and, grasping Maura's hand, ran after us.

The negrets caught up just as Savian and Maura were bolting up the stairs. Brom and I were already at the stone tomb, leaning into it, ready to shove it closed just as soon as they cleared the entrance, but even as Maura emerged, she was jerked backward when the negrets flung themselves on Savian with high, piercing cries.

"Candles!" Savian yelled as he struggled to beat them off himself. "They turn to metal when touched by fire!"

"You don't need candles when you have me." Shifting into dragon form, Maura lit up the tunnel with a blast of dragon fire that caught the frozen expressions of four extremely startled negrets before it dissolved into nothing.

Four metallic thumps could be heard, followed shortly by Savian yelling about his clothing being on fire. By the time we got him up the stairs, his head and face were black, his shirt both shredded by the negrets and burned by the dragon fire, and blood was welling across his back and chest where their sharp little claws had struck home.

He helped us heave the stone tomb across the opening, all of us slumping on it when it clicked into place.

"Is there any way to open it from the tunnel?" I asked Maura.

She shook her head and blew on a bit of Savian's hair that was still smoking. "Not that I've ever found, and Thala had us make a comprehensive examination of it."

We looked from the tomb to the stairs to the chapel.

"Which means we're trapped in the *castillo*," I said, closing my eyes for a moment and wishing I were a thousand miles away.

Brom's eyes lit up. "Cool! I'll go make some bombs. I wonder if there's any gas around. I heard about this thing called a Moscow cocktail, and I bet I could make some of them, too."

"Molotov cocktail," I corrected him wearily, rubbing my temples where a headache blossomed. It was shaping up to be a very long day.

Chapter Eight

"Fire in the hole!"

The cry forced some of the negrets swarming the metal gate at the entrance of the *castillo* to look upward. Savian leaned out through a murder hole cut into the stone curtain that surrounded the inner keep buildings.

"Take that, you murderous little bastards," he added, lighting the piece of cloth that was wedged into the top of a glass beer bottle.

"Niiice," Maura drawled, trying to peer over his shoulder.

"You'd say the same thing if they tried to eat your face, too," he snapped.

"Hrmph."

"I can't see," Brom complained. I stood on tiptoe to peer over the edge of the curtain wall, watching as the explosive shattered on the rocks behind the main group of negrets, immediately turning into a wave of fire. A few screams and metallic clangs followed.

"You don't need to see. It's enough I let you make

bombs, which is probably something that will keep me from ever being on any Mother of the Year list, but this is an emergency."

"You said the negrets don't burn up. You said they don't have guts coming out or anything like that. Why can't I watch them turn into metal?"

"Because you're only nine years old, and even I have some limits." I gave him a gimlet eye, which effectively shut up his complaints. At least for the moment.

"Yippie ki-yay, mothersuckers," Savian yelled down to the negrets, a third of which were now directly under the murder hole, trying to climb the stone wall. He lit another Molotov cocktail and tossed it out the opening.

"Savian!" I gasped at the same time Maura whomped him on the arm.

"I said suckers, not . . . er . . . I made it PG," he told me with a cock of his head toward Brom.

"It's a very fine line, nonetheless."

"Some people," Maura muttered.

"I could do without comments from the peanut gallery," he told her before turning to me. "Sorry, Ysolde. Will be more careful. How's my aim?"

"You're out about ten feet too far," Maura answered as I tried to look. "No, to the left. Lordisa, man, your *other* left."

"It's not easy doing this handcuffed," he snarled, giving her a glare.

"Then take them off!" she retorted.

"I will when Baltic says we're done with you." The words emerged as if he were grinding them through his teeth.

"I swear, if you two make me pull this fortress over, you'll be sorry," I said, giving them both a mom-look that should have scared ten years off their lives.

"Sorry," Savian said immediately.

"He started it by handcuffing me to him," Maura said, but subsided when I leveled another look at her.

"You're still a little outside the main group, Savian. If you can drop one right at the foot of the gate, I bet it would get at least half of them."

"I can't lean out that far," he said, on his knees before the murder hole, his body twisted to the side as he stuck his head out of it. "The hole isn't big enough. I have to do this at an angle as is, and even then, only one shoulder will fit through it. I think I can stretch a little bit farther, but—Christ!"

"What's wrong?" I asked as he pulled himself back onto the walkway that ran the length of the curtain wall.

"The negrets. They're making a pyramid right beneath the murder hole."

I clutched the stones and stuck my head out to see for myself. About six feet below me, the topmost negret grimaced as another one climbed to stand on his shoulders. "Sins of the saints!"

The negret leaped at me, its claws narrowly missing my face as Savian jerked me backward.

"Be more careful," he scolded, turning to yell down to the inner bailey. "Baltic! We're about to have visitors!"

"Where?" Baltic bellowed back, pausing in the middle of shoving a jeep up against the gate.

"Murder hole." Savian turned back to me. "Ysolde, you and Brom had better get off the wall. I'll stay here with Her Royal Highness and light up the little devils as they come in."

"I am not a princess! Stop calling me that!" Maura said, whomping him again.

"They can't get in the murder hole," I told him. "It's too small."

As I spoke, two little hands reached through the murder hole and gripped the sides before a brown head popped into view. The negret stared at me for a second, then bared its sharp teeth and lunged, getting its entire torso through the hole.

Savian swore and pulled me backward, pushing Brom and Maura back with his other hand. The negret cursed in what I assumed was its own language, apparently stuck, twisting and turning and struggling to get through the hole. Just as I was about to point out to Savian that even beings as small as the negrets couldn't get through the murder hole, it managed to pull itself through, falling in a heap on the stone walkway.

"Go!" I yelled at Brom, shoving him toward the stairs before pausing to pick up one of the crates loaded with bottles. It had taken the four of us—Brom, Savian, Maura, and me—to manufacture the three dozen Molotov cocktails, and I didn't want to leave them where the negrets could get them.

Savian, in the meantime, took advantage of the negret's moment of inattention to pick it up and attempt to stuff it back through the murder hole. He was hampered not only by the negret's objecting to such treatment, but also by another negret's attempting to claw its way through the hole to us. I snatched up one of the bottles, lit the rag hanging limply out of it, and said loudly, "Drop him, Savian."

"Get away while you can," he answered, grunting in pain as the negret twisted on itself and bit his hand.

"Drop him!" I yelled just as Maura shifted into dragon form.

Savian glanced over his shoulder at us, and dropped the negret, sprinting toward me, one arm around my waist as he took the bottle and heaved it at the two negrets. They both shrieked as Maura's fire and the bomb exploded around them.

"Go to Baltic," Savian ordered, grabbing Maura when she returned to human form.

I shrugged off his arm and raced back to grab one of the two crates. "I'm not going to leave you two here with them by yourselves!"

"I'm responsible for your safety, and I say you get down!" he bellowed.

"In your dreams," I started to say, but was suddenly lifted off the ground from behind, and set down onto the stairs. I glared up at Baltic when his voice rumbled over my head. "Do as the thief-taker says, Ysolde."

"We agreed that the bombs were *my* job."

"Do not even think to argue with me," he said, then spun around as the now-metal negret that had been in the process of crawling through the murder hole hit the ground, another of its brethren in the process of wriggling into the keep. Baltic planted his feet in a battle stance, spun his sword in his hand, and ordered Savian to stand out of the way.

"We'll go to the other side," I told Savian and Maura as Pavel rushed past me on the stairs, his sword in hand, his eyes—like Baltic's—alight with pleasure. "There's a murder hole on the south side of the gate, too."

"All right, but if I say stay back, you stay back."

"Are you sure you're not a dragon?" Maura said, puffing a little as we ran down the stairs, our arms laden with the crates. "You're sure arrogant enough for one."

"Ha!" Savian said.

"I agree with her. And for the record, one bossy male in my life is enough," I said, scanning the yard for intruders. It was empty of everyone. "If you keep it up, I'm just going to hit you on the head with one of these bottles, and then you won't want to work for me, and everything will go to hell in a handbasket. So lighten up. I'm older than you; I know what I'm doing."

"May says you were resurrected two months ago."

"Lovey, stay with Nico and Holland," I called out to Brom as he emerged from the second outbuilding (evidently used as a storage shed) with a plastic container of gasoline, and a couple of men's shirts.

"We're going to make more fire bombs," he said, his expression one of excited satisfaction. Nico emerged behind him, his arms filled with cases of beer.

"Keep him inside the tower," I told Nico as they passed. "The negrets are coming in through the murder holes."

"They won't get past Holland and me," he promised. I watched them go into the tower before running across the bailey to the opposite set of stairs that led to the curtain walk.

As a rule, I dislike harming any living being, but negrets were a dangerous cross between a demon and a savage animal, and although they had a human appearance and wore clothing, one look at Savian's still-bleeding wounds reminded me that their culture revolved around killing whatever living things crossed their path.

But that thought brought up an interesting question.

"How do you think—oh, there, on the left, that group is starting to build a pyramid—how do you think the negrets knew to come here?" I asked, handing Savian another bottle as I watched a small pile of metal negrets slide down the wall to the rocky ground.

"Someone called them up, no doubt. Probably that redheaded she-devil."

"Thala?" Maura asked, looking thoughtful.

Horror crawled up my skin. "She's not here, is she? I thought she was in Nepal."

"I don't know where she is."

"Whew." I wondered if she'd made her escape and slipped back to Spain without our knowing it, but a moment's consideration had me shaking my head. "She can't be here. If she was, she would have come stomping out and made all sorts of dramatic declarations and such. Not to mention probably tried to kill me."

"I just wish she were here; there're a few matters I'd like to settle with her," Savian answered with a dark note in his voice.

"She hasn't been here for a few weeks," Maura said, prepping another bottle. "I heard a rumor she was going north toward Russia, but I am not at all privy to her plans."

"Really . . . That's interesting." I filed away that fact for future consideration. "I wonder if Gareth called her. That rat, he probably did. I bet he told her we were here, and she did something to arrange for the negrets to attack."

"Necromancer," Savian said, grunting as he heaved another bomb out of the murder hole.

Maura looked vaguely startled. "What about them?"

"Necromancers can call negrets. Amongst other things, they are eaters of the dead; thus, they answer the call of anyone in the Akashic League."

"Oh. True," Maura said. "Makes sense, then."

"Ruth," I hissed to myself, wishing for a moment that I really had roasted her when I had the opportunity. "She's a necromancer, too. Not as powerful as Thala, but I bet we have her to thank for this."

"Probably called them up before she ran off with your ex," Savian agreed, snarling under his breath as a fresh wave of negrets collected beneath us.

"Ruth is a necromancer, too?" Maura asked, disbelief written on her face. "Why did she never mention that?"

"No clue, but I get the feeling she doesn't use her skills very often. Not that I remember much about our time together." I stopped myself from adding any more. I had a few choice things I'd like to say to Ruth, and kept myself occupied with them until we ran out of ammunition.

"What now?" I asked as Savian dropped the last bomb.

"Let's hope Brom has more made."

We followed Savian down the stairs into the inner bailey, but there I let Maura and him head for the tower. I went in the other direction, calling after them, "I'm going to check on Baltic; then I'll help you with the fire bombs."

"Sounds goo—holy shit!"

I spun around at his exclamation. Flames licked out of one of the windows at the bottom of the tower, scorching the stone black.

"Brom!" I screamed, and ran for the tower door. I didn't make it into the tower—just as I approached it, I saw a familiar green tail lashing the air before disappearing around the side of the tower, and I raced after it.

Nico was covered with negrets, his dragon form more red than green as the little monsters tried to shred the flesh from his bones.

Holland lay unconscious or dead—I didn't know which—and was being dragged through the bloody dirt by six negrets, their faces covered in blood as they took periodic bites from his body.

"Unlock me so I can fight them!" Maura demanded as she shifted into dragon form.

"Can't! Lost the key somewhere," Savian answered before grabbing Maura's arm with one hand, and rushing past me with a fierce battle cry that attracted the attention of the nearest negrets. Dragon fire was everywhere, turning some of the negrets to metal, but there were just too many of them for Maura and Nico to toast.

Behind Nico, Brom was pressed against the wall, his face smeared with blood and his eyes huge. Nico was using his own body to shield him, but, judging by the number of negrets that poured out of the chapel and swarmed over Nico, I knew that even in his dragon form, he wouldn't last but for a few more seconds.

"Nooo!" I screamed when one negret climbed over the top of another, and reached down to grab Brom by his hair.

I yanked hard on Baltic's fire, intending to blast the negrets with it, but got only a thin trickle of fire. Baltic, I knew, was using it himself to stem the flow of negrets into the keep, leaving me without access to his fire. There was nothing for it—I had to summon my own fire, weak though it was.

"Sullivan!" Brom's cry reached my ears as I dug deep within myself, desperately trying to rouse my fire.

Savian went down, covered in negrets. Maura screamed as some of them, slashing and biting her, climbed onto her body, keeping just out of reach of her fire.

Holland was literally being torn limb from limb before our eyes.

Nico's fire occurred in shorter and shorter blasts, his body staggering as the massive swarm of negrets was taking its toll on him.

I spun around, desperately needing Baltic, but he and Pavel were too far away to help.

"Sullivaaan," Brom wailed, the negrets viciously yanking him from behind Nico.

Fury, fear, anger, hate . . . it all spun around inside me, my soul screaming with agony and impotent rage and desperation, building to such a crescendo, I thought it would explode out of my skin.

"Brom!" I screamed, leaping forward to attack the negrets that dared touch my child. I literally saw red when my dragon fire finally answered my summons, bathing the area in a scarlet tidal wave of flame that swept across half the bailey, from the towers to the other side, where the chapel and outbuildings stood. Negrets screamed in a chorus that lightened my heart almost as much as the sight of the little metal bodies hitting the ground. "Brommy! Are you all right? Did they hurt you? Stand still and let me see if you're injured. Oh, lovey, I'm so sorry I wasn't here to protect you. Is that your blood or Nico's? By the rood, if any of them harmed you—"

"Sullivan?" Brom struggled in my arms as I tried to simultaneously kiss, hug, and check him for injuries. "You're ... uh ... white."

"White? What on earth are you talking about? Oh my god, they hit your head, didn't they? My poor, poor darling—" I stopped stroking the hair back off his face, staring in surprise at the white-scaled fingers tangled in his brown hair. I lifted the hand, startled even more to see black claws tipping each finger.

"Good lord," a weak voice said behind me. "Ysolde?"

I looked over my shoulder to where Nico was getting to his feet, his dragon body battered and bloody. Beyond him, Savian groaned and moved one arm. Unfortunately, it was Holland's arm that one of the negrets had ripped off and had been using to beat Savian, but the fact that Savian was alive gave me hope for Holland. Maura, now in human form, was covered in blood as she staggered to her feet, looking dazed.

I spun around and stared at the chapel, but Holland lay halfway in the door, with no negrets coming from within. Either we'd reached the end of that particular attack force, or they were wisely hiding from my wrath. "We have to close up the bolt-hole again. But first ... Brom, can you walk?"

"Of course I can walk." He rubbed his head, his gaze locked on my body. "They just pulled on my hair."

"I have to show Baltic this. He won't believe me otherwise," I said, taking my child by the hand and marching around the tower to the far side of the bailey.

"You're a lot bigger than I thought you would be," Brom said as he bounced against my side a couple of times.

"I'm not big. I'm statuesque," I corrected, staring down at myself, unable to keep from twitching my tail experimentally. It felt strong, as if I could take down a tree with it. "Male dragons are intimidating when in dragon form. Females are statuesque while still retaining femininity. What do you think of my tail? I rather like it."

He glanced thoughtfully over his shoulder. "It's nice. Doesn't have pointy things on it like the pictures Nico and I saw in a museum. He said mortals don't understand dragon form at all, and that they were always giving them wings and horse heads and things like that." He was silent for a few moments. "Your head isn't like a horse."

"Of course not." I took a deep breath, enjoying the sensation of power that seemed to flow through me.

"You've got small front arms, though, compared to your back ones," he continued, then frowned. "Or are they all legs, like on a dog?"

I held out my free arm. It was perfectly normal in length. I stopped and bent over to look at my legs. They were dragon legs, true dragon legs, not at all human looking, strong and powerful, and covered in white scales that shimmered in the morning sun. I looked back at my arm. "Oh, great, I have tiny little ineffectual T. rex arms!"

"I don't think they're that bad—" Brom started to say, but I cut him off by bellowing Baltic's name as we approached the stairs to the curtain wall.

"What is it?" came his answer.

I stomped up the stairs, taking a perverse satisfaction in the little tremor shocks that accompanied each step. "You never told me I was going to be a mutant dragon!"

He and Pavel both had their backs to us, the curtain walk around them covered in metal bodies interspersed with blood and gore and the remains of negrets that had been dispatched when they were conserving their dragon fire.

"What are you talking about?" Baltic asked, turning around to ask, an irritated look on his face that only grew more irritated when I gestured toward myself.

"I have tiny little arms! They aren't at all like yours!

They're minuscule! They're like baby arms or something! I cannot tell you how disconcerting this is!"

Pavel, who had also turned to look, took a step back in surprise, tripped over a negret corpse, and fell off the wall to the ground below.

"You see?" I gestured toward Pavel as he picked himself up off the ground. "Pavel is so horrified by my puny little arms that he would rather leap off the wall than stay on it with them," I declared, knowing it was untrue, but unable to keep from expressing my unhappiness.

"You choose *now* to find your dragon form?" Baltic snarled, backhanding a couple of negrets off the wall down onto their brethren. "You couldn't wait for a time where I might guide you? You had to do it now? I am *busy*, mate!"

"It just happened! I thought I was going to explode, and instead, this happened." I stared at him for a moment, unable to put into words what I most feared.

"You don't know how to change back, do you?" he asked.

I slumped a little, relief filling me that he was there with me. "No. Behind you."

He spat fire over his shoulder, sighing heavily as he walked over to us, pausing at the sight of Brom's bloody face. "You are hurt?"

"Just my hair."

"Ah. Good. Mate, look at me."

"I don't like my arms," I said, releasing my death grip on Brom to wave them at him. "They're really, really disappointing. I thought I was going to be big and beefy like you. You have powerful arms. You have arms that make people respect you. You don't have widdle runty arms like me."

His mouth twitched, but he managed to keep his expression sober as he pulled me against him, shifting as he did so back into human form. "You are female. Your arms are suited to your form. Nothing more, nothing less."

"I don't like them," I repeated petulantly, letting a little of my fire caress his chest.

"Then change your form. It is simply a matter of controlling your will, *chérie*. Will yourself to your other form, and it will be so."

I kissed his neck, breathing deeply of his scent, now overlaid with the metallic smell of blood. I thought of myself as I normally appeared, of how my body fit so well against his, of the pleasure I took in our embraces, of my true inner self, of who and what I was, and when I reached up to pull his head down to mine, it was a normal human hand that brushed back a strand of his hair. "I love you," I told him.

"I know," he answered, kissed me swiftly, gave my butt a squeeze, and released me to take care of the next batch of negrets that forced themselves through the window. Pavel limped past us, giving me a crooked smile as he picked up his sword.

"Will you be mad if I said I like you better when you look like a normal person?" Brom asked as we trotted down the stairs to see how the others were doing.

"Of course not." I put my arm around him, rubbing his back, relieved to be in my human form once again. "I liked my tail in the dragon form, but I prefer this body, too."

"You have normal arms now," he pointed out.

"Yes." I frowned as we approached Nico, who squatted next to Holland. The latter, I was pleased to see, was still alive, although mostly unconscious, and missing one arm and part of an ear. Maura had helped Savian to his feet, his shirt and pants covered in blood and dirt. He weaved as he staggered against her, gesturing toward us. "And don't you think I won't have a thing or two to say to the First Dragon about those puny dragon arms when I see him next."

"Are you all right?" Savian called.

"We're fine. The negrets got in through the crypt, though. We need to block it off again in case more try to come through that way."

Nico and I did most of the work since Savian just wasn't up to it, and Maura was still firmly attached to him. We left them to watch Holland and the door while we swung the tomb back into place, and we wedged the base with a bit of broken wood from a window shutter.

"Let's hope that holds. Nico, are you all right to come with me?"

"Yes. Just a bit worn out," he said, trying to put a brave face on what I knew were some pretty grievous injuries.

"Good. Savian, you and Maura stay here with Holland."

"If he would just unlock me, I could help you," Maura complained, shooting a potent glare at Savian.

He lifted a feeble hand at her. "I would if I could, princess, but I told you that somehow, in all of the excitement, the key fell out of my pocket."

"Great, just great." Maura huffed to herself as she plopped down on the ground next to him. "This is so how I wanted this day to go."

"At least you can heal yourself," Savian said with a soft moan as she jogged his arm.

"If Holland recovers consciousness, tell him we'll get him to a healer just as soon as we can," I told them. "You may not want to let him see his arm lying there, though. That's an awfully startling thing to see when you just come to your senses. You're sure the bleeding has stopped?"

"His, yes. He's a corporeal spirit. Me, I'm human," Savian said, leaning back against the sun-warmed stone wall with a groan of pain.

"We'll get you and Maura a healer, as well," I promised, hesitating when my gaze landed on Brom.

"Can I come with you?" he asked, and I saw fear in his eyes that I knew he would never acknowledge.

"You would be a big help." He smiled in relief as the three of us went to pick up the Molotov cocktails that Brom had managed to make before the negrets had burst in on them.

I yelled up to Baltic my intentions, receiving in return a warning to be careful. We hurried over to the other side of the wall, which fortunately none of the negrets had managed to breach.

"With luck, they've either run out or realized we're just going to toast them into extinction," I said as I hurled a lit bottle down on the small cluster of negrets.

"You wouldn't think there was an endless supply of them, would you?" Nico asked as he—taller than me—tossed a bottle over the wall.

"I sure hope not." I bent down to drop another bottle, but movement to the far right side caught my eye. "What now?"

"*What* what?" Brom asked, handing me a bottle.

I handed it back to him. "You supply Nico for a minute, lovey. I want to see what's going on over at the far side. If the negrets have found a weak spot, we need to know about it."

"Don't leave the curtain walk," Nico called after me as I hurried down the narrow walkway.

The movement that had caught my peripheral vision was around the north side of the fortress, where the wall melted into the heavy stone mountain that rose above our heads. I peered down through the branches of a half dozen lemon trees that ringed a low stone wall that formed a drunken oval outside the bailey. The ground inside the oval was much less rocky than the surrounding area, although a few large flat stones were scattered around. My eyes narrowed as I focused on one of those stones. It looked like a headstone. I turned to look behind me, into the bailey. The chapel was directly below me with Maura, Savian, and Holland propped up against the wall.

"Must be the fortress graveyard for people not buried in the crypt," I said to myself, turning back to the area and searching it for signs of life.

A little flash of red through the green leaves had me gasping in surprise and shock, followed swiftly by terror. The sight of bodies forming out of nothing sent me running back along the wall. I didn't stop to explain when I got to Brom and Nico; I grabbed my son's arm and dragged him after me as I raced down the stairs and across the bailey.

"Baltic!" I yelled as both Brom and Nico asked me what was wrong. "Baltic! We have to get out of here. Now!"

"We can't until it is safe for me to take you and Brom," he said, appearing at the head of the stairs and tossing a metal negret down onto a stack that sat at the base of the stairs. "There are fewer of them coming now. Another hour or so and we will have depleted their forces enough that I can take you away."

"We don't have an hour. We have to go now!" I insisted, starting for the chapel. "We'll have to go out the bolt-hole and blast with dragon fire any negrets that remain."

"Ysolde!" Baltic said in his most domineering voice. "I insist that you allow me to decide when it is safe for you and Brom to leave."

"Thala's here!" I yelled over my shoulder, pausing long enough to gesture toward the north. "She's not in Nepal; she's *here*!"

He froze for an instant, then smiled.

I shivered at the smile.

"Good. We will capture her and take her to the watch."

"You don't understand. Oh, for the love of the saints—" I shoved Brom at Nico and marched back to Baltic, taking him by the arm and trying to pull him after me. "She's not alone!"

"She has ouroboros dragons with her?" He shrugged, refusing to allow me to budge him from where he stood. Pavel slowly came down the stairs, looking curious.

"No, she doesn't. She's in the graveyard. And unless I'm way off base, she's resurrecting the dead people there."

I'll say this for Baltic: he may love a battle, and will happily fight when the odds are greatly against him, but he's not stupid; he knows when the time is upon him to retreat.

That time was now.

He had to see for himself, however. While Nico and I whipped together a makeshift stretcher in which we gently rolled the still-unconscious Holland and his arm (we couldn't find his ear), he and Pavel went up onto the north wall, returning almost immediately with identical grim expressions.

"Liches," Baltic said, moving me aside as I threw myself on the tomb, trying to slide it back. "We will leave now."

"I can't go with you!"

We all turned to look at the woman who stood in the doorway, Savian next to her. She held up her hand. "Someone has to get this off, because I'm sorry, but I really cannot leave."

"Look, I know you feel some sort of loyalty to Thala—"

Her face twisted in pain. "No, it's not that at all. It's— it's . . . Oh, it's too complicated to go into now. You just have to believe me when I say I can't leave."

I turned to Baltic. "She's been nothing but helpful since we got here. Would you go ahead and break the handcuffs? Savian lost the key to them, so you're going to have to use brute strength to get her free."

"He won't be able to," Savian said wearily as Baltic started toward Maura.

"Don't be silly. Baltic is extremely strong, and even stronger in his dragon form."

Savian shook his head. "These aren't mortal handcuffs, Ysolde. They're titanium, spelled, warded, and scribed with not one, but two banes. They are unbreakable, even by a dragon."

"Oh goddess," Maura said, moaning as she put one hand to her head. "What am I going to do?"

"I have another set of keys in my flat," Savian told us. "If we can get back to England, I can unlock them."

"You're just going to have to come with us," I said loudly when Maura vented her spleen on him, telling him in no uncertain—and sometimes anatomically impossible—terms what she thought of his ineptitude. "I know it's not what you want, but we have no choice, and no time to stand here arguing about it!"

The negrets in the tunnel were taken by surprise when not one, but three dragons all descended upon them, filling the entire passageway with fire. Brom and I carried Holland—over Savian's protests that he felt fine, really, and the fact that he fainted when he stood up a minute before was just the merest coincidence—while Maura and Savian brought up the rear, the latter in a drunken stagger that owed its existence to a severe loss of blood.

"It's clear," Baltic said once he and Pavel returned from reconnoitering the entrance of the bolt-hole. "She has raised only a half-dozen liches thus far. Ysolde, would you—"

"No," I told him, taking his arm. "I know you want to take her while she's so close to us, but"—I glanced toward Brom—"she wouldn't bat an eyelash over the idea of using him against us."

He hesitated, torn between the need to take care of the threat Thala posed us and the acknowledgment that Brom was in danger by being so close to her. She was absolutely unscrupulous, and I didn't doubt for a second that she would use him mercilessly to harm us.

"You are right, I know, but . . ." He snapped off the word, his jaw tightening until a muscle twitched. "You are right. We will go. There will be other opportunities to find her—ones that do not pose such hazard."

"If I weren't already head over heels in love with you, I would be now," I told him as we hurried through the rocks and scrubby plants to the area where we'd left our cars, praying as we did so that we could get Brom away safely.

Chapter Nine

"I've never truly felt like a red shirt before, but I sure do now." Holland sucked in his breath and winced when I dabbed antiseptic liquid over the six-inch slash across the right side of his chest.

"Sorry," I murmured. "I know it stings, but it's the best I can do until we get you to a healer."

"Red shirt?" Baltic asked, stalking into the portal company's waiting room, his hand held out to me. "Are you done with my phone?"

"Yes, I just had to make one call. Here it is."

He accepted the phone, immediately punching in a text message.

"It's a *Star Trek* reference," Maura answered Baltic in a resigned voice. "It means the disposable guy who gets killed. Which is basically what I'm going to be unless you let me go."

"My mate wishes for you to remain with us," Baltic said with a dismissive glance at her, still texting.

"Well, it's not so much that as Savian can't get the

handcuff off you until we get home. Besides, I know your mother and grandfather are worried sick about you, Maura, and would welcome the chance to talk with you." I wrapped a length of gauze around Holland's chest before tying it off. "Not that I owe Dr. Kostich anything, but still, I'm sure he's worried. And you're far from a red shirt, Holland. We very much appreciate your helping us. Are you absolutely sure your arm isn't hurting you?"

We both looked down to where I had, with Baltic's assistance, bound Holland's severed arm to his shoulder, trying our best to line it up properly.

"Not since Pavel found that morphine, no," he answered, his voice slower now. "With luck, the flesh will start regenerating by the time we get to England."

"I'm afraid your ear is going to suffer for the experience, though," I said, giving the healing remains of his ear a sorrowful glance. "I'm so sorry about that, Holland."

Baltic turned his back to us, speaking softly into the phone.

"It's all right," Holland said with a weak smile. "It was an adventure. Wouldn't have missed it for anything."

His eyes closed as he spoke. I looked across him as Brom returned from visiting the portalling company's bathroom, Pavel dogging his heels. "I feel just terrible about everything, Pavel. I hope you can forgive us for putting your friend in so much danger, and for letting the negrets chomp on him."

Pavel looked surprised. "You did not put us in danger, Ysolde. Thala did that. Or those under her command. We do not hold you to blame for anything."

"Nonetheless, I feel terrible about it."

"Are we going home now, or is Baltic going to draw and quarter Gareth?" Brom asked, tugging at my sleeve.

"No one is going to draw and quarter anyone. Besides, Gareth and Ruth hightailed it out of there after calling up all those wretched negrets."

"Yeah, but he said he was going to kill them just as soon as he was done killing the dragons."

"He what?" I took a deep breath and pulled Brom aside. He obviously needed a little reassurance. "Brom, I know this has been a horrible day for you, what with Gareth and Ruth, and the ouroboros dragons, and then the negrets attacking us, but you know that Baltic and I will never let anything bad happen to you."

"I know that," he said with all the insouciance of a nine-year-old. "Baltic told me he'd kill the dragons, though. The bad ones, I mean. Not Maura, because she's nice, but the others, and then he said he'd draw and quarter Gareth for what he put you through."

A horrible suspicion struck me. What if the ouroboros dragons who had been in the keep hadn't run away, as I assumed they had done once Baltic had bested them. What if . . . I eyed the dragon of my dreams suspiciously, moving over to where he stood, quickly assessing his hurts, and deciding after a few seconds that he was, as he had claimed, not in any danger of expiring on the spot. That didn't mean others hadn't done so, however. "Is there something you want to tell me?" I asked, nudging Baltic's arm when he ended his call and began to dial another number.

"About what?"

"About killing people?"

He looked up from his phone, frowning. "Negrets aren't people, mate."

"Not them. The others." I waited, but his gaze dropped, and he refused to meet my eyes. "Baltic?"

"No, there is nothing I wish to tell you." The fact that he didn't even look at me spoke volumes.

I sighed and moved around to stand in front of him. "Tell me you didn't kill any of those ouroboros dragons."

"I didn't kill any of the ouroboros dragons."

I looked into his fathomless eyes and did not like what I saw there. "You're lying, aren't you?"

"You just told me to do so." Irritation flared in those beautiful eyes.

"No, I said—oh, never mind. How many dragons did you kill?"

"Why?" One of his eyebrows rose. "Are you going to locate a priest and pay for indulgences for the deaths of ouroboros dragons, just as you did in the past?"

The second the words left his lips, I felt as if I were caught up in a whirlpool, spun around, and sucked down into dizzying depths . . . that just as suddenly disappeared, leaving a man's voice echoing in my ears. ". . . are responsible for the deaths of dragons you claimed were ouroboros, are you not, Baltic?"

"Whoa," said a thin voice, and I blinked away the confusion to see Brom standing next to me, watching with wide eyes the scene in front of us. "We're in another of your visions, aren't we? This one doesn't have Gareth and Ruth. I like it better."

"Why on earth am I having this? My dragon woke up, didn't it?" I wrapped one arm around Brom and moved over to where Baltic stood with a martyred expression on his face. Pavel, Savian, and Maura stood behind him, all three of them blinking in surprise. Holland appeared to be asleep on the couch.

"We're in a vision? I've never seen anything like this," Maura said, glancing around. "It's a vision of the past, I assume. Interesting. Who are those people?"

I leaned into Baltic and watched the two men before us. "The one standing with his arms crossed, and his back to the fireplace is Baltic. I know it doesn't look like him, but that was his original human form. The other man is . . . Who is that?"

My Baltic sighed. "It matters not. I grow weary of

your insistence that I relive episodes from the past that are of no interest to anyone, mate. And now you have brought others in, when we have little time to indulge in such matters. End the vision so that we might take that blasted portal out of Spain."

"Pavel?" I asked, ignoring Baltic's demands.

"That's Alexei, the wyvern of the black dragons," he answered with a little smile.

Baltic shot him an annoyed look.

"Alexei? The wyvern before you?"

"You refuse to answer me?" the man in question demanded of the old Baltic as he stormed past, pacing a path between the long trestle table and a massive fireplace big enough to roast two oxen side by side. Alexei, almost as tall as Baltic, bore a resemblance to the latter, with a similar shape to his jaw and chin, as well as the same dark hair and eyes. Although many black dragons had such coloring, it was obvious even in the dim light that Baltic and Alexei were related.

"Why should I bother to do so?" Baltic asked with a shrug as Alexei paced past him again. "I told you that I would avenge my mother's death, and I have done so."

"At the risk of alienating the red dragons, who are already at the verge of war against us because of you!" Alexei said, his hands gesturing wildly in the air.

"I know that can't be your father, because your father is the—" I glanced beyond my Baltic to where the others stood watching the vision with interest, and bit off the rest of the sentence. I was still coming to grips with the fact that the man I loved with every ounce of my being was the child of a dragon god. "I know Alexei isn't your father, but it's obvious you're related to him somehow."

"End the vision," Baltic growled, turning Brom and me to face him.

"I told you before—I don't know how to end them. What was that bit about avenging your mom?"

"You would have me let the murderers of your own daughter escape without punishment?" the past Baltic snarled. "You may not care that her death be avenged, but I do."

"She was my only daughter! Of course I care! I feel her loss more than you can possibly know, but that does not give you the right to kill Chuan Ren's elite guard!" Alexei snarled right back at him. "As if the situation weren't troublesome enough with your actions threatening the peace of the entire weyr, now you must do this!"

Baltic took me by the arms and gave me a little shake. "Mate, you will cease this immediately!"

I said nothing, unable to look away from the scene between Baltic and . . . his grandfather?

"I will not be dictated to," the past Baltic snapped. "Not by you, and not by Chuan Ren."

Alexei spun around, his expression as black as his hair. "You are not wyvern here, Baltic; I am. And if I choose to dictate to you, then I will do so!"

"Ysolde!" the present-day Baltic demanded, his voice filled with ire.

I glanced back to him. "Chuan Ren's guards killed your mother? Why? Wait—let's start first with Alexei. He was your grandfather?"

"End this!" he said, his patience frittering away into nothing.

"You keep saying that, but I don't know how," I pointed out, wanting to ask him a dozen more questions, but hesitating with the presence of the others.

"Then I will end it for you!" he snapped, and without concern for the fact that I still held Brom close to me, he pulled me against him, his lips claiming mine, his dragon fire spilling out in a spiral around all three of us. Brom squeaked something about being crushed, until I released him and allowed him to pop out from between us, my attention now focused on the man whose kiss dominated me, demanding a response I was unable to withhold.

"Aww," I heard Brom say a minute later, when I could catch my breath and rally my thoughts into something other than how badly I wanted to wrestle Baltic to the nearest bed and have my womanly way with him. "It's gone."

"It'll never be gone," I said without a care for grammar, staring into Baltic's eyes and reveling in the love I saw in return.

"Never," he agreed, brushing his thumb along my lower lip.

"That was fascinating," Maura said thoughtfully. "Not your kiss, the vision. I had no idea one could revisit the past in that way. What causes that, Ysolde? Do you know?"

I stepped back from Baltic, not surprised to see that he had, in fact, ended the vision by the simple method of kissing me senseless. "I used to think it was the frustrated dragon inside me trying to get me to wake it up. But it's woken now, so that doesn't make sense anymore."

"It's not woken," Baltic said, brushing back a strand of my hair. "It answered your call when you needed it, but that is all. The dragon inside you still slumbers."

"How do you know?" I asked, warmed to my toes by the gentle caress of his hand on my cheek.

"I know." He turned back to his phone, dismissing the rest of us.

"I don't have a dragon inside me, although Sullivan says when I'm older and I have children, they will be light dragons, and will be able to shift into dragon form," Brom told Maura. "I wish I could do that. I don't want to have children, but Sullivan says I probably will later on. How come you turned red when you were a dragon, if you aren't in a sept?"

"My father was a red dragon, so that is the form I take

when I'm dragonny," she answered, giving him a little smile that faded almost immediately. "My mother isn't a dragon, however."

"You know I'm going to have at least a dozen questions about that whole scene," I told Baltic as he consulted a text message he had just received.

He sighed a particularly martyred sigh. "I know."

"I'll go check to see if the portal is ready yet," Pavel said, and slipped away.

"I should check the area outside to make sure no pursuing dragons, liches, or negrets are about to descend upon us," Savian said, groaning out loud when he limped forward. "Come along, princess. You can pick up any of my body parts that happen to fall off."

"Oh, for the love of the good green earth," Maura said, snapping the handcuffs in an annoyed manner. "You're such a big baby! You don't have nearly the number of wounds that poor knocker has, and you're making a much bigger fuss about them than he is."

"You're going to drive me barking mad until I can get these cuffs off, aren't you?" Savian asked her as they left the waiting room.

"A girl has to have some fun."

"Did you get everything in order?" I asked Baltic as he tucked away his phone. "Did you arrange to have a healer standing by when we get back to England? I don't like the looks of Holland's injuries, even though he says he can heal that severed arm."

"We're not going to England," Baltic said, taking my arm with one hand, and Brom with the other.

"We're not?" I asked as he ushered us out of the room and into the portalling chamber. "Where are we going?"

"Home."

"Home is England, isn't it?"

"No."

"Then where are we going?"

"Going? Right, this is where I make my last stand. I absolutely refuse to leave," Maura said as Savian and she reentered the building. "I have told you people and told you people—I can't leave. There are things I must do, and I cannot do them if Thala finds me missing. I'll just have to do them with this giant pain in the ass attached to me."

"Like hell you will," Savian growled. "I'm not staying here to be chewed to shreds by that red-haired she-devil. You're coming with us whether you want to or not."

"Please, I can't leave Spain," she pleaded as Savian, with a grim expression and a loud groan of pain, bent down and hoisted her onto his shoulder. "Dear goddess! What do you think you're doing? Put me down!"

"I know you're anxious about everything, Maura, but you needn't be. Once Savian gets the key to his handcuffs, I will talk to your grandfather for you if you like," I offered as we stepped into the portalling room. "I know how intimidating he can be, and I'm sure with his help, he'll keep Thala from threatening you, or whatever it is you're afraid she'll do to you because we took you away with us."

"No, you don't understand at all. . . . It's not that simple."

"Where are we going?" I asked Baltic again as the portal attendant gestured us toward the oval of grey light that twisted upon itself, a never-ending Möbius that sat in the middle of the room. Just looking at it raised the hairs on the back of my neck; it was wrong, somehow, that a tear in the fabric of space should just hang in the air like that. Baltic's face was grim as he looked at it, and I knew that he and the other dragons were all dreading the experience to come.

"Latvia," he answered as Pavel, with an identical expression of complete and utter loathing, stepped into the portal.

"To Ziema?" I asked, naming the town where the forest that hid Dauva was located. Dammit, I was sure we were going home. I'd have to make another phone call.

"Riga. Pavel located a house there for us yesterday, before Brom was taken. He was going to have you look at it, but there was no time. We will go there now, and set up defenses so that the usurping bastard will not threaten you or Brom again."

I said nothing before I entered the portal other than to reassure the still-protesting Maura that I would help her deal with her grandfather and mother. Baltic waited until Brom and Savian and Maura had been sent through the portal after me before venturing into it himself, the now-comatose Holland in his arms.

He was just as rumpled and discombobulated coming out the other side as he had been going to Spain. I spent a few minutes fussing over Holland before attending to Baltic. He suffered me to smooth out his shirt, and tidy his hair (which always came undone from its leather tie when he went through a portal) before turning his attention to Pavel.

"There should be two cars waiting for us."

"Where the hell are we?" Savian asked, rubbing his chest with a pained expression on his face. "Did the portal company screw up?"

"I'll see that they're ready," Pavel said with a nod. He got to his feet and staggered out the door.

"There wasn't a screwup, no," I told Savian before turning a worried glance on Holland. "Baltic, we need a healer."

"One will be at the house when we arrive."

"Then what are we doing here?" Savian asked.

"Wait a minute—this isn't England," Maura said, somewhat belatedly, it was true, but she, being a dragon, was extremely discomposed by the portal. Nico was only now shaking his head and rubbing his face, clearly trying to recover from the effects of portalling.

"No, it's Latvia." I waited for the explosion and wasn't disappointed.

"Latvia?" Maura exploded in a flurry of oaths that were luckily in Zilant, the archaic language once used by the dragons in the weyr. "Why are you doing this to me? Why do you want me to suffer like this?"

"We don't want you to suffer. Admittedly I may have wanted that a while ago, but not since you've been so helpful in Spain. And considering that you went against Thala in order to aid us, I feel it's only right we aid you in return. Baltic, can I use your phone for a second? My battery is dead."

By the time I made a fast phone call, visited the ladies' room to tidy myself up (I may have a dragon buried deep in my psyche, but luckily, portal travel didn't discommode me much) and returned to the others, Pavel was feeling much more like himself and announced that the cars were waiting.

Baltic picked up Holland. "Brom, you may open the car door for me. Holland will travel with Pavel, while you will stay with your mother and me."

The rest of us shuffled out of the portalling office after them, Maura still protesting that she couldn't be in Latvia; it just wasn't possible, and why couldn't we understand that?

She complained the entire way through town, and into the outskirts.

"Seriously, there has to be a way to get these handcuffs off," she said, still going at it when Baltic pointed to a dirt driveway. I turned up it, trying to think of some way to calm down Maura when Savian took care of the matter for me.

"You're making my head hurt with your endless bitching," Savian said, rubbing his face.

"I'm not bitching; I'm complaining about this unnecessary abduction. And tough toenails!" was her reply.

He cast her a glance that had her opening her eyes wide. "It hurts so bad, I may vomit. On you. Savvy?"

Silence reigned in the car for a whole thirty seconds before Brom, his nose pressed to the window, asked, "Is that my lab? It looks kind of crumbly."

The drive was long and straight, the rich chocolate earth covered in golden leaves from the aspens that lined the drive, their branches arching over us in a lovely way that had me thinking warm thoughts about Pavel's house-finding abilities.

To the right, a shimmer of water could be seen through the trees, as well as a ruined red stone wall with still-intact Gothic windows.

"Oh, I'm sure that's not it. That's not much more than a shell of a building. Surely Pavel would have found us something with a basement, or a completed outbuilding." I glanced at Baltic, beside me. "Wouldn't he?"

He shrugged. "He showed me the information about the house. It is an eighteenth-century mansion with five standing outbuildings, on twenty-seven acres. It has power and water. That is all I know about it. It was up to you to approve it or not, but he did not have time to show you the pictures."

"An eighteenth-century mansion," I said, a little thrill of excitement making me shiver. "It sounds wonderful."

"It sounds full of mice," Maura said in a subdued voice.

"Pessimist," Savian told her.

"Realist, thank you. Emile has an eighteenth-century house in the north of France that is mouse central. I grew up there." She shuddered.

"Another ruin," Brom said, pointing to the other side of the drive.

"That looks like it could have been a barn or something," I commented as the trees grew denser around us, the track making a sweeping curve to the northeast. "Oh, I think I see the house through the trees! It looks big. Yes, that must be it. How excit—" The words dried up on my lips as we rounded a dense clump of trees that lurked at the far end of a large pond, revealing the three-story mansion in all its glory.

If you could use that word. Which I wasn't about to.

"Sins of the saints," I swore, letting the car roll to a stop a few yards away from the closest end of the house.

Baltic squinted at the house for a moment before opening the car door. "It needs some work."

"Needs some work?" My mouth hung open as I stared at the looming monstrosity before me. Oh, it was a mansion all right, and it looked as though it had seen every single moment of time that had passed since it was built three hundred years before.

"Told you it has mice," Maura said with grim satisfaction as Savian, wordless at the sight of the house, slid out of the backseat, pulling her after him. "Probably rats, too. And given the state of the house, I wouldn't be surprised to see badgers, foxes, and bears inhabiting it, as well."

"Cool," Brom said as he stared wide-eyed at it. "It looks haunted. What's behind it? That looks like a building back there. I'm going to go see."

I closed my eyes and rested my forehead on the steering wheel for a moment, wondering if it was possible to gather everyone back up to whisk them away to England and civilization.

"Mate?" Baltic stood with my door open, his hand outstretched for mine.

I looked up at him, then over to the house. I have no idea what the original color of the paint was, but now it was basically the color of putty. Mildewed putty on which a dog had thrown up. The ground-floor paned windows had tall, elegant dimensions that you see in homes of its age; the second floor bore gabled windows of a lesser stature, but topped with ornate hemispheres. The upper floor had more gabled windows, but without the prettiness, obviously belonging to the servants' quarters. The roof, dotted with chimneys of varying colors, was solid green with moss, as were the gables. Unkempt, scraggly grass the color of straw surrounded the house, along with some depressed-looking bare trees that drooped claustrophobically over the far end of the house, no doubt making the rooms at that end of the house extremely dark.

It looked like a deranged special effects master's idea of a house sitting over a portal to hell.

"You don't seriously expect us to live there," I told Baltic as I slowly emerged from the safety of the car. "If it's not infested with mice and bears, or haunted—both of which are frankly quite likely—then it's got to be nothing but a giant mold and mildew pit, and completely uninhabitable."

"You like fixing things up," he said, his fingers twining through mine in a gesture that I suspected owed more to a desire to keep me from running away than one of affection. "This house will satisfy your need to be domestic."

I tore my horrified gaze from the house and let it rest on him. "You're joking, right?"

"Consider it a challenge. Or if you like, practice for how you will furnish Dauva once it is completed. Ah. There are Pavel and the others."

"I found a building I can use," Brom said, running around the house toward us, as happy and excited as a boy could be. "It's got a big door and windows, and everything. There's no glass in the windows, but that's OK. It even has a sink, although there's something brown that growled at me living in it."

"This is a nightmare, isn't it?" Maura said, staring at

the house with the expression I had a feeling was also on my face. "I'm having a nightmare to end all nightmares, and this is just the capper on that, isn't it?"

"I don't think I've ever seen a house I'd use the word 'rancid' about, but this one fulfills just about every meaning of the word," Savian said, likewise staring at it.

I was about to tell Baltic that there was no way I would ever consent to live in such a horrible parody of a house, when one of the two double front doors opened up, and a man emerged onto a short, split verandah.

"There you are," Constantine said, gesturing grandly toward the house. "Welcome to Valmieras!"

Chapter Ten

"You did this on purpose!"

Faded and tattered wallpaper rustled forlornly in the wake of an agitated dragon.

"Not in the sense you mean. Baltic—"

"You went behind my back to call that bastard traitor!"

A little breeze came in through the window I'd thrown open, but even the fresh air wasn't strong enough to battle the horrible combined scent of mildew, abandoned house, and things I'd really rather not identify.

"Ysolde, my beloved one, would you like me to strike him down?" a disembodied voice asked. "He looks as if he is about to do you bodily harm, and I cannot allow that."

I stopped trying to grab Baltic as he paced back and forth in front of me, down the length of the largest bedroom that he had claimed for ours, his hands gesturing in short, jabbing movements, his eyes all but spitting fury, and instead focused my best frown on Constantine. "Of course I don't want you to strike him down, and Baltic has never lifted a hand to me. *Ever!* Such an idea is utterly ridiculous."

"It also has great appeal at this moment," Baltic growled as he stomped past me, smoke trailing him.

"Oh!" I stepped immediately into his path, transferring my frown to him. "You wouldn't!"

He looked downright deadly at that moment, every inch the famed dread wyvern, his black eyes lit with fury when they narrowed on me, his muscles bunched, his dragon fire about ready to burst from him. "Wouldn't I?"

I wrapped my arms around his waist, ignoring the fact that his arms were crossed over his chest. "Not unless you mean on a certain posterior portion of my person, and even then, that would be totally uncalled for. Unless, of course, you let me reciprocate."

He looked even more outraged than he had when Constantine sauntered down the front steps of our new home. "I am a wyvern! Wyverns are not spanked. You, however, are *not* a wyvern."

"Really? You're into that, too?" Constantine said, going from transparent to corporeal form in the blink of an eye. "Did Ysolde tell you about my spectral whip? I'm told it's not nearly as effective on non-spirit beings, but still packs a titillating sting if used properly."

"We are not into that, no," I said quickly when Baltic's fire rose even higher. "I was just making a little joke to lighten the mood, which Baltic well knows. He just likes to pretend he's more indignant than he is."

"You called him," Baltic accused me.

"Are we back to that again?" I tightened my arms around him, crossed arms and all. "Yes, I did call Constantine. No, I didn't inform you that I was telling him we were going to Latvia instead of back to England. And no, I do not desire him. I love you. I always have, I always will, and someday, you're going to realize that and be on your knees in gratitude that I love you so much, I'm willing to put up with your insecurity where Constantine is concerned."

Baltic growled, although he loosened his arms enough to let me hug him properly. "Why did you feel it necessary to inform him of your location?"

"She wants me to do a little job for her," Constantine said, fading back to nothingness. "Two jobs, actually. Neither of which *you* can do."

"Oh, for the love of the saints, Constantine! I said no baiting Baltic! And I mean it. If you can't behave, you can take a time-out in one of the outbuildings and think about what it means to have some manners. Baltic, my love, my *only* love, stop smoking."

He looked at me as if I were deranged.

I smiled and touched one nostril. "Your dragon fire is riding so high that little wisps of smoke keep sneaking out. It's true that I asked Constantine to do a job for me, but I didn't expect he would come here immediately." I paused for a moment, thinking about that. I looked over to where I'd last seen the shade. "How *did* you get here before us? I called you from the portal office when we first arrived."

"I was already in Riga. I knew that Baltic would try to rebuild Dauva, and I decided when you disappeared from England that he had brought you here. It's amazing what a little snooping in real estate offices will uncover."

"What jobs?" Baltic asked, unbending even further to wrap his arms around me, his hands on my behind. "What is it you believe he can do that I cannot?"

Constantine snickered.

"I'm serious about the time-out," I told him before turning back to Baltic, picking my words carefully. "I want my dragon shard from Kostya."

"The Avignon Phylactery?" He looked puzzled for a moment, then shrugged. "Thala has much to answer for in giving it to him solely in order to distract me. It is right you should want it back, mate, but you do not need to employ traitorous murderers in order to get it."

"You murdered more dragons than me," came the reply from across the room. "Thousands more! It's a wonder the weyr didn't charge you for them centuries ago, like they have now."

"Baltic has been cleared of those ridiculous charges that he killed the blue dragons," I started to say, but I was interrupted before I could hone my outrage to a needle-sharp point.

"I will have Pavel get the phylactery for you."

"Pavel who you said yourself was not a very good thief?" I kissed Baltic's chin, ignoring the gagging noises from Constantine's side of the room. "There are few beings more suited to the liberating of stolen items than a shade, my darling. And look at it this way—it will give Constantine something to do, and it will vex Kostya in the bargain."

Baltic's expression went from outraged to thoughtful. "That does have a certain attraction. Very well, I give my approval to him reclaiming our shard. What is the second job?"

I took a deep breath. This was going to require a more delicate touch. "Dr. Kostich refused to help us with Thala."

"Then we will use the other archimage of whom you spoke."

I shook my head, grateful Constantine was keeping quiet for a change. "I don't know her well enough to really gauge whether or not I can convince her to assist us. We're not in the weyr, Baltic, and thus not officially recognized by the Otherworld. She has no reason to help us."

"The same applies to the deranged archimage; yet you thought he would do so."

"That's because I've known him for such a long time, and worked for him, and helped Violet with Maura, although admittedly that didn't turn out very well."

"I liked the part where her men shot Baltic."

"Hush, Constantine." I gave Baltic a meaningful look. "There is another option, and that's to use someone against whom a necromancer's powers are ineffectual."

By the time I finished the sentence, Baltic understood where I was heading. He rolled his eyes in a dramatic gesture. "You can't think to use Constantine to subdue Thala! He's a shade!"

"A very good shade! You wish you could be such a shade!"

"Time-out is incoming if you don't be quiet," I told the part of the room where Constantine was lurking. "And I mean it!"

An injured sniff was the answer.

"He would not be a shade if you hadn't had him raised as such," Baltic accused me.

"Which I wouldn't have done if your father had just bothered to tell me outright what he wanted me to do, as I told him the other day in the sex shop, but he just looked at me the way he does and ignored that whole issue. He's so frustrating at times."

Baltic froze. "You summoned the First Dragon to a sex shop?"

I damned myself for that verbal slip. I hadn't intended on telling him about the little chat I had had with his father. "I didn't summon him at all. He just kind of appeared. It must have slipped my mind to mention his little chat with me, what with Brom's being kidnapped."

"Hmm." Baltic didn't look convinced, but he let that point go to pounce on what I least wanted his attention focused on. "For what purpose did he seek you out?"

"I was there, too. Ysolde admired my spectral whip. I believe she desires one."

"Constantine—" I said warningly.

"You have lost that little zest that I so admired in you in the past," he said in an aggrieved tone, but fell silent again.

"I don't want a whip," I told Baltic, just in case he believed Constantine. "Not the spectral kind, anyway. I saw a very interesting soft leather device in the fetish area. . . . Never mind."

The expression in Baltic's onyx eyes was only too readable. I cleared my throat and continued on a different tack. "The First Dragon wanted what he always wants with me—to tell me I've failed yet again, and to get on with redeeming your honor, or else. It was all too annoying, and I told him that, so you can stop looking martyred about the whole thing."

"If I look martyred, it is because I will hear about your conduct at a later time," he said with a sigh. "I've told you before not to heed what the First Dragon says. You have yet to take this advice, but I assure you it will make both our lives easier."

I took his hands in mine and rubbed his knuckles on my cheek. "He says he loved your mother, you know."

Baltic's fingers tightened in mine. "We are not here to discuss the past, mate. My objection to Constantine stands."

I allowed him to change the subject, since I knew he would feel uncomfortable talking about his parents in front of an audience. "Shades are powerful against necromancers, my love. Constantine is willing to help us with Thala, as well as the shard. Would you prefer that I prostrate myself before Dr. Kostich, or be forced to make some sort of an agreement that will make me vulnerable to him, and place us in obligation to him?"

His teeth ground for a few seconds while he thought that over. "I *prefer* to handle this myself."

"I know you do, but Thala is just too powerful when

she has all her minions around her, so you need to just let go of some of your animosity toward Constantine, and accept his help."

"I do not like your having dealings with the dead one."

"I'm dead because I sacrificed myself for Ysolde!" Constantine chimed in.

"You're dead because giving your life for hers was the only way you could pay for killing Alexei!" Baltic snarled in return.

A silence so thick you could cut it with lemon pudding filled the room.

"You . . . Did I hear that right? You killed Alexei?" I stared at the now slightly visible Constantine with stunned disbelief. "Your own wyvern?"

"I did not," Constantine said, but he couldn't look me in the eye. "Your mate, as always, attempts to divert the truth by casting guilt on others. Ask him what happened to Alexei, if you like, but do not expect to hear what really took place. I have better things to do with my time than to stay here and be abused by him. I bid you farewell, my lovely one, for the moment. I will return as soon as I can."

He faded away to nothing, and the sense of his being near disappeared, as well.

I turned slowly to face Baltic.

"No," he said, marching past me. "Not now. I am too busy. Another time."

"The questions are stacking up; you know that, don't you?" I called after his retreating form. "I can stifle only so many of them before my head explodes! And if that happens, you're going to have to clean up the mess. Baltic? Baltic! Drat that dragon! One of these days, he's going to drive me really insane, and then he'll be sorry."

*   *   *

"The sleeping arrangements leave a whole world to be desired," Maura said approximately seven hours later when one-handedly she helped me shove a small bed close to a window seat.

"I'm not thrilled about them, either, Your Royal Pain-in-the-assness," Savian replied, irritation overriding the dulled glint of pain obvious in his eyes. "And I'd better not catch you ogling my manly form during the night. I'm a very light sleeper, and I'll know if you try to have your womanly way with me."

Maura turned to face him. "Have my womanly way with you? Seriously? Because right now, the only thing I want to do to your manly form is bang it on the head with a very heavy blunt object. And then maybe find a hacksaw."

"I told you the handcuffs can't be sawed apart," he retorted.

I fluffed up the pillow on the window seat and made sure the blankets, which Pavel had brought from one of three trips into Riga, were adequate to keep the sleeper from getting a chill.

"I wasn't intending on sawing off the *handcuffs*," she answered with an arch look.

His eyes widened, but the fact that he didn't retort told much about his physical state. Although a Slavic healer had made the rounds of all the occupants of our house, spending the most time with Holland and Savian, she wasn't a dragon, and her healing abilities were not as profound as I would have liked. Holland was recovering quite nicely, but Savian was mortal, and thus couldn't regenerate like the rest of us.

Despite her veiled threat, Maura helped me get Savian into bed, although he did balk a bit when I tried to undress him.

"I'd accuse you of wanting to change my nuts to toads

again, but I suppose after today, I can trust you with them," he said, slapping away my hand when I tried to unzip his pants. "However, I can't say the same for her ladyship."

Maura blinked for a second. "You tried to change his testicles to toads?" she finally asked me.

"No, I just threatened to change them to—never mind; it doesn't matter. That was months ago, and I've long since changed my mind about Savian."

"Thank you," he said wryly.

"You can't sleep in those pants," I told him, gesturing at his legs. "They're caked in dried blood. Pavel bought some jeans and underwear while he was in town getting the bedding, so at the very least, let me get a clean pair of shorts on you."

"I have dressed myself since I was very young, and I do not need any assistance now," he replied with great dignity.

"You don't have anything I haven't seen before, and you know full well that I'm madly in love with Baltic and have no lustful thoughts whatsoever regarding you, in case you were worried, which I suspect you are, because I know what men who look like you think, and that's that every woman on the planet wants you. Well, we don't."

"I'm well aware you are harboring no desires for me, but that confidence doesn't extend to her." He pointed to Maura. "I'm not getting naked in front of her. It was traumatic enough having her hanging out the door of the loo while I used it, but I'm not letting her get another eyeful."

"Oh, for the love of the Virgin and all the little saints—Maura, turn around, please."

"And close your eyes!" Savian demanded when, with a muttered oath, she spun around, her arm stuck out awkwardly behind her. It didn't take me long to get Savian out of his filthy pants, and into fresh clothing. The wounds across his torso and legs were somewhat better, but I knew they must hurt like the dickens.

"No shirt until your key comes, unfortunately," I told him as I tucked the blankets around him. "Unless we tie one on you."

Murmuring something that didn't make much sense, he immediately fell asleep. I looked up to where Maura stood, leaning slightly to one side in order to accommodate him.

"Let me know if he gets worse during the night," I told her. "I'll leave your door cracked open a little bit so someone will hear you if you yell."

She looked down on him, her expression unreadable.

"Aggravating man," she said at last, and with my help, got out of her shirt (leaving her tank top since we didn't want to cut that off), and slipping into a pair of lounging pajamas.

"He can be, but he's also very brave, and quite nice once you get to know him." I paused, my matchmaking instincts suddenly coming to the fore. "May—that's the silver wyvern's mate—she and Gabriel think the world of him. He helped them quite a bit, you know. Some of it was locating Baltic, but really, that served to help me, too, so I don't hold that against him. Just let me know if he starts getting feverish, all right?"

"I will." She got into the bed, turning on a small lamp I'd placed next to her for reading. "Oh, and Ysolde, I feel obligated to say once more how sorry I am about what happened in Ziema a few months ago. . . . I really had no idea that Thala had plans to try to destroy you. I just thought she wanted to hold you for ransom."

"That, I think, is a subject we'll leave for another day." I bade her good night and headed for the room Brom had claimed for his own. He was happily ensconced in bed, making notes in a blank journal Pavel had bought for him in town. I double-checked that his window was locked, glanced in on Holland, and bumped into Pavel on his way downstairs.

"You're taking the first watch?" I asked him.

"Yes. Nico wished to take one, as well, but Baltic told him to recover from his wounds, first."

"That's a long shift for each of you. I could help by taking one of the watches."

He laughed. "Do you really think your mate would allow that?"

"No, I suppose not." I smiled wryly. "He'd just sit up with me to make sure nothing happened."

"Exactly." Pavel made a little gesture of annoyance. "The watch itself is probably not necessary, since the oracle or Thala could not find us this quickly, but Baltic does not wish to take chances that Brom may be taken again."

I shivered at that thought and promised to send Baltic down in a few hours to relieve him. "I hope you won't be bored sitting here all by yourself."

He sat with his back to the wall at the end of the hallway, his feet propped up on the banister as he toasted me with a glass of dragon's blood. "I will entertain myself with thoughts of those toys you said you bought me."

I laughed and wished him a good night before returning to my own room.

Right into a scene of madness.

At first I thought it was a bonfire that lit up the area, sparks of amber and gold wafting upward like fireflies into the velvety indigo of the night sky. But as I stepped forward into the pool of light cast by the fire, I realized what it really was.

A funeral pyre.

"Oh, my love," I said, tears pricking behind my eyes as I found Baltic in the crowd of silent dragons paying homage to the dead. "This is for your mother, isn't it?"

He didn't answer me, of course—the Baltic who stood with such a stoic expression was the past Baltic, but I knew by the way his jaw was tensed that he was beset by grief. I moved next to him, watching the firelight play over the hard planes of his face, gilding the soft linen of his tunic scarlet and gold. I wanted to touch him, to hold him against the pain that I knew he was experiencing, but I was as insubstantial to him as the sparks that flew upward into the heavens.

"It is done," a deep, somber voice said from behind me.

Baltic didn't respond, his gaze locked on the fire.

The dragons around us filed past the pyre, each stopping next to a page who held a small wooden casket. As each person passed the fire, he or she reached first into the box, then cast something into the fire before joining a solemn procession that snaked up the hill to the keep.

"What is it you're throwing on the fire?" I asked no one, moving closer to the page so I could see. Inside the box appeared to be sand . . . until the page shifted, and the firelight caught the contents, making it glitter with a warmth I felt down to the tips of my toes.

"Gold dust," I said, wanting to run my fingers through it. "You put gold dust on the fire? Why?"

One by one the dragons paid their respects to Baltic's mother, until only three men were left.

Baltic continued to stare at the fire, his eyes filled with pain, but his expression an unemotional mask. Constantine stood next to him.

"It is as Alexei says, Baltic—it is done. You did everything you could for her. Now you must let her go."

"I did not save her," Baltic said in a monotone. "I let them kill her."

"You couldn't have known that Chuan Ren would strike her down in order to hurt you." He gestured toward the third man. "Alexei didn't know they would go that far. I didn't dream they would do such a heinous thing. *No one* could know."

"Baltic knew," a man's voice said as a fourth person emerged from the shadows.

"I might have known you'd show up," I said, narrowing my eyes at the human form of the First Dragon. He turned to look at me, giving me a massive case of the heebie-jeebies until I realized he was staring beyond me, at the fire.

Alexei made a low bow to the First Dragon. "You honor my Maerwyn's memory with your presence, dragonsire."

Constantine looked more than a little awestruck, bowing and stammering some inanity or other before glancing nervously at Baltic, but the latter continued to stare at the fire, too bound in his grief to acknowledge even the appearance of his father.

The First Dragon stood before the fire, staring deep into its depths. I wondered if I had mistaken what he had said in the sex shop. What did he feel at seeing the body of the woman he had taken as a mate? Was he sad at her loss? Did he miss her? They had a child together—surely he must feel something at her passing.

And yet his face was as unreadable as Baltic's.

"Your Maerwyn should be alive," the First Dragon finally said, switching his gaze to Baltic. Even in human form, as he was now, the First Dragon had an "other" sort of aura to him, some intangible quality about him that warned he wasn't what he appeared. His expression, though, was usually neutral, sometimes benign. But now? I shivered, rubbing the goose bumps on my arms. His face was as austere and frigid as the cold winter air. "And she would be, had it not been for you."

Baltic at last turned his head, bowing it to acknowledge his father, but silent as a tomb.

"Will you honor my request?" the First Dragon asked of him.

"No."

The word was curt, but filled with conviction.

"You are aware of the price of such defiance?"

Baltic nodded.

Constantine moved closer to him, saying under his breath, "God's thumbs, Baltic, do not be so foolish. Take Chuan Ren as mate, and be done with this."

"Whoa now," I said, blinking in surprise a few times. "Chuan Ren is who everyone wanted you to hook up with? Nasty, backstabbing Chuan Ren?"

"I will take no dragon as a mate," Baltic answered, surprising me yet again. He gestured at Alexei. "You heard the soothsayer yourself."

"Soothsayer?" The First Dragon shifted to look at Alexei. "Explain."

Alexei's shoulders slumped. He looked weary beyond words, his grief, at least, etched into every line on his face. "Before she was killed, Maerwyn brought a soothsayer to the keep. She said it was to stop a terrible tragedy." His eyes closed for a moment as a spasm of pain flashed over his face. "It is ironic, is it not, that her prediction has caused a tragedy beyond words?"

The First Dragon said nothing, clearly waiting to be told what prediction had been made. Alexei passed a hand over his face, turning away, his shoulders jerking as he gave in to his emotions. Tears spilled down my cheeks in sympathy for a man who so obviously loved his daughter.

"The soothsayer told Baltic he would die if he took a dragon for his mate." Constantine licked his lips, his gaze skittering between Baltic and the First Dragon as he spoke. "She told him that he would find love only in the arms of a human, and that all others would bring death and destruction to him and the black dragons."

I clutched the chain that hung around my neck, holding the love token for comfort, my heart sick at Constantine's words. Baltic never should have come back for me—I was a dragon when he found me, even if I had thought I was human. It was my fault the silver dragons destroyed his sept. It was my fault all those dragons died in the Endless War. If only Baltic had found this woman he had been meant to be with, none of the tragedies of the past centuries would have happened.

I wanted to simultaneously vomit and scream my denial of such a thing. We *were* meant for each other. There could be no other woman who loved him as much as I did.

"And this is your final choice?" The First Dragon simply looked at Baltic, who met his gaze without wavering.

"Yes."

"So be it. Alexei?"

Alexei turned around. "I do not wish to strip my grandson of everything he has, dragonsire. There must be something else—"

"There is nothing."

Alexei's face worked for a moment, but at a sharp gesture from the First Dragon, he faced Baltic, and said in a voice filled with more sadness than I thought possible, "Baltic, son of Maerwyn, I hereby cast you from the sept of the black dragons, naming you ouroboros before our eyes." He slid a glance toward the First Dragon before adding, "May the gods have mercy upon your soul."

Baltic jerked backward, as if he had been struck, but he said nothing to Alexei. He bowed, instead, a short, choppy bow that must have cost him much, turning on his heel and striding away. He paused as he passed the First Dragon, however. "This changes nothing," he said.

The First Dragon's gaze slid away from him and returned to the fire. "It changes everything."

The fire swirled around me, making me suddenly

dizzy, which caused me to stumble forward, my hands outstretched as blindly I attempted to catch my balance.

I stubbed my toe on something hard, swearing under my breath as my vision cleared to show me a bed occupied by a sleeping body.

"Chuan Ren?" I said, grabbing the pillow and hitting the body smartly across its torso. "You didn't tell me it was Chuan Ren!"

Baltic rolled over, glaring at me sleepily from under tousled hair. "You wish to engage in lovemaking now? You have never wished to do so in the past when it is your woman's time. Is this some new fantasy?"

"Chuan ... Ren ..." I said with great deliberation, climbing onto the bed next to him, an abstracted part of my mind glad that I'd sent Pavel into town for fresh supplies, including bed linens. The room still smelled moldy and musty, and I shuddered to remember what state the bedding was in when we stripped it from all the rooms.

"She's dead," he said, just as if that mattered.

"She wasn't six or seven hundred years ago." I knelt next to him, hugging the pillow to my chest. "She wasn't when everyone wanted you to take her as your mate."

He rolled back onto his other side, grunting as he did so. "You've had another of those irritating visions."

"Yes, I did." I prodded his back with the edge of the pillow. "Why didn't you tell me it was Chuan Ren that everyone was pressuring you to claim as a mate?"

He sighed and let me pull him over onto his back. "It doesn't matter. I had no intention of taking her as anything, let alone a mate."

I slumped down next to him, leaning against the headboard and stared down at my feet, remembering my sadness. "All those dragons, Baltic."

"All what dragons? Why are you dressed and outside of the blankets? Is your woman's time bothering you? Do you wish for me to fetch pain tablets?"

I twined my fingers through his, drawing strength and comfort from his touch. "All those dragons who died because you met me instead of the woman you were supposed to spend your life with."

"A woman? What woman?" He sighed again. "You will remove your clothing and climb into bed so that I may comfort you. I would prefer to make love to you, but I know how you are at this time, so I will simply hold you as you said you enjoy."

I slid from the bed, slowly unbuttoning my shirt, not with the intention of teasing him, but with a sense of regret so strong, it made me want to weep. "The woman you were supposed to mate with. The human woman that some soothsayer told you would bring you untold happiness, or something like that. And instead, you met me, and we fell in love, and I brought death and destruction to the sept and the weyr. Oh, Baltic, what have we done?"

I wanted to curl up into a little ball, so heavy was the guilt that weighed me down.

Baltic marched around the bed, his hands on my shoulders as he gently shook me. "You insist on having these visions, and now you see what comes of it. I demand that they stop, Ysolde. They distress you, and I do not like to see you unhappy."

"I can't help it," I said, sobbing now. "If only you hadn't met me. If only you hadn't come to my father's castle—"

"*You* are the woman I was supposed to meet. *Chérie*, do not weep for such a foolish reason." He tipped my head back, brushing off my tears with his thumb. "And do not look at me with such accusation in your eyes. I have never lied to you, and I do not do so now."

"But . . ." I swallowed back the ache in my throat. "But in the vision, Constantine said the soothsayer foretold that your mate was a human."

"You are human. You retain a dragon consciousness, but until that has fully claimed you, you appear human."

I thought about that for a moment, letting him kiss along my jaw, my fingers digging into the warm, satin-covered muscles of his arms. Despite having attained dragon form in Spain, the dragon being within me was still, I knew now, slumbering. It had woken once, and I had hope I could bring it to full awareness again, but for now . . . well, he was right. I *was* human.

But I hadn't always been so.

"I wasn't human when we met."

"You thought you were. You had been raised as one. To everyone but the mortals who gave you sanctuary, you were human." He pulled back enough to look down at me, his eyes glowing with mingled passion, love, and annoyance. "You heard Constantine talk about the sooth-sayer? That happened the night of my mother's sepulture."

"Sepulture? You mean her funeral?"

"Dragons do not have funerals. We burn our dead in a ceremony called sepulture." His eyes narrowed. "Is that the vision you had?"

"Yes." I slanted him a look. "We have a lot to talk about. I've got oodles of questions."

He sighed a third time, quickly divesting me of my clothing before picking me up in his arms and carrying me to bed. "You always have questions."

I giggled at the martyred tone in his voice. "At least you can't say your old Ysolde never asked you questions, because I know full well I did. Why did the First Dragon force your grandfather to kick you out of the sept just because you didn't want to hook up with Chuan Ren? Why did he say your mother's death could have been avoided, and that you were responsible for it? And why—"

"Enough!"

"I want answers!"

"And I do not wish to give you anything but extreme pleasure." He paused, his mouth a hairbreadth from my breast as he glanced down my torso. "Is your woman's time over?"

"Oh, for the love of the saints. You are the most irritating, annoying, arrogant man I've ever met."

"Yes, I am," he said, not batting so much as one single eyelash. "Is it over, or must I wait to make love to you?"

"Baltic, I'm tired of your never answering my questions. And I have a lot of them."

"Your woman's time is not here?" he prodded.

"By the rood, Baltic! Do we have to discuss this right now?"

"Is it here, yes or no?"

"No!"

He looked down at my breasts with a speculative glint to his eyes.

"Wait! I'll make a deal with you." I held him back as he was about to dive for my chest, my fingers taking the opportunity to gently massage the tendons in his shoulders and neck.

"What sort of a deal?"

I smiled to myself. There was nothing dragons loved more than negotiating. "For every question you answer, I will bring you untold, immense sexual gratification."

He looked thoughtful, but shook his head. "You do that regardless of whether I answer your unimportant questions. I will make love to you now."

"How about this—" I said, squirming to the side as he started to rub his cheek against one breast. "For every question you answer, I'll let *you* bring *me* untold, immense sexual gratification."

"You receive that pleasure regardless, as well."

"Yes, but this time," I said, sweeping my hand up his

chest and purring at him, my leg sliding along his. "This time I'll let you be in control all the time. You're always telling me you don't like me being dominant—although heaven knows you don't seem to mind it once you stop complaining and let me get on with things—but this time, it's all you. One question earns you one minute of mindless lovemaking with you in the driver's seat. Do we have a deal?"

He smiled, one of those "I am the man, and you are the merest puddle of goo in my seductive hands" sorts of smiles. Unfortunately, I knew I *would* be a puddle of goo in his hands, and I quickly sorted through all the questions I had, deciding which ones to ask while I could still speak with any sort of coherence.

"I agree to your bargain. But tell me, *chérie*, just how many questions do you believe you will be able to ask me?"

"Oh, I imagine about ten or tweeee!" The last word ended on a gasp of surprise and pleasure as Baltic suddenly dipped a finger into very sensitive flesh, using his thumb to torment me into instant insensibility.

His fingers stilled. I glared at him. "That was not at all fair. You have to answer a question first, then you can . . . er . . . do that again. As many times as you like. And maybe just a smidgen to the right."

"What is your question?" he asked, bathing me in a light wave of fire.

"No fire!" I said quickly, slapping out the flames on the blankets around me. "We haven't dragon-proofed the bedding yet. At least, you can, but confine it just to me, and not anything else."

"Your question?"

"Why did the First Dragon say you were responsible for your mother's death?"

His head dipped to take one of my nipples in his mouth.

I gasped again. "Gently, my darling. Oh yes, just like . . . Wait, Baltic, you're supposed to answer first."

He released one extremely happy nipple to cock an eyebrow at me. "The First Dragon claimed that my refusal to take Chuan Ren as a mate made her lose face, for which she retaliated. He also claimed that she believed the only way to hurt me was to destroy the one person who loved me. He was wrong. Chuan Ren was searching for a reason to war, and knew I would not suffer the murder of my mother without appropriate action. It had nothing to do with saving face."

Even now, I felt the pain deep inside him at the loss of his mother, and I knew that despite his claims, he did feel guilty. I slid my hands into his hair and pulled him down to kiss him. "Your father is an ass."

He chuckled as he turned his attention to my other breast. "So my old Ysolde said on many occasions. I have never had the desire to argue otherwise. What is your second question?"

"Is that why the First Dragon wants me to restore honor to you? Your mother's death is the death of the innocent he was talking about?"

"I have no knowledge of what passes through the mind of the First Dragon," he said with obvious evasion that I instantly forgot when he laved my belly with his tongue, his fingers dancing in and around me in a manner that left me squirming on the bed, desperate for the feel of him. "You will have to ask him if that is what he meant."

"Typical . . . oh yes, right there, my darling . . . typical dragon answer."

He slid down my body, hooking my legs over his arms, a wicked smile on his lips as he looked over my pubic bone. "You have time for one more question, mate. I would advise you to make it a quick one."

I clutched the sheets with both hands, trying desperately to remember what I was going to ask. "About your talisman . . . Why would Thala want to take it from your lair? I assume it's something that only you can use if your father gave it to you to mark you as one of his children, so why would she—"

Never a man with much patience, Baltic had run to the end of his. He dipped his head and filled me with fire, making me arch off the bed at the sensation of all that heat in very sensitive areas, my hands scrabbling for a hold on the sheet when he added his tongue into the proceedings.

By the time he finished tormenting me and slid upward, rocking against me with urgent movements that sent me flying, I knew my time was up. I reveled in the sensation of him moving against and inside me, holding him tight when he found his own moment of exquisite pleasure and cherishing not just the feel of him, but also the knowledge that until the end of my time, his heart was mine.

"You owe me an answer," I told him sometime later, when I could restart my brain and utter things other than moans of purest ecstasy. "I'd make you answer it now, but that performance has earned you some rest, so you have a pass until tomorrow morning. Really, Baltic, I swear you're getting better at this. I didn't think it was possible, but you are."

He grumbled as he pulled me against him, one leg draped protectively over mine, his breathing soft against my head as he fell asleep.

There were so many things to worry about, so many concerns that nagged me. I examined them all as I lay in his arms. Prioritizing them, I decided which ones demanded my attention, and which could wait.

"At least we're all together again," I said softly, snuggling into Baltic's chest. "Brom is safe. Holland and Savian are recovering, and Constantine is going to help make everything right again. I guess there's nothing more I can hope for."

"Go to sleep," Baltic murmured against my temple, his arm tightening around me as he pressed a kiss to my forehead. "You are tired. You need rest."

I glanced up at him, wondering . . . then shook my head, and did as he said.

Chapter Eleven

"Ysolde, you insult me. *Again*."

I gave my hair an annoyed flip while passing Baltic, who was seated in the chair in the hallway, a newly purchased laptop on his knees. "You're the only one who thinks that checking on Brom is insulting to you."

"I will not allow harm to come to my son again." He looked up from the laptop and leveled a frown at me. "The first time you checked on him was forgivable. This is the third time."

"I'm a mother. I worry. It's what I do best, all right? You're just going to have to learn to deal with it."

"You will trust that I will protect you and Brom, and return to bed where you should be," he announced, his gaze once again on the laptop screen. "And you are incorrect."

"I am?" I hesitated at the door to our room. "About what?"

A little smile curled the edges of his mouth, although he didn't look up. "Worry is not what you are best at."

I blushed at the heat in his voice and returned to bed, intending on going over again the plans for Constantine, but despite my nagging need to repeatedly check that Brom was safe, sleep once again claimed me until morning.

It took some doing to get Savian up, washed, and dressed, but we managed it in the end.

"Of all the embarrassing, annoying things I've ever had to do," Maura grumbled as she climbed out of the bathroom window, tucking her shirt into her jeans.

"Look, you wanted privacy, and having one of us stand right outside the window while the other does her business is the best we can do. It's my turn now, so I'd appreciate it if you turned on the radio, because I have an extremely shy bladder."

"Mind your owies," I told Savian as he hoisted himself up and into the bathroom. "They look much better, thanks to the healer's attentions, but you're not fully healed up yet."

He gave me a stern look down the long length of his nose. "I am not Brom, Ysolde. I do not have *owies*."

"My apologies. Just mind your wounds."

He inclined his head in acknowledgment, and with a glare at Maura, pushed the window down until it was just wide enough for her arm to dangle inside.

"Radio!" we heard him bellow.

"How about I talk to her instead?" I yelled back.

"All right, but no stopping to listen. My bladder can't take it."

Maura rolled her eyes, a little giggle escaping her. "Just when I think I can't stand another minute of it, and I'm ready to kill him, he says something funny."

I laughed. "I know the feeling."

"I'm sure you do, although . . . this may sound rude, and I don't in any way intend for it to be so, but Baltic has such a sinister reputation. I've heard him referred to my entire life as the 'dread wyvern Baltic,' and yet he doesn't seem that bad to me. I mean, a man who would sit up for half the night just so that you wouldn't worry about your son doesn't scream badass to me."

"He isn't bad, but he can be very protective." I thought for a moment. "How did you know he was sitting up for four hours?"

"Eh? Oh." To my surprise, she blushed. "I . . . er . . . He came to check on us once. Er . . ." She cleared her throat, not meeting my gaze.

"Why would he do that?" I asked, sensing a mystery. I loved mysteries! "I told him before he went to relieve Pavel that Savian had fallen right asleep when I tucked you in for the night."

Her blush deepened. "Savian was making . . . noises."

"What sort of noises?"

"Just noises! Does it matter what sort of noises? A noise is a noise is a noise!" She took a deep breath.

I eyed her, wondering what was going on, but decided now was not the moment to press her. Not when I had other things to discuss. "He wasn't in pain, was he?"

"Not in the way you think." The words sounded as if they were being ground through her teeth. How very intriguing this was. "What was it you wanted to talk to me about?"

I let her change the subject, making a mental note to ask Baltic later about what he heard. "You're not going to like it."

"What else is new?" she said with a slump of one shoulder.

"It's about Thala. . . . I know you're probably going to resent my questions, and I think you know me well enough now to be aware I wouldn't wish to cause you undue distress, but my son's welfare is at stake here, as well as everyone else's. I know full well that you are bound in loyalty to Thala and the other dragons in your tribe. I'm not trying to undermine the sense of camaraderie or friendship that you feel with them. And I know it's going to be a difficult thing for you to go against everything you swore to uphold with the tribe, but I really have to ask if you know where Thala is right now, and if she has any intention of trying to harm Brom or the rest of us."

"Ysolde, I don't—" Maura started to say, but I lifted a hand to interrupt her. I knew she wouldn't betray her tribe unless I gave her a very good reason to do so.

"Let me just add that I am well aware that there is a price on your head, and that if something doesn't change very soon, thief-takers the world over will be looking for you and the rest of your tribe of ouroboros dragons because you guys broke into the L'au-dela vault in Paris."

She blinked in surprise. "You know about that? How—oh, Emile."

I nodded. "Actually, it was your mother who mentioned it, but your grandfather was very angry with her for telling me about it. She had to, though, in order to bring me up to speed if I wanted to help you." I looked thoughtfully at her. "Which I failed to do, but loyalty to Violet prompts me to again make the offer of assistance I made two months ago in Ziema: I will help you return to your family, and I can just about guarantee that if you promise to leave Thala and the tribe, Dr. Kostich will remove the bounty for your capture that he swore he was going to put into place if you didn't return the things your tribe stole."

"Ysolde, I think you—yeouch!" Maura's arm was jerked painfully against the windowsill, causing her to glare at the window, the privacy glass making it impossible to see in. She slapped a hand on the glass. "Hey!"

"Sorry," came the reply. "I normally use that hand to—never mind."

"Thank the saints you can heal bruises quickly," I

commented when she rubbed the abused part of her arm.

"If he thinks he can get anywhere with that sort of treatment—what? Oh yes." She stopped grumbling to herself and gave me a long look. "What I was going to say is that you've got hold of the wrong end of the stick."

"I do?" I stopped considering her and Savian as a couple and wondered where the flaw in my reasoning lay. "How so?"

"I am not beholden to Thala. I do not feel a sense of obligation to her, or loyalty, or, in fact, any of those things you mentioned." My disbelief must have been obvious because she gave me a weak smile. "I've split from the tribe. I'm no longer a part of their plans—at least not in the sense you think—and have nothing to do with whatever it is Thala is now up to. And no, I don't know where she is right now, although I suspect . . ." She hesitated a moment, her expression thoughtful as her gaze drifted over my shoulder.

"You suspect what?"

"I suspect she's going to Russia."

"You said that earlier." That was uncomfortably close to Latvia, and Dauva. "Whereabouts in Russia? Moscow?"

Maura shrugged. "I don't know. Wherever the sepulcher is."

"The light sword," I said softly, my mind whirling with a thousand things to say to Baltic. Part of me wanted to demand we leave the country immediately and go somewhere safe, but I knew that if I did get him to take Brom and me elsewhere, he'd return to oversee the building of Dauva. Not even the pain of temporary separation would keep him from that. And that would only leave him exposed to whatever foul plans Thala had for us. "Far better for us to stay together," I murmured.

"Safety in numbers," Maura agreed.

My gaze slid back to her. "If you're no longer working for Thala, then why were you in the Spanish *castillo* with her tribe of dragons?"

She glanced at the window, slapping her hand on the glass again.

"What?" Savian responded with annoyance.

"How much longer are you going to be in there?"

"I'm trying to shave. Stop moving your arm or I'll cut my throat. And don't say what you're going to say, and yes, I know you're thinking it."

Maura gave me another considering look, then made a short nod, as if she'd come to a decision. "Mum said you were her friend for many decades, so I'll trust you. When I returned to Spain from Ziema two months ago, I was appalled and shocked at Thala's plans for you. I told her so. I objected to the fact that she had undermined my authority with men who were placed in my charge, but more, I objected to her plan of violence. Thala told me I had no voice in the matter, and my job was simply to get the location of the sepulcher from Emile, and that she'd had her plans in place for too long for them to be messed up by the likes of me, and . . . and . . . oh, just buckets more of that sort of thing. I was never comfortable having to use my family like that, but the violence against you and Baltic was the final straw. The end result was that I renounced the tribe and prepared to leave them."

She stopped, the fingers of her free hand playing with the belt loops on her jeans.

"I'm glad to know you weren't a part of the plan to harm us," I said somewhat dryly. "And I'm sure Dr. Kostich will be relieved to know you won't be pumping him for information that he surely would not tell you."

Pain flashed across her face as she leaned against the

house. "That's just the trouble—he's got to tell me where it is."

"So you can tell Thala?"

She nodded, her eyes closed, her face weary.

I studied her for a moment, trying to piece together the bits of what was puzzling me. "Is Thala blackmailing you for it?"

She nodded again.

"What, exactly, is she—"

"Ysolde!"

The roar that carried my name from the other side of the house was a familiar one, the fury in it warning me that it would be folly to remain where I was in order to pin down Maura for more information.

"My beloved! Do not heed the traitorous one. He is weak, as he has always been."

"Traitorous!" Birds squawked like crazy as they flew out of the nearby trees in protest of Baltic's bellow. It was amazing how well the sound carried. I imagined the people in town some four miles away could hear him. "I am not the traitor here!"

"You stole the black sept from me!"

"I challenged you and won it from you! You lost!"

"Because you cheated!"

"Sadly, that voice is also familiar," I said, sighing.

"You shouldn't have had me summon him, then," Maura said with a wry smile.

"Hindsight, twenty-twenty, and all that," I told her, heading off to interrupt what was sounding like a huge fight between Baltic and Constantine. "We'll continue this discussion later."

Unfortunately, that hindsight didn't just fail me when it came to the subject of resurrecting spirits—it also let me down with regard to Maura.

It took a good hour to get Constantine out of our hair,

and by then, Savian had taken off for parts unknown with Maura in tow. Pavel left shortly after that to return to England in order to gather up our belongings, leaving Holland to complete his recovery with us.

Duty-bound, I tried calling Maura's mother, but for the third time in a week, I wasn't able to reach her. After some thought, I decided that I owed it to Violet to contact her father. Again. "He'd just better not try to turn me into anything this—hello?"

"Yes," a sharp voice snapped into the phone. "What do you want?"

"Good morning, Dr. Kostich. It's Ysolde de Bouchier, again. I haven't been able to get a hold of Violet, but I wanted to tell her that Maura is with us, in case she's worried about Maura running around in Spain with a bunch of nutball ouroboros dragons."

"I still have nothing to say to you, dragon."

"I'm sorry to interrupt whatever it is you're doing, but I thought—"

The phone clicked in my ear.

I sighed and hung up. "Evidently you don't want to know how your own granddaughter is. You rotter."

Between getting the monstrous house into a habitable state, doing copious amounts of shopping in town with Brom firmly at my side—much to his disgust, until Baltic and I took him into Riga to buy equipment for his new lab—keeping Baltic and Constantine separated (not to mention focusing the latter on locating Kostya's lair), and generally trying to settle into a new home, two days passed during which I didn't have time to do much beyond collapsing exhaustedly into bed each night.

"You are working too hard," Baltic told me the morning of the third day, watching me chop basil for the bacon and goat cheese frittata I was making for breakfast.

"You have dark circles under your eyes. I do not like this. You will take more naps."

I glanced up at him, startled for a second. "*More* naps?"

"Yes. The ones you are taking are too short, and you are restless at night, and not sleeping well." He frowned. "Are you still worried about the safety of our son? The electronic security system put into place yesterday is more than adequate, mate, and I will engage a firm of Guardians to place wards on the house every few days. Thala will not be able to do us any harm here."

"I'm not worried about that any longer. At least, I *am* worried, but not to the point I was. You'll notice that last night I didn't get up once to check on Brom."

"I noticed. You still did not sleep well. You are doing too much."

"Not since you hired a veritable platoon of cleaning ladies to scrub down this mausoleum. But as we're on the subject of things I should do, I've been thinking about what you told me." I cut a quarter of the frittata and placed it on a waiting plate, alongside some fresh berries, chicken apple sausage made locally, and two croissants. Baltic accepted the plate with a murmur of thanks. I picked up a small walkie-talkie. "Moonbase one to Brom. Breakfast is ready, and your attendance is required pronto."

His response, somewhat crackly, was immediate. "I'm just setting up my draining table. I'll eat later."

"You'll eat now, and thank you very much for putting the image of a draining table in my mind when I'm about to have breakfast. I expect you to be washed up and in here in five minutes."

"Aw, Sullivan . . ." Luckily, he stopped transmitting before continuing. I yelled up the stairs to Nico and Holland that breakfast was ready, and started on the second frittata when Baltic, his attention now happily diverted to breakfast, asked, "Where is the thief-taker?"

"He and Maura went into town to get some clothing. They should be back soon."

"Ah. What is it you believe you should do?"

I listened for a moment but didn't hear anyone coming down the stairs. "It's about that last vision, when your mother was being sepultured."

"Sepulture is not a verb," was all he said before he slathered his croissant with grapefruit marmalade. I grimaced at the action—Baltic had an insatiable sweet tooth, but that was no reason to ruin a perfectly lovely croissant.

"I know it's not; I was just being quirky. You love it when I'm quirky. But that's beside the point. The other night you said that the First Dragon blamed you for your mother's death. That's got to be the death of the innocent that he was referring to when he told me I had to redeem your honor."

Baltic sighed, just as I knew he would. "Still you insist on listening to that foolishness. I have told you many times that my honor does not need your attentions, despite what the First Dragon would have you believe. I grow tired of repeating myself, and if you continue to make me do so, I will be forced to take action."

"What sort of action?" I was unable to resist asking.

"Perhaps I will punish you as I did a week ago."

I thought for a few seconds. "That wasn't punishment! That was you being bossy as usual, and making incredibly hot love to me outside when everyone in the pub was asleep. And don't you even think you can distract me with thoughts of just how wonderful that outdoor interlude was, because it won't work."

Baltic set down his fork and raised one eyebrow.

"All right, it's working a little bit, in so much as I think I'll take a couple of blankets out to the north ruins, but that's as far as I'll go. Baltic, whether you want to or not, I'm going to restore your honor to such a state as will make your father happy, and by the saints, you will help me!"

He frowned as he took the last bite of frittata. "I do not care what the First Dragon thinks of me."

"He's your father!"

"And about this, he is wrong. I have explained that to you." His black eyes glittered dangerously at me, but I knew that underneath his anger, a little morsel of pain existed.

I pulled the second frittata off the stove and went over to sit on Baltic's lap, gently kissing his face and smoothing back his hair as I said, "My love, I do not doubt that you are right. The First Dragon is wrong to blame you, but he *is* the First Dragon. He is the ancestor of us all, and he has placed a task upon my shoulders. Would you have me fail when he has done so much for us?"

"He has done nothing but give us grief all our lives." Baltic's fingers tightened on my legs as he turned his face into my neck, kissing all those spots that made me shiver with delight.

"He resurrected me twice, and for that I will be eternally thankful, because it meant that you and Brom are in my life. I can't refuse to do what he asks, not when it concerns you. I know you think this is nothing but folly, and I don't blame you in the least for being offended that you're in this position, but please, my love, my most adorable love, do it for me."

His sigh ruffled my hair, but dragon fire wrapped around us. "What is it you wish for me to do?"

"I think the First Dragon wants you to pay penance for your mother's death. No, don't say it. I know you weren't responsible, and you shouldn't have to do it, but if it will make him happy and fulfill the task he's bound to me, then you're just going to have to do it."

"Bah," he snorted, gently pushing me from his lap and giving my behind a swift pat in the process. "If I do what you ask of me, you will understand that it is for your sake alone that I do so."

"I understand." I smiled up at him as he stood and stretched, enjoying, as I always did, the sight of his shirt pulled tight across his impressive chest. I fought the need to stroke that chest, reminding myself that this was more important.

"What must I do in order to fulfill this penance?"

"Well . . ." I thought for a moment. "I'd say in this case it was to make reparation for the damage done. When your mother died, you killed Chuan Ren's guards, didn't you?"

"Yes."

I kissed his chin and returned to finish the frittata. "Which prompted her to attack the black dragons?"

"In a way. She declared war against us and the green dragons, and within six months, the entire weyr was at war with one another."

"Right, so really, I think the First Dragon wants you to pay for that, for causing the Endless War."

"I didn't cause it!"

"Of course you didn't! As much as I hate to speak ill of the dead, Chuan Ren was a vindictive woman, and one, I suspect, who loved to be at war. I have no doubt she set you up to provide her ample reason to declare a weyr-wide war. But your father obviously views things differently, and thus, you're going to have to make reparations for that."

He thinned his lips and stood with his hands on his hips. "How do you expect me to do that?"

"A good start would be to lift the curse off the silver dragons."

"No."

"It would show everyone—the First Dragon included—that you were sorry for how things turned out."

"I will not lift it. I have no reason to do so."

"But—"

"No!" He marched over to the door, obviously about to leave, but paused and sent me a scathing look. "If that is all you have to suggest, then I will go into town and meet the builders. They are arriving today, and I must take them to Dauva."

"Wait a second. I'm not done talking about this." I yanked the frittata off the burner again and ran after him as he left the house and started for the car. "If you won't lift the curse, then what about the light dragons joining the weyr? Then you can formally apologize to everyone for the events of the past, and maybe even, I don't know, set up some sort of a fund for needy dragons whose families were decimated by the war. I think that might placate the First Dragon."

"We do not need to join the weyr. They have nothing to do with us."

"Because you won't let them. Baltic, I really would like for us to be a part of the weyr."

He stopped at the car, gave me a swift, hard kiss, and yet another pat on the behind, and said simply, "We do not need them," before hopping in the car and leaving.

"Gah!" I yelled, wishing for a moment that I knew some sort of spell to make dragons less stubborn.

"Are you going to yell at me because it's been six minutes instead of five?" a voice asked behind me.

I gave my own little sigh and turned to usher Brom into the house. "No, as long as you washed your hands."

"I did."

I looked at his hands. "They don't look any too clean to me. What did you do—hold them near water but not actually in it?"

He sighed the put-upon sigh common to those under the age of ten. "I found some owl pellets out back and had to collect them so I can dissect them later. You can't do that without getting a little dirty, but I washed off most of it at the faucet outside."

I stared in horror at the child I had borne. "You did . . . No, Brom, just no! It's bad enough that you make mummies from whatever dead things you can find. That, I suppose, has some sort of scientific value, although just what escapes me at the moment. But I draw the line at your collecting owl poop!"

"Owl pellets, not poop," Brom said, and with blithe disregard to my reaction, he took his plate and started shoveling eggs into his mouth before nodding toward the two men who entered the kitchen. "Nico, Sullivan thinks an owl pellet is poop. It's not, though."

"No, it's not," Nico said with a bright smile. He accepted the plate of food I handed him with an appreciative sniff. "Owl pellets contain the undigested food that owls regurgitate once they are done consuming their prey. Brom has long wished to study them, but I wanted to wait until we were settled to find a local source for them."

"Uh-huh." I gave Holland a swift, assessing glance, but he appeared to be wholly healed. He thanked me as I gave him a plate, taking his place at the table with the others.

"I assure you, Ysolde, they're fascinating objects, and there are several companies who make pellet dissection kits available to children. Am I to take it that Brom found one on his own?"

"Yeah. It's a big one, too. I bet it used to be a cat or something."

"You are an unnatural child," I told Brom, and took my own plate to the far side of the kitchen table, where

I proceeded to ignore the discussion of just what grue-some things one might find in owl barf.

Pavel arrived soon after that, driving a large moving truck that I greeted with cries of happiness. It took a few hours to unload and put away our things, but by the time that had been done, and the day's squad of cleaning women had worked their way through the remainder of the house that previously had been left uncleaned, I was beginning to feel more at home.

"Well, it's certainly not anywhere I'd like to spend the rest of my life, but at least it's habitable," I said aloud to no one as I stood in the empty front hall, looking around for traces of cobwebs or dust that had been missed. The cleaning ladies knew their stuff, however, and if the house wasn't attractive, at least it was no longer caked in dirt and grime.

"Was that a moving truck I saw leaving the road?"

I turned at the voice and smiled. Maura's color was very high as she and Savian entered the house, while his hair was tousled, and his shirt buttoned up incorrectly.

"Yes, Pavel got here with our things. Including ..." I pulled a small jeweler's box from my pocket. "Ta da! The spare key to your handcuffs that your landlady allowed Pavel to retrieve."

"Ergh," Savian said, looking sideways at Maura. "My ... uh ... landlady. Yes. Just so."

"I'm sure you two will be delighted to finally have them off," I said, my expression innocent as I handed over the key. "I know how wearing it's been to be con-stantly together, day and night, every single moment, with no privacy, just the two of you. Especially since we haven't seen much of you these last few days while you've been out doing ... What is it you've been out do-ing?"

Maura shot me a startled look. "Savian has been doing some research for a job he says you hired him for, but he won't let me see the computer screen while he's doing it, so I have no idea what is going on other than I've been forced to forgo all of my plans and spend every day doing what he wants."

Savian grinned wickedly at her for a second, then cast a glance toward me, cleared his throat, and said, "In part, I've been trying to locate your ex-husband, but I lost his trail somewhere in Switzerland, and just haven't had a lot of time to devote to that because you told me the other project was to take priority."

"It is the more important of the two, yes," I said, watching them, hesitating to tell Maura that we, too, were searching for the location of the sepulcher. I had no idea with what Thala was blackmailing her, but I would never let the light sword go, not while I had such a desperate need for such a valuable object.

"And then we . . . got a bit . . . distracted." Maura fidgeted uncomfortably.

Savian seemed to realize just how obvious she was being, for he murmured something noncommittal before using the key to unlock three different sections of the handcuff.

It opened with a loud click, and a louder sigh of relief from Maura. She rubbed her wrist, and with an unreadable look at Savian, excused herself. "I'm going to take a shower by myself for a change."

My eyebrows rose. "Oh?"

She blushed and stammered, "Not that Savian and I have taken a shower together."

"That's not quite the truth, princess," Savian said to her with a wink. "Just yesterday you were taking a shower with me."

"Not *with* you," she said, a tad desperately, I thought. "It's not like that at all, Ysolde. Savian was in the room with me, but not in the shower!"

"I know that full well," I said, taking pity on her face, which was now beet red. "I brought in some towels while you were having your shower." My gaze slid to Savian. I'd caught him peeking in through the shower curtain, but decided their budding romance—if they were destined for one—would benefit from a blind eye turned once in a while.

She shot Savian another look and ran up the stairs.

I turned my attention to him.

"There are no flies on you, are there?" he asked.

"No. I'm very fond of her mother, though, and would not take kindly to anyone toying with Maura."

"Oh, but there's so much to toy with." He grinned unashamedly for a second.

"I take it you haven't found the sepulcher yet?" I asked.

His grin faded. "Not yet, although I'm down to just four possible locations. I hope to narrow it down further tomorrow."

"The sooner, the better. I don't know if Maura's told you, but Thala is on the hunt for it, as well, and we need to get there before her."

He saluted. "Aye aye, mon capitaine." His expression sobered as he rubbed his chin, saying thoughtfully, "My landlady, eh? I'll have to see to her before—"

I waited for him to finish, but he simply thanked me for the key, and, whistling to himself, slowly mounted the stairs.

An hour later, I tracked down Pavel already at work in the kitchen, Holland at his side. "Can I see you for a minute?" I asked Pavel, gesturing toward a dark pantry that sat off the kitchen.

He followed, giving me a curious glance as I clutched a plastic shopping bag to my chest.

"I want to know three things, and I expect you to answer them, and not give me the usual dragon runaround."

"I will do my best," he answered, looking as if he wanted to smile.

"First of all, do you have any idea why Thala would want Baltic's talisman? The one the First Dragon gave him?"

"The talisman?" He rubbed his ear and looked thoughtful. "She is not a full-blooded dragon. If her mother had been a mortal human, then yes, I would understand. But Antonia von Endres was an archimage, and thus her daughter's blood was not pure by dragon standards."

"Why would you understand if Antonia had been mortal?"

"You remember about wyverns, yes?"

"I know they have to have one human parent, if that's what you mean. Except Baltic, of course, but that's because his father was the First Dragon."

Pavel nodded. "All of the First Dragon's first generation children founded septs, including Baltic. They were able to do so because they bore the talisman."

A little chill ran down my spine. "It has that much power?"

"Not power so much as it is an artifact recognized by the weyr. If the bearer is a dragon, he or she can form a sept and no one in the weyr can deny its existence. Have you never wondered why ouroboros dragons did not form their own septs rather than tribes?"

"They didn't have a talisman," I said slowly.

"Hence they can only form tribes," he agreed.

"But . . ." I bit my lip in thought. "But Constantine formed his own sept, and he didn't have a talisman."

"Didn't he?"

I narrowed my eyes at Pavel. "He isn't one of Baltic's brothers, if that's what you're implying. Baltic said all his siblings were dead, and besides, Constantine told me his father had died many centuries ago."

"No, no, I did not mean that he formed the silver sept

because he was the child of the First Dragon. I meant simply that he did possess a talisman in order to create the sept."

A flash of insight struck me. "He stole Baltic's talisman, too? Or did he take one from some other dragon? Are the talismans handed down to wyverns, like the dragon heart shards are?"

"I do not know—I am not privy to the intimate details of other septs."

"Baltic must have gotten it back from Constantine," I mused, wondering if the day would come that my memory would ever return to me. Then again, perhaps Baltic—not the most forthcoming of individuals when it concerned private things—had never told me about the theft of his talisman. "Did I know about this before I was killed?"

He shrugged. "You would have to ask Baltic that."

"Fat lot of good that'll do me." I made a face at the wall. "He hates answering questions about the past."

"What were the other two things you wanted to speak to me about?" Pavel glanced toward the door behind him. "I was about to put the rib of beef into the oven, and I wished to put a rub on it first."

"Oh, I wanted to ask you . . . Rib of beef? How are you cooking it?"

"Just roasting it with thyme, potatoes, and some root vegetables."

"Thyme? What an excellent idea. Would you like me to make a salad?"

"If you wish to, although I'd planned on grilling some courgette, and tossing it with feta, mint, and pine nuts as the salad."

I started salivating at the thought. "No, no, you go ahead with that. Um. What was it I wanted to ask . . . oh, Baltic said when we came here that he was having someone in England try to locate where Gareth and Ruth went when they left the *castillo*. Did you happen to find out if they've been tracked?"

"I did, and they haven't." He made a little gesture. "I'm sorry, Ysolde. I told Baltic yesterday that the tracker reported they disappeared after going to Geneva."

"Damn. That matches what Savian said." I let myself dwell with much satisfaction on what I wanted to do to Gareth once we did find him again.

"And the third thing? I really must baste the vegetables before they are put in with the beef."

With an effort, I pulled my attention back from thoughts of a cattle prod being applied to Gareth. "Hmm? Oh, this." I held out the bag. "I bought these in London the day Brom was taken, and I meant to give them to you to use with Holland, but things went to hell in a handbasket that night, and they got shoved into the wardrobe with my things."

Pavel pulled out the toys I'd purchased for him, his eyes widening at the sight of the bed restraint system. "The cuffs alone would have been enough," he said, then blinked as he pulled out the C-shaped item. "Christos."

"I didn't know whether you like that sort of thing or not, so I got a couple of different ones," I said, pulling out a stimulator. "This one is ribbed. I assume that's good, although I wouldn't want . . . never mind. And this wand can be used by two people at the same time, which I thought was pretty handy. Now, the electric jobby is brand-new, and Dido, the lady at the sex store, says it's a huge hit with gentlemen, although you have to be sure to attach *both* electrodes before turning it on. Oh, and she said because of the shape, there's a special way to . . . er . . . use it. She said you need to lie on your side—"

"Thank you," Pavel said quickly, snatching the toy from me and stuffing it into the bag along with the others. "You've been more than generous, but I believe I will be able to work out how to use everything."

I beamed at him, pleased that he was so enthusiastic. "I hope you enjoy them. And Holland enjoys them, too. Do let me know how that bed restraint goes, and whether or not the electric thing works as well as Dido said it does."

I swear he choked as he hurried out of the pantry, but I put it down to his being overwhelmed with the number of toys I'd brought. "Now, if I can just get Baltic to agree to play with the toys I bought for us, we'll be set."

Chapter Twelve

A few minutes later, when I was arranging a vase of rather aphidy wildflowers in a cracked vase, I heard noise from upstairs.

"Oh good, you're still here," Maura said as she walked briskly down the stairs, a small duffel bag in her hand. "I didn't want to leave without saying good-bye, and thanking you for making my imprisonment as charming as it could be."

"You weren't imprisoned," I said with a bit of exasperation.

"My kidnapping, then. Thank you for making it a pleasant kidnapping. Or as pleasant as it could be having been chained to that man."

"I know it wasn't pleasant, but Savian isn't that—"

The front door was suddenly flung open, the breeze from the action whipping my hair around.

"I knew it!" The silhouette of the man in the doorway resolved itself into a familiar form as he entered the house. "I knew you were here in Riga!"

"Kostya? What are you doing here? And why are you banging my front door around like that? I hope you're not treating my door at Dragonwood that way, because if you are, I'll have a few things to say to you about it."

"Dragonwood is not yours, so what I do with my own front door is—" He stopped, took a deep breath, and said in his most dramatic voice, "*What* are you doing in Latvia?"

"Will you move, you great big . . . You could help me, you know!"

Kostya jerked as if someone had shoved him, stepping aside to glare down at the woman who dragged a huge suitcase in after her. "You shoved yourself—uninvited, I'd like to point out—into my car. Since I no longer recognize you as my mate, I am not responsible for you, the immense amount of luggage you crammed onto the backseat, or the hotel bill you tried to force me to pay."

"Hello, Cyrene," I said, suddenly weary. "I take it by the suitcase that you've come to visit us? I'm afraid you'll have to share a room with Maura now that Savian is on his own again, unless you wanted one of the attic rooms, but I didn't have the cleaning ladies do anything with them, so they're no doubt full of spiders and bats and really nasty things like that."

"You can have my room, because I'm leaving. I'm in a world of trouble for having been away this long as it is," Maura said, trying to scoot around the couple.

"Thank you, Ysolde," Cyrene said, smiling broadly at me as she leaned into Kostya. He promptly moved away. "We'd love to stay with you for a bit!"

"Wait, Maura, just a second. I want to talk to you."

Her shoulders slumped a little when she gave a longing look to the door. "If you're going to apologize again, you needn't do so. I know the kidnapping wasn't your fault."

Kostya gave me a considering look. "You kidnapped that woman?"

"No! Not really. Kind of. It was an unforeseen, and very regrettable accident, that's all, and Maura, don't you dare take another step toward the door."

"Almost free," she said in a dramatic voice, her eyes locked on the door. "Freedom, the sweetest of all balms to the immortal soul."

"Oh, for the love of . . . no, Cyrene, Kostya cannot stay here. You may share Maura's room if you like, but even though Baltic no longer wants to kill Kostya on sight, there's no way he can stay in this house."

"I don't want to be in the same house as Baltic. I have a perfectly nice home in St. Petersburg." Kostya shot a harried glance toward Cyrene. "Or I used to, before a certain watery tart tried repeatedly to break into it."

Cyrene hung on to her smile for all she was worth. "Isn't he cute?" she said, patting him on the arm. The expression in her eyes was less amused, however. "Kostie does enjoy his little jokes. But that is so kind of you to ask us to stay. We'd love to, naturally. I don't think we'd be comfortable in a room with someone else, though, so if you could just give us a room with a nice big bed, we'll be happy as two little clams."

I ran my hand through my hair, feeling more than usually harried. "Just wait a few minutes, Cyrene, then we'll talk about the situation. Maura—"

"No." She stood at the front door, a firm, decisive expression warning that she had reached her limit. "No more excuses, no more good-byes, no more conversation. I'm in far more trouble than you can imagine, and I have to go call Emile in an attempt to keep the most horrible event you can imagine from happening. I don't want to be rude, and I do appreciate the fact that you made my incarceration here as pleasant as possible, but the answer is still no."

"But—"

"Good-bye, and good luck with whatever it is that Savian has undertaken on your behalf."

The door closed firmly behind her as she left. I frowned at it for a moment, trying to decide what would be best to do with regard to her. I wanted to help her, and yet at the same time, I needed to know the location of the sepulcher. Perhaps if she got that information from Dr. Kostich, she would tell me, as well as Thala?

"Hellfire," I swore, deciding that would never happen. If Savian didn't come through with a location in the next twenty-four hours, I'd just have to try to get the information from Dr. Kostich myself. *Somehow.*

"And damnation," Kostya said, giving Cyrene an irritated frown.

"Look, I'm trying to be nice to you; I really am," Cyrene said, frowning right back at him. "You could work with me!"

"I don't want to do anything other than to wish you to the devil," Kostya snapped before turning his back on her to face me. "Why are you here?"

"I live here," I said, making a helpless gesture.

"In Riga?" His eyes narrowed in suspicion. "That insane mate of yours intends on doing something here, doesn't he?"

I set his feet on fire. He did nothing other than tighten his lips, although the fire made Cyrene squawk and leap back. "Baltic is not insane, which you very well know."

"Does he intend to rebuild Dauva?"

"Of course he's going to rebuild. Did you ever doubt he would? You know how much he loved it."

"I cannot allow that," Kostya said loftily, his voice rife with impatience. "It is too close to St. Petersburg, where my home is located. I will not have Baltic on the black dragons' back doorstep."

"Will you cease bothering my mate!"

I folded my arms over my chest and waited for the explosion. Baltic strode into the house, his dragon fire simmering inside him, his attention focused on Kostya.

"You don't deny you are building here deliberately to threaten my sept?" Kostya spun around to ask.

"Has he annoyed you, Ysolde?" Baltic asked, his eyes as hard and shiny as hematite when he looked at Kostya, but warm and full of mysterious depths when they turned to me. "You will not let me kill him, as I ought, I know, but I will see to it that he does not bother you in such a manner again."

Kostya sneered. "As if you could —"

"What is going on, here? Are you having a party without me, my most beloved of all females?"

"Oh, that's all we need," I said, sighing and moving over to take Baltic's arm, when he turned toward the voice at the open doorway. "Constantine, you have the worst timing of anyone I know."

"Thank you," he said, materializing just so he could grab my hand and press a wet kiss to it. "It warms me to my cods to know that you care."

"She does not care about you or your cods!" Baltic snarled, snatching my hand away from Constantine. "She cares only about me and mine!"

"The current derangement of her mind is not as important a subject as one I have to impart to her regarding—godson!"

Constantine evidently just noticed Kostya standing to the side, because he turned to him with delight written all over his face. "Now you cannot escape me. I will challenge you once and for all for my sept."

"You what?" Kostya asked, all astonishment.

"I was the heir to the black wyvern before Toldi even met your mother. Thus, the sept is mine by rights. If you do not hand it over, I will challenge you for it, although I shouldn't have to challenge anyone for what is mine."

"It is *my* sept," Kostya said between grinding teeth. "I have no intention of letting you challenge me any more than Gabriel does, ghost."

"I am a shade, not a trivial, unimportant spirit," Constantine said with much dignity, straightening his shoulders. "And you have no choice in the matter. By the laws that govern the sept, I, Constantine of Norka, do hereby issue a formal challenge of transcendence to Konstantin Nikolai Fekete, who falsely claims the title of wyvern of the black dragons. You will not refuse if you have even a shred of honor to your name."

"I have more than a shred, but I'm not going to fight you for my sept. You aren't alive. You can't be a wyvern," Kostya said, looking somewhat pugnacious now. I couldn't blame him for that—Constantine tended to have a one-track mind, and was currently clearly obsessed with the idea of fighting Kostya.

"You are a base coward," Constantine said in an obnoxious voice, waving a hand toward Baltic. "Baser even than Baltic, who at least was not afraid to fight me."

Baltic snarled something rude.

"I'm not afraid of you," Kostya said, looking irritated.

"Oh, come on, Kostie—fight the ghost and then you'll prove you're the big bad wyvern," Cyrene said, yawning and looking around the hall. "Which room did you say was mine, Ysolde? I'm a bit tired since the hotel was incredibly noisy."

"What is this?" Baltic asked me, just as I was about to tell Cyrene where Maura had been staying. "Mate, I insist you stop inviting everyone you meet to stay with us!"

"I didn't exactly invite her," I said in a low voice.

"Fine!" Kostya bellowed, drawing our attention back to the two men who stood toe-to-toe in the middle of the room. "I accept your challenge. You will meet me body to body. I name as a second . . . I name . . . er . . ." He looked around the room. His gaze lit on me for a second, and I thought he was going to demand I act as his backup for the challenge, but with an annoyed click of his tongue, he finished, "I name Baltic."

"What? You can't name him," I said, wrapping an arm around Baltic in case he was about to charge Kostya. "You guys don't like each other."

To my absolute surprise, Baltic didn't say anything right away. He looked hard at Kostya for a few seconds before his gaze shifted to Constantine. "I accept," he said with a smile that had Constantine looking wary.

"Good," Constantine said with one last look at Baltic. "Then I name Ysolde as second."

"No," Baltic snapped.

"Why not?" Constantine asked.

"Yes, why not?" I asked, prodding Baltic in the side. "I've never been a second before. It sounds rather dashing. I think I'd like to do it."

"A second must be prepared to fight in place of the principal," Baltic answered, his eyes flashing something unreadable at me. "Constantine may not care if you are injured, but I do."

"Oh." I thought for a moment, then nodded. "I'm sorry, Constantine. I don't want to seem like a coward, but I wouldn't be an effective second. Kostya doesn't fight women, and he definitely wouldn't fight me. That wouldn't at all do if I was called upon to fulfill my duties as your second and fight in your place, and, of course, if Baltic was fighting for Kostya . . . well, you must see that it just wouldn't work."

"Very well," Constantine said with an annoyed sniff. He waved his hand toward Cyrene, who was looking somewhat bored. "I'll take the naiad as my second."

"Me?" Cyrene squeaked. "But I'm a woman, too, and Kostya wouldn't fight me."

"I'd make an exception for you," Kostya told her with a grim smile.

She looked indignant for a moment, then straightened her shoulders and gave Constantine a quick nod. "All right, I accept the position. I'll be your second. But I get to beat the holy hell out of Kostya."

"The gloves are off now, I see," I said softly, elbowing Baltic. "You needn't look so anticipatory, my darling. I'm sure Kostya will have enough spleen venting to do on Constantine to make your assistance unnecessary."

"Kostya is weak. He will fall quickly to Constantine. I will not."

"We will conduct the challenge now," Constantine announced with a grand gesture. "A body-to-body challenge can take many forms. Which do you choose, Kostya?"

"Swords are always good," Kostya answered, flexing his arms.

"We don't have any swords," I said, distracted when Cyrene tugged on my sleeve and said, "I need a bath. Which room is mine?"

"Second on the left. Bathroom is at the end of the hall."

"Thank you." She sniffed and looked at Kostya. "Since you are being silly about this whole thing, and not letting me stay with you, as a mate should, then I will remain here with Ysolde. When you get over your little snit, you can find me here."

Kostya, who had been in the process of saying several snarky things to Baltic in Zilant, paused berating him to give Cyrene a dirty look. "That day will never come."

"We'll see." She sniffed again and moved toward the stairs.

Kostya ignored her, saying to Baltic, "You overestimate your prowess, Baltic. As for your accusations, I have never failed a challenge. About Dauva—"

"I do not care about Dauva—I care about the challenge," Constantine interrupted.

"Dauva will be rebuilt. I never overestimate anything, and you are tiring Ysolde. Leave, and take *that* with you." Baltic gestured toward Constantine.

"Your boorish manners do not offend me; I have long been used to them. And I cannot leave just yet. First, we must have the challenge. Following the reclamation of my sept, I have business with Ysolde," Constantine answered, turning his charming smile upon me. "You will want privacy for what I have to tell you, my lovely one."

By dint of extreme control, I managed to keep from glancing at Kostya. "Oh. Um . . . yes. I'm sure we needn't bore everyone else with such a trivial matter. There's a small sitting room to the left. Why don't we have our chat there now, and you can deal with the challenge later."

"Ysolde—" Baltic said warningly.

I kissed his chin. "It's all right; it's just that little project I discussed with you earlier. There's no need for your feathers to be ruffled."

"I am a dragon, not a bird. I have scales." His phone buzzed at that moment. He glanced at it, frowned even more, then heaved a sigh. "I am wanted at Dauva. The builders need guidance. I will trust that you will not allow that murderous whoreson spirit to impose upon your gentle nature, mate, but I will also remind you that I do not like having him in our lives, and just as soon as you have used him, he must leave and not return."

"You can't leave yet. We haven't conducted the challenge, and I'm sure my godson will need you, given how ineffectual he appears," Constantine said, swearing when he started to fade. "God's toes, now you've made me use up almost all of my energy. Ysolde, most beloved of all dragons, let us go sequester ourselves away from this rabble, and we will conduct the challenge later, as you suggest."

"Wait a minute," Kostya said, looking as if he wanted to throw a tantrum as Baltic started for the front door,

Cyrene thumped her way up the stairs with a suitcase, and Constantine and I headed for the small, damp room off the main hall. "You can't all just leave. I'm here to protest Baltic's rebuilding on my land."

I paused at the door to the sitting room. "You just asked him to be your second. I hardly think it's nice to ask a favor from him, and then make a fuss about his building on land that you don't even own."

"The black dragons—" he started to say.

"Have nothing to do with us," Baltic said with finality. "Dauva was my home before I was wyvern, and it will be so again. If you wish to lead that pathetic group of stragglers you call a sept, then do so, but your choice of location does not impact us in any way."

Kostya clearly wanted to argue the point, but his grudging admittance of the truth—and the fact that Baltic walked out of the house—stymied that desire.

"I still say Dauva should be left in the past, where it belongs," he grumbled before turning on his heel and walking swiftly to the door.

"Well, it's not. And while we're on the subject, let's talk again about Dragonwood," I yelled after him. His shoulder twitched as he left, but he didn't respond. The rat.

My hand was on the doorknob to the sitting room when my phone bellowed out my name. I glanced at the caller, answering it with a cheery, "Hello, Aisling."

"Hi, Ysolde. Has Kostya left yet?"

"Er . . . yes, he just left. How did you know he was here?"

"We're keeping tabs on him. She says he's gone, sweetie, so we can keep driving."

Curiosity got the better of me. "Where are you driving to?"

"To see you, of course. But we didn't want Kostya to know we're in the area, because then he'll want us to stay with him, and if we do that, he'll tag along when Drake goes to the L'au-dela vault you mentioned, and *that* would just be all shades of awkward."

I shuddered at the thought. "It would indeed. But . . . um . . . I guess we can find room for you, although it may mean doubling up if Drake's guards are with you."

"Oh, we're not moving in!" Aisling gave a little laugh. "Drake takes security very seriously when it concerns the babies, so he rented us a house in the suburbs of Moscow. We just flew into Riga—it takes only two hours, which means we won't have to leave the babies overnight—so that we could meet with you and get this shindig under way."

"Oh dear." I panicked just a little bit.

"We should be there in about half an hour. Drake insists that we take back roads so Kostya won't see us."

"All right. How did you know he was here?"

She giggled. "Drake is having him followed. For his own good, of course."

"Of course." She hung up with another giggle, leaving me struck mute with mingled horror and worry.

Pavel, who was on his way through the hall to one of the back rooms, paused as he strolled past me. "Are you all right? You look upset."

Slowly, I put my phone back into my pocket. "Drake and Aisling are on their way out to get some information from me, and I don't have it."

"Information about what?"

I hesitated, torn with conflicting emotions. I trusted Pavel completely, but his devotion and dedication to Baltic were absolute. It just wouldn't be fair for me to tell him something he knew Baltic would be desirous of knowing but wouldn't be able to impart. "If I said I couldn't tell you, would you be annoyed?"

"No." He smiled suddenly. "Is it something that will enrage Baltic?"

I couldn't help but sigh. "I'm sure it will, although that's not anyone's intention. I'm just trying to fix things."

He inclined his head in a little bow. "Then I will wish you Godspeed. Is there anything I can do to help you?"

"Other than spread dinner for another"—I counted mentally—"four people and one hungry demon, no. Plus Cyrene. And possibly Kostya, if he's here for Constantine's challenge."

Pavel's mouth worked a couple of times before he said, "Constantine has challenged Kostya for the black dragon sept?"

"Yes. Kostya named Baltic as his second." I nibbled on my lower lip for a few moments. "Maybe I should make a few snacks for the prechallenge part of the evening—"

"Ysolde!" An indignant Constantine appeared behind me, in the doorway. "You said you wish to have a tête-à-tête with me!"

"My apologies," I said, soothingly. "I was caught up in the thought of canapés. Pavel, can you—"

"Holland will help me put together something, and do not worry about the dinner—it will be enough for everyone."

"Bless you," I said, and meant it.

Chapter Thirteen

"Well, isn't this . . . nice."

"Man, what a hole. And I thought Aisling used to stay in some crappy places."

"Jim!" Aisling stopped looking around the entryway of the house and whapped the demon on its head, giving me an apologetic smile in the process. "I'm sorry, Ysolde. Jim swore it was going to be on its best behavior, because *it knows what will happen to it if it's not.*"

The emphasis on the last few words was not lost on Jim, who winked at me. "Soldy knows I'm just teasing. It's a great house if you like the Addams family. I especially like that tarantula over there in those cobwebs. Very atmospheric. Hey." The demon sniffed the air a couple of times. "Is that dinner I smell?"

"We are not staying for dinner," Aisling said quickly, giving Jim a stern look before preceding me into the sitting room when I gestured toward it. "We just came to . . . er . . . you know."

"Of course you're staying for dinner. Pavel's cooking, and there's plenty for everyone."

"Now, that's what I'm talking about," Jim said, plopping itself down on a couch before Aisling shoved its butt off and pointed to the floor.

"Is Baltic here?" Drake asked as he followed us into the room, trailed by his two redheaded bodyguards.

"He's at Dauva, although"—I glanced at my watch—"he should be back in the next hour or so. Dragon's blood, anyone?"

I handed out the fiery drink at the polite murmurs of assent, pouring a bit of Perrier into a bowl for Jim.

"Oooh, fancy, lemon slices," it said, slurping at the water. "Any time you want to dump me on Solders and Baltic is fine with me, Ash."

"One more, and you're out," Aisling warned the demon.

"Sheesh. Bully much?"

"We would like to extend greetings to Pavel," István said as I handed him a glass of the dragon's blood wine. "Is it allowed that we do so?"

"Of course. He's in the kitchen, but I'm sure he would welcome the opportunity to exchange greetings with you, as well." I made sure to keep my language as formal as István's, despite the urge to giggle. So far as social niceties went, dragons preferred to cling to the old ways, and that meant elite guards of one wyvern had to present their greetings to the elite guards of other wyverns in a very formalized way.

Pál and István took themselves off with a nod from Drake, who, after a somewhat scurrilous look at the battered and dismal couch that I hadn't yet had time to replace, sat down next to Aisling.

"So!" Aisling said brightly, leaning a bit into Drake as he put his arm across her shoulders. "Here we all are.

Drake's like a cat on a hot tin roof, just about dancing with anticipation, so the sooner he gets started on breaking into the sepulcher, the better."

"*Kincsem,*" Drake said sternly, shooting her an emerald-eyed glare. "I am a wyvern. You do not tell people I dance over any emotion, and certainly not anticipation."

"My apologies." She patted his leg, her eyes sparkling with amusement. "Although you are an incredibly good dancer. That last dream you sent me, where you taught me to dance the sevillana, and you spun me around so hard my dress came off, and we ended up—er—yes. We'll just leave it at you're an excellent dancer."

"You have visions with Drake, too?" I asked in surprise, correcting myself when both Drake and Aisling turned startled faces to me. "That is, you have visions about your wyvern, too?"

"They're not really visions, no, not like that one you had at the *sárkány,* or a few months ago when you tried to stab Drake in that vision. Drake and I share an ability to have, for lack of a better term, lucid dreams. Extremely lucid dreams. So much so that—" Drake made an abbreviated gesture, causing Aisling to clear her throat. "Yes, well, we've strayed from the original point, which was that we are both very eager to undertake the job you spoke about. So, where is the sepulcher?"

"Er . . ." My brain, normally a pretty reliable organ, just shrugged and told me I was on my own when it came to thinking up an excuse as to why I hadn't yet found the location of the sepulcher. "That's a really good question. And the answer is that . . . erm . . . Why don't we save that discussion for after dinner?"

They exchanged glances.

"If you desire," Drake said in a smooth voice, his fingers gently stroking Aisling's shoulder in a way that had her shivering, and shooting him a heated look. "About the recompense you will be providing me for these services. I take it you have in your possession the valuable object that you indicated earlier?"

"Not in so many words," I said, thinking back to the hurried conversation I had had with Constantine a short while before. He'd assured me that he had found Kostya's lair, and getting into it, and removing the shard, would be no problem. I had been obliged to persuade him that I needed it now, rather than waiting for him to take over the sept, when it would be his to hand over to me, but after a few minutes of persuasion, he had agreed to retrieve it. "But I should before tomorrow, assuming everything goes as planned."

"Oh man, if that isn't jinxing us, I don't know what is," Jim said, flopping down on the floor, coughing loudly when a cloud of dust rose around him.

"Don't be silly. I don't believe in jinxes," Aisling said firmly. "I do, however, believe in accidents, and derailments of best laid plans, etc. So you'll be sure to tell us if something goes awry, won't you, Ysolde?"

"Of course."

"What, exactly, is this object?" Drake asked, his fingers now tangled in Aisling's hair. She kept sending him little glances that should have steamed his eyebrows.

"I think," I said slowly, "that I would like to hold off on telling you about that until I have it in hand."

"And I would prefer to know now."

I sat up a little straighter at the tone in Drake's voice. "I'm sure you would, but I am not comfortable with explaining the whys and hows of the object to you just yet."

"Not comfortable?" he asked, his green-eyed gaze sharpening on me. "What about it makes you uncomfortable?"

"That's really none of your business," I said, growing rather annoyed. While I was willing to admit he had a right to know what he was bartering his services for, he also had to know I wasn't going to try to cheat him. "I will tell you tomorrow, once I have the item in my possession."

Drake was silent for a moment, then said in a drawling voice, "You forget my consequence, Ysolde. I must insist on knowing what object you use to barter with before I risk myself and my men. You will tell me what it is now, or I will not go forward with this agreement."

"Drake Fekete," I said, deliberately using his original name in an attempt to remind him of his place, "I am well aware of your consequence, your history, *and* the terms of our agreement. It is you who have forgotten that you agreed to do the job based on my word alone. I have said I will describe the object tomorrow, and so I shall. Either you will honor our agreement, or you will renege on it." I rose while making an imperious gesture. "But I will waste no more time on this. Decide now."

My heart was beating like crazy as I basically bluffed Drake, part of me worried sick what I'd do if he called that bluff, and left me without a thief, but the other part, the one who had absorbed much from Baltic's dealings with other dragons, told me that there were times when arrogance had its place, and that time was now.

"Oooh," Jim said on a big breath, its expression watchful as it turned to see how Drake would respond.

Drake's eyes flashed molten green fire, his body tense, as if he was going to storm out of the room. Aisling opened her mouth to say something but evidently thought better of it, for she just put her hand on Drake's and raised her eyebrows at him.

After a moment's silence that seemed to last a thousand years, Drake gave a sharp nod. "Very well. I will wait until tomorrow. But that is as long as I will wait."

"You won't regret that decision," I assured him. "You may think I'm trying to blow smoke up your ... er ... but I'm not. You'll see that tomorrow—"

*   *   *

A sudden crash from the hallway came at the perfect moment . . . perfect for lessening the tension so rampant in the room, that is. On every other front, it caused me no end of worry. I fretted, as I leaped up and ran for the door, over whether a wall had caved in, or the stairway collapsed, or any of the million other forms of destruction that seemed to hang like a particularly brooding miasma over the house.

"By the rood!" I yelled, charging out to the hall. "What is going on—really, Constantine? You have to do this now? It's almost time for dinner!"

Two dragons, identical expressions of chagrin on their faces, stood before me, one covered in shiny black scales, the other in glittering silver. The silver of Constantine's chest was splattered crimson, blood from the three slashes dripping down onto the floor.

Constantine's nostrils flared. "We are conducting a challenge for the black sept, Ysolde. This is a sacred fight, one honored by all dragonkin since the First Dragon set forth the laws of the weyr, and it will not be stopped by something so mundane as a mere meal."

"You clearly haven't tasted Pavel's cooking," I told him with a glare, pointing to the floor. "And you're dripping all over the tile. I just hope you plan on cleaning that up, because it took the cleaning ladies three hours yesterday to scrub off all the muck and dirt, and I'm not having the tile stained again."

Constantine straightened his shoulders and looked down his long dragon snout. "I am wyvern! I do not clean floors! Now, stand aside so that I might beat my godson into submission and reclaim that which should have been mine in the first place."

"I grow weary of hearing you make such ridiculous claims about the black dragons," Kostya said, whipping his tail around in an annoyed manner. It caught the edge of a small occasional table, knocking it against the wall, and sending a small, ugly ceramic vase to the floor.

"Now you know how we feel," Aisling said, sotto voce. Jim snickered. Drake shot her a long-suffering look.

I transferred my glare from Constantine to the vase where it lay smashed on the tile floor. "Konstantin Fekete!" I bellowed, marching over to him.

"Uh-oh, someone's in trouble with Mom," Jim said. "Again, since the last time you did something to piss her off, she had exactly that same look on her face."

Kostya backed up a couple of steps before he obviously remembered he was a wyvern. "My apologies, Ysolde, but it is only a small vase."

"One that I particularly liked!"

"I thought you said it looked like something a donkey pooped," Brom said from the safety of the doorway to the small, damp sitting room.

"That is beside the point." I took a deep breath and couldn't keep from adding, "I really don't think a challenge is suitable for you to witness. If you're through mucking about in your lab, you can go wash your hands and face. Dinner will be ready shortly."

"Boy, I didn't think it was possible, but she out-bosses even you," Jim told Aisling.

"Quiet, demon, or I'll dump you on her for a week and see if she can't arrange for an attitude adjustment."

Jim's eyes grew large as it backed up a few steps, but it kept silent.

"Aww, Sullivan. I want to watch the challenge. Nico says it's an important part of dragon stuff, and I should know about it even if I won't ever be a wyvern."

I looked around the hall. Everyone was there, Brom (with Nico standing protectively behind him) next to Savian, who leaned against the wall with a grin on his face. Beyond them, Pavel and Holland were at the head of the hallway that led back toward the kitchen. Behind Constantine, Cyrene sat on the stairs, texting someone while chewing gum with blithe unconcern for anything that was happening. My gaze settled on Baltic as he stood to the rear of Kostya, his arms crossed, and a bored expression on his adorable face. Despite that, I could tell he was aching for a chance at Constantine. "I don't think seeing two men beat each other up is particularly vital to your well-being, even if one of those men is incorporeal some of the time."

"Please, Sullivan?" Brom came perilously close to a whine, which he knew annoyed me. I tipped my head in question to Baltic. He looked consideringly at Constantine for a few seconds, then nodded.

"All right, you can stay, but if you have nightmares about shades bleeding all over the place—not that I knew shades could do that in the first place—then I don't want to hear any complaints."

"My corporeal form is exactly the same as yours," Constantine pointed out haughtily.

Jim snickered again.

Constantine set it on fire.

Kostya apparently just noticed that his brother and Aisling were present. "What are you doing in Latvia?" he asked them.

"Housewarming," Aisling said after a moment's pregnant silence. She waved a hand at the hall. "Ysolde invited us to see the new place."

Kostya snorted his disgust.

"Will you stop setting Aisling's demon on fire," I told Constantine. "It's just rude, and besides, this house hasn't been fireproofed yet. Jim, are you all right?"

Aisling had beaten out the fire by the time I was done speaking. "It's fine, no thanks to Casper the Not-so-friendly Ghost over there."

Brom covered his mouth to stifle a giggle.

"You know, the more I think about it, the more I feel the whole idea of a challenge is stupid."

Around me, five dragons simultaneously sucked in outraged breaths. "Stupid?" Kostya asked with equal amounts of disbelief and indignation.

"Yes, it's archaic and sexist, to boot. What if I were wyvern, and you challenged me to a physical fight? I wouldn't stand a chance against a strong male."

"Which is why females should not be wyverns," Constantine said.

"Oh, you do not want to go there," Aisling said at the same time I snapped, "Get over yourself, Constantine."

Cyrene looked up from her phone and inquired, "Would you like me to fill the room with water, Ysolde? I've found nothing brings reason to pigheaded dragons like the act of nearly drowning."

Kostya wanted to argue the statement, but I intervened. "No, I think we'll forgo that, but Constantine won't find himself invited to dinner if he keeps up that sort of crap." I thought for a moment. "Do shades eat?"

"Yes, we eat! We're just like non-shades, other than we sometimes lose power and fade into the beyond until we regain enough energy to join the mortal world again."

"That's fascinating, but it doesn't negate the point that I think these challenges are idiotic. Even Baltic, who loves nothing more than a reason to fight, looks bored to tears by it."

"That is only because I'm waiting for Kostya to fail, so that I can take over," my love said, cracking his knuckles.

"I am not going to fail. You're my second only because I must have one," Kostya snarled at him, "and because the only other choice was that watery twit."

"Oh!"

I held up a hand to stop Cyrene as she leaped to her feet. "My original statement stands, and to it, I add a new rule—no more dragon form. It's too destructive."

"Aw, man," Jim started to complain.

I set its toes briefly on fire. Jim yelped.

"Oh, it's all right if *you* set it on fire?" Constantine asked in an arch voice.

"Yes, it is," I said, examining my fingertips. "I'm a mother. It's part of our arsenal of behavior management."

Aisling grinned.

"Baltic!" Constantine swaggered toward me (dragon form is very prone to swaggering), stopping in front of me with a peeved expression on his face. "Inform Ysolde that she cannot interfere in a challenge, and that by the terms of this challenge, we must fight body to body. That requires dragon form."

I raised an eyebrow at Baltic. He was silent for a moment, then made a short, annoyed gesture. "It pains me greatly to say the words, but about this, Constantine is correct. You may not interfere in the challenge, mate."

"I will *not* have this house destroyed because you boys don't want to play nice!" I said loudly, turning back to glare at Constantine.

"I really hate it when she refers to us as boys," Kostya said in an aside to Baltic. "We're older than she is, after all."

Baltic nodded. "She was always that way, though." He smiled suddenly. "Do you remember the time when she dragged you out of Dauva by your ear for swiving that milkmaid in the main hall?"

Kostya rubbed his ear and shot me a surly look. "I haven't forgotten. My ear has never been the same since."

Aisling laughed openly. I ignored them to address Constantine. "Either you beat the crap out of each other while you're in human form—and without breaking anything but each other—or you can just take it outside."

"Ysolde—" Constantine started to say, but I interrupted him with brutal disregard.

"Out!" I flung open the two front doors and made a grand gesture. "You go outside with your challenge, or you call it off."

"Are you going to allow her to speak this way to us?" Constantine asked Baltic, clearly expecting him to do something.

Baltic looked thoughtful for a few seconds, then shrugged. "She is my mate. If she does not wish for the challenge to take place in our home, then it will not. I do not desire her to be unhappy. You will conduct the challenge outside."

Constantine was obviously about to explode, but in the end, he stomped his way out the door, down the verandah, and out into the yard, grumbling the entire way. "I have never been so treated, and I have been abused by the very best! To speak that way to *me*, the wyvern of her own sept, is unthinkable. Were she *my* mate—"

"If I had been your mate, I would have been insane a long time ago," I called out after him as Kostya, with a martyred sigh, trundled after him. The others followed, Baltic bringing up the rear with a slight twitch to his lips that told me he found the situation as amusing as I did.

As I walked down the steps to the yard, faint sounds caught my attention. I paused for a moment, trying to pinpoint where the yelling was coming from, but it was too distant, almost on the edge of my awareness.

"Do you hear that?" I asked Baltic as I approached him, counting on his exceptional hearing to locate what I couldn't.

Baltic stood with the others in a loose circle around Constantine and Kostya as they pounced, tails whipping through the air, claws flashing, grunts and oaths rising upward on a reddish cloud of dust from the disturbed ground.

"Hear what?" he asked without turning toward me.

"That noise. It sounds like . . ." I paused and closed

my eyes in order to focus my attention. "It sounds like someone is doing bodywork on a car. I can hear metallic pounding and yelling."

"I hear nothing." Baltic stepped backward as Constantine and Kostya, now fully engaged in battle, rolled toward us. He grabbed my arm to pull me back, but the second he did so, a familiar feeling washed over me.

"Oh no, not now," I said as the afternoon light shimmered, dimming into that of predawn.

"Ysolde—"

I held up my hand to stop the complaint I was sure was to follow. "Don't tell me to stop the vision, Baltic. I've told you repeatedly I can't. And besides, I don't want to. They are the only way I ever find out anything, since you refuse to tell me things I evidently need to know."

"Ooh, another vision," Cyrene said, looking around us with bright, interested eyes.

"I'm beginning to enjoy them, I have to admit," Savian told her.

"They do bring back some fun memories of times long past," she agreed. "Although Ysolde never has visions about anyone I knew."

"You're not going to get hurt, are you?" Brom asked, moving over to stand next to me. "Pavel told Nico you had dreams of when someone killed you a long time ago."

I pulled him between Baltic and me, smiling at him when Baltic put his arm around us both. "No, I'm not going to be hurt, and you don't have to worry, lovey—I would never let you see that vision. This one looks like . . ." I looked around us at the images of the past. "I—I don't know where this is. Baltic?"

"It's Latoka, isn't it?" Drake asked, sidestepping when his brother, still fully engaged in fighting with Constantine, was thrown backward. "Baltic, is this Staraya Latoka?"

"What's Latoka?" I asked Baltic, nudging him when he was obviously reluctant to answer.

"It was the holding of Alexei." He glared around him at the vision people as they fought in an oddly ironic mimicry of Constantine and Kostya. Only the dragons in the vision all belonged to the black sept, and they were armed with swords. "It was destroyed."

I looked at the two squat round towers that towered over us, noting the men running along the ramparts of the stone wall. It wasn't a very big fortress, nor did it look to my unknowledgeable eyes as being nearly as protective as Dauva was, but clearly this stronghold was built centuries before the latter.

"It looks fine to me now. When was it destroyed? And why are all the dragons fighting one another?"

Baltic's expression grew grim, and, much to my surprise, he took my hand and led me toward the nearest tower. I grabbed Brom with my other hand, pulling him after us. "For once, you have chosen a fitting vision. No, do not bring my son. He may stay out here with his tutor."

I caught his eye and read a warning in it. I turned back, expecting to see everyone still watching Constantine and Kostya despite the vision, but they had all fallen into place behind us. "Nico, would you mind?"

"Not at all," he said, obviously lying, but his dedication to Brom won out over his interest to see whatever event Baltic wanted to keep Brom from seeing. He held out his hand for Brom.

"Why can't I stay with you?" Brom asked.

"Because there are some things that even I, a mother who allows you to help firebomb negrets, have issues with your seeing, and this is obviously one of those things."

"But you don't know what it is," he pointed out.

"Go!" I said firmly, pinning him back with my best

annoyed-mom look. He walked slowly over to Nico, muttering under his breath about no one letting him have any fun.

"Jim will stay with you, won't you, Jim?" Aisling said, nudging her demon.

Its eyes grew big with an obvious plea in them.

"You can talk, but only because I want you to keep Brom and Nico entertained."

"Seriously, Ash, you've got to stop taking mean lessons from Soldy." Jim walked just as slowly as Nico, casting plaintive looks over its shoulder as we all moved toward the tower. "We never get to see any of the really good stuff."

"What about them?" Cyrene asked, pointing to where Constantine was in the process of head butting Kostya, while the latter was trying desperately to pull Constantine's legs out from under him.

"They can stay where they are. I'd much rather have them keep each other busy than have to cope with more attitude from either of them," I said, squeezing Baltic's hand.

"It's too bad Maura isn't here," Savian said as we entered the tower. "She really enjoyed the last vision."

I expected there would be more dragons fighting inside the tower, but it was empty. Or so I thought at first. Across the vast space was another door, obviously leading to an antechamber. Before it, two men stood, both in human form, with one bearing chain mail armor, and a huge sword.

"You cannot do this," the armor-bearing Constantine said, the anger in his voice audible even across the centuries. "Allowing him to return to the sept will be the last straw. Chuan Ren will not tolerate that insult to pass. She will bring war to the black dragons, and the blame for that will lie directly at your feet."

"The First Dragon was wrong to force me to remove

Baltic from the sept," Alexei said, waving a weary hand at Constantine. "I am making peace with my own conscience."

"Who's that with Constantine?" I heard Aisling whisper to Drake. He murmured an explanation. Aisling sounded astonished when she asked, "Baltic's *grandfather* kicked him out of his own sept?"

"Does Alexei know that all the black dragons are fighting one another outside?" I asked Baltic, my fingers tightening around his in acknowledgment of how hard I knew it was for him to watch this.

"I don't think he did. Constantine never expected that Alexei would go against the First Dragon's command, and he struck out in fear and anger."

"Those guys fighting are with Constantine?" Aisling asked. "The black dragons, I mean—wait, they're all black dragons at this point, aren't they? This is so confusing. But some of those fighting are the same dragons who followed Constantine to the silver sept?"

"I think so," I answered, watching Baltic's face. His eyes were filled with anger, his dragon fire running very hot within him as he watched the scene in front of us.

"You can't do that!" Constantine yelled, his voice filled with frustration as he slammed his fist into the wall. "I am your heir! You named *me* as heir."

"Baltic is heir now. You lost the challenge to him before he was removed from the sept," Alexei said, holding up a hand in an obviously placatory gesture. "Do not lash me with your ire, Constantine. I am aware of your feelings, but I must think about what's best for the sept, and the future of the black dragons lies with Baltic."

Constantine struck Alexei's hand aside. "Because you wanted him for your heir all along, did you not? You named me as heir while he was young and unlearned, but all along you intended for him to take the sept when you could no longer hold it. You lied to me! You took my oath and swore the sept would be mine; yet you never intended for me to have it!" Constantine stormed around Alexei, his free hand gesturing wildly.

I watched his other hand, the one holding the sword, knowing in my heart that Baltic had been right, and that Constantine was responsible for the death of Alexei. Was this the moment when he died? It must be—there would be few other reasons but murder that would prompt Baltic to send Brom away.

"I will not have it!" Constantine screamed.

Alexei frowned. "Recall yourself, Constantine. You allow your anger to overrule your mind, and forget who and what you are, and what you owe to me. You will not—"

"No! It is you who will not." Constantine took a deep breath. "You will not destroy me in this fashion. You will not bring Baltic back into the sept."

"It is already done," Alexei said, his shoulders slumping a little. "I have accepted his fealty and granted him status within the sept once again. There is nothing you can do to change what fate has already written."

Constantine was working himself up into a frenzy, screaming curses at his wyvern.

Baltic's grip on my fingers turned painful as without warning, Constantine lunged forward. I spun around at the move, but not before I saw the sword flash and blood spray out in an arc.

"Oh my god!" Aisling gasped in a choked voice.

Baltic pulled me against his chest, his hands hard on my arms. I clung to him and bit back a sob, the emotions of the scene too much for me.

"I will never suffer Baltic as wyvern! This sept will be mine, or I will see it destroyed!"

"He really was mad, wasn't he?" I asked Baltic, wiping my eyes on his shirt before looking up at him. "You weren't exaggerating when you told me he wanted to see you and the sept destroyed."

"I wasn't exaggerating," he said, his muscles tight as Constantine stormed through the middle of us, blood dripping from his sword, a fanatical light in his eyes.

"But he seems so normal now. Well, somewhat normal," Aisling said, shuddering as she looked away.

"His madness was always cold by nature rather than hot," Baltic said, his eyes still on the figure of his dead grandfather. "He had sane moments, but it was the madness that drove him on and kept him attacking the black dragons when others would have ceased."

"And now?" I touched Baltic's cheek, drawing his attention away from tragic memories. "Is he being coldly mad now?"

"No. I thought at first he was, but I see now that the act of being raised as a shade has changed him, leached the madness out of him."

Behind us, present-day Constantine yelled, "You call me a douche canoe? I am not the douche canoe—you are. No, you are more than that—you are a douche speedboat!"

"*Most* of the madness," Baltic qualified.

Savian laughed, then immediately looked guilty. "Sorry. Didn't mean to make light of a somber occasion."

"It matters not," Baltic said briskly, turning with me and striding out of the tower. "That event was long in the past. Constantine paid the price for his actions of that day."

"By sacrificing himself for me when I was killed?" I asked, trotting after him.

"That was later. He suffered most when I threw him and his followers out of the sept."

I stopped so quickly that Aisling, directly behind me, bumped into me, immediately murmuring an apology.

"You threw them out? No, that's not right. Gabriel told me that the silver dragons left the black sept."

"Gabriel was not there. I was." Baltic stopped, saw the look on my face, and sighed one of his highly perfected martyred sighs. "I can tell by your expression that you are not going to let this rest in the past, where it should remain."

"Damned straight, I'm not." I approached him, searching his face for signs of distress, but he had once again mastered his emotions. "Are you sure you kicked them out? Because everyone else seems to think that Constantine left the sept because he didn't want to be a part of it while you were wyvern."

"That's what Drake told me," Aisling said, looking to Drake for confirmation.

He shrugged. "It is what Constantine told us when the silver dragons joined the weyr."

"Now, just wait a second," I said, stopping Baltic when he would have continued. Dimly, the noises of Constantine and Kostya yelling at each other were still audible, letting us know they were still engaged in their battle. I wanted badly to ask him about whether Pavel was right in hinting that Constantine had taken Baltic's talisman, but I didn't feel right mentioning it in front of Drake. Instead, I went back to the main point of my confusion. "From what I've gathered, all along Constantine has made a big deal about the silver dragons forming because they didn't want to stay in the sept while you were running it into the ground." I made air quotes about the last few words. "Which is stupid, because you did no such thing, but that's always been Constantine's big thing . . . they left to form their own sept."

"They formed a sept, but only after I removed Constantine and the dragons who attacked the rest of our sept." Baltic's eyes were unreadable. "You have some memories of Constantine. Do you expect that he would have made it known to all that he had been made ouroboros?"

"No," I said after some thought. "He always did have a bit of a sensitive ego."

"Just playing devil's advocate, I'd like to point out that no one knew Baltic was kicked out of the black dragons, too. At least I don't think anyone knew. Sweetie?"

"No," Drake said, his face as placid as ever. "That fact was not known to me until just a few minutes ago."

Baltic shrugged. "I did not hide it, the way Constantine has hidden the truth. It simply did not matter, since Alexei reinstated me as his heir."

"I don't know about anyone else, but I find it very interesting that Constantine got the boot," I said, stumbling after Baltic when he took my hand and returned through the complex tapestry of the past to the present day.

The battle was over by the time the last few tendrils of the vision had faded away into distant memory, at which point, Kostya soundly beat Constantine . . . or he would have if Constantine hadn't suddenly run out of energy.

"No!" the spectral voice of Constantine howled, echoing through the half-dead trees as he faded from our view. "Not now! I cannot lose power right when—"

Kostya picked himself up from the ground, where he'd been thrown by Constantine, breathing heavily as he wiped blood from his eyes and shifted back into human form. "What . . . happened?" he panted, looking around for his missing challenger.

Baltic swore profoundly. "I knew he would do that before Kostya failed and I could take over."

"Will you stop saying I'm going to fail!" Kostya snapped, wiping the blood flowing from his nose.

"I'm sorry that you can't vent your animosity a bit by

beating him up, but I'm not sorry that you can't fight," I told Baltic, somewhat confusedly.

"I did not fail!"

"You will cease being concerned that I will be hurt. Unlike you, I have not died repeatedly," Baltic said with lofty disregard.

"I would not have failed, either, which you would see for yourself if Constantine had not disappeared!"

"Neither death was my fault, I'd like to point out," I said with much righteousness. "It's not like I go around getting killed just for the fun of it."

"I am wyvern! I do not fail!" Kostya weaved as he staggered toward us, suddenly sitting down very hard.

I sighed and looked over to him. "I suppose I'm going to have to call the healer again."

"I am not hurt. I don't need a healer," Kostya said, and promptly fell over onto his side as he moaned softly to himself.

"Take him into the sitting room," I said with a dispassionate eye as Drake, looking somewhat annoyed, scooped up his brother, tossed him over his shoulder, and started for the house, Aisling and Jim trailing behind.

Chapter Fourteen

"I knew I would find you here. Always when you are upset, you retreat to the garden."

"You know me so well." I moved the camping light a foot to the side and knee-walked after it to settle in front of a choked tangle of weeds and daisies. "If we're going to stay here for a while during the rebuilding of Dauva, I'd like to be able to enjoy the garden area. It will be quite a nice little spot once the beds are weeded, although not many of the flowers have survived. Just a few aphidy roses, and what I suspect are wild daisies."

"We will hire someone to do this work," Baltic told me in his usual bossy tone.

I slanted a look up at him and sank my fingers into the earth, gently separating the roots of the weed from that of a daisy. "I enjoy weeding, as you well know."

"I know it, but I do not wish for you to overwork yourself."

I looked up again, searching his face, but there was nothing there to indicate anything other than mild concern. I murmured something noncommittal before asking, "Did Kostya take off?"

"The green wyvern took him once the healer was done. Why did you leave? Pavel was distressed that you missed the meal he prepared."

I yanked out a few more weeds, trying to find the words to explain the sense of despair that had come over me while the healer was fixing Kostya's ills. "Does it ever seem too much to you, Baltic? All the death and betrayal and inevitability? And don't tell me you don't care—you may have the reputation of being a heartless fiend, but you feel things just as deeply as I do."

He knelt beside me, not touching me, but close enough that I could feel his warmth. "I should not have allowed that vision to continue. It distressed you."

"It isn't that. Well, yes, it did distress me, but only because I don't like seeing anyone die, even if that event was almost a thousand years ago." I jerked out a clump of crabgrass and swore when the tough fibers of the plant slid along my hand and cut my palm.

"You always were fairly squeamish despite your blood-thirsty nature," Baltic said, taking my hand and blowing a little fire across it.

"I am not bloodthirsty! Nor am I squeamish. I've never been squeamish. I just don't like people killing one another. Is that so wrong?" Another wave of despair washed over me, causing me to lean into Baltic, needing him to bring hope and happiness back into my life.

"This is not about Alexei's death," he said, brushing a tear off my cheek. "What distresses you, *chérie*?"

"Everything." I made a vague gesture. "Your refusing to let me make the First Dragon happy. Constantine's fighting everyone for a sept. The business with Kostya and stealing back our shard from him. And having Drake—" I stopped.

"I wondered when you were going to tell me why the green wyvern came to visit you," Baltic said with deceptive mildness. He kissed the palm of my hand, now healed. "You bring the woes of the world upon yourself, my love. It was ever so, but I grow tired of seeing you with dark circles under your eyes. You will cease to worry about the First Dragon. What he thinks is of no importance to us. And I will speak to Constantine, and make it clear he is not to trouble you again. As for Kostya—"

"No, I don't want you cutting everyone off. Don't you see?" I clutched his shirt and shook it. "You're so insular, Baltic. You never used to be this way, but you are now, and I just can't live like that. Constantine may be an annoying remnant of a former madman, but he was once your friend."

"He was also my bitterest enemy."

"I grant you that, but that was when the madness took over. And Kostya was your closest friend."

"Until he killed me."

I ground my teeth for a few seconds. "You allowed him to kill you. You admitted that yourself."

"Only because I knew you had died, and I did not wish to live without you."

I melted against him, kissing him even as I pulled on his dragon fire. "You have always been able to distract me just by saying things that you know will make me a puddle of goo in your hands."

"If that were true, then I would never hear a dissenting word from these sweet lips." His mouth was hot on mine, as demanding as ever, his tongue twining itself around mine, firing up both my passion and my need for him until they blazed within me, singeing my soul with their strength.

I moaned when he kissed his way along my collarbone, sliding off my shirt to gently cup my breasts, his fingers teasing the flesh above my bra. "Baltic, we shouldn't, not here."

"I wish to indulge your fantasy for making love outside," he murmured, his hands moving around behind me to unhook my bra, the slight stubble on his cheeks making me arch backward as his cheeks brushed the underside of my breasts.

My fingers worked rapidly down the buttons of his shirt, tugging it out of his pants as I moaned again. "Someone could see us. The garden is visible from the house."

"Only from our room." He got to his feet when I tugged on his belt, quickly removing his shoes and pants before sliding his hands up under my skirt, his fingers teasing the sensitive flesh of my thighs.

"Brom," I panted, licking a path along his collarbone to his jaw, which I nipped, my own hands stroking up his chest and arms.

"Watching a DVD on ancient cultures with Nico."

"Then I guess—oh yes, right there, my darling—then I guess we are safe out here." I released the earlobe I was sucking and leaned backward, reaching for the gardening bag at the same time I gave him my very best sultry-eyed look. "Which means we can finally try—"

"There you are. I wondered where everyone got to after dinner. Are you gardening at night? Isn't it hard to see the plants?" Cyrene loomed up out of the darkness, her eyes bright with interest as she took in our state of undress. "Oh, you're naked."

I made an eeping sort of sound as Baltic pulled me behind him. I grabbed his shirt and tossed it onto his lap, getting to my knees to peer over his shoulder at the intruder. "Hello, Cyrene. I thought you went into town to visit the local spa."

"I did, but their pool was too small to really enjoy." She pursed her lips. "I'm *de trop*, aren't I?"

"Yes," Baltic told her, frowning.

"Sorry. It's just . . . well, everyone's gone. Brom and that teacher of his are watching a movie on how ancient Egyptians made mummies, and Pavel and his friend disappeared right after dessert, and Savian took the car as soon as I got back, but he didn't say where he was off to, so I thought I'd see if you wanted to play cards or something."

I ignored the wistful tone in her voice, my fingers tightening on Baltic's shoulders when he was obviously about to let her know what he thought of the interruption. "No, thank you, Cyrene. We'd rather be alone."

She sighed heavily and gave us a wan smile. "All right, but if you want to play cards when you're done, I'll be in my room."

"Don't say it," I told Baltic when she disappeared into the night. He eyed me as I moved around to his side. "I didn't invite her; she invited herself. And I felt sorry for her. Now, where were we?"

"You were about to placate my anger," he said sternly, pulling me over him as he lay back, deftly catching the tip of my nipple in his mouth.

"Ah, yes. And I have just the thing for truly world-class placation." I squirmed away from him, reaching into the bag to pull out a soft blanket.

He cocked an eyebrow at the two items. "A blanket?"

I grinned as I spread the blanket out, gesturing to him to scoot over onto it. "I know you as well as you know me, my darling."

"You were so sure, then, that I would seek you out here?"

"Oh yes. Sure enough to bring this, as well." I reached into the bag again and pulled out a small device made up of four round metal balls connected by an arched handle in the shape of an X.

"What is—"

Before Baltic could finish his question, a voice could be heard calling my name. "Ysolde! Where are you? That child of yours said you were out here. Ysolde?"

I tucked my toy away into the bag, snatching up Baltic's shirt and pulling it on before laying my shirt over his lap.

Baltic fairly growled when Constantine suddenly appeared out of the laurel hedge. "Ah. I have found you. I wanted to tell you—you appear to be nude under that shirt. Are you engaging in sex?"

"Not if people insist on parading through the garden." Baltic's voice was deep and filled with ire. "What are *you* doing here?"

"I came to report to Ysolde that my job is done. My first job, that is." He stretched in order to see over Baltic to me. "Are you using the gold dust on him? I told you how effective that is. Or did you opt to go with the body paints?"

"Your job is done?" I asked, ignoring his rude questions. "You mean you have it?"

"Yes." He held out a small wooden box, chased in silver with intricate designs of stylized dragons. "It is your shard, my lovely one."

"She's my lovely one, and now that you have given her our shard, you may leave," Baltic said in a haughty tone.

"But . . ." I glanced at Baltic's watch, lying on top of his pants. "But Kostya's lair is in St. Petersburg. That's a couple of hours away from here, and you didn't fade away until it was almost dinnertime. How did you get there and back so quickly?"

"Mate, do not encourage him to speak. There is nothing more he likes than the sound of his own voice. We'll never be rid of him if you ask him questions."

"And there is nothing you like more than to belittle me in front of Ysolde!" Constantine spat, looking down his nose at us.

Baltic started to get up, but I pulled him back down onto the blanket. "Stop it, both of you. I've had enough posturing and arguing today to last me a good month. How did you get the shard so quickly, Constantine?"

He sniffed and brushed off a minute speck of dirt from his sleeve. "One of the benefits of being a shade is that portals no longer discompose me. I portalled from St. Petersburg to Riga while Kostya was behaving like the weakling he is."

I opened the box, smiling when light from within bathed me in a warm, golden glow. The shard was in a long crystal tube, chased in gold, the glow deep inside it triggering a sense of well-being and happiness. "Our shard."

"You have done as Ysolde asked; now you may leave," Baltic said abruptly.

"I like that! I've gone to all the trouble, not to mention considerable risk, of bringing that to you, and you simply snatch it from me and try to throw me out?" He put his hands on his hips. "I've a good mind to let you cope by yourself with that lieutenant of yours, but I have too much affection for Ysolde to go back on my word."

"A good mind? *You?* You wouldn't know a good mind—"

"Baltic," I interrupted, pinching the back of his arm.

"What?"

"You're arguing with him when we could be doing much more pleasant things." Gently, I bit his shoulder. "Thank you for the shard, Constantine. I'm sure I'll have the opportunity to be more expressive in my thanks tomorrow."

Constantine bowed. "Words of gratitude from your luscious lips, my lady, are all—"

"Get the hell out of here!" Baltic roared, and started to get to his feet.

Constantine sniffed again and made an obscene gesture. "You don't have to be so rude, Baltic. I know when my presence is not welcome. I was simply indicating to Ysolde—"

He finally left us, but only after Baltic chased him across half the garden. By the time Baltic returned, still naked and no longer aroused, I was beginning to rethink my plan of seducing him under the stars.

"Perhaps we should go to our room," I said thoughtfully, my fingers stroking over the lid of the phylactery box. "Less traffic that way."

"No," Baltic said stubbornly, taking me into his arms and divesting me of both his shirt and the box. "It is your desire to make love out here, and that is what we will do. Now lie back and let me pleasure you."

"You know the rules," I said, stroking my hand down the thick muscles of his chest. "If we play that way, I get to ask you questions."

"No questions," he said, leaning over me until I did as he said and lay back on the blanket, giggling a little at the scowl and firm-set jaw. It never failed to amuse me how he could be simultaneously annoyed and seductive. "Just lovemaking. We will commence with—"

"Oh no, I get to use my toy on you. That's what I was going to do before we were disturbed."

His scowl darkened. "I do not need sexual aids to arouse me, mate. And neither do you!"

I laughed at the outrage in his voice, and softened my amusement by wiggling against him. "No, of course you don't, and you know full well I don't need anything but you to make me a mindless blob of sated woman, but that doesn't mean we can't try something new now and again, just to broaden our minds."

He glared at the object I retrieved. "What is it?"

"It's, for lack of a better explanation, electric knuckles. Here, sit up and I'll show you."

Reluctantly, he rolled off me and sat up, his eyes suspicious as I turned on the device and ran it over his shoulder muscles.

"See? It's like when someone massages you, using the knuckles to dig into your muscles. It feels good, doesn't it?"

"I prefer your hands to a metallic substitute," he said, but he leaned into it when I pushed harder on the tendons at the base of his neck.

"Obviously hands are best for a massage," I agreed, running it down his spine. "But this can do more than just what it was intended for."

His eyes narrowed as I moved it around to his leg, letting it vibrate on his thigh muscle for a moment. "In what way—"

He sucked in his breath as I slid the little machine up toward his genitals, just teasing the sides of his testicles.

"Now, tell me that isn't fun," I cooed, pushing him down onto his back so I could have access to all those spots I wanted to torment.

"It is . . . not unpleasant," he admitted, squirming just a little when I let the machine buzz his inner thighs.

I bent down to take one tasty little nipple in my mouth as I ran the machine up his thigh again until it reached the apex, allowing it to vibrate against the base of his penis. He froze for a few seconds; then suddenly I was on my back, and he was looming over me, the machine in his hands. "Now it is my turn!"

"But I bought that for yoooo—" The sentence ended in a howl as I writhed beneath him. He was merciless with that blasted machine, touching me with it first on my breasts, then my thighs, then back to my breasts, my neck, my belly . . . following each touch with his mouth, his tongue burning a hot brand on my even hotter flesh, his fire sweeping around us both in a spiral that seemed to go on forever. By the time he got done teasing me to a frenzy, I was mindless with pleasure and cried my rapture up to the night sky.

It took a very long time for me to pull my wits together again; when I did, I found Baltic lying next to me on his back, his big chest heaving as he struggled to catch his breath, the electric knuckles clutched in his hand still buzzing gently.

"I am so going to stock up on batteries," I told him, taking it from him and switching it off.

"Get a case of them," he agreed.

"Now, aren't you glad you let me try something—"

"Ysolde? Is that you I heard? Do you have a minute? I really need to—lordisa!"

I sighed as Baltic jerked the blanket over me. "I swear, there's more traffic through this garden than Grand Central Station." I grabbed my shirt and jeans, quickly pulling them on.

Baltic, with a few choice words muttered under his breath, donned his clothing, as well.

"Good evening, Maura. I'm delighted to see you again, although I do wish you hadn't seen quite so much of Baltic."

"I'm so sorry," she said, her back to us. "I only got a glimpse. I had no idea you were out here doing what you were doing. And I'd go inside to wait for you, but I'm afraid this concerns my mother, and is rather important, and . . . and . . . I'm really at my wit's end."

Baltic, who had continued to mutter some very rude things under his breath, helped me to my feet.

"It's all right; we have been a bit distracted, what with one thing and the other." I folded the blanket and picked up a few things that had slipped out of the gardening bag, repacking it with a significant glance at Baltic.

"I will be inside," he said, shaking his head. "You have ten minutes before I come to find you. Do not make me hunt you."

I just smiled as he stalked off.

"Hunt?" Maura said, turning around to look at me. "He doesn't want to hunt you? But that's a dragon game. All males like it."

"I think he's warning me that he's at the end of his very limited patience. What's worrying you about Violet?"

She slumped down onto a mildewed stone bench bedecked with somewhat obscene cherubs. "Everything."

"Is something going on between her and your grandfather? I don't have a lot of memories of my time with your mother, but I do remember that she was always able to get him to do things that no one else could. Have they had an argument or something?"

"I wish it was that. No, it's something much more horrible." She looked up as I sat next to her, ignoring a stone cherub that seemed to be about to do a most inappropriate act to another cherub. "You remember the talk we had a few days ago, about why I couldn't leave the *castillo* in Spain?"

"You said Thala was blackmailing you."

She nodded.

"Is she trying to convince your mother that you're in trouble?"

"My mother doesn't have to be convinced of that—she knows it very well by now." Maura stopped pleating the material of her pants and took a deep breath. "Thala is holding my mother prisoner until I give her the location of the sepulcher. Yes," she said when I gasped in surprise. "The very same sepulcher that you've been looking for."

I eyed her. "How did you know I am searching for it, too?"

"Savian told me a few minutes ago. He said he didn't think you'd mind, given the dire nature of the situation.

Please don't be angry with him for betraying your confidence. I begged him for help, and once he heard what I was trying to do . . . well, it just kind of came out. I'm the one who deserves your wrath, not him."

"Don't be silly. I'm not mad at him. Or you. But kidnapping your mother . . . that's very extreme of Thala."

Maura sighed. "She wants that sword that she says belongs to her mother, and since I left the tribe and she couldn't make it a condition of my membership that I find out the location, she took my mother, and she's holding her hostage for the information."

"So when you were in Spain and said you couldn't leave . . ."

"Thala told me I couldn't go anywhere without her permission. I don't know what she thought I'd do—perhaps present my situation to the L'au-dela Committee and bring them down on her head—but she warned me against doing anything but convincing Emile to give me the location of the sepulcher."

"And we took you away with us. Oh, Maura, why didn't you tell us this at the time?"

"What good would it have done?" She ran a hand through her hair. "There was no way to get those stupid handcuffs off, and besides . . ."

"You didn't trust us," I finished for her.

She nodded, sadness quite evident on her face. "I realize now that I was wrong about your conveniently losing the key just so you could keep tabs on me. But at the time, I wasn't sure, and I just didn't know what to do. So I kept quiet about it, and, in hopes that she wouldn't hurt Mum, I explained to Thala that I'd been kidnapped by you."

Fear gripped my gut. "Oh no! Tell me she didn't hurt Violet."

"She didn't, or at least she says she didn't, and I think that about this, she's telling the truth. Evidently enough people in the town were witness to my struggles to convince her that I was taken against my will."

"So when you left us here, that was to talk to Dr. Kostich?"

She shook her head. "I thought I'd try to find the sepulcher myself."

"But why?" I cried. "Surely Dr. Kostich would move heaven and earth to save Violet."

"No, he wouldn't." I stared at her in abject horror. She made a frustrated gesture in response. "I'm saying it all wrong. He would if he could, but the Committee has a strict no-negotiations policy with people who are, to draw a modern-day analogy, terrorists. He told me that if he makes an exception for Mum, then he'll have to make exceptions the next time someone comes to him with a family member or loved one held hostage. He said there was nothing the Committee could do to help my mother. It breaks my heart, but I understand why he has refused to tell me the location. I just . . . I just wish they would make an exception for me."

I was silent for a few minutes, the soft sounds of the night surrounding us. An owl hooted in the distance. A low drone indicated a car passing on the borders of our property. A high-pitched whine warned of a mosquito in search for a warm meal. At last I said, "I assume you told all of this to Savian?"

"Yes. I didn't want to, because I felt it would add unnecessary stress to . . . things."

"A relationship?" I asked with arched brows.

Even in the dim light of the camping lamp, I could see a faint stain of color on her cheeks. "Such as it is, yes. But when I got this message, I knew I had to get some help."

She pulled out her phone, punched a few buttons, and showed me a text message that read simply "You're out of time. You have eight hours to find it, or your mother will pay."

I handed back the phone. "That sounds like Thala. How long ago did you get it?"

"About two hours ago. It took me some time to get here. I was in St. Petersburg."

"Why there?" I asked, wondering if everyone was in St. Petersburg at that moment.

"Thala told me that was where she thought the sepulcher was. There or outside of Moscow, but she felt St. Petersburg was the better choice due to the number of watch members in the area."

I bit my lower lip in thought, then patted her hand in a reassuring fashion. "Don't worry. We still have six hours, and we're going to make the most of them." I got to my feet and gathered up my bag.

"If Savian couldn't find it in the three days he said he's been looking—" she started to say.

"We don't have time for that. I don't say he wouldn't find it, but he himself would be the first to admit that sometimes it takes a while to locate objects that have been hidden well. No, we're going to go to the source for the information."

"The source?" Her forehead wrinkled as she followed me back into the house. "What source?"

"Dr. Kostich."

She put a hand on my arm to stop me. "Ysolde, I just told you—"

"I know what you told me, and I also know what your grandfather didn't say. I may not have many memories, but I know this—he loves your mother, and there's no way he'd sit around and not take any action when her life was threatened. We just have to get around that whole "no negotiation with terrorists" thing, and I'm confident we can do that."

"How?" she asked, standing in the doorway to the kitchen when I headed up the back stairs.

"Leave that to me," I said with calm reassurance, and

hastily trotted up the stairs before she could ask me for details.

The truth was, I hadn't a clue how I was going to get Dr. Kostich to give me the location of the sepulcher. I just knew that somehow it had to be done.

Chapter Fifteen

"Explain to me why I must do this."

Ten minutes after my conversation with Maura, I sat on Baltic's lap to keep him from getting out of the chair and leaving the room, as he had threatened to do just a moment before.

"Because it's important to me. Surely that is enough?"

"The archimage's daughter is nothing to me."

"No, but Violet is my friend, and she helped me before, so I'm not going to turn my back on either her or her daughter."

"The same daughter who led the attack on us at Dauva," he pointed out.

"She's explained that, and apologized, so move on." I kissed the tip of his nose. "It's important to me, Baltic. But mostly, it's important to *us*."

He frowned. "How is taking a portal to St. Petersburg to locate my mage sword important to us? You do not like the sword. You are jealous of it because Antonia was my lover when she gave it to me. You told me that you would skewer me with it yourself if I ever so much as thought of her, which was ridiculous since I have never thought of any woman but you since I took you from the humans."

"I miss my parents," I said, suddenly homesick for a home that hadn't been mine in five hundred years. "They may have been human, but they were very nice people. Wait . . . When did I tell you I'd stab you with it?"

He gave a little half shrug. "When I moved it from my lair in Dauva to the one in England. It was a half century before we were killed. You accused me of wanting to be with Antonia again, and threatened, amongst other atrocities, to geld me with it."

"Boy, I had a serious jealousy issue back then," I mused, but couldn't keep from wondering if there wasn't a reason I'd been jealous. I eyed Baltic suspiciously until he laughed and kissed me soundly.

"You have exactly the same look on your face that you did when you threatened the gelding. Must I reassure you again, mate?"

"No. Well . . . another time. Right now we have to get our butts to St. Petersburg to intercept Dr. Kostich. Maura called him and told him of Thala's ultimatum, and of the deadline."

"Why then must we go?" He was back to looking disgruntled.

"Because Dr. Kostich told Maura there was nothing he could do. He was lying, of course. Or not so much lying as avoiding the strict truth. I know how he thinks— he doesn't want to involve her, and he can't go against the laws of the L'au-dela, so he's going to find a way to slip the information about the location to Thala, and be on hand when she arrives at the sepulcher."

His eyes narrowed. "How do you know he will proceed in that manner?"

"Because it's what I'd do, and, like I said, I know how

he thinks. The man is a master at getting around rules and finding loopholes. Come on. If we get out of here in the next half hour, that will leave us with four hours to lurk around the portal office in St. Petersburg so we can follow Dr. Kostich when he arrives, plus it will give Drake and Aisling time to get there."

I started to get off his lap, but he pulled me back down onto it. "You will tell me now why the green wyvern is involved."

"Oh, are we playing sharing time? Excellent. I will tell you just what problem I've asked for Drake's help with, and you can tell me a number of things, starting with how Constantine got your talisman to make his own sept, to how you got it back, how you're going to get it back from Thala, and what you know about the location of Gareth and Ruth. And don't deny you know something, because Pavel told me you had people looking into it for you. Do we have a deal?"

He growled deep in his chest, a little puff of smoke lazily wafting from one nostril. But after a moment's silence, he said, "It's the light sword. You know I desire to possess it again. Green dragons are notable thieves; therefore, you've asked Drake to steal the sword for you."

"Dammit," I snapped, getting off his lap and marching to the door in a fine approximation of someone in high dudgeon. "I just hate it when you figure things out! I'm going to call Aisling and tell her to meet us in St. Petersburg. I hope you can be ready to go in twenty minutes, because that's when I told Pavel to have the cars ready."

I closed the door on the sound of his swearing in Zilant, smiling to myself. I never doubted that the moment he found out that Drake had something to do with my plans for the sepulcher, he'd realize that the mage sword was my goal. But what he didn't realize was how I intended on returning it to him. "And I just pray he doesn't find out until it's too late."

"Until what's too late?" Brom emerged from his room pulling a wheeled suitcase behind him. He looked at his watch. "It's almost eleven. You said I had to be in bed by ten on weeknights. How come we're going somewhere now?"

"I'm sorry about keeping you up late, but you can sleep in late in the morning. How would you like to stay with Aisling and Jim for a day or two?"

He shot me a puzzled look. "I like Jim. Aisling makes me play with her babies. All they do is crawl around, put everything in their mouths, and get slobber on it. And they spit their food onto the floor. It's gross."

"Babies are notorious for both their slobber and finicky eating habits, and you, my dumpling of delight, were no different. I may not have many memories of the past nine years, but I distinctly remember someone objecting to his strained carrots by spewing them all over his father."

Brom grinned. "I bet Gareth was pissed."

I ruffled his hair and smiled with him. "Extremely so. He was just about to leave to meet an important client, as I recall, and had to change his suit. It really was one of your finest baby moments."

"How come I can't go with you and Baltic?"

I walked downstairs with him to where a bag with a few hastily tossed-together items waited. "Because I'm not sure how long we'll be, and Thala is most likely going to be present. When Aisling was here earlier, she offered to have you stay with her and Drake in their house in Moscow, with Jim as company. I thought you'd like that for a day or possibly two."

His expression turned sober as he gave me a long look. "OK, but it's not going to be like last time, is it?"

"No," I reassured him. "Baltic and I won't be alone with Thala. We'll have others with us to keep us safe, all right?"

"OK," he repeated, and dropped his bag at the door,

next to the three others already waiting. "I'm going to go see if there's any more owl barf before we go."

"I want you back inside in ten minutes. Ten minutes!" I yelled after his swiftly retreating form.

A quick phone call to Aisling later, I was upstairs to inform Cyrene of the plans. "Do you wish to come with us?"

"To St. Petersburg? Are you kidding? That's where that slimy, scaly, horrible naiad-hater lives," she said with haughty grandeur. "I'd rather die than let him think I was chasing after him. In fact, if you don't mind, I'm going to leave in the morning. I think I need a vacation from all this stress and negativity. So thank you, but no. I will go to the Riviera, instead, and be with nice people, not insane black dragons."

I left her to her own plans, and made a fast perusal of my mental checklist of what needed to be done before we left. I was about to go into the kitchen to see if Pavel was there, but a low moan of pain caught the very edge of my hearing, causing me to whirl around and run for the small, damp sitting room. "Brom?" I threw open the door and came to a skidding halt in the middle of the room, my eyes wide with surprise.

Two people locked together in an embrace on the sofa flung themselves apart with such energy that one of them ended up on the floor.

"Oh," I said, trying not to grin as Maura hastily tucked one exposed breast back into her shirt. Savian, on the floor, also had an open shirt . . . and lipstick marks down his chest to his belt line, where they stopped. "Sorry, I didn't mean to interrupt."

"Savian was just . . . was helping me with . . . He was—" Maura began an explanation that all three of us knew wasn't going to go anywhere.

"Give it up, love; she's cannier than that," Savian said, buttoning his shirt while winking at me.

"I suppose it is going to be kind of hard to explain why you had your mouth on my boob when she came in," Maura said, her face beet red. She finished tidying herself up and cleared her throat. "I'd appreciate it if you didn't mention any of this to Emile, though, Ysolde."

"Really? Why? Is Dr. Kostich that protective of you?"

Savian rubbed his whiskery cheek and put an arm around Maura. "It's more that he has a bit of a grudge against me."

"You're a thief-taker. One who works for the Committee. Why would he have a grudge against you?"

"He found out I was taking jobs on the side for May and Gabriel, and he felt it was a conflict of interest. The truth is . . ." He glanced at Maura. Wearily, she nodded. "The truth is, I've been stricken off the thief-takers' roll. I'm freelance now."

"Ah. So he wouldn't welcome the news that you and Maura . . ." I nodded. "Gotcha. I assume those are your bags out in the hall?"

"Yes, we're ready to go," Maura said, brushing a hand down her shirt.

"Some of us are more than ready," Savian growled in her ear.

"Mmm, well, perhaps you can hold that thought until a more suitable time. We'll be leaving in about ten minutes. You got all the information you needed from Aisling, I assume?"

"I did. I think I'll go see if there is such a thing as bubble wrap in the house," Maura said, the sentence ending an octave higher than it started when Savian's hand slid down her back to her behind.

"Why bubble wrap?" I asked as I pulled out my cell phone.

She paused at the door and made a little face. "If I have to take a portal to Nepal, which is where your friend Aisling says the aerie is, then I'm going to want a restorative when I get there. If I wrap a bottle of dragon's blood and hold it tight to my chest, I should be able to bring it through the portal with me." She looked sadly at Savian. "I just wish you could come with me."

"I'll be there just as soon as I locate the sepulcher for Ysolde," he promised. "I'll take the first portal out to you and help you beat the daylights out of the dragons holding your mum."

"Are you sure you're going to be able to handle all the dragons by yourself?" I asked her, worried that our plan wasn't as well thought out as it should be.

"They're the least of my concerns," she said with a little smile. "One of the dragons at the *castillo* told me there were only two guards at the aerie simply because it's so impossible to get to . . . and get out of."

"I hope Aisling's directions were enough to get you there in time."

"Actually, I'm using her wyvern's directions. Evidently when Aisling went to the aerie, she took a longer route. It should take me only two hours of climbing, which leaves me enough time to disable the guards and get Mum out of there before Thala can call and order them to hurt her."

"I'd be happy to send Pavel with you," I offered for a second time.

She shook her head. "I'll be fine on my own. You need everyone to capture Thala. She won't have time to order anyone to harm my mother if she's fighting off an attack."

I said nothing but worried nonetheless.

"I'll help her find some packing for the bottle," Savian said, following Maura out of the room. He winked as he passed me.

"I just bet you will," I murmured to myself, then rang up Aisling, apologizing for the second call within ten minutes.

"That's fine. The twins don't want to go down for the

night, so we're trying to wear them out. Iarliath and I are having a rousing game of 'fling the toys against the wall and laugh hysterically when they bounce.' What's up? Need more info about the aerie?"

"No, I think that's fine. I forgot to tell you earlier that I have Drake's reward, and I wanted to reassure him that it'll be waiting for him when he has the sword."

"I'm so glad it's finally happening," Aisling said in a confidential tone. "Drake has been itching to do this job ever since we got home. He's trying to teach Ilona how to use a Wii controller, but she's teething and insists on sucking on it rather than pressing buttons as he insists she should. This will give him something more constructive to do."

I heard the masculine rumble of a voice in the background.

"She's six months old, Drake. She's not going to benefit from the honed-to-razor-sharpness hand-eye co-ordination that you get from playing Super Mario Brothers," Aisling said. "Sorry, Ysolde. You said you were going to leave shortly, yes? We'll meet you in St. Petersburg in . . . How long will it take us to get there, sweetie? Drake says it will take two hours to get the plane ready and fly out there, Ysolde, so expect us around one a.m. You're absolutely certain Dr. Kostich will take a portal at that time of night? He doesn't seem to me to be the sort of guy to do rash things like take red-eye flights."

"He has only a few hours to save his daughter, so yes, I think he will. We'll meet you outside the portal place, then."

"We? You're not bringing Baltic, are you?" She sounded appalled. "You didn't say you were bringing him."

"I was a bit rushed then, but yes, we're all going. But . . . er . . . Aisling, Baltic thinks I've arranged for Drake to steal the blade so that I can give it to him."

"Ah. Well, you will be, in a roundabout way."

"Yes. It's just the route it takes to get to him that will no doubt annoy him. So if you and Drake could keep mum about that, I'd appreciate it."

"Our lips are zipped. And by that I mean I'll leave Jim at home, so it can't spill the beans to Baltic, which we both know it would do in a heartbeat."

"Thanks. Nico will continue on with Brom to Moscow, if your offer of a pickup at the portal office is still open."

"Of course it is. We'll be delighted to have him stay with us for a couple of days. The babies love to play with Brom!"

I giggled to myself as I hung up, and made a mental note to give Brom a bonus to his weekly allowance to compensate for all the baby drool he would be encountering.

Less than an hour later, I grilled the employee at the St. Petersburg portal station about whether Dr. Kostich had arrived.

"No one's come through for two days," the man said in a mild Yorkshire accent, eyeing the money I held just out of his reach. "Just you lot, and we don't normally see dragons using portals around these parts."

"It's a bit of an emergency," I explained.

He glanced to the side, and I turned to consider the sight of two mussed-up dragons sitting on the floor, each clutching a paper cup. Taking a cue from Maura, I also brought a bottle of dragon's blood wine with me. Holland and Savian were off finding two cars to hire.

"Aye, must be."

"We'd like to use your waiting room for a bit," I said, adding a few more bills to the ones I waved at him. "If your portal isn't that much used, you won't mind us doing that, I'm sure."

His gaze snapped back to the money, watching as I gently waved it in the air. "No, I don't see as that would be a problem. So long as you're a customer."

I smiled and handed him the money, then spent the next five minutes coaxing Baltic and Pavel into the waiting room. They were both prone to be a bit snappish, which I put down to having had to use a portal multiple times in the last week. Evidently, the cumulative effect of portalling was a bit more devastating than I had anticipated.

I called Brom to make sure that Nico and he had arrived safely in Moscow, and that one of Drake's men was waiting for them (he was), answered a call from Maura to assure me that she, too, had (barely) survived the portalling, and then set about rallying my crew.

"Honestly, I don't know what you're making such a big fuss about," I told Baltic, when he refused to get off the couch he had collapsed on some fifteen minutes before. "You're acting like a big baby. You don't see Pavel demanding to be left alone so he can die in peace, do you? He's just fine and dandy."

Pavel lurched past me, ran face-first into a wall, rebounded off it with a shake of his head, and fell over onto his back with a little gurgle.

Baltic looked up from where he lay prone on the couch, and he glared at me just as if I were to blame.

"Fine! I'm to blame! You can yell at me later if you like, but Savian and Holland are going to be back with the cars any minute now, and I want you up and ready to follow Dr. Kostich the second he arrives."

He growled. He actually growled.

I bent down and kissed him, saying softly into his mouth, "Just keep in mind that when this is all over, I'm going to be so grateful to you, I'll be willing to let you be bossy in bed for a long, long time."

He stopped growling and started looking interested, but I caught his roving hands and stepped backward, pulling him to his feet. "Come along, handsome. We have work to do before we get to the rewards."

"Rewards, plural?" he asked, giving Pavel a hand up. "It had better be plural, because my temper will need much assuaging after this."

I pinched his butt as I passed him. "Right. I think a few jogging laps around the block will do much to clear your respective heads. I'll stay here in case Dr. Kostich shows up. Would I be out of line if I asked you to hold hands so no one gets into trouble? Oh, Pavel, ouch, is your head all right? Yes, I agree, that doorjamb really is in the way. Maybe next time you should keep your eyes open when you walk through a doorway. And I think perhaps you should *walk* around the block, not jog."

Another fifteen minutes later, and not only had Savian and Holland arrived with two vehicles, but the dragons were all more or less operating on all thrusters again, although Pavel's run-in with the door left him with a nasty cut on his forehead that was taking its own sweet time to heal, no doubt due to his general state of discombobulation.

"Are we late?"

I spun around to see a familiar woman step out of the portalling office. "May?"

"I hope we didn't miss anything. Aisling said we had to be quick, and here we are."

"Ah," a dark-haired, dark-eyed man said as he followed her out onto the sidewalk. He looked around, taking a deep breath, his face alight with pleasure. "St. Petersburg. The pillaging that went on here. The violence that ensued. Surrounding villages fired to the ground . . . the sweet sound of screams filling the night . . . the many captives I took back to my palace later, for even more fun . . . good memories, every one!"

I gawked at the man.

"This is Magoth," May said with a deep breath. "He's a former demon lord."

"The best there was, eh, sweetness?" the black-haired

Magoth said, turning his eyes to me. His brows rose as he shimmied toward me, all undulating power and rampant sex appeal. He wore leather pants, and a black silk shirt open nearly to his navel. He reminded me of someone, but I couldn't put my finger on it until a little breeze caught his hair and lifted it back. "And who do we have here? Sweet May, who is this delicious-looking blonde, and is she into threesomes?"

Baltic was still far enough away down the sidewalk that I risked setting fire to Magoth's feet.

"Oh, don't do that," May said quickly, causing me to tamp down briskly on the fire. "He just enjoys that sort of thing. Trust me on that."

"Oooh," Magoth purred, trailing a finger down my arm. His touch was icy, as if he'd been sitting in a refrigerator. "Someone likes to play rough. Go ahead, sweetheart—fire me up!"

"Magoth, you promised!" May said, punching him in the arm. "This is Ysolde. She's the mate to the dread wyvern Baltic, and he won't tolerate any crap from you any more than Gabriel lets you hit on me, so stop it right now, or the whole thing is off."

"Ysooolde," Magoth drawled, bowing over my hand and kissing my knuckles, his tongue snaking out to lick between two of my fingers before I snatched my hand back. "Would you like to see my curse?"

"Say no," May advised.

"No," I told him, then asked her, "Is there a reason you felt it necessary to bring a demon lord with you?"

"Magoth is a *former* demon lord," she corrected. "He's without about ninety-seven percent of his power, so he's mostly safe to be around. Although he has a libido the size of Montana."

"So kind of you to say, sweet May. Now," he said, rubbing his hands together, "where do we start?"

"Gabriel says we need a demon lord for the lifting of

the curse; although he only has three percent of working abilities, they should be enough."

"Ah. I thought Aisling could do that since she's a demon lord, as well."

"Yes, but she's a good demon lord, and she can't be used for this purpose because it'll proscribe her again. Thus, Magoth. He's the only demon lord we can deal with safely, now that Abaddon is in uproar over recent happenings."

"What recent happenings?" I asked.

May waved away the question. "Bael was overthrown. It doesn't really matter to us now, except in so much as all the demon lords are fighting for ascendancy. Magoth is our best shot."

"In so many ways," he said, waggling his hips at me. "Would you like me to show you three or four of them?"

"I'd like to give you a big old whack upside the head, but I suppose that wouldn't fly," I told him.

To my horror, his eyes lit up with sexual interest. "Oooh, you like it rough, too? Excellent. Perhaps you and I can get together a little later on and compare our favorites list, hmm?"

"You know, you make me appreciate just how noncreepy Constantine is," I told the former demon lord. "I'm going to have to thank him for that, later."

"Did I hear my name invoked?"

My shoulders slumped as Constantine shimmered into view.

"What do you have to tell me, my adorable little squab?"

I turned to face him. "Squab, Constantine? Really? Squab?"

He grinned. "They're cute. And I like to bite them."

"Do you really?" Magoth said, giving Constantine a once-over. "I suppose it would be preferable to bats, as that one rock star was known to do, but I myself prefer a nice, poisonous tree frog if I'm going to bite off the head of any animal. The tang of the poison as it courses through one's blood nicely counterpoints the robust, earthier flavor of the frog. There are some salamanders that are almost as nice, but not quite the same sort of a rush, if you know what I mean."

Constantine blinked at Magoth. May groaned, and turned, suddenly realizing her mate wasn't with her. "Gabriel? Where are you? What are you doing in there?" She reentered the portal office.

"I don't bite the heads off anything, let alone a frog," Constantine corrected. "Who the devil are you, anyway?"

I made the introductions, providing brief explanations of who each of them was before watching as May led Gabriel from the portal office.

"I didn't know dreadlocks could stand on end," I commented as she fussed over him, straightening his shirt and his eyebrows, then handing him one shoe, which evidently had come off during the portalling. "It's a good look, though. Where are Maata and Tipene?"

"In Australia, where any sane dragon should be," he answered, feeling his hair, and smoothing it down to its normal state. "When they found out we'd have to take a portal to reach here, they refused to join us, although they send their regards to you, and compliments to Pavel."

"This is going to sound horribly rude, and I don't for a second mean it to be taken that way, but why *are* you here?" I asked as Baltic, his eyes narrowed on Gabriel, approached, the air bristling with electricity.

"Aisling said you—" May stopped at the sight of Baltic, shooting me a questioning glance. I shook my head just enough to warn her against finishing the sentence.

"Look who's here," I told Baltic as he stopped beside me. "It's May and Gabriel and May's former demon lord, Magoth."

"Ah, the dread wyvern we've heard so much about,"

Magoth said, giving Baltic a quick visual examination. "Any time you and the so-luscious Ysolde wish to join me in a quick orgy, just say the word."

Baltic rolled his eyes, but Constantine said, "Orgies? We're having an orgy? What sort of an orgy? A bondage orgy? Or just a regular one?"

"I vote bondage," Magoth said, waggling his eyebrows at May.

"Seconded," Constantine said.

"No one is having an orgy, bondage or otherwise," I said firmly, trying desperately to reclaim control of the conversation. "I do have to say I'm a bit surprised to see you here, May."

"Aisling said you were going to need some help, so we thought we'd pop over to Russia and see if we could be of assistance."

Gabriel looked in surprise at her but said nothing.

Baltic's favorite scowl was firmly in place as he faced Gabriel. "We do not need the help of silver dragons."

I rounded on him, slapping my hand on his chest hard enough to make him look down in surprise. "That is enough!"

"Mate, you—"

"Oooh, she *does* like rough play," Magoth said sotto voce. "I like her."

"You can't have her," Constantine said somewhat prosaically. "If she leaves Baltic, I have a claim on her. She was my mate for about five minutes before he challenged me for her."

"So she plays around, then, hmm?"

I ignored the comedy team to focus on Baltic. "No! It's enough, do you hear me? Far and away beyond enough. There will be no more slurs made against silver dragons—do you understand? No more! It's through, Baltic. This war between the black and silver dragons is done, finished, ended once and for all."

"I will not forget what they did to us," Baltic snapped, his fingers tightening.

"Well, you'd just better learn to live with it, because I have had enough! We are all going to get along if it kills us. Do you hear?"

"It killed me," Constantine quipped.

"They probably *can* hear you; we could hear you two blocks away, and we had the car windows closed."

I spun around to see Aisling climbing out of a car, Drake at her side. I was about to greet them when Aisling added, "Oh no, not you again."

Magoth turned to her and to my absolute surprise, leered. "If it isn't the delectable little Guardian. No longer pregnant? Pity. I like fecund women."

Drake snarled something extremely obscene as he took a step toward the man.

"Is your lovely and inventive mother here?" Magoth asked Drake, rubbing his hands together in a manner that made my flesh crawl.

Drake shuddered. "Fortunately, she is well out of your grasp."

"Do I want to know why he's here?" Aisling asked May, gesturing at Magoth.

"Not really," May said with a weak smile.

"Well, I'm glad you guys got here in time, nonetheless," Aisling said before greeting Gabriel. "At least I hope we're in time. Are we?"

"Yes. We've been here for half an hour, but it took that long for some of us to get over the effects of portalling."

Drake gave Baltic and Pavel scathing looks. "Portals are not pleasant, but they are not that disorienting."

"They are if you've been forced to take three of them in four days," Baltic replied, sending the scathing look back to Drake.

"*Three* times?" Drake looked incredulous. Gabriel

appeared to be sick at the thought. "I withdraw my statement, and offer, instead, my congratulations on surviving with all your limbs intact."

"I feel guilty enough; you really don't need to drive the point home," I told Drake with a thin-lipped expression I've found works well. "The answer to the question is yes, you're all in time. We haven't seen hide nor hair of Dr. Kostich."

"What is this?" a male voice asked behind me. "Why do you concern yourself with my hair? Why are you and that behemoth of a dragon lurking in wait outside the portalling office? And what are they doing here, too?"

I turned around slowly, slapping a pleasant smile on my face. "Hello, Dr. Kostich."

Dr. Kostich's expression, lit by the soft yellow glow of sodium lights, was grim to start with, but it became even grimmer on beholding me. "I might have known I'd find you here. No doubt you intend on getting in my way."

"Hey now," I said, about to tell him a thing or two, but then I remembered that he was probably quite worried about Violet. There was a strained look about his pale blue eyes that hinted at emotions not evident on the surface. Instead of protesting his slur, I simply said, "We're here to help you. As a matter of fact, we've gone to considerable expense, and quite a bit of personal discomfort, in order to do that—something you would do well to remember when you start calling Baltic's dragon form fat. Which it isn't, but I know you have an issue differentiating between a really buff dragon form and Jabba the Hut."

Dr. Kostich's eyes narrowed as he looked from Baltic and me to the others. "You're not here to help me," he said slowly, his head whipping around until he could pin me back with a glare that came close to stripping my eyebrows right off my head. "You're here to steal the von Endres blade!"

"Now why would you think that?" I asked, trying to force an innocent expression to my face.

He pointed at Drake. "The green wyvern is here, the only being who has ever been able to break into the L'au-dela vault until last year, when my misbenighted granddaughter and her band of lunatic dragons repeated the act."

Drake pursed his lips. "Someone else broke into the vault?"

"In a manner of speaking. Maura bribed a guard to allow her and her band of thugs into it." Dr. Kostich looked about to explode at the memory.

Aisling patted Drake's hand and said softly, "It's all right, Drake. Your record still stands. You can stop thinking about new ways to top Maura's break-in."

"Hmm," he said thoughtfully.

"Yes, well, we have more important things to focus on right now," I said, taking Baltic's wrist to look at his watch. "When do you expect Thala to arrive?"

Dr. Kostich looked at me as if I had suddenly turned into a tiny pink elephant.

"Look, we know you're here to trap her at the sepulcher. We also know you must have given her the information about its whereabouts. We're here to help you make sure that you do, in fact, capture her. Er . . . just for curiosity's sake, how did you get the information about the location of the sepulcher to her?"

"That is my business, Tully Sullivan. Do not try to deny that you are here so that you can pretend to assist me in rescuing Violet, but secretly plan to steal the von Endres sword," Kostich countered.

"We promised Maura to help, and by the saints, we are going to do so."

Dr. Kostich's gaze shifted to Baltic, who was looking somewhat bored. "You planned this, didn't you? You planned it when I took the sword away from you months

ago. Don't deny you had a hand in this—it was your lieutenant who kidnapped my daughter. You swore to have
the sword back, and this is your way of achieving that
goal, isn't it?"

"It's a way, yes," Baltic said.

I looked at him in outright surprise. "You didn't tell
Thala to kidnap Violet, did you?"

"No. I thought simply to rob the sepulcher to reclaim
my sword. But so long as Thala did kidnap the archimage's daughter, we might as well take advantage of it."
He turned back to Dr. Kostich, his gaze shrewd. "As my
mate has said, we will help you capture Thala, and force
her to return your daughter . . . for a price—my sword."

Gabriel made an unhappy little noise. I shot him a
warning glance, which was fortunately enough to keep
him from speaking up.

Kostich was silent for a few seconds, but after some
general seething, finally said, "I would not risk my own
daughter's life for something so trivial as a sword. But
neither will I give it up to a dragon. It belongs to a mage,
and you are not one. I refuse your offer."

"What?" I cried as he pushed past me, and with a
quick glare at Savian, strode past him toward a car that
had just pulled up. "You can't refuse. We're talking about
Violet. Even now, Maura is on her way to the aerie where
Violet's being held, so she can release her and bring her
back home."

"What I *can't* do is stop my granddaughter from con-
sorting with dragons any more than I could stop her
from involvement with the ouroboros tribe she insisted
on joining, more's the pity. I can, however, draw a line
at what I will and will not countenance, and turning a
blind eye to the true purpose of that insane necromancer is simply not acceptable. I will take care of the matter myself, without the assistance of you or any other
dragons."

"You have really got a chip on your shoulder about us, don't you?" I couldn't stop from saying. "Does Violet really matter so little to you? Is your pride so overbearing that you really believe you can take Thala on by yourself and beat her?"

"I have called up the local members of the watch," he told me as he opened the car door. "We will deal with this dragon just as we've dealt with everything else—the right way."

"You are the most obnoxious mage I've ever met," I said, wanting to set him alight with my dragon fire. "Even considering the stress you're under."

"And you are the most objectionable dragon I've met. Next to your husky mate, that is."

"Objectionable!" Aisling said at the same time that I asked of Baltic, "If we all worked together, do you think we could bring Dr. Kostich to his knees?"

"Dominatrix," Magoth said, nodding. "I approve."

Dr. Kostich's fingers twitched as he glared at me, but when Baltic moved protectively in front of me, he simply raised an eyebrow at us.

"I know I could," Aisling said softly.

Dr. Kostich's gaze flickered her way, making her take a step backward, and causing Drake to move in front of her in the same gesture of warning as Baltic had just made.

"Your threats do nothing but waste my time," Dr. Kostich said with a grim note of finality. He climbed into the car without another look back at us.

"Now what?" Aisling asked as the car pulled away and disappeared into the night.

"Now we find the sepulcher," Savian said, grinning as he cracked his knuckles.

"I thought you knew where it was," Aisling said.

"Er . . . not really. Savian's been trying to find it but hasn't had much luck. He says it could be one of four places, and he just didn't have time to investigate the possibilities before this business with Violet happened. That's about to change, though, right, Savian?"

"Yes. I'll take the first car," he said, heading for that vehicle.

"Call when you know where he's going," I yelled after him.

He waggled his hand as he got into the car.

"But how—" Aisling started to say. Drake murmured something in her ear. "He can? Really? I thought May was the one who could track people."

"I can," May said, and with a secretive smile, disappeared from sight, her voice distant and muffled as she said, "I'll follow Dr. Kostich's traces in the shadow world while Savian follows him here. One way or another, we'll find him. Gabriel?"

"Would someone mind if my body accompanied them in their car?" Gabriel asked. "I can walk in the shadow world with May, but only in incorporeal form."

"Been there, done that—hate it when it happens during a challenge," Constantine's voice said, his body having faded from view several minutes before. "I shall ride with Ysolde."

"Like hell, you will," Baltic grumbled as he pushed me toward the first car. "You can ride with Gabriel."

"I still don't understand how we expect to save Maura's mom and take the sword if Dr. Kostich gets to the sepulcher first," Aisling said as Drake opened a door to his car so Gabriel could get in and, assumedly, take his consciousness off to the beyond, that alternate version of reality mages and the fey inhabited.

"We won't be able to take the sword from him without a fight," I agreed as Baltic held a swift consultation with Pavel. "That's why we're going to try to get there first. Once Savian knows which of the four locations Dr. Kostich is headed, we'll head straight there."

"But Dr. Kostich," Aisling said as Drake tried to push her into their car.

I smiled. "Savian will see to it that he's delayed. He's a very good tracker, Aisling. And he's dating Dr. Kostich's granddaughter, so he'll be very interested in making himself look good in Maura's eyes. And what better way to do that than to be on the winning team? Anyone need a potty break before we head out? We should probably be ready to go the second we hear which location is the target."

A squabble broke out between Constantine and Magoth over who got to ride with whom, but in the end, everyone squeezed into one of the two remaining cars present and waited for Savian's call.

Chapter Sixteen

"So this is the famed sepulcher," a male voice said behind me.

I smiled as Savian appeared around the edge of a clump of tall fir trees. It was then I noticed his condition.

"What happened to you?" I asked, walking in a circle around him. He was shirtless, his jeans tattered, revealing rather surprising tiger-striped underwear in a few spots, his chest and arms covered in soot. His face was as black as his chest, with fingers of lighter color fanning out along his laugh lines. A little blood leaked out from under a strip of material that had been bound around one of his upper arms, and he appeared to have lost both of his eyebrows.

"Dr. Kostich," he said, twitching slightly.

"Oh dear. Do you need a healer?"

"No. I'll live." He squinted at the sepulcher. "I take it Thala isn't here yet?"

"Not yet."

"Are you sure that's it?" Aisling asked, nodding

toward the building. "It's a ruins. Dr. Kostich would never put a vault in a ruins. Would he?"

"It looks like a ruins, but trust me, it's not. It's layered with prohibitive arcane magic."

"That doesn't affect May, does it?" Savian asked, gingerly feeling his forehead.

"No, it doesn't, but May has worked through the protection and made it to the inside. She and Gabriel's ethereal self are having a look around in there to see what's what before Drake takes over."

"I had a feeling it might be this place." Savian considered the redbrick ruins of what must have once been a glorious Russian Orthodox church. "It felt wrong for what it was, if you know what I mean."

I studied the building that the L'au-dela had turned into its sepulcher. Nearest us was a tall round columnated tower, topped with a spire bearing the Orthodox cross. Gothic rounded windows and columns ran down the body of the church, ending in a huge dome on the far end, most of which was still standing. Surrounding the remains of the church was a thick stand of firs, and the air, even at night, was sharp with the scent of pine. Bats flew overhead as they searched for their evening meal, the waxing moon partially hidden by some clouds, but peeping out now and again to shine down an almost unearthly glow upon the building.

"It certainly is atmospheric," Aisling said, rubbing her arms as she glanced around somewhat nervously. "I wonder where Drake's gotten to."

"How did it go with Dr. Kostich?" I asked Savian. "Other than his attempt to blow you up."

His expression hardened. "It went. I caught up with them about three miles outside the forest. I tried to take them by surprise, but Kostich saw me just as I jumped him. That was when he got off the arcane blast, but despite that, I managed to knock him out long enough to restrain him with some duct tape and nylon rope."

"I hope that doesn't make things worse for you and Maura."

He shrugged. "It had to be done." He slid me a look from the corner of his eye, then suddenly grinned. "I can't tell you how good it felt to use that neck pinch on him. He dropped like a sack of mages. Then I tied up his driver and him, and drove them off a side path into the woods where I hope no one will find them until we're done here."

"The watch is still on its way," I reminded him.

"Yes. Hopefully not so many that we can't handle them." He looked around. "Where are the others?"

"May and Gabriel are inside, as I said, although Gabriel's body is propped up next to the building. Drake and his bodyguard, István, are securing the perimeter. May's demon lord got too close to Aisling, and Drake set him on fire, which he just seemed to enjoy, so he went off with Constantine to discuss something about spectral whips. I really don't want to know more than that. And Baltic, Pavel, and Holland are doing something I also don't want to know about with a couple of electric mantraps that Drake brought along with him. I should check on Baltic, speaking of that. He needs to discuss with Constantine what has to be done to deal with Thala, and there's no way he'll do that without me there to nag . . . er . . . guide him."

He laughed as I headed around the side of the building, calling after me in a soft voice, "I'll go back to town, unless you think you need me here."

"No, you go to Nepal. I'm sure Maura could use your help more than we will need you. Thank you for everything, Savian."

He saluted me. "A pleasure, as always. Except the arcane blast. I'll call when we have Maura's mum to safety."

"Godspeed," I called after him, then made my way through the encroaching forest around one side of the sepulcher, passing Gabriel's relaxed form on my way. I paused to check that he was all right, then continued on around the far side of the church, where the huge round dome sat over a semicircular bulge of brick and stone columns. In the shadow of one of the columns, I could see the faint images of Baltic and Pavel as they stood together, consulting about something. "Did you set your traps?" I asked when I was close enough for them to hear me.

"As a matter of fact, I did," a voice answered, but it didn't belong to Baltic. It wasn't even male. I gasped as I spun around, a noise that was cut short as Thala, emerging from the nothing that was the beyond, slapped a hand around my mouth, and before I could so much as blink, wrapped a thin, very sharp wire around my neck. "I didn't think it would be you I caught, though. However, this will work, too."

Baltic glanced toward me, did a double take, and roared his fury to the night sky even as he leaped toward us, a brief glimpse of moonlight shimmering along the white scales that covered his dragon form.

Thala spun us around so that I was between the two of them, the wire digging painfully into my neck. "This is a razor garrote. Any closer, and I'll decapitate your mate."

That stopped him. He stood just out of reach, softly panting fire.

"I don't know what you think you're going to do here, but you should be aware that we're not going to let you get away with anything," I said, being very careful to not move as I spoke. "Nor are we going to let harm come to Violet."

She laughed, tightening the wire just enough to make me gasp in pain. I ground back a snarl, keeping my gaze steady on Baltic. "You always were an interfering bitch. Do you really think I care the least about you or Kostich's daughter? I'm here for one thing only, and nothing will stop me from taking it."

Baltic crossed his arms as he returned to human form. "The sword is mine, Thala. It was given to *me*."

"To hold until such time as it was needed again, and that time is now," she countered, jerking me around until we faced the wall of the sepulcher. The wire, unfortunately, tightened even more. Wetness trickled down my neck and chest as I tried to look out of the corner of my eye to see what Baltic was doing. I knew full well that he wouldn't allow Thala to slice off my head, but I worried that he might not have the patience to wait to attack her before the others—including Constantine—realized that she had arrived. I prayed that Pavel had slid off around the other way and was warning everyone.

"And how do you expect to take it?" Baltic inquired, gesturing toward the building. "The archimage has placed much protection on it, mostly arcane, and necromancers have a particular aversion to arcane magic."

I felt, rather than saw, Thala's smile as she said simply, "I am not as weak as you believe, Baltic. I will destroy the sepulcher just as I destroyed your house. I will sing an earth song."

In the distance, I heard a shout of alarm as Pavel had evidently reached the others. Thala must have heard it, as well, for without further ado, she opened her mouth and began to sing.

I have little recollection of the dirge she sang that destroyed our previous house around us, but Baltic told me later it was an air song, a spell that literally exploded the house with a force equivalent to several traditional bombs. I dug through my faulty memory as Thala inhaled and began to sing.

Dirges, I knew, were a form of dark magic, spoken in the form of a song, and mastered only by those who were very adept. I watched in amazement when black, twisted roots boiled up from the earth around the sepulcher, twisting and twining around the building like so many horrible tentacles, and it was then I realized the full power of the earth dirge.

The noise issuing from Thala was horrible, a low, grating sound that seemed to be made up of tormented screams from the very depths of the earth, tortured and tainted by darkness, filled with hopelessness, scraping away bits of my soul as it continued to urge the earth itself to destroy that which had been made by man.

The roots wrapped around the building, and with one final swelling of Thala's song, exploded outward in a flying mass of bricks, stone, and wood.

Centuries of dust, decay, and despair filled the air, swirling around us in a dense cloud, choking the lungs and vision. The garrote dug in even deeper as I coughed, my eyes widening when the cloud started to dissipate. Behind me, I could hear the sounds of people approaching, and the cries asking for an explanation of what just happened.

"What the—" Aisling's sentence ended in a violent attack of coughing as she approached.

"Hmm," Baltic said, waving his hand through the air to clear the air of dust as he eyed what remained of the side wall. A good third of it was missing, leaving a jagged, raw entrance into the sepulcher. Inside, part of the ceiling had come down onto the stone floor. A hand emerged from under the debris, shoving it aside.

"Still think I can't circumvent Kostich's protections?" Thala asked him with a note of smugness that made me want to slap her.

"Mayling!" Gabriel shot past us from outside the sepulcher, hurdling the fallen stones to yank bricks and chunks of wood off May.

"I'm OK," May said, coughing as she crawled out of

the mass of stone. "There was some sort of statue here, and it gave me shelter. What happened?"

"Who . . . oh, the shadow walker," Thala said dismissively. "That will teach her to be where she shouldn't be. Stand back or Ysolde will die. And when *I* kill, they stay dead."

This last was spoken to Drake, who approached us with István.

Baltic jerked, his eyes narrowing on Thala. Briefly, I wondered what had startled him so, but my attention was soon claimed elsewhere as the others formed a semicircle around us.

Thala's voice was amused as she spoke to Baltic. "You don't really believe you can stop me with a few dragons, do you? Really, Baltic, I thought you knew me better than that."

"I thought I did, as well," he said softly, once again causing me to roll my eyes toward him in surprise. He had an indescribable look on his face, something akin to speculation and confusion. "You will release Ysolde."

Thala was silent for a moment. "You really would give up the sword for her, wouldn't you? When I was held prisoner, the green wyvern told me you did, but I didn't believe him. I thought Kostich must have tricked it from you, or that you gave it to him as part of your plan to take over the weyr, but it was true that you willingly gave it up for a mere woman?"

"She is my mate," Baltic said, his face now completely unreadable, but his fire was burning extremely hot, just beneath the surface, barely contained. I had a feeling that the slightest spurt of emotion would unleash it.

"You have become as tiresome as she," Thala said, and to my utter surprise, whipped away the razor wire and shoved me toward him. "If you wish to be a fool, then far be it from me to stop you. You will not see my sword again, however."

She started toward the destroyed wall, but Baltic was instantly there in front of her, in dragon form once again.

She stopped a few feet from him, laughing and shaking her head. "And now you prove to me that in addition to your heart having grown soft, so has your head. Do you believe there is any way you can stop me from doing exactly as I want, dragon?"

"Yes," Baltic answered simply.

"We outnumber you, Thala," I pointed out, tearing off the sleeve of my blouse and wrapping it around my neck.

"I am not so foolish as to come alone," she said, gesturing to the side.

"Bloody hell," Savian muttered as a group of about twenty or so dragons emerged from the woods, each armed with weapons used in centuries past, all of them in their natural forms. Red, blue, black, and even two green dragons came toward us, the clouds shifting just enough to allow the icy fingers of moonlight to caress the metal of their weapons.

But it was the two people who trailed behind them who had my blood boiling.

"Oh goody," I said, flexing my fingers. "Retribution time."

"Retribution?" Aisling asked, quickly drawing protective wards over Drake and everyone around her.

"That's Gareth, my bigamous former husband, and his evil wife, Ruth." I smiled, wondering which of my spells would be best for them.

"Oy. I think we're going to need help more than Brom needs distracting," Aisling murmured, and added in a whisper, "Effrijim, I summon thee."

The demon dog appeared before us, popcorn spilling out of its lips as it blinked in surprise. "Man, Ash, give a guy some warning next time. Brom and I were going to have a *Monty Python* fest ... fires of Abaddon! It's that crazy lady and her badass posse! And Magoth! What's he doing here?"

"About to enjoy some roast demon," Magoth said with a smile that sent a little shiver down my spine.

"You do, and you'll find your ass back in the Akasha," Aisling warned before turning her attention to the dragons who moved en masse toward us. "Effrijim, I command thee to attack Thala!"

"What?" Jim shrieked.

Thala spun around to face her just as I caught a flicker of movement from my peripheral vision. Drake slid into the shadows of the interior, and disappeared. No doubt he was off to break into the vault while Aisling distracted Thala. I was surprised he allowed her to do such a dangerous thing, but that surprise faded away instantly when Baltic, Pavel, and Gabriel all rushed Thala at the same time, pushing Aisling a safe distance away.

"It seems we're always fighting someone," I grumbled as Thala went down underneath a pile of dragons, only to send them flying a few seconds later. "Toads. Maybe I'll turn Gareth and Ruth into toads. Would you like that, Gareth?" I bellowed as the dragons in front of him came into range. "Would you like to be a big, fat, slimy toad? That's what your character is, so you might as well be one in truth!"

Gareth didn't react, leading me to believe that he hadn't heard me. He ran after the dragons, a gun in his hand, and Ruth bringing up the rear.

I eyed the nearest of Thala's cohorts as he approached. Aisling had sent Jim off to tackle the oncoming group of dragons, her hands flying as she started throwing out binding wards. Holland and Pavel rushed past me to the onslaught, Pavel—like the other dragons—in a more robust form. His tail slashed through the air as he caught the first dragon across the chest. Holland, with a battle cry that would do William Wallace proud, leaped across him and onto the dragon as he went down. Jim flung itself onto the next dragon, leaving me standing alone as Gareth, catching sight of me, veered off from the pack and headed toward me with a wicked look on his face.

I smiled, waiting for him. As soon as he got close enough, I would whip into my dragon form and beat the living daylights out of him. I remembered just how much power I wielded in that form, and even though Gareth was armed, I knew I could take him.

Behind me, I heard Baltic call out as he and Gabriel struggled to contain Thala. Just as soon as I took care of Gareth and Ruth, I'd fetch Constantine, and I'd demand he do whatever it was he could do to disable her, but until then . . .

"I knew I'd find you here," Gareth sneered as he raised the gun to me, Ruth dancing behind him and urging him to shoot. "I'm going to take care of you once and for all. You're coming with us, and you're going to manifest some gold, or I'll kill you where you stand."

"You pathetic little snotball! You'll get no more gold from me," I said, yelling an archaic oath as I shifted into dragon form.

Or rather, I tried.

"Oh holy—ack!"

I ducked when Gareth opened fire on me, swearing when I stumbled over the prone form of a dead ouroboros dragon.

"Then you'll die, you stupid woman. I'm tired of you and your brat always messing up my life. Ruth's right— it's time to take care of you once and for all!" Gareth snarled. The gun spat out more bullets, but either Gareth's aim was atrocious, or I was extremely lucky, because none of them struck me.

Snatching up a morning star that the dead dragon nearest me still clutched, I swung it as I bolted for the woods, once again trying to shift my form into that of an attractive, if slightly puny-armed, white dragon. Nothing happened other than I immediately got a stitch in my side.

"Great, now I'm going to die because I'm out of shape and my shifter is broken," I panted as I lunged past the first tree, desperately trying to think of a spell that would disable Gareth so I could beat the crap out of him.

"You can run, but you can't hide from me, you coward," Gareth shouted as he followed me into the woods.

"Pot, kettle, black," I yelled back. In the distance, I heard Baltic calling for me again. I hesitated for a second, wanting to reassure him, but not wishing to take him away from containing Thala.

"I will blow your brains out, and while you lie writhing on the ground, I'll tell you exactly what I think of you," Gareth spat out as he leaped out at me, raising the gun.

"Oh please, like anyone cares what you think." Before Gareth could pull the trigger, I took him by surprise by running toward rather than away from him. I swung the morning star as I did so. Gareth squawked and ducked, leaping to the side. I dashed around a huge ash tree, saying as I did, "Sky below and earth above, sinners all repent, tree of butter and sea of dove, be thee now absent."

There was a pregnant silence that lasted for the count of four, and then . . . nothing. "Be thee now absent? Really, brain, that's what you came up with?" I stood up and peered around the tree, braced to find Gareth and his gun, but rather than a flesh and blood man, a life-sized statue of one stood in the classic shooter's pose, one arm outstretched as he was evidently about to fire again.

I put my finger out and touched the gun. It came away slightly damp. I looked at the surprised bird that sat on top of the statue, showing it my finger. "It's butter."

The bird, a dove, blinked at me, and ruffled its tail feathers.

I sighed. "When I said tree of butter and sea of dove, I was actually referring to colors, not actual . . . oh, never mind." I considered my former husband for a moment, then nodded. "Fitting justice, I think, Gareth. I hope it's a really, really hot day today. If I'm feeling benevolent later, I'll send someone out to scrape up what's left of you."

The dove flew off as I turned and marched out to where the battle was in full force. "One down, one to go. And there she is."

I smiled as I emerged from the trees with my morning star in hand. Ruth, who had been hiding behind a large boulder, spun around when I called her name.

"What are you doing there? Why aren't you dead? You're supposed to be dead!" She stomped her foot. "Where's Gareth? What have you done to him? Dammit, he was supposed to take care of you!"

Behind me, a couple of men ran toward us.

"Gareth is a bit busy melting right now," I told her with a satisfied smile. "And I think, I really think I've just about had enough of you."

"Are you insane as well as stupid?" She tossed her head. "I'm the daughter of Antonia von Endres. I'm a necromancer of great repute. You're not even dirt beneath my feet. You're below dirt. You're subdirt! I loathed you when we first found you, and I've loathed you every minute since. Gareth was always too soft where you were concerned, but I'm not soft, Sullivan." Her face was red and twisted with hate as she swept a hand toward a wild patch of tall grass and broken headstones. "And now you're going to see just how insignificant you really are. I will raise the dead, and they will rend the flesh from your bones, which I will grind into dust, and sprinkle on my doorstep so that I can walk over your remains every single day!"

"Seriously? Rend my flesh? You don't think that's a little over the top?"

She screamed and turned to run for the tiny graveyard. I looked over at the two men who approached. "Are you the watch?"

They paused. "Yes." The nearest one narrowed his eyes at me. "And you are . . . ?"

"That's really not important right now. But you should know that the woman over there, the one waving her arms around in the graveyard, is a necromancer, and she's about to raise some liches so she can kill Dr. Kostich, whom, incidentally, she just admitted she has bound and gagged and hidden away in some woods."

The two men looked at each other, then at Ruth.

"Dr. Kostich told us we must protect the sepulcher. Is that fighting I hear?"

"Yes, a wacked-out necromancer—sister to that woman, by the way—is trying to get into it." I smiled. "I used to be Dr. Kostich's apprentice, you know, and I'm positive he'll be very pissed if you let Ruth get away. If I were you, I'd take care of her first, then go nab her sister. It'll be a hundred times harder to catch either of them if Ruth raises some liches to do her bidding."

The men hesitated, then with a nod, dashed off toward the graveyard. I turned on my heel and ran toward the audible sounds of fighting that came from the other side of the church. "I'm not proud of that, but it's better than turning her into butter. That leaves us with just one crazy woman to go."

As I ran around the north side of the church, it was evident that Team Baltic was getting the better of the ouroboros dragons.

It was clearly time to stop the bloodshed and take charge of the situation. "All right, I'm here, I'm armed, and I have the power of butter behind me! I want everyone to stop fighting and settle down!"

No one, of course, paid the slightest bit of attention to me. Drat them all.

"I'm getting sick and tired of everyone always fighting around here," I yelled as I stomped my way toward the mass of dragon bodies engaged in full battle. I paused at the sight of Magoth, now stark naked, his face painted blue, as he twirled a sword in one hand and leaped on the back of one of Thala's dragons before immediately beating him on the head with the flat side of the sword. "Where on earth did you find blue paint?"

"Ysolde!"

"I'm fine," I answered Baltic, who paused in the act of slashing at a dragon who was foolish enough to think he could take my darling dread wyvern. I raised the wooden handle of my morning star. "I picked up a toy."

He nodded as he handily backhanded the dragon before turning back to where Thala was fighting Gabriel and István. I gave myself a moment to admire the fact that he was actually dual-wielding swords, one in each hand as he flung himself on her. His face and upper chest were covered with blood, but I could see by the light in his eyes, and the spiral of dragon fire that wove around him, that he was having a fine time. "We really have to find you a hobby," I said to myself as I searched the crowd for Constantine.

"You OK?" Pavel asked as he danced past me, parrying a thrust from a green dragon. He, too, was armed with a sword. I gathered that as the ouroboros dragons fell, our people were picking up their weapons.

"Annoyed, but unharmed. Have you seen Constantine?"

"Over by the hole," he grunted, leaping high into the air when the dragon tried to cut off his legs. A roar of anger ripped through the night, followed by a black shape as Pavel shifted and attacked the green dragon.

I hurried over to the blasted wall, leaning inside it to bellow, "Constantine!"

"Holy Mary, you needn't yell, I'm right here," came the disembodied answer. "I think you deafened me."

Constantine's form appeared, somewhat transparent, but solid enough that I could grab his sleeve. "Come on. We have to stop Thala. Baltic's been using arcane magic and he's run out of steam, and she's not wearing out at all. Time for you to do your thing."

"What thing is that?"

"The shade thing that you can do to stop her. Come on! Stop dragging your heels."

"What will you give me if I help you?"

I stopped and turned to stare at him. "*What* did you say?"

He brushed his wrinkled sleeve and looked down his nose at me. "What will you give me as a payment for my assistance with the archimage's deranged daughter?"

Damned dragons and their intense need to bargain! "You said you'd help me because you loved me!" Outrage poured through me, igniting my own fire.

"I changed my mind," he said with a sniff. "I'm allowed to change my mind. I got you the shard, after all. I think I should have something for all my hard work."

I hefted the morning star, tempted to tell him exactly what I was going to give him, but reason tempered that desire. "What do you want?" I snapped.

He stroked his chin in a contemplative gesture. "I want you."

"Well, you can't have me."

He stroked some more. "Then I want a sept."

"You challenged Kostya and lost, remember? You can challenge him again, but the same thing will happen. You're dead, Constantine. You're a spirit. You can't be a wyvern and be a spirit. How do you expect to protect your sept if you run out of power every couple of minutes?"

He grimaced. "If I can't have you, and I can't have a sept, then I want to be with you in your sept."

I couldn't believe what I was hearing. "You want to join the light dragons?"

"Not particularly, but since that's where you are, it will have to suffice."

I blinked a couple of times, not sure what else to do. I couldn't begin to imagine what Baltic would have to say to me when I informed him that his most hated enemy, the madman responsible for the destruction of so many lives, wanted to be a part of our sept, but now was not the time to dwell on the impossible.

"Fine. You stop Thala, and I'll get Baltic to let you into the sept. Deal?"

"Deal," he said, grabbing me by the shoulders and planting his mouth on mine.

"Try that again, and you're going to be wearing this upside your head," I snarled, shaking the morning star at him.

He just grinned as he slipped into incorporeal state and walked straight through the battle. I eyed it with some misgivings. About half the dragons lay dead or wounded, the remainder fighting with a ferocity that took me—and the others—by surprise. Just as Constantine reached where Baltic and Gabriel were keeping Thala busy, two things happened in short succession. The first was Drake suddenly emerging from behind me, a long ebony box in his hands.

"You got it!" I cried.

"Yes." His gaze flickered out to the battle, obviously looking for Aisling.

"Jim and Aisling are over there, on that big rock. Holland is there with her," I said, pointing.

"Ah." He gave me a curious look, and somewhat reluctantly handed me the box. It had a long leather strap attached to it, which I slung over my chest.

"Oh, thank you! You really are a talented thief."

"My reward?" he asked with one raised eyebrow.

I edged toward the destroyed wall. "Can it wait until after things calm down?"

"No." He held out his hand.

I reached into my pocket and brought out the case containing the phylactery, handing it to him.

He opened it, both eyebrows raised. "The Avignon Phylactery?"

"Yes." I gave him a long, hard look. "I expect you to keep it safe, Drake."

He bowed and tucked it away inside his jacket. "I will treasure it."

"You'd better, or Baltic will want it back."

He was about to answer, but at an angry shout from István, he jumped through the destroyed wall, snatching up a sword in the process before he joined the fray.

"Now we're getting somewhere," I said, applauding lightly when Pavel chased off a wounded dragon, returning to go after a pair of blue dragons who were attacking Baltic.

"But not where you think you're going," a voice said behind me. "Give that to me!"

"No," I said, my jaw dropping a smidgen as Dr. Kostich, trailing bits of duct tape, strode toward me with a furious expression. "Savian said you were tied up and out of our way!"

"I am an archimage," he said through clenched teeth, his eyes all but spitting ire. "I am not put out of anyone's way, let alone someone as nefarious as you and your gang of hoodlums. Return that sword to me this instant, or you will pay the penalty, and I assure you, Tully Sullivan, that it is a debt you do not wish to incur."

"My name is Ysolde de Bouchier," I said, squaring my shoulders. "And it's Baltic's sword, not yours. You can just—"

Luckily, there was an interruption at that moment to keep me from finishing what was going to be a very inappropriate suggestion. Unluckily, the reason for the interruption was imminent death and destruction.

A blast of air and light sent everyone flying backward a few feet.

"What the—that was an arcane blast," I said, shaking my head as I stood up. "Baltic needs to watch where he's aiming that."

"It wasn't your gargantuan mate who cast that spell." Dr. Kostich also got to his feet and was in the act of brushing himself off when he froze, his eyes narrowed as he stared toward Baltic.

"It had to be. Only mages can call up arcane power like that."

"It was the woman," he said, his lips barely moving.

Goose bumps crawled down my arms. "Thala? But she's a necromancer. She doesn't have arcane power."

"She's singing!" Pavel yelled, turning to face the rest of us as everyone, friend and foe alike, slowly rose from the ground. "Take cover!"

"Sainted Mother, she's going to sing another dirge," I gasped, spinning around to find a place to hide. I grabbed Dr. Kostich by the arm and jerked him to the side, toward the missing wall.

"No," he said, pulling me back. "That building is about to collapse."

"Ysolde!"

The world seemed to slow down at that point, time itself lagging until each second took five times as long to pass. I watched with an odd sense of detachment as Baltic vaulted over the still-fighting dragons, shifting as he did so back into human form, his face a mask of fear—fear for me, I knew. Beyond him, Thala stood with her arms outstretched, a horrible wail starting to scrape across the night sky. I knew it was a matter of only a few seconds before she completed the dirge, too long for Baltic to reach me.

A sob choked in my throat as I dropped my morning star and ran toward him, needing his strength not to protect me, but to complete me.

The dirge swelled into a sound that threatened to burst my eardrums . . . and then it stopped, the air around us vibrating as it waited for the final note, the final word of the dirge to complete it. A golden light gathered itself before me, tiny little motes spinning around and around until they elongated into the shape of a man.

"Your time has run out, daughter," the First Dragon said, his eyes filled with sorrow.

I stared at him for a second. Then, slow as molasses, my gaze shifted over his shoulder, to where Baltic still ran toward me in slow motion. Thala appeared to be frozen in time, what remained of her tribe staring with open mouths at the First Dragon as he strode forward.

"Run out of time? You're going to kill me?" My voice was pathetic and tiny, reflecting perfectly the uncertainty I felt at that moment. Was he so pissed at me that he'd kill me for failing to save Baltic's honor? He wouldn't do that, would he?

His gaze flicked to the side as Baltic stumbled over a dead dragon, skidding to a stop next to me. "Baltic."

"I would have you cease harassing my mate," Baltic said somewhat breathily, his chest heaving as he tried to catch his breath.

I elbowed him and whispered, "A little more humility might be in order, my darling."

Baltic ignored me. "If you wish to punish me for the acts of the past, you will do so to me, not Ysolde. She is not to blame for any of my actions."

"You are correct. You alone are answerable for your sins." The First Dragon glanced around at the gathering, his gaze pausing for a moment on Thala before returning to me.

"I'm sorry. I haven't yet managed to do what you

wanted me to do," I said, clasping Baltic's hand for support.

"This will end where it began," the First Dragon said, and in the fraction of time between instants, we were no longer standing outside the sepulcher. Instead, we stood, all of us, in a cleared section of woods that surrounded a tall, grey structure.

"Dauva," I said, staring at it before spinning around, trying to look in all directions at once. "It's Dauva."

"Fascinating, absolutely fascinating. I believe this translocation requires a few notes," Dr. Kostich said, pulling out a small notebook and a gold pen.

Jim snuffled the First Dragon's shoes. "Wow. Those are some pretty awesome teleporting skills you got there, Your First Dragonness. Don't suppose you're looking for a devastatingly handsome demon sidekick, are you?"

"Jim!" Aisling smacked it on its butt.

"So the fighting has stopped for good?" Magoth put his hands on his naked hips and looked around in dismay. Suddenly, he brightened up. "I recognize this place. It's where my sweet May enjoyed playing with me. May, my darling—"

"No!" May said in a disgusted voice, but her eyes were large as she moved to press herself next to Gabriel, whose arm immediately went around her.

"Fine, be that way. I'll find someone else to tail-slap me." He eyed Pavel, who looked more than a little startled.

"So this is what the famed Dauva looked like all those centuries ago," Holland said, strolling toward the wall. "I've always wonder—oof!"

He bounced off the wall, taking himself—and the rest of us—by surprise. He rubbed his nose and reached out to pat the wall, turning to face us with disbelief in his eyes. "It's real."

"It can't be real," I said, shaking my head. "Baltic

hasn't rebuilt it yet, and besides, I told him no moat. That clearly is a moat." Everyone looked at where I pointed. "This has to be a vision of past Dauva."

"This is no vision," Baltic said slowly, crossing the drawbridge upon which we all stood. He touched the stone gateway.

"If it's not a vision, then . . . what? It's real?" Aisling asked, looking curiously at the First Dragon. "Can he make something as big as a castle appear out of thin air?"

The First Dragon smiled.

"He created the race of dragons, *kincsem*," Drake told her. "A castle would be as child's play to him."

"Well," I said after giving Baltic a chance to thank his father for magicking up his heart's desire, "that's awfully nice of you to save us the trouble of rebuilding. Thank you."

The First Dragon ceased smiling. I felt as if the sun had gone behind a cloud. "The choice of whether this place is a reward or punishment is yours, daughter."

"You will not punish my mate," Baltic said, and would have continued if I hadn't stopped him.

"Fine," I told the First Dragon. "You've made your point. I've failed you again. If you'd just tell me exactly what you want Baltic to do, I'll convince him that it's within his best interests to do it. But please, no more mysterious comments and hints at unknown things and references to events I have no memory of ever happening because, to be honest, I'm really getting sick and tired of it all."

The First Dragon's eyelids dropped over his eyes, making me feel even more as if I were on trial—and my defense was made up of the Marx Brothers. "The end is within your grasp, daughter. The choice of which end it will be is yours."

"Oh, for the love of . . . See? That's exactly the sort

of mysterious crap—" His eyes widened. I cleared my throat. "Mysterious comments that drive me bonkers."

"That's not an awfully long tri—ow!" Jim yelped as Aisling leaned down and whispered furiously in its ear.

"You refuse, then?" The First Dragon began to turn away. "So be it."

"No, I don't refuse!" I started toward him, but Baltic held me back, saying, "Mate, do not distress yourself. It is a game he plays. He enjoys trying to destroy my happiness."

"Well, I'm not going to let him. Now, you just listen here," I threw caution to the wind and marched over to where the First Dragon was strolling out of the circle of people. I caught at his sleeve, my temper getting the better of me even though I knew it was the sheerest folly. "I've done everything you asked, not that you ever really came right out and said what I had to do, but I've tried. I've wheeled and dealed . . . dealt . . . whatever, and I've made sacrifices, and I've tried to keep the peace to the very best of my ability, but that's evidently not good enough for you!"

"Man alive, is she yelling at the First Dragon?" Aisling asked Drake, her eyes huge as I shook the First Dragon's sleeve.

"I believe she is," Drake answered. "It is not something I ever wish to see you doing, in case you were thinking along those lines."

"I'd be afraid to," Aisling admitted.

"Ysolde, maybe you should take a few minutes to calm down," May said, taking a few hesitant steps toward me. Her gaze kept skittering to the First Dragon as she added, "I think your emotions are running a bit high right now."

"Of course they're running high!" I let go of the First Dragon's sleeve to run my hand through my hair. "He's trying to drive me insane."

"Baltic?" May asked, nodding toward me, obviously hinting that he should do something to stop me.

Baltic crossed his arms and leaned against the wall of Dauva, but he said nothing.

"Look, I don't mean to be rude—"

"Too late," came a soft voice behind me.

"But if you're frustrated with me, I'm doubly so with you. So if you'd just once and for all tell me—"

"This is beyond tolerable," Thala said suddenly. "I have better things to do with my life than witness your pathetic little dealings. You'll be mud beneath my heel soon enough."

She shot a look of pure loathing at pretty much everyone, and leaped on me, sending me flying backward with a wicked blow to my face. Pain stretched across my back for a second before there was a snapping noise, and then Thala was off, racing away with the black sword box in her hands, the broken leather strap trailing behind her.

Baltic, who had caught me before I could hit the ground, gave a shout and tossed me forward to Drake before he ran after Thala. Pavel sprinted after him with only one backward look.

"Really, Thala," I yelled, my hands on my hips. "You have to pick now to do this? You don't see that I'm busy with the First Dragon?"

"Should we go after them?" May asked Gabriel.

"She has the sword. I suppose we should." Gabriel glanced toward the First Dragon before making a bow.

"You stay here—I'll go. He'll never let you get the sword, but he'd let me have it," I told Gabriel before racing past the First Dragon.

"Running is so tiresome unless one is being chased by a being with a barbed cat," Magoth said in a bored voice.

I heard the others calling after me as I ran, but I ignored them, focusing on trying to remember the lay of the land. Dauva sat on the rim of a solid granite ledge that dropped several hundred feet down to a marshy wooded area, leaving only one side and the front vulnerable to attack. That was one reason why it was so successful at resisting attacks, but that didn't matter to me at the moment; what did matter was where the game trail I raced along was taking me. I had a vague sense that the ledge was fairly close by on the left side, but the terrain had changed in the last few hundred years, and I could no longer rely on landmarks to guide me.

The sound of crashing bodies through the underbrush warned me the others were following. It just drove me faster. I had to get that sword before Baltic, assuming he could get it away from Thala. I hoped Constantine had the presence of mind to come after me, so he could restrain Thala, but I had a feeling he wasn't going to be as trustworthy as I'd hoped, not after the most recent experience with him.

"I really hate it when I'm right about things like this," I panted a few minutes later when I emerged from the heavily wooded area to a narrow stone ledge. I stopped a good dozen feet from the edge, but I had to take a minute to catch my breath before I could address the two people who stood there.

"—betray me now as you have done in the past?" Baltic was in the middle of saying. He stood facing Thala, who held the black sword box in both hands. "What have you done with my talisman?"

"What do you think I did with it?" she answered in a snotty voice, a cruel smile on her face. She pulled a narrow gold chain out from under her shirt, allowing a flat disk of gold hanging from it to dangle before him. "If it means so much to you, you should take better care of it."

"I did. You betrayed my trust there, as well."

"I did tell you it was folly to trust anyone," she answered with a little shrug, then yanked the chain off her neck and threw it at his feet. "Let it not be said that I am not generous. I am through with it, so you can have it back. You may thank me for giving your mate one less thing to fuss over."

Baltic didn't even look at the talisman lying in the dirt. "Do you think I care what you do, so long as it does not involve the light dragons? If it is your desire to avenge yourself against the archimage, then do so, but do not involve me or those I am responsible for."

"You really believe that's what this is about? *Revenge?*" Thala laughed softly, gesturing toward him with the sword. I eyed it, wondering if I could snatch it and shove her over the edge of the cliff. It was high enough that the fall would likely kill even an immortal. . . . Mentally, I shook my head as the idea occurred to me. I couldn't do that to her, not even when she had tried to destroy us. "Perhaps it *is* about revenge . . . of a sort. But not the type you or your precious Ysolde would understand."

She didn't even look toward me as I edged a hair closer to her. I wanted the talisman, but more important, I wanted that damned sword.

Behind me, voices called as the others tried to find our path. I assumed they were having a bit of difficulty finding us since they didn't have Savian to find our tracks.

"The sword is mine," Baltic said, holding out a hand. "It was given to me, not you."

"That was a mistake," Thala said, smiling. "Not one that will be repeated. Now if you don't mind, I'm going to kill you once and for all, and then I think I'll kill your mate, and after that—"

I never did find out what horrible plan she had in mind, because Baltic sprang at her before she could finish her threat, sending her flying backward a good eighteen feet, right up against a sharp obelisk of stone that seemed to have erupted out of the earth. The force of the blow knocked the sword box from her hand, causing me to scramble forward and snatch it up before she could grab it again.

I tied the broken leather strap around my waist even as Thala screamed an oath at Baltic. "You will not triumph again! Not after all this time!"

"Mate, stay back," Baltic ordered as Thala lunged at him, her hands dancing in the air as he sidestepped her.

I gaped at the gestures she was making, recognizing them. "Baltic, she's—"

He, too, must have recognized them, for with a roar of fury, he sprang on her again . . . but she had finished casting her spell, and this time, it was Baltic who went flying.

Right over the edge of the cliff.

Chapter Seventeen

Time as I knew it stopped. No, the world stopped. The *universe* stopped. I stared in dumbfounded horror at the empty space at the edge of the granite cliff where a nanosecond earlier, Baltic had stood.

"My sword, if you don't mind."

I continued to stare at the spot, my brain unable to process what it had just witnessed. With another oath, Thala ripped the box from the leather strap. I took six steps forward until I stood at the edge of the cliff.

"Baltic?"

The word came out as light as the wind.

"Baltic?"

"There she is. Ysolde, you're a hard woman to track.... Erm . . . where are Baltic and Thala?"

"Look, there's Thala, running that way. Drake—"

"You stay here, Gabriel," Drake said. "István and Pavel and I will go after her."

"Are we chasing someone? I love a good chase. I love

it even more when I catch the prisoner and can take her back to my palace, to my toy room, where I—"

"That's enough, Magoth," May said. "You can go with Drake if you behave yourself."

"I will stay and guard my beloved one," Constantine announced. "Unlike some, I do not need to take prisoners to enjoy myself."

I peered down into the dark depths of the ravine. There was nothing—no flicker of color or movement, just . . . blackness. "Baltic!"

The scream was horrifying to hear, filled with agony of such depth, it brought me to my knees.

"Holy shit! Ysolde? Are you OK? That was the single most horrifying noise I've ever heard. Oh my god, May, she's going to throw herself over."

Hands jerked me back from the edge as I was about to leap down and find Baltic.

"What happened? Ysolde, what happened?" May's voice was filled with concern.

He couldn't be . . . I shook my head. I couldn't even put into words my worst fear.

A black shape stood next to me. "Oh man, did what I think happen just happen?"

I looked down at Jim as it peered over the edge of the cliff, then backed up hastily. "Man, it did. I never thought the dread wyvern could be killed twice, but I guess I was wrong."

"No," I said as Aisling gasped in horror.

"Who's wrong? What's happening?"

I ignored the voices behind me, shaking my head as I focused on Jim. "No, you're wrong. He's not . . . He can't . . . He didn't . . ."

It was the sympathy in the demon's eyes that made me realize the horrible truth.

Baltic was dead. He was gone, just like that, one minute standing before me, demanding that Thala give him the sword. . . . "No, that's wrong. Not Thala."

"Who's not Thala? What is going on?"

It was Constantine's voice that spoke.

I continued to stare at the demon as my brain tried desperately to pull together the pieces of a puzzle I didn't know existed until that day.

Hushed voices murmured in the background.

"Baltic's dead? Are you sure? Ysolde, my darling, my love, allow me to comfort you."

I shoved Constantine away without even thinking about it, aware of something behind me, a presence that seemed to compel me to turn.

"He's dead," I said, ignoring everyone and everything that wasn't at that moment important.

The First Dragon just looked at me.

"He's dead," I repeated, a bit more forcefully, striding toward him until I was a foot away.

I was on fire, literally on fire, but even that didn't distract me. I had one mission, one goal, one purpose to my being, and I would not let anything, not even the First Dragon, stand in my way.

He inclined his head in acknowledgment of my statement, his eyes, his damned all-knowing eyes, simply watching me as if I were a particularly interesting form of insect.

I punched him in the chest, just to see some sort of a reaction in his face or eyes. "Resurrect him."

There were a couple of gasps behind me.

Slowly, the First Dragon closed his eyes.

"Resurrect him!" I hit him again, harder this time, my fire burning so bright, it spilled out of me and crawled over him.

"Why should I do so?" he asked.

"You're his father!" I screamed, tears washing my

cheeks, the pain inside me so great it almost brought me to my knees.

"I am the all-father."

"But he's your son. Your last son."

"I did not resurrect my other sons when they died," the First Dragon said.

"You have to bring him back because I love him." My voice was mostly a wail now, one painful to hear.

"Some of my other sons, too, had mates who loved them."

"But this is different," I gave in, sinking to my knees. "I can't go on without him."

"You are willing to die, as well? What of your child? Are you willing to leave him behind in your desire to quit the mortal world?"

I thought of Brom, the best part of me, my adorable, quirky child, and my heart contracted even more. "No. I can't leave Brom. I can't leave . . . no. I'm not willing to die. But if I have to live without Baltic, my heart will be dead. My soul will be dead. I will continue on because I must, and I will love and cherish those dear to me, but I will not truly live. I will just . . . be."

He said nothing. I had to try to reach him. I had to try to make him understand. "You have to bring him back. He's the last of your children."

"All here are my children," he said gently, waving a hand at the people collected. "Even you. Even the child growing inside you."

"Whoa!" Jim said, squinting at my midsection. "You're preggers?"

I put my hand protectively over my belly. "How do you know about that? I haven't even told Baltic."

He just looked at me with those wise eyes, and an emotion boiled up within me until I knew it would spill out like acid.

"I hate you," I snarled, getting to my feet, ignoring the

distressed murmurs of everyone present. "You are an abomination. You call yourself the ancestor of everyone, but you don't want the responsibility that goes along with that. I am ashamed to know that my child will bear your blood."

"Ysolde," May warned, her voice filled with shock. "Think of what you're saying. Think of whom you're saying it to."

"I don't care," I answered, never taking my eyes from the First Dragon. "If you won't resurrect Baltic, then I will scour the world to find a necromancer who will. I don't care how long it takes, or how much it costs, or what I have to sacrifice to do it, I will bring him back. And when he is safe in my arms, then you will know my full wrath."

He tipped his head to the side as he considered me. "You think to threaten me, daughter of light?"

"Yes," I said evenly, letting him see the soul-deep intention in my eyes. "I am threatening you."

"Oh, Ysolde, I really don't think that's wise," Aisling said, starting toward me. She stopped when May put out a hand.

"No one has ever threatened me," the First Dragon said meditatively. His gaze sharpened. "What would you give to return Baltic to your side? Would you give your son's life?"

"No!"

"That of your unborn child?"

"Never." I thought for a moment I would vomit, so sickened was I, but I managed to quell my emotions enough to speak. "You're truly a monster, aren't you? Are we all just a game to you? Something to amuse yourself with whenever you're bored? You reprehensible, disgusting, vile—"

He held up a hand, stopping me. "You would not give your own life, and you would not give your child's life. What, then, do you have to offer me?"

I stared at him, absolutely flabbergasted. "You're . . . bargaining? You're trying to cut a deal with me to resurrect Baltic?"

"I am asking what you would give to have him returned to life." He was silent for a moment. "I did not ask you what you would give before, when I had him brought back. Now, I do so."

"Before?" I shook my head. "You didn't resurrect him. Thala did."

I swear I saw a twinkle of enjoyment in his fathomless eyes. It just made me want to scream and rip his head off. "Baltic is my son. Even the most gifted of necromancers could not resurrect him without my guidance."

I stumbled forward, tears once again filling my eyes as I knelt before the First Dragon. "Then do so again. Please. I will give you whatever you want, so far as I can. I love him with every ounce of my being, and I swear before everyone here that whatever you want, you will have."

"I've heard those words from you before," he said, half turning from me. "I gave you a task, and you have not completed it."

I closed my eyes for a moment, agony twisting sharply inside me. "I tried to redeem his honor. I tried to get him to apologize for his part in the death of Alexei and Maerwyn. But he doesn't—didn't—seem to understand how important that was."

"I asked for you to ensure he paid for the deaths of the innocent," the First Dragon said.

"That's Alexei, isn't it? And by extension, Maerwyn. I tried, but—"

"They are part of it, but they are not the only ones who have suffered because of my son." His gaze went beyond me, to scan the face of everyone there. "Baltic is flesh of my flesh. He was intended to make the weyr stronger in times when it was weak."

I closed my eyes again, insight smacking me upside the head. "But instead, the results of his actions tore it apart."

"The endless war?" Aisling asked.

I nodded, wiping my face with my sleeve. "When Baltic refused to take Chuan Ren as his mate, the red dragons started the endless war."

"Thousands of my children died. Hundreds of thousands of mortals did so, as well," the First Dragon said.

"I don't quite understand how," Aisling said, looking warily at the First Dragon.

My stomach twisted with grief and rage and regret. "The red dragons killed Maerwyn, Baltic's mother, which triggered the separation between silver and black dragons."

"So Chuan Ren really *did* start the war," Aisling said softly with a little whistle of amazement. "I knew it. I just knew she had to be behind it."

"The black dragons were all but destroyed."

"As were the silver dragons," Constantine said, only faintly visible. "We suffered gravely because of Baltic's actions."

My gaze returned to the First Dragon. "You hold Baltic responsible for the deaths of all of those dragons? Everyone who has died since the onset of Endless War?"

"The deaths of the innocent weigh heavily on his soul," he said, a typical dragon non-answer. "You were to redeem that sin."

"The flesh of your flesh," I said softly, fighting the pain so I could think. I knew that everything I was and would be depended on getting this right. "He was supposed to bring strength to the weyr—" I stopped, once again insight striking me with an almost palpable blow. "You want him back in the weyr. You want our sept to join the weyr. But why? Baltic doesn't care anything about the weyr."

"Man, what is it with you humans?" Jim asked, shaking its head. "You guys fall off the obvious wagon when you're young or something?"

"Jim, hush," Aisling said quickly, turning to apologize.

I looked at Jim. It winked at me. Obvious? What was I missing that was so obvious?

"You had wanted Baltic to take Chuan Ren as his mate." The words came out slowly, as my brain once again frantically squirreled around trying to piece things together. "But Baltic didn't care about that, didn't care that his actions would enrage the red dragons. He didn't care to the extent that he was booted out of this sept, until Alexei accepted him back as heir when Constantine's treachery was exposed."

"Constantine's treachery?" Gabriel frowned. "What treachery is this?"

"Nothing! There was no treachery," Constantine said quickly, then glanced at the First Dragon and immediately disappeared. "I'm ... er ... low on power. I'll claim you as my mate later, Ysolde, when everyone is gone."

I waved a dismissive hand, not willing to be distracted. "It's old history, Gabriel. I'll tell you later." I met the First Dragon's gaze again. "You wanted Baltic to bring strength to the weyr. He was your only living child, and you wanted him to bring stability to a weyr that was imploding upon itself."

"My children have always been fractious," he said with the barest hint of a smile. "The dragon fire that burns within us manifests itself in many ways."

"But Baltic didn't do that. He didn't care about bringing the weyr together. He cared about the black dragons, instead. He—"

"He cared about you," the First Dragon interrupted.

At that moment the penny dropped. Memory after memory tumbled in my mind—Baltic telling me five hundred years ago that the weyr could go about its busi-

ness so long as it left him alone; Baltic not three weeks
ago telling me the same thing. "You want him to care
about dragonkin."

"Oooh," Aisling said on a long breath.

"He must pay for the deaths of the innocent," the
First Dragon said in that enigmatic way he had.

"You're really irritating, do you know that?" I squared
off as if about to fight him. "You couldn't just say that—
you had to make me jump through five million hoops?
I've wanted him to rejoin the weyr all along."

"But you have not accomplished that task."

"What more do you want from me?" I yelled, slapping my hands on my legs. "I've tried and tried and
tried, and I swear that I'll continue to move heaven and
earth to make you happy. I swear I'll redeem Baltic's
soul. I swear I'll do anything, anything at all. Just bring
him back!"

"Mate, do not grovel."

The First Dragon's lips tightened, as if he'd heard it all
before.

"I can't offer to do anything more than that!" I
grabbed the First Dragon's arm and shook it. "I love him.
Do you understand that? Our love goes beyond death.
It's . . . It's . . . It's *everything* to me."

"Always you must make dramatic scenes. He enjoys
them; you do know that, yes?"

"Baltic is the beginning, and the end, and . . . and . . ."
I stopped, my heart beating wildly as a warm, familiar
presence made the skin of my back tingle.

My heart, my soul, the very essence of who I was,
came to life once again. I staggered a step to the side
with the overwhelming surge of emotion. "When?" I
asked the First Dragon.

He knew exactly what I was asking. "When I felt his
loss."

"You bastard!" I swore, slapping my hand on his chest. "You let me go through all that when he was already alive? You heartless bastard! You cruel, manipulative—"

"*Chérie*, do not finish that sentence," Baltic rumbled behind me, his arms sliding around me. I turned, tears of happiness spilling over my lashes. "I have already had to endure one lecture from the First Dragon this day—I do not wish to hear another, and if you continue, that is exactly what will happen."

"You're alive," I said, taking his face in my hands and gently kissing him.

"I am." He brushed away a long trail of tears. "You wept for me?"

"I offered my soul for you."

"This is the most romantic thing I've ever seen," Aisling said, sniffing and dabbing at her eyes with a tissue. "I wish Drake were here to see it."

"Serious chick flick stuff," Jim agreed, nodding.

May wrapped her arms around Gabriel and held him as he stroked her hair.

"It is not good for you to be so upset," Baltic said, frowning down at me. I could have cheered for joy at the sight of that lovely frown. "You must remember your condition."

"My—you know?"

"Of course I know. I am not stupid. I can use a calendar as well as you."

"Congratulations, by the way," Aisling said, still sniffling.

"Oh boy, another pregnant mate in the weyr. *Sárkánies* are sure going to be fun."

"We are not in the weyr," Baltic said, allowing me to kiss the breath right out of his mouth.

"Oh yes, we are." I took a step back from him, my foot tripping over something hard. I bent to pick up Baltic's talisman, leveling him with a look that didn't just read volumes; it could have filled an entire library with my ire. "We are joining the weyr."

He crossed his arms.

"Don't you dare cross your arms at me." I stormed forward, gesturing toward the First Dragon. "After what I went through with him, we are joining the weyr, and that's that."

"Mate—"

"We're joining the weyr! And you're going to start caring about other dragons!"

"That madwoman/psycho/scary face is good on you, Soldy," Jim said, tipping its head to the side. "Kind of a 'three bread crumbs short of a meat loaf' look, but effective."

Baltic sighed, glanced at his father, and made an annoyed gesture. "Very well. I will give in to your demands this time, but only because I do not wish for you to be further upset. I will allow the weyr to accept the light dragons as members."

"Thank you," I said, kissing him again before turning to face the First Dragon, Baltic's arms around me. "And thank you, too. For everything, but mostly for giving me Baltic."

He was silent for a moment, then smiled, his body shimmering into that of a dragon, one whose scales held all the colors of the spectrum. The colors seemed to dance along his scales; then he was gone, leaving behind nothing but the faintest sparkle of color in the air.

Chapter Eighteen

"Sweetie? Baltic was dead, but he's alive again. I thought you'd want to know. Ysolde's talking to Maura now. She says that she has Violet, and they're starting down the mountain, so assuming they make it to the town OK, Operation Save Violet is good. Oh, you missed Ysolde punching the First Dragon." Aisling, who had moved a short distance away to speak on her cell phone, listened for a few seconds. "No, she's alive and well, too, despite the punching and saying some pretty harsh things to him. Did you find Thala? Rats. Well, come on back. Things have settled down here. Is Magoth still with you? Ah. OK."

Dr. Kostich, who had evidently taken his own sweet time finding us, strolled up as Aisling was finishing her call. "Ah. Here you are. Where is the dragon ancestor? I wish to return to the sepulcher to secure it against thieves."

His gaze was rather pointed when he looked at Baltic.

"Just a second, Maura. I think someone will want to

talk to you," I yelled into the phone, it being difficult to hear over the howl of the wind on the side of whatever mountain it was Maura and Violet were descending. "Dr. Kostich, Maura has rescued Violet. Would you like to talk to her?"

"I already have. She called me a few minutes ago," he said with a sniff. "I expected nothing less from my granddaughter. She is very resourceful, if foolish about many things."

"Never mind, he says you talked to him. My love to Violet. Yes, he's on his way. He'll probably catch you guys on the way down, so tell him everything's fine here. Call when you get back to town." I hung up the phone and considered my former employer. "I'm afraid the First Dragon has gone back to wherever it is demigods hang out when they're not busy with us lesser beings. Aisling, I take it that Drake and Pavel weren't able to grab Thala?"

"No. Drake says they were close to tackling her, and she just poof! Disappeared. Oh, and we should be blighted with May's demon boss any second now. Evidently he decided it was too much work chasing Thala and turned around to hit on us some more. Lucky us."

May muttered something quite rude.

"Thala," Baltic said, looking thoughtful. "She must have gone into the beyond."

"No," I told him. "Absolutely not. I know you can go in there—"

"Which he shouldn't be able to do, since dragons cannot wield arcane magic," Dr. Kostich argued.

"But I don't want you tangling with her in her natural habitat, so to speak."

Pulling out a cell phone, Dr. Kostich snapped an order into it for some mage in the region to pick him up and take him to the nearest portal shop.

"Is Thala really that powerful that everyone should be so worried about her?" May asked, rubbing her arms against the chill of the night air. Gabriel immediately moved to her side.

"She destroyed an entire house with her song," he pointed out. "You saw the damage she inflicted on Baltic. She is to be feared."

I hesitated, touching Baltic's shoulder. His muscles tightened in response. "Thala, I think, is not that powerful. Is she, Baltic?"

"No."

"Then why are you guys so jumpy about her?" Aisling asked, a frown between her brows.

"Ash, babe—"

"Don't you dare tell me I'm missing something obvious, Mr. Would-you-like-a-demon-sidekick," Aisling said, glaring at her demon.

"Sheesh! It was just a joke. You know, ha-ha? Man, you used to be able to enjoy a good joke."

"I used to have a demon that didn't lip off every five seconds," she told it grimly.

Jim cocked a furry eyebrow.

"All right, you always lipped off, but at least you used to want to be my demon, and not offer yourself up to every godlike being who wandered past."

"Aww." Jim butted its head against her leg. "I still wuvs ya, babe."

"I have returned," Magoth announced as he emerged from the shrubs. He was still naked, and he struck up a pose next to Aisling, giving her a thorough examination. She blinked at his penis, which appeared to bear a curse on it. "Who wishes to have a post-fight orgy? I should tell you all that I'm equal opportunity when it comes to sexual congress, so don't let your gender stop you from initiating the fun."

Dr. Kostich, to whom the comment was addressed, rolled his eyes and, with a stern look bent upon me, informed us all that he was leaving. "Naturally, the Watch will be pursuing the necromancer who stole the blade belonging to us. As for your attempt to break into the sepulcher—"

"We didn't break into it," Aisling said quickly, batting her eyelashes.

"No, we didn't," May added just as quickly, an innocent expression on her face.

"That's right. Thala blew it up. If you want to go after anyone, you can nail her," I said with a smile so sweet, it could have been mistaken for honey.

"Someone stole the light blade," Dr. Kostich insisted, his eyes on Aisling. "The green dragons are, I believe, noted for their ability to take things that belong to others."

She smiled. "Did you see Drake with it?"

"No. But I saw Tully with it."

I shrugged. "Thala blew up the sepulcher to get the light blade. We all heard her say that. I must have picked it up when the boys jumped her."

The other ladies murmured agreements. Baltic rolled his eyes and moved off a bit to search the ground. Gabriel nodded, his dimples obviously fighting to come out. Magoth hit on Aisling until Jim lifted its leg in response.

"Bah. Between the wyvern and the doppelganger thief"—May shot Dr. Kostich a bright smile at that slur—"it's obvious that you're trying to pull something over on me. I won't have it."

"Get it from Thala," Aisling said. "Unless big bad you are afraid of her, as well."

"I think Dr. Kostich has every right to approach her with caution," I said slowly while he sputtered in anger.

Aisling turned to me. "All right, what am I missing? Jim, don't you dare speak. Yes, it's an order. Ysolde?"

My gaze dropped to the object I held in my hands, my fingers tracing the intricate design on the flat, golden disk. "*Thala* is not the danger," I said carefully.

Baltic glanced over to me. My fingers closed around

the disk. He held my gaze for a minute before nodding. "I believe you are correct, mate."

"Then what's the big deal with her?" May asked. "I'm just as confused as Aisling."

"As am I," Gabriel added.

I bit my lower lip, watching Dr. Kostich as I said, "I asked you once what happens to a mage when she diminishes. You said she goes into the beyond and remains there, unable to return to the mortal world."

"It is the way of our kind," he allowed.

"It's impossible for the mage to ever return?"

"For a mage? Yes."

"And an archimage?"

Gabriel looked thoughtful, his eyes on Baltic, who had returned to searching the ground for his talisman.

Dr. Kostich took longer to answer the question. "It is not impossible, but very unlikely. The archimage would have to find a willing vessel into which he would place his consciousness—"

"Holy cow!" Aisling gasped. "You mean that Thala . . . that she's . . ."

"She's Antonia von Endres."

"Really," Magoth said thoughtfully. "I do love a woman of power. I wonder if she has a spectral whip."

Baltic's black eyes were almost as full of mystery as his father's eyes. "Antonia always resented the act of diminishing. I'm surprised it took her so long to finally convince Thala to allow her access to this world."

"You don't think she was Antonia all along, do you?" I asked him.

He shook his head. "I believe the last we saw of Thala was in Spain, when she raised the dead. Antonia would have no more need of her after that, and she would be content to take over Thala's body in order to reclaim her sword."

Dr. Kostich was oddly quiet at this, no doubt chewing

over the ramifications of one of the most notorious mages in history having gone rogue. "This is a matter with the gravest of consequences to the Magisters' Guild. I will have to consult both them and the committee to see what steps should be taken."

His phone jangled a little Mozart tune. He gave us all his somber consideration for a few seconds, then said, "I will return to Paris. If you locate this individual, inform me at once."

"Nice seeing you again, too," Aisling said sotto voce as he strode off into the forest.

"Glad we could help save your daughter from impending death!" I bellowed after him.

May giggled.

"What a pain in the behind," I grumbled before eyeing Baltic. "You can stop looking for it. I have it."

His usual frown was in place as he walked over to me, his hand out. "You found my talisman where Thala dropped it?"

"Yes." I held it up by the chain, allowing the disk to shine in the lamplight.

"Ah. Good."

I looked at him for a long, long minute, then handed the talisman to Gabriel. For a few seconds, I thought Baltic's eyeballs were going to pop out of his head.

"Oooh," Aisling said, her eyes round.

Gabriel smiled as he examined the talisman. "Thank you, Ysolde."

"Mate!" Baltic, furious and hurt, stood before me, his fire wrapping around us in a manifestation of his anger. "Why do you betray me in this manner?"

"I'm not betraying you. I'm simply forcing you to do something you've been too stubborn to do despite my many requests."

"What—" He stopped, suspicion crawling over his face as he whipped around to face Gabriel.

"I've never seen a talisman of the First Dragon before," Gabriel said somewhat contemplatively as he admired the object.

"It looks powerful," May said, touching it with one finger.

"It is. Very powerful." Once again, Gabriel's dimples threatened to show themselves.

"Pfft," Magoth said, absently scratching one naked butt cheek. "Dragon relics. No use to anyone but you scaled ones."

Baltic's fingers clenched convulsively. "Ysolde!"

"Oh, you deserve every moment of this," I told Baltic a second before I slid an arm around his waist.

His fingers twitched again. "No," he finally managed to say after unlocking his teeth.

"Yes. It's time. It's well past time. Gabriel?"

Gabriel held up the talisman. "I offer you a bargain, Baltic. In payment for the act of lifting the curse you placed upon the silver dragons, I will return to you this talisman."

The look Baltic turned on me warned of all sorts of acts of revenge, but I wasn't frightened. Oh, he was angry now, but I knew in my heart that he loved me above all else, and sooner or later, he'd accept that this was right.

"You leave me no choice but to accept," Baltic snarled, facing Gabriel again, but only after letting me see in his eyes just how hot his emotions were running. "I will remove the curse."

"Oh! I think this is where Magoth comes in," Aisling said, gesturing toward us.

"Very well, but only because my sweet May offered to build me a film studio of my own."

"It was the only thing I could think of," May explained with a little wave of her hand.

"I appreciate you making that sort of a sacrifice," I told her as Baltic, with a sour look at Magoth, put his hand on the demon lord's shoulder before growling some phrases in Latin that I didn't understand.

"No sacrifices?" Magoth asked, disappointed. "You dragons have so much to learn from me. Well, then, so be it." He spoke a phrase in a language I'd never heard.

Gabriel and May took simultaneous deep breaths, both blinking as if they'd seen something wondrous.

"It's . . . It's gone," May said, throwing herself on Gabriel. He tossed the talisman to Baltic before wrapping his arms around her and swinging her around in a circle as he kissed her. Immediately, both their phones went off.

"No sugar for Daddy?" Magoth asked.

May and Gabriel ignored him.

"I do so love a happy ending. I think we'll go find Drake," Aisling said, nudging Jim before they set off through the forest.

"Hmm." Magoth looked from me to May, then to Baltic and Gabriel. "I shall come with you, Guardian. Perhaps your mate would be interested in a threesome?"

Magoth toddled off after Aisling.

"We have much to celebrate," Gabriel told May as he set her on her feet. His eyes held a light that had May rubbing herself against him.

"I think this calls for a little chase," she said, and with a quick smile at us, dashed off into the forest.

Gabriel managed to make a bow, and say, "I thank you for all that you have done for the silver dragons, Ysolde. We will always regard you with honor."

"And Baltic?" I asked, unable to keep from smiling at the look of sheer joy on his face.

"Er . . . we will be grateful that the curse is lifted," he answered somewhat stiffly.

I laughed. "As am I. Go find May."

With another bow, he was off, leaving me alone with one very angry dragon.

"Thank you, my love," I told Baltic, leaning into his back and kissing his shoulder. "I know it annoyed you to do that, but now, at last, we can live in peace with all the other dragons."

"First you must make your peace with me," he said, turning to pin me back with a look that would probably have killed a lesser being.

I bit his chin. "You may be the dread wyvern Baltic to everyone else, but you don't scare me. I love you too much to be frightened of you."

"That is your first mistake," he growled a second before his mouth descended to mine. I gave in to the heat of his desire, wriggling against him even as I welcomed his fire with my own, allowing the two to blend together into an inferno that I knew would burn bright for an eternity.

Or until the next time one of us was killed.

"Wait a minute," I said, pulling back and frowning when a thought occurred to me. "You were just resurrected."

"That fact has been established, yes."

I bit back a very rude word. "Dammit, Baltic, that means you're back to being younger than me again! I'm a cradle robber! I hate that! Where's your father? If I were to fling myself off the cliff, maybe he could—"

The word he spoke was much ruder than mine, but the light of love in his eyes did much to assuage my irritation.

Epilogue

"I am here—"

"No one cares why you're here, you horrible scaly dragon!"

"I am here to formally disavow all connections—"

"A lying, cheating dragon! One with horrible fashion sense, and no understanding of anything elemental!"

"Relationships, past or future, honors, duties—"

"You wouldn't know honor if it bit you in your great big butt!"

"Cy, really!"

It was a struggle, but I managed to keep from giggling along with Aisling. Next to me, Baltic sat tense and unhappy. I didn't have the heart to break it to him that he was about to become a whole lot more unhappy. Instead, I took his hand and rested it on my stomach. Instantly, his body language changed to one of seduction.

"And responsibilities owed to or from the individual known as Cyrene Northcott, naiad and all-around pain in the ass."

Cyrene gasped and sputtered. "You're the pain in the ass! I'm sorry I ever let you sully my pristine self, you horrible, vile, disgusting—"

"Cy, really, that's enough." May frowned at her twin across the long oval table, but Gabriel, at her side, was clearly fighting a smile.

"Henceforth from this moment on, the sept of the black dragons, and I, Konstantin—"

"Big ass!"

"Nikolai—"

"Water hater!"

"Fekete no longer claim Cyrene Northcott as a mate."

Cyrene, who had been held back by Mikhail, Kostya's weedy guard, screamed and stamped her foot. "Fine! I don't want you anyway! You're arrogant, and self-obsessed, and . . . and . . . and selfish in bed."

Kostya, standing at the *sárkány* table, ground his teeth, but did not respond to Cyrene's slurs.

"The weyr no longer recognizes Cyrene Northcott as your mate," Gabriel said, his lips twitching slightly. "I believe there is one other bit of business to be conducted before we conclude this *sárkány*, and partake of the lovely meal that Ysolde has cooked for us."

"Pavel did most of the work," I said quickly, casting a grateful smile at where he sat on the other side of Baltic. "He made the most divine Peking duck. I hope you're all in the mood for Chinese food, because it's all I can think of lately."

"Chinese sounds yummy," Aisling said, beaming at me. "And I totally hear you on the cravings. When I was having the twins, potato chips were all I wanted. Didn't matter what flavor—I wanted them all."

"I believe we've strayed from the point," Gabriel, who was taking his turn to head up the *sárkány*, gently observed.

"Yes, we have. The point is that Kostya is a big fat

baby pants, and I am formally demating him, so he can't kick me out as his mate," Cyrene said, breaking free of Mikhail. "He's a horrible dragon, and if you had any sense, you'd boot him out of your precious weyr. Not that I care anymore because I'm through with dragons. Totally through with dragons. Really, really through." She stopped, her eyes on the blue wyvern Bastian, who immediately donned a worried expression.

Gabriel cleared his throat. "If we could return to official business? It's my understanding that we have an application for a new sept to be accepted into the weyr."

Everyone looked at Baltic.

He glowered in return.

I leaned in and whispered, "You promised."

"I did not. You told me I would do this, and I, not wishing to upset you, agreed." -

I pinched his side. "The sooner you get it done, the sooner we can eat all that lovely food that Pavel and I have spent all day cooking."

"I do not desire food," he said in a low growl with just a hint of petulance.

I leaned in closer. "I'll let you eat it off me."

"The sept of the light dragons wishes to join the weyr," Baltic said, leaping to his feet and striding across the hall of the newly restored Dauva to where the long oval table sat in the center of the room. "You will accept us now so that I may go devote myself to my mate."

"Subtle," I told him, getting up.

"Do you agree to abide by the laws set in place by the weyr?" Gabriel asked Baltic.

"If I must."

Aisling covered her mouth as she giggled again. Cyrene made a disgusted noise and stomped over to the row of chairs along the paneled wall, plopping down next to Pavel. "I don't suppose you'd like to come to the Riviera with me?"

Pavel, with a panicked look, immediately rose and took up a position behind Baltic.

Cyrene looked at Maura and Savian, who were present as guests of the weyr.

"He's taken," Maura said, putting her hand on Savian's thigh.

"I'm not, but my heart will always belong to my beloved Ysolde," a disembodied voice said.

Cyrene rolled her eyes and slumped back, pulling out her cell phone.

"You must abide by the rules, as you well know, having once been a wyvern in the weyr," Gabriel said, his lips once again twitching a little. May was suddenly possessed with a coughing attack that didn't fool anyone. "I believe we can dispense with the rest of the formalities due to the candidate's previous experience as a wyvern. How say you all?"

"The Green Dragons welcome the new sept into the weyr," Drake said promptly.

I tucked my arm through Baltic's and leaned into him, so happy I could have burst into song.

"Despite the misunderstandings of the past, the Blue Dragons are happy to welcome the light dragons, as well," said Bastian, with a genial smile toward us.

Kostya, who sat with his arms crossed, was in the middle of a glaring battle with Baltic, but after a few minutes of pointed silence, he snapped, "The black dragons will recognize the light sept. Grudgingly. So long as they stay out of Russia."

"Oh, get over yourself already," I told Kostya. "You can't ask Baltic to be your second one day, and then be snotty to him the next. Let bygones be bygones. I have, for heaven's sake. You don't see me ripping your head off over the fact that you killed Baltic, do you? No, you do not, because I have enough common sense to know that what's in the past is in the past, and we've all changed since then. Well, most of us have. And those that haven't just need to pull their heads out of their butts and get with the program."

"Amen, sister," Aisling said, applauding.

"Hear, hear," May said at the same time.

Kostya stiffened up, but other than muttering some things about mates who didn't know their places, stayed silent.

"I never thought the day would come that the silver dragons would have cause to agree with the others and extend a welcome to Baltic and his sept, but we have only ever wanted peace, and for that reason, we agree to allow the light dragons to join the weyr."

Everyone looked at the empty chair to the right of Drake.

"Still no word of Jian?" I asked the room in general.

"No," Drake said, frowning slightly. "He did not respond to the summons for the *sárkány*, nor did any red dragons contact the weyr with an explanation."

"Taking that into consideration, the weyr now recognizes the sept of the light dragons, with Baltic as wyvern, and Ysolde de Bouchier as his mate. Welcome to the weyr."

"Thank you, all," I said, sniffling just a little as Aisling and May applauded again. "This means so much to me. I can't wait to tell Brom that he's officially a dragon, even if he isn't physically one."

"I believe this concludes all weyr business," Gabriel said, rising.

"Excellent. We'll just set up this table as a dining table, and then we can eat."

"Not just yet."

I looked at Baltic in surprise. "What other business do we have?"

He gestured at Kostya. "It is his business."

We all turned to Kostya.

"You have something more to say?" Gabriel asked.

Kostya took a deep breath, shot Baltic a look that literally set him on fire, then said through obviously clenched teeth, "Be it known to all that the black dragons hereby gift Dragonwood to Ysolde de Bouchier. As of this moment, it is hers, and hers alone."

I stared in stunned surprise at him for a few seconds, joy filling me as I finally turned to Baltic. "How?" I asked.

The others in the room applauded and congratulated me.

"We made a deal," Baltic said, his expression grim.

"What did you give him?" Dread quelled some of my joy. "Your talisman—"

"No, not that," he interrupted, a disgusted look on his handsome face.

"Then what?"

"Me." Constantine appeared out of nowhere to take my hand and press a wet kiss to it. After a moment's consideration, he continued up my arm.

Baltic growled and snatched my hand away. Constantine gave me a little leer.

"Oh my god, he didn't just make Constantine a member of his sept, did he?" Aisling asked.

"I think he did," May answered. "I'm just . . . wow."

My gaze met Baltic's. Martyrdom was rife in his beautiful black eyes. "You did that for me?"

"Yes."

I kissed him, murmuring, "Just when I think I couldn't love you any more, you go and prove me wrong. This is the sweetest, the most thoughtful, kindest thing anyone has ever done for me."

"I don't say it will be an easy thing to live under Baltic's reign again," Constantine said, striking up a pose. "But for Ysolde, I will bear it."

"And not be able to challenge Kostya again," Aisling

said, nodding at her brother-in-law. "Smart thinking, Kostya."

"Hmm. Now that I'm officially in your sept, I can challenge you for control of it," Constantine told Baltic. "And Ysolde. I like that idea!"

Baltic growled and lunged at Constantine, who shrieked and faded just as Baltic lifted him overhead in preparation for flinging him into the nearest wall.

"Baltic, really! Don't be breaking Dauva. The First Dragon went to considerable trouble to have it rebuilt, which really was a very nice present, when you think about it, although I would have preferred something along the lines of a large house rather than an exact reproduction of a medieval castle. Still, we'll have lots of room for Brom and the baby to play, and for everyone to come and visit us when we're not at Dragonwood."

Behind me, Constantine appeared on the long table, and started into reasons why Baltic should step down and let him be wyvern. Baltic, moving too fast for Constantine, leaped onto the table and caught him up by the throat, shaking him like a terrier does with a rat.

"A happy end to another successful *sárkány*," Aisling said, biting the end of Drake's nose. He looked outraged for a moment, then, with a grumble, pulled her up to kiss her mindless.

I watched Baltic a bit nervously. I knew how much it must have cost him to accept Constantine into the sept, and that he did so of his own accord just to return Dragonwood to me. . . .

There was a smile on his face as he throttled Constantine, who squawked, his arms flailing around wildly.

Baltic's eyes met mine.

"I love you," I mouthed to him down the long length of the hall.

"By my mate's grace, you are allowed into the sept, but I reserve the right to name you ouroboros at any time," Baltic warned, tossing Constantine aside. He jumped off the table and stalked toward me, his body moving with a sinuous grace that never failed to make my stomach tighten in pleasure.

"You're going to make me suffer for this, aren't you?" I said as he approached me.

"You will pay for making me go through this hell, yes," he said, his eyes molten with desire. "Every single day of your life you will pay. Every. Single. Day."

I shivered in heated anticipation. "Oh good. Let me tell you about this new restraint system I picked up for you in England. It hooks over the door, and with it, we can—"

He picked me up and carried me to the stone stairs leading to the upper level. "You will have to refrain from your more inventive fantasies until after my son is born, *chérie*. I would not have you or the babe hurt in your enthusiasm to placate my temper."

"Our daughter is going to be just fine with a few little additions to the normal routine, not that I find anything wrong with how you normally do things, but still ... hmm. I wonder if we could summon up another vision of when you and I used to live in Dauva. I bet there are some good ones to be had."

"Always you wish to engage in a foursome," Baltic said, shaking his head while rounding the landing and starting down the hall that led to the master bedroom.

I gasped. "Oh, I do not! Well, OK, I do now and again, but just with ourselves, and that's not really a foursome as much as it is two twosomes. Oooh, if I could get two visions of us going at the same time, we could have a six-some!"

Baltic's laughter rolled down the hallway, filling Dauva—and me—with happiness I knew would last an eon.

Katie's Guide to All Things Dragon

Aisling Grey: Thirtysomething mate to Drake Vireo, the green dragon sept wyvern. Aisling is a Guardian (demon wrangler), and technically a demon lord since she is responsible for Jim, the demon she inadvertently summoned in the first Aisling Grey novel. Aisling and Drake have two children.

Baltic: The dread wyvern Baltic is the first-generation child of the First Dragon, the demigod who created dragons many millennia ago. Baltic is the former wyvern of the black dragon sept, which ceased when he was killed by his heir, Kostya Fekete, immediately after Baltic's mate, Ysolde de Bouchier, was struck dead. He was recently resurrected, and he found Ysolde, his beloved mate (also resurrected), in the first Light Dragons book. He formed the light dragon sept upon his resurrection.

Bastiano (Bastian) Blu: The wyvern of the blue dragon sept, Bastian is the uncle of Fiat Blu, the former blue wyvern, who is pretty much insane and running around causing havoc.

Brom Sullivan: Ysolde's child by Gareth Hunt, her former husband. Brom has an unnatural interest in mummifying things, and is claimed by Baltic as his son.

Constantine Norka: The former heir to Alexei, the black dragon wyvern, Constantine refused to stay in the black sept when Baltic was later named wyvern, and he left it to form the silver dragon sept. He spent many centuries at war with the black dragons. He was resurrected as a shade (corporeal spirit) at Ysolde's request.

Cyrene Northcott: Naiad, and twin of May Northcott. Cyrene fell in love with Kostya, and was happy to be named as his mate even though she was not technically a wyvern's mate. Cyrene created her doppelganger twin, May, via her then-lover, the demon lord Magoth.

Dauva: Baltic's former home in what is now Latvia, and the heart of the black dragon sept. It was destroyed when Ysolde and Baltic were killed in 1701.

Dragon heart/shards: The dragon heart is one of the most powerful artifacts on Earth, and consists of five shards, which are scattered amongst the various dragon septs. The heart can be brought together and re-formed, but this has happened only twice in the last millennium. Dragon shards are immensely valuable relics of the First Dragon, and thus valued beyond almost anything else.

Dragon mate: The man or woman who was born to be the mate to a dragon. Wyvern mates, much more rare than dragon mates, can handle and control the wyvern's fire, which would destroy an ordinary mortal.

Dragonwood: The house that Baltic had built in England for Ysolde. It is currently in possession of Kostya, since he claims it belongs to the black dragons.

Drake Vireo: The wyvern of the green dragon sept, and

a master thief. Drake has homes in London, Paris, and Budapest, and he divides his time amongst the three. Despite his black dragon father, he became a green dragon via his grandmother, who was a reeve (a special type of dragon with unusually pure bloodlines). He has two children with Aisling Grey, his mate.

Effrijim (Jim): A demon sixth class who is bound to Aisling Grey. Jim's preferred form is that of a Newfoundland dog, and he complains nonstop if he is forced into human form. Jim resides with Aisling and Drake, has a passionate love for an elderly Welsh corgi named Cecile, who lives in Paris, and greatly enjoys eating.

First Dragon: The demigod who created the dragonkin, he can be summoned by means of the dragon heart, or in extremely rare cases, by those who have wielded the dragon heart. As befitting a god, it is not always clear whether his intentions are benevolent.

Gabriel Tauhou: The wyvern of the silver dragon sept, and mate to May Northcott. As a silver dragon, Gabriel was cursed by Baltic to never have a mate born to him until a black dragon ruled his sept. Luckily, he found May, who, as a doppelganger, was created rather than born. Gabriel has houses in London and Australia, and he alternates his time between the two.

Gareth Hunt: Ysolde's former (bigamous) husband, and actual husband of Ruth Hunt. Gareth is an oracle. He has an apartment in Spain where Ruth and he used to live with Ysolde and her son, Brom.

Dr. Kostich: The current head of the L'au-dela (Otherworld), as well as the head of the Magisters' Guild. He is an archimage, and thus extremely powerful. He is the father of Violet, and the grandfather of Maura Lo. Ysolde de Bouchier was apprenticed to him for several decades before he threw her out of the Magisters' Guild upon discovering she was a resurrected dragon.

Konstantin (Kostya) Fekete: Named for Constantine Norka, his godfather, Kostya is the wyvern of the black dragon sept, and brother to Drake Vireo. Kostya stated before the weyr that he was accepting Cyrene Northcott as his mate, an event he later regretted.

Maura Lo: Half-dragon Summoner, and granddaughter to Dr. Kostich, she is a part of an ouroboros dragon tribe under the leadership of Thala von Endres.

Magoth: Former demon lord, he bound May to him at her creation, and he used her doppelganger abilities to acquire many precious objects. He was later thrown out of Abaddon (hell) and stripped of almost all of his powers. He did a stint in Hollywood during the early twentieth century, and he is still recognizable by the astute viewer as a famous silent movie heartthrob.

May Northcott: Doppelganger and wyvern's mate to Gabriel Tauhou. May is an identical twin to Cyrene, although she does not cast a shadow and has no reflection in a mirror. May was formerly bound to the demon lord Magoth, and later became his consort, but she was happily stripped of her title when Magoth was booted out of Abaddon. A shadow walker, May can slip out of the view of most people when she desires.

Ouroboros dragons: Dragons who have been kicked out, or have voluntarily left, a dragon sept. Usually outlaws who are up to no good, ouroboros dragons form tribes, and they are not governed by laws of either the weyr or the L'au-dela.

Ruth Hunt: Wife of Gareth Hunt, and a necromancer. Ruth is sister to Thala, although their relationship is somewhat distant.

Savian Bartholomew: Thief-taker and tracker extraordinaire. Savian is the only person ever able to catch May Northcott when the L'au-dela put a price on her head. He later became a friend to both May and Gabriel, and occasionally does work for them.

Thalassa (Thala) von Endres: Necromancer, dirge-singer, and former lieutenant to Baltic, Thala is the daughter of the famed archimage Antonia von Endres. It was Thala who resurrected Baltic almost forty years ago.

Visions: Ysolde is prone to having visions of events in the past that her inner dragon feels are important for her to know. Since her memory was mostly destroyed by Gareth and Ruth, the visions provide her with a link to the past, and a connection with the present. Her visions can encompass other individuals, and sometimes they include events that happened before she was born.

Wards: A drawn symbol of magic that has various effects, including binding, protection, clarity, etc. Many individuals can draw wards, but the most powerful are drawn by Guardians.

Weyr: The collection of dragon septs. The wyvern of each sept can call a *sárkány*, a meeting of all the wyverns, to discuss weyr business. The weyr laws govern each sept, and the weyr has diplomatic relations with the L'au-dela.

Wyvern: The leader of a dragon sept, a wyvern has one human parent and one dragon parent.

Ysolde de Bouchier: Born to the silver dragon sept some five hundred years ago, she was raised as a human and was later claimed as a mate by both Constantine Norka and Baltic. She was subsequently killed during an attack on Dauva by Constantine. Resurrected almost immediately thereafter by the First Dragon, she spent the remaining centuries in a mental fog due to a nefarious plot by her bigamous husband, Gareth. She is subjected to fugues every six months where she transmutes lead into gold. Although she appears to be human, she has a dragon self who is dormant inside her psyche. She has one son, Brom, via Gareth, and she is the long-lost mate to Baltic.

Gretl and I moved down the center aisle of the Goth-Faire. "This place is wild. How did you hear about it, Gretl?" I asked.

"An old friend of mine works here. I went to see if she was here, but her booth was closed. The Wiccan lady next to her told me that she was off shopping, though, and she should be back any time. What would you like to do while we wait for her?" Gretl stopped and looked around.

I looked with her. The GothFaire was a traveling fair, with two rows of booths set up in a U shape and a large main tent standing at the bottom. Flyers rippling in the breeze proclaimed that two bands would be playing later in the evening, but a couple of magic shows were sched-uled earlier. I glanced at my watch. "I'd love to see the magic acts, but those don't start for an hour. How about we check out the palm reader? Or they have some sort of aura-photography thing. That might be fun. I wonder what sort of camera tricks they use to give people auras? Maybe I could examine their setup and figure it out."

Gretl laughed and nudged my hand, which was still holding my camera. "Trust you to want to see the photography booth."

"That's why I'm here, after all," I said lightly, gesturing down the length of the fair to where a booth with a giant eyeball was painted on a wooden sign.

"You are here to recover from recent events in your life, nothing more," Gretl said firmly, stopping me when I began to protest. "I would never be able to look your father in the face if he thought I made you work while you were staying with me. You relax. You rest. You get your feet under you again, and then you will return to the States and find yourself a new job—a better one, one that will not have an employer who tries to grope you."

"I could have handled Barry's octopus hands if it had just been that, but when he found out I filed a sexual harassment charge, he cooked a few accounts to make it look like I messed up. Lying, despicable, boob-grabbing bastard." I took a deep breath, reminding myself that I had two and a half long months to get over losing my job and my apartment in the same week. A new home shouldn't be too hard to find, although this time, I'd make sure the owner of the building didn't plan on selling it out from underneath all his tenants. "And photography is relaxing to me, Gretl. This is going to be the best summer I've had since . . . well, since the last time I spent the summer with you."

She laughed. "You were sixteen then. Much has changed in St. Andras in that time."

"It still seems to be the same cute little Austrian town to me." I nodded over her head to where a ruined castle perched on a hill. "Picturesque as hell, and so charming I probably won't want to go back home at the end of the summer, just like I didn't when I was sixteen. Have I told you that you're the best cousin ever for inviting me to stay with you?"

"Yes, and I have an ulterior motive, you know," she answered, pushing me along the line of booths. "Now that Anna is married, I have the empty tree."

"Empty nest? Yes, I suppose you do. But it's not like you don't have a lot going on in your life, what with your yoga classes and that program for encouraging new artists that you were telling me about on the way here."

"*Pfft.* I am never too busy for family. Oh, look! Imogen is back. That is my old friend. I have known her for, oh, over thirty years. You will like her—she has a way about her that makes everyone very comfortable. Imogen!"

Gretl hurried forward to where a tall, elegant woman with long curling blond hair was arranging bowls of small polished rocks on a black velvet tablecloth. I followed slowly in order to give Gretl time to greet her friend. The woman turned and Gretl checked for a moment.

"Gretl? Can it be you?" The blonde started toward Gretl with a surprised but welcoming smile.

"Yes, it is me," my cousin answered, her voice sounding odd. "But you! You have not changed since the last time I saw you more than twelve years ago. How is this? What magical face cream are you using to look so young?"

Imogen laughed, but the lines around her eyes were stark rather than happy. Her complexion was pale, normal for blondes, but it struck me that she was a little too pale, as if she was under a great strain. "It is nothing but genetics, I'm afraid. You, however, look as wonderful as you did when we last met! And you are a grandmother! It must be all those yoga classes about which you wrote to me."

The two ladies hugged, and I was pleased for Gretl's sake to see genuine affection in her friend's blue eyes.

"I do not look even close to wonderful, but I am content as I am," Gretl said as she released Imogen. "Now I must introduce to you my cousin from the States. Iolanthe, this is Imogen Dvorak. Iolanthe is staying with me for the summer."

We murmured pleasantries and shook hands. "You are being a tourist?" Imogen asked a few minutes later when she and Gretl had caught up on the most immediate of news. "Are you traveling around Austria, or staying here?"

"A little of each. I'm using this break as kind of a working holiday," I said, holding up my camera. "I'm trying to make a start in the photography world, so I'm poking around St. Andra looking for interesting locations. Luckily, there's a lot to choose from here."

"There are many lovely sites in this region," Imogen agreed.

I eyed her. There was an air of fragility about her that intrigued me, and I wondered if there was any way I could capture that on film. She was certainly lovely enough to model, but a sense of tension seemed to wind around her, as if she was only just being kept from fracturing into a million pieces. It prompted me to ask, "Would you . . . This is going to sound awfully presumptuous, but would you be willing to let me take a few pictures of you? I can't pay you, I'm afraid, but I'd be happy to give you copies of any of the prints you want."

Imogen looked startled for a moment before smiling. "How very sweet of you. It's been . . . oh, so long I can't even remember when someone has asked to take my photo. I would be delighted to, although we are only in St. Andra for four days before we move on to Salzburg."

"Well . . ." I glanced at the skyline. It was dusk, and a dark purple had started to creep across the sky from the inky black silhouette of the mountains. "I know you're busy tonight with your pretty stone things—"

"Rune stones," she interrupted, touching with reverence a deep purple stone bearing an etched symbol on one side. "I have an affinity for them, although I do occasionally read palms as well."

"Ah. Rune stones. Interesting."

She flipped a long curl over her shoulder. "Right now Fran is doing palm reading because she and Benedikt are ... er ... helping. Benedikt is my brother," she added, turning to Gretl. "Do you remember meeting him in Vienna that time we met in the 1990s?"

Gretl's round face lit up, a faint blush pinkening her cheeks. "Who could forget him? He was absolutely gorgeous. And he's here?"

"Yes, with Francesca. They were married a few months ago. You'll like Fran—she's very sweet, and she absolutely adores Benedikt, although she teases him mercilessly about the fact that women are prone to swooning over him."

"Wow. He must still be quite the looker," I commented before steering the conversation back to where I wanted it. "I know you're busy tonight, but perhaps I could shoot you tomorrow, if you are free."

"Benedikt is very handsome, yes," Imogen answered, ignoring my attempts to steer her. "He resembles our father in that way."

The sense of tension in her increased, and I noticed she glanced over my shoulder, a flicker of pain passing across her face.

"Your father must have been a very handsome man, then," Gretl said with a dreamy look in her eyes that made me want to giggle. "I don't believe you've ever mentioned him before."

"He died when I was twenty-two," Imogen said swiftly, her gaze now on the stones that she stroked with long, sensitive fingers. "He was killed by his two half brothers."

"Oh, how horrible!" both Gretl and I said.

"It was very tragic. He inherited our family home, and they coveted that, so they lured him into a forest one summer night and destroyed him." She stopped, obviously hesitant to go on. "It is why I am here, as a matter of fact. The anniversary of his . . . death . . . is two days from now. I try to make a pilgrimage to the location he died whenever I can."

"I'm so sorry," I said as Gretl murmured sympathetic platitudes. "I should never have mentioned your father."

She sniffed back a few unshed tears. "No, no, I don't mind talking about him. Before that horrible night, he was a good man, an excellent father, and I loved him very dearly."

"You must miss him terribly. I assume they caught his killers?"

"They disappeared before they could be tried, unfortunately."

"That's terrible. But I'm sure that wherever your father is, he knows how much you loved him."

She looked up at me, her eyes wide with surprise. "Wherever he is?"

I gestured toward the sky. "You know, looking down on you." I had no idea what religion, if any, she subscribed to, so I didn't want to be too specific in my attempt to provide her with a little comfort.

Imogen gave a delicate little shrug, returning her gaze to the stones. "Ah. Yes, I'm sure he does. At one time I had hope that Ben and I would find Nikola's brothers, but we were unable to do so."

"Nikola is your father?" I couldn't help but ask. I didn't want to be nosy, but my curiosity got the better of me, and she honestly didn't seem to mind talking about him, so long as we kept off the subject of his manner of death.

"Yes." She set down a stone she was stroking and looked up again at us, a little smile lighting her pure blue eyes. "Nikola Czerny, the fifth baron von Shey."

I blinked at her. "Your dad was a baron? A real baron? Does that make you anything?"

She laughed aloud, patting my arm for a second. "Yes, it makes me a woman."

"Oh, I'm sorry," I apologized again, blushing a little at the stupidity that had emerged from my mouth. "You have to excuse me—I'm an idiot. But I've never met someone who was from the aristocracy before."

"Most of the nobility lost their power in Austria almost a hundred years ago," Gretl said gently, giving me a little squeeze on my arm. "Although I, too, did not know that Imogen's father was a baron. The title passed to Ben?"

"No, it didn't," Imogen said, her expression darkening for a moment before she gave us both a bright smile. "It was all a long time ago, and we have much more pleasant things to speak of, yes?"

It was a not very subtle hint that she was through talking about the subject.

"Of course," Gretl said soothingly, and made a date for the next afternoon to have tea and pastries.

"I hate to bother you if you're busy," I said, not sure whether she had responded to my request for a photo session because she was polite or because she really wanted me to take some pictures of her. "If so, then I will totally understand. But if not, I'm sure we can find somewhere locally that would make a good backdrop."

Imogen looked up with a genuine smile. "No, I am not too busy. I would love to be your model."

"Oh, you must go to Andra Castle!" Gretl said, clasping my arm. "It would make a lovely setting—"

"No," Imogen said quickly, her expression as brittle as ice. I blinked at the sudden change in her demeanor. She suddenly relaxed and gave a forced little laugh. "I'm sorry. You must think me very odd, but Andra Castle holds . . . bad memories for me. I would prefer not to go there again."

"Of course we won't use it," I reassured her, curious at such a strong reaction to a ruined castle. Perhaps she'd been frightened there—when Gretl had told me about the ruins, she said that it had a bad reputation by the locals as being unpleasant to visit. "There are lots of other places around here we could use."

"The rose gardens?" Gretl suggested. "The town hall? The church? It is quite old."

"Mmm . . ." I scrunched up my nose as I thought. "To be honest, I'd like to try something a little different as a backdrop for Imogen. Something to contrast with all that fair delicacy."

Imogen laughed, her expression once again changing like quicksilver. "I'm sure you meant that as a compliment, but I assure you, I am anything but delicate. Fair, yes—I got that from my mother. But delicate? No."

"Appearances are often deceiving," I agreed. "I think I'd like to see you set against something dark and gritty. That would make for some wonderful depth to the picture."

"As you like. You're the expert," Imogen said with another of her little shrugs.

"I'm far from that, but I see you . . ." I narrowed my eyes and thought about an image of Imogen against the ruined castle. That would have been ideal, but there were other places that I could use. "Oh! Gretl told me about this haunted forest near here—"

"No!" Imogen all but squawked, drawing attention from the people moving past us. She shot them a reassuring smile before turning it on me. "I'm so sorry. You must think me terribly emotional, but if you are talking about the Shey Woods, then I must again say no. It is not a good place, that forest. I will not step foot in it again."

"I'm so sorry; I didn't mean to suggest somewhere that would make you feel uncomfortable." I thought for a moment. "I don't really know many places around here, but surely there must be some other location we can use that would give the same sense of—oh, I don't know—something otherworldly."

"Otherworldly? Yes, of course I can do that." She shot me a startled glance that quickly turned speculative, then amused, as if we shared a secret, something that struck me as hugely odd. I had only just met her—how could we share a secret? When Gretl turned to greet an acquaintance who had called her name, Imogen leaned over to me, saying with a little nod at Gretl's back, "I had no idea you were not mundane."

"Er . . ." Mundane? Was she making a dig at Gretl? I bristled righteously in defense of a much-loved cousin. "I've always thought of myself as something . . . different, but just because Gretl chose a more traditional path in life doesn't mean she's not a wonderful person."

"Of course she's wonderful. She's been my friend for many years." Imogen smiled and squeezed my arm briefly. "And we all feel *different* at some time or other, don't we? At least until we settle in with our own kind. But who exactly are you? I realize it is rude to just come right out and ask you, but I'm sure you do not wish to speak of your true nature in front of dear Gretl."

I blinked at her, once again taken aback and unsure of how to respond, but luckily Gretl finished her chat and turned back to us, so I was content to simply smile in answer to Imogen's wink, and made a mental note to ask Gretl or her daughter to accompany me on the photo shoot. It was becoming clear that Imogen was a few apples shy of spiced cider.

"Oh, there is Benedikt and Fran. Come. I must introduce you both to them. Benedikt will be delighted to see you again, Gretl."

I followed as Imogen bustled off with Gretl in tow over to where a tall man with shoulder-length black hair stood with a woman who was almost as tall as he was.

The woman, who faced me, looked to be in her early twenties.

"Well, now, that's interesting," I murmured to myself, eyeing the woman named Fran. No matter how good Imogen looked, she had to be nearing fifty for Gretl to have known her for thirty years. Which meant her brother was either older than he looked, or he was a whole lot younger than Imogen. "Even if there is a big age difference," I said as I strolled toward them, "he would be close to my age."

And yet his wife was probably twenty-two or -three. I glanced at Gretl as the couple stepped forward to greet her. A puzzled frown pulled her brows together for an instant before she smiled, quickly returning to her usual charming self. When the man turned to greet me, I saw why Gretl had frowned. I stared at him for a moment, unable to believe what I was seeing. He was in his mid- to late twenties, at least ten years younger than me, which meant Imogen was old enough to be his mother. Not an unknown situation, but not a common one, either. I realized that everyone was staring at me as I gawked so obviously at Imogen's handsome, much, much younger brother, and I pulled my wits together.

"Sorry," I murmured, shaking first his hand, then Fran's. She gave me an amused glance before leaning into her husband, her arm around his waist in a possessive move that I'd have had to be blind to miss.

I chuckled to myself, wanting to assure her that I might be single and not averse to finding a man, but I wasn't about to stoop to husband stealing and cradle robbing. "It's a pleasure to meet you both," I murmured.

"Iolanthe wishes to take my picture tomorrow," Imogen told her brother. "She is a photographer. She wishes to take me somewhere *otherworldly*."

The emphasis Imogen put on the word seemed to have some meaning for them, because they both raised their eyebrows for a few seconds. Ben slid a gaze to Gretl before returning it to me, saying in a low voice that couldn't have been heard by anyone but his wife and me, "Are you with the Court of Divine Blood? I don't recognize what you are, but I'm not very familiar with members of the Court."

"I'm a woman," I answered, ironically echoing Imogen's words as I moved a few steps away from him. Clearly there was some sort of mental instability in Imogen's family.

"Yes, of course you are," Fran said with a comforting smile that I didn't for one minute buy. Ben turned to answer a question Gretl asked him, leaving Fran chatting with me in a low voice. "What Ben meant was what *are* you? You're not a therion or a Guardian or a Summoner. I've seen those, and you don't look like them."

"I used to be an accountant," I told her, feeling that diplomacy was going to be my best bet if I wanted to get pictures of Imogen. It wouldn't do to offend any of Imogen's family by calling them crackpots. "But Barry, my boss, kept hitting on me, and when I tried to turn him in, he got me fired. Illegal and reprehensible, but true."

"No, I meant—" Fran stopped talking when Gretl turned back to us.

"Io, you don't mind that Imogen has asked me to sit with her for an hour or so while she reads the rune stones, do you?"

"Not at all. I'll just wander around the fair and see the sights."

"We'll take care of your cousin," Fran told Gretl as we moved off. I couldn't help but notice that Fran wore a pair of long black lace gloves that disappeared into her shirt cuffs. "We'll show you around and introduce you to all the people who work here. You might find someone you'd like to photograph in addition to Imogen, you know. There are lots of interesting folks. My mother is—Ratsbane! What's he doing here?"

Fran had been steering me down the center aisle when she suddenly froze and glared to the side, where a blond man with a short goatee was strolling toward us. The man also froze when he caught sight of us, an expression of joy on his face as he waved an arm in the air and bellowed, "Goddess Fran! We have returned!"

"I thought you said they'd gone back to Valhalla?" Ben asked in a tight, low voice.

"They had. Dammit, they promised me they wouldn't come back until I asked for their help again. . . . Excuse me a minute, Io. I have to deal with an old . . . *friend*. . . ."

She hurried off to the blond man, who was joined by two others, all of whom enveloped Fran in a group bear hug with cries of, "Goddess!"

"Oh, Christ, not all three," Ben said, rubbing a hand over his eyes.

"You don't have to escort me around the fair, you know. I'm quite capable of trotting around by myself."

"I'd much rather show you around than deal with those three lunatics," he said, nodding toward the nearest booth. "What would you like to see first? I can't vouch for the tattooing, but the demonologist is a friend of mine and can be quite interesting if he's holding a private group session."

"I'm fine just people watching, if truth be told," I said politely, the hairs on the back of my neck standing on end. The words "demonologist" and "private session" just seemed like an incredibly bad juxtaposition. "People are so fascinating if you have the time to really study them."

"True words. I won't ask you any more about yourself since I'm sure Imogen will pump you for all the information you're willing to divulge," he said, laughter rich in his voice as we moved on at a slow amble. "My sister appreciates people watching, as well. Some might call her nosy, but in reality she just likes mortals."

Keep in the open, I told myself. *Stay around other*

people. Do not, under any circumstances, go off anywhere alone with this bizarre man. "I really am not all that interesting, I assure you. I do feel bad about my horrible foot-in-mouth disease with Imogen, though."

He paused in front of a booth dedicated to personal time travel, shooting me a curious look. "Pardon?"

I made a little face. "I said I wanted to take photos of Imogen at the place your father met his end."

"My father?" Ben blinked. "My father is in South America."

"Oh, I'm sorry." A blush warmed my face as I realized that once again I'd verbally embarrassed myself. "I thought you and Imogen had the same father."

"We do. He's in Brazil, I believe. Or Argentina. Somewhere with lots of nearly naked young women and a high level of debauchery."

I stared at him in incomprehension. "He's not dead?"

"No." He leaned in close and said in a low voice, "My father is a Dark One. He can't die unless someone goes to quite a bit of trouble, and I can assure you that no one has done that in several centuries."

"Several centuries," I repeated, just as if that weren't the least bit startling, although, of course, my brain was screaming at me to run far, far away from the crazy man.

And then the thought hit me—what if Imogen and her brother were having me on? What if they were teasing me, the ignorant little American tourist? What if they were waiting to see me freak out, whereupon they'd all have a good giggle at my expense?

The bastards. I wouldn't give them the pleasure!

"Well . . . three hundred? That seems about right. I think it was in 1708 that he flipped out. So three hundred and four years."

I may not have had a lot of pride left that wasn't in tatters after the smear campaign by Barry of the Many Hands, but what I did have I gathered around me. "Oh, *that* kind of Dark One. I thought you meant the . . . um . . . non-three-hundred-year type."

He looked at me as if potatoes had started a cabaret act on my head. "The what?"

"You know, the kind that aren't around for three hundred years."

I think the potatoes may have begun a trapeze act, because the look he gave me was one of utter incredulity. That killed my idea of his pulling my leg—people who were teasing you seldom bore that sort of expression when you sussed out what it was they were doing.

"You did say three hundred years, didn't you?" I asked, suddenly worried that I misheard him. Maybe he had every right to look at me as if I was the odd one.

"Yes." He continued to eye me. "My father is actually older than three hundred years. He's . . . Let me see. I'm three hundred and nineteen, which means he must be around three hundred and forty. Or three hundred and forty-two. Somewhere in that range."

What do you say to a man who claims he's over three hundred years old? I don't know what you would say, but I decided that the best thing to do was to agree with him and try to get rid of him.

"Just so. Those are my favorite kind of Black Ones."

"Dark Ones."

"Sorry." I cleared my throat and tried to sidle away. "I think I'll just—"

Ben evidently wasn't having any of it. He followed after me, giving me a look of much consideration. "There are only two types of Dark Ones, Io—redeemed and unredeemed. My father is the latter, naturally."

"Naturally." I wondered if I dashed into the big main tent if he would come after me, or if I could lose him in the crowd that was starting to gather.

"Although he did love my mother. In his own fashion.

It was only afterward that he lost the ability to feel any such emotions."

"Well, you know how it is with Dark Dudes—that happens."

He stopped me by taking hold of my arm, swinging me around to face him, his eyes narrowed on my face. "You do know what a Dark One is, don't you?"

"Of course," I lied, giving him what I hoped was a serene smile. "They're . . . um . . . They live a long time, and they . . . uh . . . hang out at fairs, and . . . er . . . do other stuff like . . . urm . . ."

"Being vampires," a female voice said behind me.

Eyes wide with disbelief, I spun around to find Fran smiling over my shoulder at Ben.

"Sexy, sexy vampires," she added with a little sigh of pleasure.

Panic hit me then, hard and hot in my gut. I looked around wildly for an escape, throwing to the wind my desire to photograph Imogen. There was no way on this green earth I was going to spend any more time with people who thought they were three-hundred-year-old vampires!

"Io, let me introduce you to my ghosts. They're Vikings, and although they're supposed to be in Valhalla, they claim they were sent back to help Ben and me with a little project—"

I didn't wait for Fran to finish her sentence. I bolted, wanting nothing more than to escape the insanity that suddenly seemed to possess me.

New York Times bestselling author

KATIE MACALISTER

The Novels of the Light Dragons

Love in the Time of Dragons

Tully Sullivan is just like any other suburban mom—except now she's woken up in a strange place surrounded by strange people who keep insisting that they're dragons—and that she's one too. But not just any dragon. She's Ysolde de Bouchier, a famed figure from dragon history.

Tully can't shape-shift or breathe fire, and she's definitely not happy being sentenced to death for the misdeeds of a dragon mate she can't remember. Yet she'll have to find a way to solve the crimes of a past she has no memory of living.

The Unbearable Lightness of Dragons

Ysolde de Bouchier is still coming to terms with the dragon part of her, while at the same time trying to free a friend of Baltic— her Black Dragon lover—from the weyr, get Baltic to meet with the dragons who want him dead, rescue a half-dragon damsel in over her head, raise the shade of the man everyone says killed her, and once and for all clear Baltic's name of the murder charges that continue to plague him. For Ysolde, being a dragon is starting to bite.

Available wherever books are sold or at
penguin.com

S0304